Bedtrick

Bedtrick

Jinny Webber

Cuidono • Brooklyn

Bedtrick
© 2021 Jinny Webber

Cover image: Betsie Van der Meer/Getty Images
Map: Wenceslaus Hollar. Ad Londinvm epitomen
& ocellvm. 1647. Folger Shakespeare Library.

ISBN 978-1-944453-14-5
eISBN 978-1-944453-15-2

Cuidono Press
Brooklyn NY
www.cuidono.com

CONTENTS

CHARACTERS

Playwrights, Players, Poets, and Musicians

* **Edward (Ned) Alleyn,** 1566–1626, leading actor with Admiral's Men.

* **Robert Armin,** 1563–1615, joined Lord Chamberlain's Men in 1599 or 1600, replacing Will Kemp as the clown and prompting Shakespeare to write new sorts of clowns and fools.

* **Amelia Bassano,** later **Lanyer,** 1569–1645, member of a musical family; mistress of Henry Carey, Lord Hunsdon (d. 1596) from approximately 1588 until she became pregnant with his child and was married to the musician Alfonso Lanyer in 1592. She's been suggested as the Dark Lady of Shakespeare's sonnets. In 1611 she published a book of poetry, *Salve Deus Rex Judaeorum,* notable for its feminist perspective.

* **Antonio Bassano,** court musician and uncle of Amelia Bassano Lanyer.

* **Francis Beaumont,** 1584–1616, playwright who came into his full powers under King James I.

* **Christopher Beeston,** c. 1579–c. 1638, boy actor who later became manager of Queen Anne's Men.

* **George Bryan,** d. 1613, actor with Lord Chamberlain's Men.

* **Richard Burbage,** c. 1571–1619, actor and original shareholder in Lord Chamberlain's Company, famous for playing Shakespeare's leading male roles. Son of James Burbage, who built The Theatre in Shoreditch. With his brother Richard built the Globe on the South Bank in 1599.

* **Alexander Cooke,** d. 1614, began as a boy player. Listed in the First Folio as an actor in Shakespeare's plays. Edmond Malone, c. 1780, introduced the hypothesis that Cooke originated Shakespeare's principal female roles. Member of Lord Chamberlain's Company, later a shareholder. In this novel: born as **Kate Collins,** 1576.

*Johnny Cooke, brother of Alexander. Performed onstage and later wrote plays, including a successful comedy performed for King James I and Queen Anne: *Greene's Tu Quoque, or The City Gallant* (1611). In this story, born as **Johnny Collins**, 1578.

*Henry Condell, d. 1627, actor and close colleague of Shakespeare, shareholder in Lord Chamberlain's Company. With John Heminges, edited the First Folio of 1623.

*Samuel Daniel, 1562–1619, poet and dramatist.

*Thomas Dekker, c. 1572–1632, dramatist and pamphleteer. Satirized by Ben Jonson in his *Poetaster* and *Cynthia's Revels*; retaliated with *Satiromastix*. Later the two playwrights collaborated on spectacles for King James' coronation. Dekker wrote *The Roaring Girl*, a play about Moll Frith, with Thomas Middleton.

*John Donne, 1573–1631, poet born into a Roman Catholic family. Married Anne More in 1601 against the wishes of her family. In later life he became Dean of St. Paul's and wrote as passionately about religion as he earlier wrote about love and sex.

*John Dowland, 1563–1626, lutenist and composer, said to have been born in Dalkey, Dublin.

*Füzuli, c. 1494–1556, Azerbaijani Turkish poet who wrote in Turkish, Persian, and Arabic. Noted for romantic and epic poems; also an astronomer and mathematician.

*John Heminges, 1566–1630, actor and shareholder in Lord Chamberlain's Company who with Henry Condell edited the First Folio of Shakespeare's plays, published in 1623.

*Philip Henslowe, d. 1616, manager of Admiral's Men and owner of the Rose Theatre and later the Fortune. Kept the famous 'Henslowe's Diary' full of information about the London theatre.

*Ben Jonson, 1572–1637, dramatist and self-educated classicist. In 1598 he killed Gabriel Spencer, actor with Admiral's Men, in a duel; escaped execution by "benefit of clergy" (being able to read Latin), but his thumb was branded as a murderer.

*Will Kemp, d. 1603, comic actor and one of the original shareholders of Lord Chamberlain's Men, which he left in 1599. *Kemp's Nine Day's Wonder* (1600) is his account of his Morris dance from London to Norwich.

*Alfonso Lanyer, 1563–1613, member of a family of court musicians.

Cousin by marriage to Amelia Bassano, whom he married in 1592 when she was pregnant with Lord Hunsdon's child. He disappears from musical records in 1603.

* Innocent Lanyer, brother of Alfonso. Court musician who becomes apprentice master to Amelia Bassano's son, Henry Carey Lanyer.

* Henry Carey Lanyer, 1593–1533, son of Amelia Bassano Lanyer, known as Harry in this book. Became a court musician to King James I.

* Thomas Lupo, court musician and cousin of Amelia Bassano who led the royal musical consort.

* Tom Nashe, 1567–1601, satirist, poet and playwright. Collaborated with Christopher Marlowe, Ben Jonson, and possibly Shakespeare on his earliest plays.

* Augustine Phillips, d. 1605, shareholder in Lord Chamberlain's Company who represented the company when summoned before the Queen's Privy Council about their special performance of *Richard II* which Essex's supporters hoped would raise Londoners to arms against the Queen.

* Tom Pope, d. 1603, comic actor and shareholder in Lord Chamberlain's Company.

* William Shakespeare, 1564–1616, dramatist and poet from Stratford-upon-Avon. London theatre career from roughly 1590–1611. Married to Anne Hathaway, who for the most part remains in Stratford with their children, Susannah, and the twins Judith and Hamnet (d. 1597).

* John Taylor, 1580–1653, Thames waterman and poet.

Royalty and Court

* Queen Elizabeth I, 1533–1603, second daughter of King Henry VIII, by Anne Boleyn. Succeeded her half-sister Mary to the throne in 1558.

Queen Elizabeth I's ladies of importance include *Lady Helena Snakenborg Gorges; *Anne Russell, Countess of Warwick; Elizabeth's cousins the Carey sisters, *Philadelphia Carey, *Lady Scrope, and *Katherine Howard, Countess of Nottingham, whose death in February 1603 hastened the Queen's decline; and Lady Isabel, her youngest attendant.

* **King James I** of England, 1566–1625. Ruled as King James VI of Scotland until he succeeded Queen Elizabeth I. Ruled England 1603–1625. Married to Anne of Denmark; had many male favorites.

* **Queen Anne**, 1574–1619, married to James I; mother of Henry, Charles, and Elizabeth. Her marriage was often divisive, but she took a leading role at court and fostered extravagant masques.

* **Sir Robert Cecil**, 1563–1612, Queen Elizabeth's chief advisor continued in that position with King James I, who made him the 1st Earl of Salisbury.

* **Lady Anne Clifford**, 1590–1676, a favorite of Queen Elizabeth when she was a child, went on to participate in Queen Anne's masques and to write a famous diary. She and her mother, Margaret of Cumberland, were important patrons of Amelia Lanyer, whose poem, "The Description of Cooke-ham," depicts their country house.

* **George Carey, Lord Hunsdon**, 1547–1603, son of Henry Carey, who was cousin (or half-brother) of the Queen. After his father died in 1596, George succeeded him as Queen Elizabeth's Lord Chamberlain and patron of Shakespeare's acting company.

* **Robert Devereux, the Earl of Essex**, 1565–1601, the politically ambitious favorite of Queen Elizabeth who led the Irish campaign, exerting more authority than she had granted him. In 1601 Essex staged a rebellion and was executed for treason. Married to Frances Walsingham, widow of Sir Philip Sidney, and thus the stepfather of Lady Elizabeth Sidney Manners. Fellow rebels of the Earl of Essex include Lord Monteagle; Sir Charles Percy; Sheriff Thomas Smyth, among others.

* **Henry Herbert, 2nd Earl of Pembroke**, c. 1538–1601, husband to Mary Sidney Herbert. Properties include Wilton House, his country estate, and Baynard's Castle, a large dwelling on the Thames which once belonged to the House of York. His eldest son William Herbert succeeded him as Earl of Pembroke in 1601.

* **Mary Sidney Herbert, Countess of Pembroke**, 1561–1621, renowned as a patron of poetry and the arts. Married Henry Herbert in 1577, his third wife. Mother of William and Philip Herbert. Sister of the poet Sir Philip Sidney, she translated psalms with him and became his literary executor after his death in battle in 1587.

* **Philip Herbert**, 1548–1650, second son of Henry and Mary Sidney Herbert, succeeded his brother William as 4th Earl of Pembroke in 1630. A favorite of King James I, he became one of the first gentlemen of the King's Privy Chamber.

* **William Herbert**, 1580–1630, succeeded as 3rd Earl of Pembroke in 1601. Became King James' Lord Chamberlain in 1616. Like his mother, he was a patron of the arts. Founded Pembroke College, Oxford, with King James I.

* **Roger Manners, Earl of Rutland**, 1576–1612, noted for his intellect and learning. He married Lady Elizabeth Sidney in 1599; evidently the marriage was never consummated, either because he had syphilis or was homosexual. He joined the Essex Rebellion against Queen Elizabeth and did not return to royal favor until King James I succeeded to the throne.

* **Lady Lucy Russell, Countess of Bedford**, 1580–1627, a noted beauty and patron of the arts, married Edward Russell, the Earl of Bedford. He participated in the Essex Rebellion and was not returned to royal favor until King James I took the throne. Lady Lucy Bedford championed John Donne and encouraged Amelia Lanyer with her poetry.

* **Lady Elizabeth Sidney Manners**, 1485–1612, daughter of Sir Philip Sidney and stepdaughter of Robert Devereux, the Earl of Essex; married Roger Manners, the Earl of Rutland, in 1599. A gifted poet praised by Ben Jonson, no known works of hers have survived.

* **John Whitgift**, c. 1530–1604, Archbishop of Canterbury who knelt beside Queen Elizabeth for hours when she was on her deathbed.

* **Henry Wriothesley, Earl of Southampton**, 1573–1624, pronounced 'Risley.' A handsome young man whose literary patronage was much sought after. Shakespeare dedicated "Venus and Adonis" and "The Rape of Lucrece" to him. He's regarded as the most likely inspiration for the young man addressed in Shakespeare's sonnets. Joined the Earl of Essex's rebellion; his life sentence in the Tower was commuted by King James I.

Others

* **Abd el-Ouahed ben Messaoud**, 1558–?, Moroccan ambassador to Queen Elizabeth in 1600; influenced Shakespeare's depiction of the "noble Moor" Othello. His portrait is exhibited at the Shakespeare Institute in Stratford-upon-Avon.

* **Compte de Beaumont,** the French ambassador who sent home an un-flattering report of Queen Elizabeth's fashion sense after he met with her in 1603, her last official visitor before her death.

Frances Field, 1578–1645, Silkwoman to Queen Elizabeth and owner of a dressmaking shop on London Bridge.

* **Dr. John (Giovanni) Florio,** 1553–1625, scholar and dictionary writer, married to Rose Daniel, sister of poet Samuel Daniel.

* **Dr. Simon Forman,** 1552–1611, astrologer who kept famous casebooks that include descriptions of Shakespeare's plays as well as of his female clients including Amelia Bassano Lanyer.

* **Mary Frith,** known as **Moll Cutpurse,** dressed in breeches and doublet and went about blatantly as a man. Notorious in the 17th century as a thief, bawd, and fence, dramatized in Middleton and Dekker's play *The Roaring Girl,* c. 1607–1610.

Dr. Simon Garnet, alchemist, astrologer, philosopher; student of Dr. John Dee, the Queen's astrologer.

Ibrahim ben Messaoud, fictional nephew of Abd el-Ouahed ben Messaoud; votary of the poet Füzuli.

* **Sir Lewes Lewknor,** 1560–1627, translator and master of many lan-guages, he escorted the Moroccan Abd el-Ouahed ben Messaoud on his state visit to Queen Elizabeth in 1600 and served as trans-lator. Later became King James' Master of Ceremonies.

PART ONE

FOLLY AND HOPE

Never till tonight, never till now,
Did I go through a tempest dropping fire.
Either there is a civil strife in heaven,
Or else the world, too saucy with the gods,
Incenses them to send destruction.
CASCA, *JULIUS CAESAR*

CHAPTER I
March 1599

The crowd surged close around me, the drizzling rain adding to the stench of unwashed clothes and sweaty bodies. My brother and fellow players were nowhere to be seen in the melee, and my ears rang.

"Defeat the rebel Tyrone!"

"Death to the Irish!"

"Essex is our man!"

"On to victory!"

"Long live the Queen!" drowned out by "Death. Death. Death."

Nothing I wanted more than to escape the ferociousness that underlay this show of patriotism, but it was all I could do to hold my own. We'd come to see the Earl of Essex and his men on their nobly caparisoned horses parading toward their ships bound for Ireland. Instead, the mob pushed and shoved to get a closer view, shouting and cheering. I stumbled against them pushing my way out, along with a father clutching the legs of the small boy on his shoulders.

Finally I broke free, heart pounding and doublet wetter by the moment from the shower that deterred the barking crowd not at all. The day had started bright and hopeful for Essex's glorious departure, worthy of King Henry V off to France in our play. But this was no theatre, this crowd more frenzied rabble than enthusiastic groundlings edging toward the stage. Why such excess? I dreaded what it presaged.

The horses' plumes would be falling limp, though no doubt their aristocratic riders would be elated at their send-off. Not so much the common soldiers, who I pictured huddled by the ships in damp, ominous silence. I sensed that Essex's campaign was doomed one way or another, but larger disasters threatened. Leaving behind the mass of rank-smelling men, I stowed my worries and fled toward London Bridge, as they'd blocked my way north on Gracechurch street.

As I'd learned on arrival, London wasn't all palaces, grand houses, markets, taverns, and jollity. Filthy tenements lay behind handsome inns and craftsmen's shops, many streets were so closely lined with tall buildings that light could barely penetrate, cemeteries of ruined churches housed the poor in shanties, and dangerous alleys abounded, especially across the Thames in Bankside, where also lay amusements, legal and otherwise. Yet despite the noise and odors and throngs of every sort of person, London's bustle made it exciting. After eight years I still found it wondrous.

But today's throng resembled the rowdies at a hanging on Tyburn Hill, times a hundred, times a thousand.

A waterman's haunting call rose from the Thames, and an occasional disreputable character shoved past me on his way to Bankside, along other folks with their heads down, fleeing as was I. No hurrying throngs on the Bridge, no peddlers shouting their wares, no goods spilling out of shop fronts. Doors were shut tight, all but a bake shop where I bought an onion pie.

I intended to continue on to Southwark to visit my old prentice master Tom Pope, who favored his home fire on such a day, but rain began to fall in earnest. In the upstairs window of Frances Field's dressmaking shop midway across the Bridge, a candle flickered. Better to share supper with Frances.

I knocked.

"Sander! Come in. I'm much in need of good company."

"Me as well, and refuge from rain and madness."

I followed to her upstairs chamber, the onion pie leaking grease down my breeches. Setting it on the table I glanced at her, a soft brown curl straying across her cheek. Frances had a lovely way about her, feminine and strong, but her face looked troubled.

"What madness?"

"A crazed mob cheering the Earl of Essex. Londoners at their worst."

"You've escaped to a safe harbor."

Her words were welcoming but her face pinched. I'd wanted to tell her my apprehensions at the riotous display I'd fled, but my worries about the world outside her door meant nothing in her presence.

"Are you all right, Frances?"

"Yes, yes. Let's have a cup of wine." She poured two from a flagon on the shelf next to her diminutive fire. Everything in her chamber was compact, the neat bed, the table beneath the window overlooking the Thames, two wooden chairs with embroidered cushions.

I moved an embellished sleeve from a chair, avoiding a poking needle, and sat by the fire. "Do you do anything besides work?"

"If I'm lucky, I share a pie with a friend."

"And a walk with that friend along the Thames, as soon as the weather improves."

"Perhaps."

Was there any question? True, Frances worked harder than I, blessed with free time between rehearsals and performances. Her shop was always busy, the worktable stacked with fabric, clothes rail hung with partially sewn garments, her apprentice bustling around and often a customer or two as well. Still, walking out together on a fine day was a delight for us both.

She set the pie on the hearth and sat beside me. "Why ever did you go out on such a rain-threatening day?"

"Johnny dragged me to watch the parade of Essex's troops. I lost him in the war-crying rabble. No doubt by now they're soaked to the bone and seeking their supper, but we beat them to it." As I lifted my cup to her, I wondered why no smile brightened her face. "To you, Frances, and friendship."

She took a sip, her expression scarcely changing.

"Are you sure nothing's upset you? Have you been summoned to the Royal Wardrobe?"

"The Queen doesn't upset me. She treats me like a pet, her youngest Silkwoman."

I'd found out for myself how Her Majesty favored young people of ambition. Once, after I played Kate in *Taming of a Shrew*, she spoke to me privately as I sat beside her on a cushioned bench, a magical, portentous memory.

"You've been as close to the Queen as a lady of her chamber."

"I suppose so. I've touched her royal skin when fitting a ruff and learned the actor's tricks they use to make up her face."

"Touching the body of Gloriana! That's what fitting bodices amounts to, I suppose. touching women's bodies." I glanced at the silken sleeve she'd been stitching. "Women of the best sort."

Frances shook her head. "I've concealed men's breeches in a gown for a Winchester Goose, and another asked for a reversible skirt with a false seam down the front to display her hose. With a codpiece!"

"Poor girls. They costume themselves for trade."

"As a dressmaker, I'd say most women costume themselves for one reason or another."

"I wish you could work for our company, Frances. Regularly, I mean, not just when we're allowed aristocrats' cast-offs for Court performances."

"I have more than enough business here. Anyone with a needle can alter a costume."

We addressed our slices of pie, though Frances barely nibbled hers. I wanted to distract her, tell tales about recent shows or reminisce about how we met, but Frances seemed closed into herself. I might have said no one had ever touched me so kindly as she did the day we played *Love's Labours' Lost* at Whitehall Palace. Taking a tuck in the bodice of my gown, her fingers slipped to the linen band wrapped tight around my chest. She'd looked me in the eye—and never spoke a word. I wanted to tell her how much I valued her discretion, how my fate had lain in her hands. But right now her fate seemed the issue, not mine.

Frances took my empty plate and her half-full one to the narrow sideboard. For all the bits of her story she'd told me over the years, I couldn't guess what distressed her.

She stood staring down at the Thames from her high window.

"You're not considering a voyage, are you Frances? I thought only I'd yearned for the sea." Silly words I knew, but somehow I had to bring her back to this moment, here with a trusted friend. The river looked dark and frightening as it rushed to the sea. My onetime dream of becoming a cabin boy on the ship of an explorer or pirate had become a joke between us, but now no laugh from Frances. Could I put a comradely arm around her? Shake her awake? Refill her cup?

"Do sit, Frances. Whatever your worries, you can tell me."

We gazed into the fire, her expression inscrutable.

"Tell me, Sander: have you ever loved a man?"

"Me?"

"If you were to love a man, even from a distance, he'd be a poet. Not a courtier and certainly not one of your fellow players. You would choose a man of passionate words."

"Since when have you played wise woman? Looking inside others' lives and drawing strange conclusions?"

"I know you. All I'm saying is 'if.' Did you ever love such a one? Do you now?"

I coughed and took a calming sip of wine.

"I'm not so much a wise woman as an observant one. I have an idea who you might have loved."

The way she said "love" and "loved" struck me. Frances wasn't curious about who I may or mayn't have loved, though her query made my cheeks burn.

She was in love herself.

"Who, Frances? Not the name of my supposed poet but the man

you love. Who captured your heart?" No response. "I'm not wrong. I can read love's pain in your face. But I cannot guess who he is."

"You don't want to know."

"You have no closer friend. Tell me." I pictured a flirtatious young man who brought his new wife to her shop for a gown and stole her heart. "Is he married?"

"He might as well be. Oh Sander, it's worse than you imagine."

"And you've kept it to yourself. What's worse than loving in vain?"

She frowned. "That's merely a subject for poets, Cupid's cruel arrow and such. What's worse for a woman? Think."

I took a deep breath. "Surely you aren't."

"I am. Pregnant."

"That's wonderf—"

"I have no husband."

"The father—?"

"The father—" She faltered. "The father is your brother Johnny."

"My dear Frances. You shall have a husband. You'll be my sister!" I was flooded with emotion. Surprise—their connection had been a secret even from me—and delight. How grand to have a sister and a baby in the family—

"I wish that were true."

"What do you mean, you wish?"

"When I told Johnny I was with child, he said he loves me but cannot marry me."

"That's outrageous!" Picturing his smug, handsome face I wanted to slap him silly. Not only was this a betrayal of Frances but me as well. Why she gave her virginity to him, I could only wonder at.

"Johnny can well afford a wife. He's a hired man now, good roles and good pay."

"That makes no difference. He refuses to marry me."

"He must!" I softened my voice. "How can a brother of mine behave so badly?" My past with Johnny flashed through my mind, back to our childhood after Mam died birthing him when I was just two years old. As small children Gran raised us, and we remained the closest of companions until I had to flee the village. He'd managed to join me as prentice to Tom Pope and we'd been acting together ever since. After he finished his apprenticeship he became something of a gallant about town, but he was forgivably young.

"Maybe that's the problem. I thought Johnny was like you, in character, I mean. You and I have been such good friends that I thought—" She broke off. "I'm a stupid fool."

"Johnny's more knave than fool. You'll be a perfect wife."

"He doesn't want a wife."

"Why not?"

"He says he's obligated to Lady Elizabeth Sidney, that she can make his future. He'll live in her noble house and be part of her *artistic coterie*." Frances said the last two words with derisive emphasis. "She'll introduce him to the wits of London and encourage his playwriting."

"Is he out of his mind? Lady Elizabeth may have taken up with him on a whim, but how can he possibly benefit from her? Johnny's obligation is to you, Frances. He can write a play on his own time."

"He says he'll support my child and be ever my friend."

"I can imagine what he means by friend. He'll pay you a night-time visit now and then. He's treating you like a Bankside wench!"

"Please, Sander."

"Please nothing. Aren't you enraged? I am! You can't raise a baby on your own. The Queen has locked women in the Tower for less."

"Queen Elizabeth cares about the behavior of her ladies. I have no such status. If I appear at the Royal Wardrobe pregnant, she'll assume I'm married and get on with fitting her gowns."

"You cannot let him off."

"He gives me no choice. What am I to do, cling to his doublet and wail, or report him to the constables?"

"Most women would. Johnny must be mad!"

"He may be, but I have no power to shake him into sense." Frances scanned the room with an assessing eye. "I'll keep my business going and raise the child myself. Right here." She pointed to a space by the fire just the size of a cradle.

"A mother must be married. If not to the father, then to one who takes that role. Look at Amelia Bassano. When she became pregnant with his child, Lord Hunsdon found her a husband. He wouldn't have dreamt of leaving her to fend for herself. Amelia was no noblewoman. Even so, Hunsdon made sure to save her reputation."

She exhaled a long sigh. "My reputation."

"You cannot stay in London and give birth to a—a—" I couldn't say the word.

"Who would marry me? Johnny is no lord, quick to buy me a husband." She blinked back tears. "I—I love him." She returned to the window, staring out as if looking for an answer.

I thought about Gran, a healer who possessed deep knowledge. Johnny and I would not have survived had we been left to our hard-drinking father. Gran taught us to do what was right, not because of sermons in St. Mary the Virgin but because of our own consciences. Occasionally a girl came to her lamenting an unwanted pregnancy. Perhaps Gran gave her herbs; perhaps she advised her on motherhood. I now knew that a woman could attempt to end a pregnancy with strong elixirs or more drastic means. Frances wouldn't likely risk such, but birthing a bastard would end her flourishing life.

As Frances gazed at the rushing Thames, I feared she might leap as had many a girl before her and seized her hands. "Please don't do anything rash. I'll speak to Johnny."

"If only that would help."

I kissed her cheek. "Take care, Frances. I'm sorry to leave you, but I must find Johnny. Promise me you'll go to bed."

"I shall," she answered in a small voice.

"Try to sleep. I'll do all I can. You needn't face this alone."

While I was in Frances' shop, night had fallen. A flash of lightning was choppily reflected in the river as I turned north. I ran fast through the drizzle, my fury growing. Not only Gran's teachings but every force of church and society condemned Johnny's behavior.

He lived in my street, just off Bishopsgate. I found him outside his door. "Hallo, Katy."

I grabbed his arm. "How dare you!"

"Sander. I mean Sander. Let me go. I have to meet—"

"Me, as it happens." I yanked him into the Spread Eagle.

"Just one cup. I have places to go."

The tavern wasn't one I frequented. It had a low timber ceiling blackened from an ill-drawing fire and multitudinous smokers' pipes. But I'd been in many a place with worse. Apparently, the Spread Eagle appealed to solitary drinkers. The barmaid was older than most, likely the tavern-keeper's wife, with ruddy cheeks, stringy grey-blonde hair tied back with a green kerchief, generous bosom and smile. She waved us to the table near the door, away from the dour men with their clay pipes. Perhaps they were drawn here by her jolly manner.

As she came our way, I saw that the tavern had a homey charm: a dresser with earthen cups fancifully painted next to the bar, a bunch of dried wild flowers amongst the tankards, and panels of stitchery stuck on the walls. Stronger than the smoke and stale beer aroma was the scent of rosemary drifting up from the fresh reed-strewn floor beneath our feet. If I weren't here on such an errand, I might even like this place.

She filled two tankards. "Haven't seen you lads here before. Stay for a while. When he gets his drink on, Old Ben," she nodded at a fellow with hair longer than hers, "plays a mean fiddle."

"Ah, entertainment." Johnny looked relieved, as if Old Ben would spare him.

"The best. I'm Maud. Glad to see you." She bounced away with her ale jug, making the rounds.

I leaned in and spoke in a quietly menacing tone. "I've talked with Frances."

"Then she told you. I cannot marry her." He started to lift his ale, as if that were his final word.

I stopped his hand midair. "You have no choice, Johnny Cooke."

"Of course I have a choice."

"You know right from wrong."

"Sometimes there's more than one right."

I looked into his arrogant face, resembling mine in coloring and features but not expression. "Don't equivocate. You fathered a child on Frances. You're responsible to her and to the baby."

"Oh, don't worry. I plan to give her money." This time his tankard reached his mouth before I could stop it.

"That is not being a father. The baby needs your name. Surely you loved Frances." I ignored the noncommittal look on his face. "How can you not love her more now, when she carries your child?" I thought of how I would feel in his place, every tender emotion aroused.

Johnny slugged down his ale. Maud stirred the fire, drawing the solitary drinkers to the hearth. No one paid attention to the two of us in our corner.

"Give me one good reason you cannot marry her."

"I'm contracted to someone else." Maud was approaching with a fresh jug, but my expression made her reverse course.

"You played love games with two women?"

"It's not how you think."

"I can't think anything at all from what you've said." I lifted my untouched tankard and gulped down half before he replied.

"I made a vow to Lady Elizabeth Sidney."

"Worse and worse! She's a noblewoman. You aren't important to her, not as you are to Frances."

"Oh, I am, I am. Lady Elizabeth's husband, the Earl of Rutland, is off fighting the Irish rebels. It's up to me to look after her." At my shocked expression, he added, "In the most chaste sense. She needs a friend."

"You've lost all reason."

Old Ben began scraping his fiddle, apt accompaniment for our dissonant conversation.

Johnny raised his voice over the music. "Lady Elizabeth is little more than a girl. She needs me."

"You choose her over Frances?"

"Frances is strong and independent."

"Yes, and pregnant. The Queen will frown on a husbandless Silkwoman with a child."

"Frances owns her own shop. She doesn't depend on the Queen."

I wanted to kick his self-righteous knee beneath the table. "The more you say, the more disgraceful! Frances' position as Silkwoman is an extraordinary accomplishment for such a young woman. You can't simply dismiss it."

As Maud passed by with her jug, Johnny gave her two coins but I gestured for her to refill our cups. "You're right, Maud. Ben's good on that fiddle." The grin was still on his face as he turned back to me. "Lady Elizabeth will be my patron. I'm going to be a playwright."

"I've heard Ben Jonson encourage you. So sit down and write a play."

"Much easier while living at Lady Elizabeth's London house, using her library, meeting her friends, working in leisure."

"Sounds like the vainest of dreams, brother. You have a pregnant woman who loves you and you've attained a worthy position in our company. Surely you won't sacrifice those to play gallant to a spoiled young noblewoman."

"You're not listening. I've made up my mind." He started to rise.

I grabbed his arm and pulled him down. "Your mind is twisted." I spit out the last word.

"I won't desert Frances, but I cannot marry her."

"She'll give birth to a bastard!"

Ben's song ended just before my last word, echoing in the abrupt silence. Drinkers looked over, grinning, and Maud laughed aloud.

I whispered, "You're behaving abominably." We said no more until Ben took up his bow.

"What Lady Elizabeth offers me will benefit Frances as well."

"It will not benefit her."

"So all of a sudden you're worried about Frances?"

"Of course I am. She's my friend."

He sipped his ale reflectively as Ben played on.

"Well then, here's a plan, Sander. Handily, your name is Cooke.

If you care so much, why not marry her yourself? You can grant her child legitimacy. A brilliant idea, I call it."

"What? You can't mean it!" I choked on the ale. When I'd caught my breath, I lowered my voice. "That's a horrifying idea. If discovered we could be called out as witches! Two women marrying is against God and nature." I gave him a hard look. "You're asking me to risk my life, Johnny—and Frances' and the baby's—to save you. The righteous course is for you to marry her. Frances will make you happy."

"That may be true, but it's not going to happen, Sander. I thought I made that clear. You want a solution, then you go ahead and provide it."

I was at a loss for words. Is this the brother who shared our motherless childhood? Who followed me to London? Lady Elizabeth clouded his mind.

"Think about it, Sander. It's not such a bad idea. You like Frances."

"Of course I do, but that doesn't mean I should marry her."

"It's the best plan. Just give it some thought. Your marrying Frances will solve all our problems, what a grand lark it would be for you. Now I'm off!"

The storm had become no more than an occasional splash, but I was in no hurry to leave.

What was it with marriage in the Collins, now Cooke, family? I'd fled Saffron Walden to avoid wedlock, and now Johnny was doing his version of the same. No, nothing like the same. I'd have been under the thumb of an unlettered lout whereas Johnny would marry the warm-hearted mother of his child. Then I remembered Frances saying how dangerous marriage could be to her position.

I let Maud refill my ale, my thoughts tossing with the complexities of this peculiar day. I'd sought refuge at Frances' shop from war fever and stormy weather and now what concerned me was her future, and not only her pregnancy. If she wed Johnny, Frances' business would become Johnny's. Her position of Silkwoman she could maintain, but as I understood the law, her husband would legally control her money. I sighed. Just as well Johnny wasn't taking that into consideration. Still, it was true, especially in London, a mother should be married.

Not only had I fled our village rather than marry Martin Day, sheep man and tanner. Frances had been all too right. I had loved a poet and he me. Beautiful, gifted John Donne. The sound of his name still warmed my heart. But to marry him I'd have had to renounce acting and become a woman again. That I could not do, for all that I yearned to be with John forever. Losing him would always be an ache in my heart, nor could I love any one else and remain a player in the Lord Chamberlain's Men.

The fire flared and my mind with it. Would serve Johnny right if I did marry Frances! She and I had been friends since before she met Johnny.

Absurd idea for us to marry. I glanced down at my codpiece, which kept idle minds from guessing the truth. I took enough risks as it was. Marriage to a woman would be far riskier. I would actually be a better husband for Frances than Johnny, making no claims on her business or her person. But it was impossible and besides, I knew what love was, as did Frances. Her heart doted on Johnny.

Carrying my ale with me as Old Ben played on, I took a closer look at the embroideries around the walls of the Spread Eagle. Nearest the door, the panel was simple, like a child's first sampler. Each one became more complicated until, behind the bar, the panel looked like something one of the Queen's ladies would make, a springtime scene thick with silken flowers.

"Pretty, isn't it?" Maud waved to the potboy to refill her jug. "Done by my daughter Joan. Now she's prentice to one of the best dressmakers in London."

"Well done!" I paused. "Joan? Does she work on London Bridge?"

"She does. Do you know her?"

"No, but I see her in Frances Field's shop."

"That's the place."

I took a seat closer to the fire, facing Joan's best work. Now she was set on a profitable future. But not as impressive as what Frances had achieved, leaving an impoverished village near Leicester with nothing but her skill with a needle. She'd managed to apprentice herself to a fine seamstress and now had inherited her shop. No doubt Frances too started by embroidering simple panels and stitching practical garments of worsted. Now she used silk thread on satin and velvet.

But for all her achievements, against Lady Elizabeth Sidney Frances didn't stand a chance. Lady Elizabeth was fathered by the courtier poet Sir Philip Sidney, and her new husband was an Earl. Johnny's head had been turned by such highborn company. Like seamstresses, players and playwrights were of an utterly different class. Our companies needed noble patrons, especially to go on the road. Otherwise we could be arrested as vagrants. A shop owner was better off, but nothing was guaranteed for the likes of us.

Christopher Marlowe had studied at Cambridge University thanks to a benefactor, but his father was a cobbler. The more I reflected on the differences between what Johnny aspired to and our reality, the more despair I felt for Frances. Yet the aura he carried simply by association with Lady Elizabeth and her ilk might make him even more attractive to her. Well as I knew Frances, I didn't know her heart.

The solitary drinkers were now talking and laughing together, some singing along off-key with Ben's fiddle. They reminded me of the easy sociability of Tom Pope's big house where I spent my apprenticeship, his sister cooking up delicious meals every day for family who stopped with them for a while, random guests arriving spontaneously, and Johnny and me in our room behind the warm kitchen fire. Though I didn't feel part of the camaraderie in the Spread Eagle, I had to admit I was tired of lodgings and would quite enjoy a convivial house of my own.

But to marry out of necessity, a necessity not of my own doing and to a woman: unimaginable. If found out, Frances would be worse off than if she raised her baby alone. And me? God only knows.

I left the Spread Eagle more hopeless than when I arrived.

O that I were a man for his sake! or that I had any
friend would be a man for my sake!
BEATRICE, *MUCH ADO ABOUT NOTHING*

CHAPTER II
April 1599

I did my best to avoid Johnny, who seemed blithely unconcerned about Frances' predicament. Once he was such a good brother! But I was too angry for nostalgia. His spurning Frances for the sake of Lady Elizabeth Sidney infuriated me.

How could he have imagined I'd agree to this marriage, no considerations of Frances nor worst consequences? Hardly what I'd call a brilliant idea! Even if we wanted to, how could Frances and I manage such a feat? Why wouldn't Johnny choose to live happily with her and their baby in a cozy house?

That would be the sensible course, one I envied more every time I thought about it. Masquerading as Sander Cooke in doublet and hose, I defied the divine order of the world. It had proved no huge leap to play parts on stage. Ever since girlhood I'd been an actor. But a husband? A dangerous proposition I'd never considered.

Leaving early for rehearsal one dreary day, I walked along the Strand with its majestic palaces: Essex and Durham house, Somerset and Savoy. Eating houses and taverns were tucked in here and there including one of our company's favorites, the Nag's Head. Fitting for this ancient Thames-side thoroughfare with its grandeur and hustle, Moll Frith walked toward me, colorful as ever.

Like any man of moderate means, I wore loosely fitting hose with a codpiece, nondescript doublet and jerkin, a dagger strapped inside my boot. Moll, however, sported a striped doublet and ballooning breeches that made her look broader than she was, soft boots with wide cuffs folded over, a charcoaled scruff of whiskers edging her chin and upper lip. Wearing male apparel was forbidden to women, but Moll cheerfully defied the rules and maintained a den of thieving lads, though she wasn't much older than me.

Johnny claimed that Moll could get away with playing the man because she was so ugly. She was younger than she looked, but nothing about her was delicate except her hands, usually concealed in rough leather gloves. I admired Moll's ferociously jutting chin and grey eyes, wild as a wolf's. Early in our acquaintance, she'd pulled me to her chest in a bear hug and confirmed her suspicion that my sex was not as it appeared. Since then, those boys of hers had saved me from one of my two closest encounters with disaster.

Once at the Mermaid Tavern, four lads I'd first assumed were hers circled round me, and before I knew what was happening edged me out the door into a gloomy alleyway, the shops and houses of Cheapside obscuring day's last light.

No quick sidestep could elude them. I couldn't see their faces with their caps pulled low and raggedy beards. They were short, but hardly lads, a solid block of manhood pushing me forward.

They spoke in grunts, but I began to make out their words.

"We dunna' kill him. We cut his balls."

"Lame him, keep that gal's voice high."

"Leave him bleeding, fancy player boy."

They pushed me onto the filthy ground and ripped at my breeches, me fighting with all my might, but who was I against the gang of them?

One pulled the fabric of my breeches apart, exposing the padding in front. "Devil take me! This ain't no boy!"

"I know damned well what to do about that," their leader said, loosening his placket. "You'll get your chance m'boys. First me. We'll do more than hired for, doubling our payment and our fun."

He tried to thrust his hand between my thighs. I held them tight shut, fists beating on his back. The others were too stunned to jump into action.

"You lying jade," my assailant muttered. He slapped my face and redoubled his efforts. I bit his arm through his jerkin, which only angered him.

"Come on, men, give me a hand! It's cunt for us all."

They were on me. One's dagger slit the front of my doublet and another fumbled ineptly to loosen the band around my breasts. These clumsy men couldn't pay the price of a disease-ridden whore, their enraged leader thrashing about at my thighs, locked against him, my fingers scraping at his face.

"Be off, you poxy curs!" Moll's unmistakable bellow. As her boys chased my attackers down the alleyway, heads popped out of windows above. I tried to pull my clothes together.

"Throw us a blanket," Moll called to someone above us, and a moment later, a tattered piece of worsted fell to the ground. She tossed it to me, one end wet from falling into the sewer conduit down the alleyway. That didn't stop me from wrapping it round myself.

"Did we get here in time?"

"Just." I laughed feebly.

"Foxy buggers. One minute you're coming toward me, the next, vanished. Took three o' my lads to find you. They don't leave a trail, these alley rats."

"They were set on by someone who wanted them to—to cut my balls!"

Moll's guffaw became a cough. "The rotters, planning to cripple you as a player or let you bleed to death. Or worse, as it turned out." She pulled me to my feet. "We have a problem. Those rats want to be paid, but now all they have to sell is information."

"Can you silence them?"

"Ain't worth risking my boys. We need a better plan." She walked me down the alley.

"Whoever set them on could report me to the Master of Revels."

"He won't dare. We'll put your Will Shakespeare on him."

I couldn't imagine how that could be done, but neither could I stand half-dressed under a ragged blanket.

Moll spoke to Shakespeare as promised, but before Gabriel Spencer, the man we suspected of setting them on, suffered any consequences, he was killed by Ben Jonson in a duel. Moll had been my savior since then, I'd not again faced such a threat nor even rumor, so far as I knew.

Today, she was in her gossipy mood. "Did I hear right? Your brother Johnny is infatuated with Lady Elizabeth Sidney, bride of the Earl of Rutland?"

"It's worse than that."

Moll had started toward a tavern, but after a glance at my face drew me into an alley. It was narrow, a foul gutter running from the privy at the back of the tavern.

"Ooh!" I held my nose.

"I'll wager this stinking place suits your news. Tell me."

"Johnny fathered a child on Frances Field."

"So?" Moll gave a theatrical shrug. "He can marry her and end this nonsense with Lady Elizabeth. I hear he regards her as his lady." She looked up, her eyes suddenly sharp. "Wait. Rutland's off with Essex's troops in Ireland. Don't tell me Johnny's doing Rutland's duty in Lady Elizabeth's bed?"

"He claims not. Lady Elizabeth will be his patron, he says. He'll be part of her artistic coterie."

"Johnny's more fool than I guessed. What a pity that he has your good looks and none of your courtesy. I'll put my lads on him. As you know, they're like a pack of wild dogs."

"To drag him to church?" I snorted a laugh.

"Why are women so stupid?" Moll shook her head. "I'd have given Frances more credit. She's worked too hard to throw it all away." She threw a loose stone at a rat dashing by, but it kept going. "Women will be women, but I hate that Frances fell like this. Will she return to her village?"

"I doubt it. She can't give up her business."

"Has she tried an old woman with wicked herbs—or worse? I know one down there." Moll waved toward Bankside across the Thames, where one could find every pleasure and every vice.

"I doubt Frances would consider it."

"Then we persuade Johnny." Moll's voice resembled a growl.

"Believe me I've tried everything short of your lads."

"Frances can't keep her shop with a wailing baby upstairs. Even if she conjures up a dead sailor as the father, the bairn would be a bastard."

"There's another solution." I pushed myself against the wall as another rat darted past.

"Let's hear it, but not here." We pushed past tavern-goers to a shadowy chapel porch. "All right, spit it out."

"Johnny says I should marry Frances myself."

The unperturbable Moll staggered. "Say that again."

"You heard right."

"Don't tell me you're considering it."

"I know better." But her question shocked me into recalling a dream where Frances had a huge pregnant belly—and I lived with her. My face flushed. "All right, yes. I might consider it."

Moll shook her head. "Do you recall the words of the marriage service?"

"The couple promise to love and be true to one another."

"That's it?" Her laugh set her hat feather aflutter. "Weren't you once on the brink of marriage yourself? Didn't you tell me the banns were pronounced? Wasn't a ceremony planned and a feast afterwards? Didn't you get out by the narrowest of escapes?"

"Yes, but—"

"But nothing. The ceremony of marriage is no light matter."

"I don't need a lecture from you, Moll."

"I fear your soft side under your male audacity. Or maybe it's your manly side, the urge to take care of an abandoned pregnant woman." She turned tack so fast my head spun. "Do you recall the vows of matrimony in the *Book of Common Prayer*?"

"You're the last person I'd expect to tell me to read the *Book of Common Prayer*, Moll Frith. Even if we do stand on a church porch."

"I know all about religion. A sour uncle of mine was a priest. You can imagine what he thought of me. Wanted to ship me off to the New World with the other misfits." Her jolly face sobered. "You would have the church courts on you in no time, Sander. Believe me, a dead sailor would be a better father for that baby than you."

"No sailors. I'm the only likely candidate. But I doubt Frances would consent. We'd be cried for witches."

"All of London believes you're a man, Sander. Very few of us know otherwise."

"Let's suppose desperation made Frances consider it. We couldn't be married by some hedge priest. She would want a real marriage, and who would marry us?"

Moll looked thoughtful and I expected her to throw up her hands in disgust. Instead she gave me a sly grin. "You'd need a real priest who's bleary-eyed."

"I suppose you know such a man."

"I might. But I'm not sure he'd do it. He couldn't in good faith. The first thing he'd have to say is that marriage is for one man and one woman, meant for the procreation of children, a remedy against sin, mutual society, help, and comfort. Father Daniel may not be that bleary-eyed. And could you make such vows?"

"As you say, all of London thinks I'm a man, and the rest is no problem."

"Oh, the priest doesn't stop there. At the dread day of judgment the secrets of all hearts will be disclosed, so now is the time to confess 'any impediment why ye may not here be lawfully joined together in matrimony.'"

"Why do you tell me this?"

"So you know the ceremony is serious."

"Yes, and necessary to make Frances' baby legitimate."

"In the eyes of God and man. That's what Father Daniel would declare."

"Man!" I couldn't help laughing.

"This is no laughing matter."

"I shall sign my name Alexander Cooke. You surprise me, Moll. I'd expect you to agree, or indeed, fancy the idea. A woman marrying a woman: now that's daring!"

Moll's gave me a conspiratorial smile. "You passed the test."

"What?"

"I was making sure you know the hazard of such a marriage. You risk prison."

"Frances and I are ordinary folk. I doubt the Queen concerns herself with the likes of us any more than she does with you."

"I challenge the law, but I have the right friends. Not in the highest places, but high enough. Bishops don't care how I dress, not if I stay out of their way. Still, I have a healthy fear of the bishops. They're capable of burning anyone they consider heretic."

"Or being burned themselves, back in Queen Mary's day. Things are different now. Queen Elizabeth says one's soul is one's own. The priests executed have been accused of plotting against Her Majesty. So tell me, Moll. Who is this bleary-eyed priest? I would need to offer Frances a proper wedding."

"A proper wedding!" Moll guffawed. "You dream. I might be able to get you married, but make no promises about the wedding. There would be one, that's what counts. If Father Daniel can hold the pen steady, it will be registered.

"Where do we find him?"

"You're serious." Moll shook her head.

"I want to offer Frances a solemnized marriage."

"Father Daniel serves at St. Alfage's, deep in Bankside. Never heard of it? No one has, just them as who avoid more regular churches. You'd be surprised how many who live by questionable means seek spiritual comfort. Old Father Daniel provides it in his fashion."

"Is he ordained?"

"He's so well ordained he lives on communion wine, and any other drink that comes his way. His church would be falling down if not for his parishioners. They keep the place up, and Bankside working women decorate the church with embroideries made between customers."

"I don't know how far that will go in convincing Frances."

Moll dragged me toward the nearest tavern. "Let's drink to it."

"I can't. Rehearsal."

"Then I'll see you onstage at The Theatre. What's the play?"

"*Henry V*. I don't know the full story yet, but I'm to play Mistress Quickly, hostess at the Boar's Head Tavern, and a French princess."

"A right bawdy old tart is Mistress Quickly, but French royalty!" Moll brayed her laugh. "Don't tell me you have to speak that girly language."

"I can speak enough." In truth I'd been studying French all through Lent, tutored by Lady Mary Sidney Herbert, the Countess of Pembroke. Lady Mary delighted in befriending a player born female. "Now I'm really late!" I took off running.

Is not the truth the truth?
FALSTAFF, *HENRY IV, PART 1*

CHAPTER III
April 1599

Rain had begun on my way to Shoreditch. Muddy and wet, I dashed through the back door of The Theatre and dark attiring room onto the wooden stage surrounded by empty galleries. The stale odor of ale and woodchips wafted up from the pit as I took my place among the actors on stage. Here was my family, the Lord Chamberlain's Men, and my true father Tom Pope who, bless him, never imagined that I was a girl, though Shakespeare guessed early on.

Shakespeare, offstage so quiet as to be overlooked, outlined the plot of *Henry V* with theatrical animation. Instead of simply reading the plot card we'd all seen posted backstage, he began by reading the first speech of the Chorus, the part he would play. I'd never heard an apology in any of our plays, and certainly not one spoken by the playwright himself.

> *But pardon, gentles all,*
> *The flat unraised spirits that have dared*
> *On this unworthy scaffold to bring forth*
> *So great an object: can this cockpit hold*
> *The vasty fields of France? or may we cram*
> *Within this wooden O the very casques*
> *That did affright the air at Agincourt?*

The Chorus asks the audience to use their imaginations to carry us to the battle fields—while feeding those imaginations with vivid pictures. At the end of plays a character like Puck might ask for the audience to applaud, but begging their humble patience from the beginning? An intriguing device. 'The vasty fields of France' was a hint: this war was on a grand scale. Prince Hal in the two Henry V plays fooled away his days with Falstaff and his drinking buddies, but by an almost magical conversion, he's now the daring and patriotic king.

We all had our parts, so Shakespeare glided over the beginning of the play, and following Shakespeare's lead, Sincler, Bryan, and I read our best scene together. I spoke as Mistress Quickly, hostess of the Boar's Head now married to Pistol. John Sincler read Pistol, George Bryan, Bardolph.

Me: *Prithee, honey-sweet husband, let me bring thee to Staines.*

Sincler: *No; for my manly heart doth mourn. Bardolph, be blithe; Nym, rouse thy vaunting veins; Boy, bristle thy courage up; for Falstaff he is dead, And we must mourn therefore.*

Bryan: *Would I were with him, wheresome'er he is, either in heaven or in hell!*

Me: *Nay sure, he's not in hell; he's in Arthur's bosom, if ever man went to Arthur's bosom. 'A made a finer end, and went away and it had been any christom child. 'A parted ev'n just between twelve and one, ev'n at the turning o' th' tide; for after I saw him fumble with the sheets, and play with flowers, and smile upon his finger's end, I knew there was but one way; for his nose was as sharp as a pen, and 'a babbl'd of green fields. "How now, Sir John?" quoth I, "what, man? Be a' good cheer." So 'a cried out, "God, God, God!" three or four times. Now I, to comfort him, bid him 'a should not think of God; I hop'd there was no need to trouble himself with any such thoughts yet. So 'a bade me lay more clothes on his feet. I put my hand into the bed and felt them, and they were as cold as any stone; then I felt to his knees, and so up'ard and up'ard, and all was as cold as any stone.*

We had to read it, in honor of Will Kemp, the best Falstaff imaginable. Indeed, Shakespeare had written the part for him. As Sir John Falstaff, he stole the show in both parts of *Henry IV.* Audiences had loved Kemp, the funniest man in England. Perhaps that was the problem. He didn't confine his creativity to his famous jigs after each play. In many a performance, his extemporaneous jesting convulsed the audience with laughter, especially the groundlings, drowning out our lines. There no room for that rowdy sack-drinker after Prince Hal was crowned. When I heard Shakespeare speak of Kemp in the past tense, it felt as if his era had passed. Burbage speculated that Shakespeare had a new sort of clown in mind. No more of Kemp's imitable jigs. I owed my career to Will Kemp and treasured him, treasured the belly laughs of those less complicated times. One distant day, may he too lie in Arthur's bosom. But first: many more jolly days to him!

My attention returned to our reading when Richard Burbage as King Henry declaimed his lines to the governor from outside Harfleur as if an audience filled the theatre.

> *If I begin the battery once again,*
> *I will not leave the half-achieved Harfleur*
> *Till in her ashes she lie buried.*
> *The gates of mercy shall be all shut up,*
> *And the flesh'd soldier, rough and hard of heart,*
> *In liberty of bloody hand shall range*
> *With conscience wide as hell, mowing like grass*
> *Your fresh fair virgins and your flow'ring infants.*
> *What is't to me, when you yourselves are cause,*
> *If your pure maidens fall into the hand . . .*
> *What say you? Will you yield, and this avoid,*
> *Or, guilty in defence, be thus destroy'd?*

No one but me seemed to mind this violent rhetoric. I couldn't help but think, as Henry later addresses his troops as a band of brothers, that these were the brothers he'd have commanded to despoil Harfleur, violate its daughters, and murder the children. I would play little part in the fighting, just brief appearances as the soldier Williams, who picks a quarrel with Henry in disguise the night before the battle of Agincourt. He's the one who tells Henry that at the final reckoning, all the deaths and maiming of his soldiers will be on the king's head. Williams does not totally get away with that.

My lesson in French as I play Katherine, princess of France, Henry's bride-to-be, brought a light, domestic touch. For that I must make use of the French pronunciation my friend Mary Sidney Herbert taught me. In the final scene, Katherine and Henry do their best to communicate despite their lack of a common language. Some humor at last, after all the warfare.

Hearing the story we felt echoes of the present crisis over the Irish campaign: poor men pressed into military service, grief caused by ambitions of the powerful. I nudged Richard Burbage. "Bubble reputation: does that sound like Essex?" His finger crossed his throat as if cutting it.

King Henry was a confusing character, combining the valor of a heroic warrior with those threats of gruesome violence on civilians and an order to kill the French prisoners. Was warfare grandly patriotic or evil? It was up to us to speak the lines and the audience to decide.

Though Henry's marriage to Princess Katherine brings peace to the two monarchies at last, the epilogue, spoken again by Shakespeare, dims the English victory. All that King Henry gained would soon be lost. Such were the vagaries of history, as could happen even to our celebrated theatre. Not every monarch would love plays as Queen Elizabeth did. Puritans who hated play-acting might one day triumph.

No doubt this play would be another success. My more immediate concern was for Frances. Instead of joining my fellows at the Nag's Head, I slipped into the afternoon drizzle and headed home. My room was damp and chill, but I didn't take time to light the fire, smaller that the one that warmed Frances' upstairs chamber. I'd added a thick counterpane to the bed and made my attic room in the house of Mistress Mountjoy and her husband in Silver Street as comfortable as I could.

I lit the half-burnt candle on the table and penned a brief note to

Mary Sidney Herbert, Countess of Pembroke. Some years ago, she had taken a fancy to me for reasons mysterious at the time.

After a performance of *Richard III*, at the Theatre, she said she wanted to invite me to her grand London establishment on the Thames, Baynard's Castle. To my surprise, she did. In her private closet she offered me wine and delicacies, not that I had much appetite sitting with a Countess in such rarified surroundings.

She wanted to know me better. After all, a young man needs connections. That made me uncomfortable. I'd learned all too well that women found boy players appealing, and I resisted them as much as I did men.

"I appreciate talent and ambition. Collect it, some would say. And I see you as both talented and ambitious. Shall I call you Alexander?"

"I go by Sander."

"Then Sander it is."

And, still more disquieting, she said, "My poets call me Corinna or some such name. You may call me Marie."

"I doubt I can do that."

"Of course you can. We must be friends."

Her unflinching eyes invited confidences, so when she took my hand and asked how I came to be an actor, I told her. Fathered by a glover in Saffron Walden, I left one summer to seek my fortune and ended up joining Lord North's Men, a company of traveling players. When Will Kemp met up with us at the faire on Midsummer Commons outside Cambridge, he told my fellow player Jack and me to look him up if we came to London. Playing companies were in need of experienced boy players.

When I added that I was no gentleman born, Marie smiled.

"Nor are most actors, playwrights, poets. Including those in my circle. At Wilton House, chemists extract their elixirs and poets hone their skills. All men, of course. Women inspire the arts, women may patronize artists, but few women practice art and fewer still dare consider alchemical studies."

I felt a tingle of misgiving. Where was this going?

"You must be a quick study to play one role after another. But in our ways we all play roles."

"You too?" I paused, then dared, "I have noted your eyes, lady. They show much wisdom, but sorrow as well."

"You see that? Well, it's true. Those that I loved most in the world have died, my dear brother Philip, the daughters my heart desired. But one cannot dwell on grief. I'm fortunate in husband, sons, nieces—and now you. I hope you will trust me."

"Pray forgive me, but what is it you desire of me, my lady?"

"Marie."

"Marie."

"Had my daughters lived, I would have desired them to express themselves as artists, poets—even actors, for surely one day our stages will allow women. So I wish for my nieces. I've only gone so far as to translate a play. And of course prepare my dear brother Philip's poem *Arcadia* for publication after he died."

"A niece onstage? I can't imagine your kin as stage players." One of those nieces was Lady Elizabeth!

"Perhaps not, but what a charming idea. Now I have a question for you."

I set down my wine goblet, as if whatever she had to say might shatter it.

"Tell me. Were you christened Alexander?"

"N-no."

"Alice, perhaps?" My heart thudded and I couldn't get a word out. "You are a superb actor. And a girl, am I not correct?"

"I—I—" My face supplied her answer.

"What you have endured to transform yourself and maintain yourself is beyond imagining."

"You invited me here because—"

"Because I want to become acquainted with such a rare person as yourself. Will you tell me your true name?"

It was difficult to get the words out; I'd not mentioned that name since I fled Saffron Walden. "K-Kate. Kate Collins."

"I'm curious to see, Kate. How far can a woman go in this man's world of ours? I've gone uncommonly far myself. I would like to help you. I can provide you with books and introductions—"

"As Alexander. Or Sander."

"Of course."

"That's very kind." Risk sizzled round me warmer than her fire.

"You hesitate." She gazed at me. "I promise to keep your secret."

"Dare we be friends, Marie? I cannot walk into Baynard's Castle as if it were the Mermaid or The Theatre. We rarely cross paths in London, and Wilton House must be days' journey from here."

"My words are not empty, Sander. Count me as your friend. Soon our household leaves for Wiltshire. When I return here, you're welcome to call any time. The doors here and at Wilton House are always open to you. Pembrokes are patrons of theatre, so why not of a particular actor?"

Since then we'd occasionally exchanged letters when she stayed at Wilton House where I'd once visited. Now she was as near as Baynard's.

I sealed the note. If ever I needed to talk to Marie, it was today.

Darting through Shoreditch, I nearly collided with an old woman carrying a basket of squirming eels and avoided more collisions until I reached the Thames, where stately homes stretched along the waterfront. Grandest and most ancient was Baynard's Castle.

The butler who opened the smaller door cut into the massive oaken one gave me a cold look. "Please deliver this note to the Countess," I said with more confidence than he inspired.

He took it with aloof disdain, clearly disapproving of a player in these hallowed halls.

The reception chamber felt like the medieval castle it once had been. Elsewhere in the vast edifice, the geometric tiled floor and roughly plastered stone walls had been replaced or covered, but this room still resembled the one where dwelt the Yorks, including their duke eventually crowned King Richard III.

The butler left me standing alone under a sputtering torch amidst

York ghosts, hesitant to sit on any of the carved wooden benches pushed against the walls. At last Marie's maidservant Jane bounded down the stairs with a coy smile that left no question: to her I was a marvel, a stage player she found fascinating.

Blandly pleasant, I followed her up the broad timbered stairs, woven hangings along the whitewashed stairwell dimly lit by her candle.

Jane opened the door to the Countess' closet, a bower of firelight and candles blushing the dove grey skirt that fell around her. She turned with a welcoming smile. "What a pleasure to see you, Sander. Do sit down."

I took the small upholstered chair facing her, its back intricately carved with entwined flowers. "I hope I'm not intruding."

"No, Sander. You are welcome. Did you come to tell me about your new play? I understand it's about King Henry V."

"True. Historical pageantry and war."

Jane filled two etched glass goblets from the flagon on the table between us and, with a wistful smile in my direction, left.

"That's not why I've come today. I must speak to you as a friend."

She lifted her goblet to me and we took sips of the sweet golden wine. A fine vintage from Spain, far better than what I was accustomed to.

I held the precious glass between careful fingers. "My concern comes close to you, in a way. You remember my brother Johnny?"

"I've oft seen him onstage. A prepossessing young man."

"So he is, Countess. Dismayingly so."

"Remember? You're to call me Marie."

"I fear what I have to say requires more formality."

"Not in private." Her russet eyes held mine. "How do you mean, 'close to me'?"

"Indirectly, regarding your niece Lady Elizabeth. I'm sorry to say, Johnny's in trouble."

"Nothing to do with her, I trust. Elizabeth needs no more trouble."

"I know her husband has gone to Ireland. May he return safely."

"Umm," was all she said.

I drank the last of the wine and set the glass down for fear of crushing it. "Johnny has made a friend of mine pregnant and refuses to marry her."

"That's dreadful! What reason does he give?"

"He says Lady Elizabeth will offer him patronage, and he owes her fealty."

"Fealty to my niece? Elizabeth is a virtuous young woman and newly married, as I'm sure you know."

"Johnny will not compromise her virtue. He honors her like his lady, as in the poems of old."

"You mean when knighthood was in flower? His behavior seems anything but chivalrous."

She set down her goblet, retrieved the flagon from the long table along the wall, and began to pace the thick carpet. Her movement agitated me, though I remained rooted to my chair, holding her with my eyes.

"Nonetheless, Marie, he's convinced he owes Lady Elizabeth his service as a knight does his lady."

"And owes the mother of his child nothing? Elizabeth would never tell him to abandon a woman who carries his child. I doubt she knows anything about this sorry situation."

"She ought to."

"Who is this woman?"

"Frances Field, owner of the dressmaking shop on the Bridge. The Queen's Silkwoman."

"Ah yes. Capable and enterprising."

"Perhaps that's the problem. Johnny thinks that Lady Elizabeth needs him more than Frances does, as she's better at taking care of herself."

"With a baby coming! He must marry her; that's all there is to it."

"He absolutely refuses." I paused, willing her to sit.

She looked at the flagon in her hand, as if she didn't know she'd held it all this time. She poured wine into her goblet, taking a sip before filling mine and sitting down at last.

"In fact, Johnny suggests that *I* marry Frances."

"What?" Now she was the one who looked about to shatter the goblet she gripped so tightly. "I cannot believe it. You're telling me he wants you to marry this girl to rescue her from his wickedness?" Marie looked out the window for long silent moments. "There's no excuse for Johnny's refusing his responsibility to Mistress Field. But I can almost imagine what he's thinking. Have you met Lady Elizabeth?"

"I've seen her, strawberry gold curls, gracious manners—and now, I understand, a Countess."

Marie sighed. "I'm not confident her marriage is destined for happiness. The Earl of Rutland is unlikely to offer her his full devotion, nor father children on her." She added quickly, "Surely you don't imagine—"

"Johnny's refusing Frances is shameful. But he does recognize propriety. We can trust him so far."

"I would hope so. As for Elizabeth, she'll not risk her advantageous marriage, whatever its failings, with her husband in Ireland and all. I suppose Johnny offers what she yearns for, a connection to the world of theatre and poetry. She has aspirations, which I no doubt have encouraged, though not me alone. Still, she knows the limits of a charming young man's attentions."

"Do you mean that Lady Elizabeth can offer something in return for Johnny's loyalty?"

"That's not what I'm saying. I fear your brother is drawn by her promises, which are likely less than his hopes. Lady Elizabeth must seem an almost mythic creature to him, the only child of my late brother Philip, courtier poet *par excellence* and the most splendid person I've ever known. The Queen's funeral, long may it be from now, can scarcely surpass Sir Philip Sidney's in grandeur. Think of what such a woman represents to a village boy."

I bristled at "village boy." Yet what was I but a village girl? By coming to London, Johnny and I not only changed our surname but our identity. Now our destinies vastly outshone our Saffron Walden childhoods. However, the Sidney-Herbert line stretched back to

William the Conqueror and the nobility of ancient Wales. Johnny and I could trace no ancestor of note.

"You're right, Marie. Your niece has turned Johnny's head."

"She may enrich his life, though so far as Mistress Field is concerned, at unforgiveable cost."

"So I told him. He'll not be moved."

She gazed out the window, looking thoughtful. What at last she spoke, I could scarcely believe my ears.

"What a novel idea, that you should marry Mistress Field."

I coughed on my wine. "Even if I could imagine such a thing, Frances never could."

"Under the circumstances she might regard such a marriage as a saving grace. Unless you can think of someone else for her—"

"I cannot, but that doesn't mean she will accept *me*."

"I expect you came here in hopes that I would convince Elizabeth to release your brother. I regret I haven't that power, Sander. She's a married woman. I doubt she knows anything about Frances Field."

"Will you tell her?"

"I'm sorry. That's up to your brother."

"And he won't," I said under my breath.

Placing my hopes in Marie had been folly. She was a grand lady who had no power over her own sons, let alone a married niece. Who was I, or Frances, to her? Even less, Johnny, a bauble for her niece.

"Think about marriage for a moment, Sander. I was Henry Herbert's third wife, wed when I was sixteen."

"A fine match."

"Yes, in the eyes of society. But how fine is it for a young girl to marry a man nearing fifty? Make no mistake, I'm content. The Earl has been a kind and indulgent husband. Marriage is sanctioned in the eyes of God, but also based on status and position."

"Forgive me, Marie, but you speak of the nobility."

"Not altogether. A farmer marries a sturdy woman who can help work the farm and give him children to assist and to inherit. The woman marries a man who can provide for her and her children. A tradesman marries a woman who can support his endeavors.

She marries a man who provides her with security and handsome clothes. We're better as two in this world."

I wanted to say, "Tell Johnny that." I gazed into my goblet, fighting tears of frustration. "What about love?"

"Generosity toward each other and mutual caring can, with time, grow into love."

"I understand what you're saying, but do you mean—" I paused, confused. "You're not talking about Frances and me, are you? We're fast friends. But two women! How could we marry?" I banged down my goblet hard enough to crack, but neither of us even glanced at it.

"I'm not telling you what to do, but it wouldn't be impossible. After all these years as a man, no one questions you. By marrying, you would guarantee Frances her business and position, and she would be a helpmeet to you."

A helpmeet. I ran my fingers through my hair as if the gesture could clear my perplexed mind. "I do like the idea of a companion."

"And Frances needs a husband. You two could make something of this marriage, peculiar though it be."

"Worse than peculiar. I've read the ceremony of matrimony in the *Book of Common Prayer*—" I couldn't go on.

Then I realized. In the world's eye I was but a player. Marie had served as lady-in-waiting to Queen Elizabeth. She knew I was female, as she had befriended me for that very reason. But perhaps, as my status was so far removed from hers, she believed I needn't worry about those binding words. She herself was known for her piety, but not all nobility took church dictums seriously. The Earl of Rutland married Lady Elizabeth knowing, if Marie's intimations were correct, that he'd not father children with her. I'd seen enough of noble marriages to know that not a few were contracted more for titles and lands than mutual comfort and love.

"Even if Frances consented to say the words in church, which I doubt, what would Queen Elizabeth think? Frances is her Silkwoman."

"Why would she care?" Marie asked.

"I'm afraid Her Majesty more than suspects that I'm a woman.

We spoke after I played Kate in *Taming of the Shrew* and she said as much. She expects Shakespeare and me to bring brand new women to the stage."

"Oh! Well, it may have slipped her mind by now. The Queen has bigger worries." Marie played with her goblet. "I think you might at least consider this marriage."

Sadness weighted my spirits. Marie's advice missed the essential, the love that animates body and soul, transcending logic and lust. I thought of myself and John Donne when our ardor flourished. Passion—and pain.

Perhaps she was right to disregard intense emotion in favor of loving companionship. Frances and I might have that much. Perhaps such a love as John's and mine could happen only outside marriage. More poetry than real life, its embraces no more than embroidery on harsh reality. My hopeful visit to Marie had failed.

"In her husband's absence, Lady Elizabeth will stay here. I leave for Wilton House tomorrow, and she has the run of Baynard's. She may entertain guests such as Johnny, of course, but this is not her household."

So Johnny was mistaken. He'd have no special privileges at Baynard's Castle. Would he listen if I told him so?

"Thank you for listening, Marie."

"I have faith in you, Sander."

So, I thought as I left her sturdy fortress, Marie cannot help, and Johnny has no reason to change his mind. I felt like crying.

Instead, I gathered my forces like a man and strode forth. On the morrow I must persuade Frances to accept me as her husband.

I have thrust myself into this maze,
Haply to wive and thrive as best I may.
PETRUCHIO, *THE TAMING OF THE SHREW*

CHAPTER IV
April 1599

In the morning, with clouds riding on the wind and the streets muddy, I headed to Frances' shop. As I approached London Bridge, I stopped to look down at the Thames, full of wherry boats and barges. Past the docks at Deptford, a huge vessel sailed out to sea. Watching it billow through the dun-colored water, I was reminded of my girlhood dream. My idol was Lady Mary Killigrew who, disguised as a man, became a pirate captain. From what I'd learned since about pirates, better that I joined stage players. Still, a ship with flags unfurled entices the imagination to other places, other lives.

In no hurry to fulfill my errand, my mind idled, looking toward the sea as random thoughts fluttered by. Never had I imagined anything beyond friendship with a woman. The one girl who fell for me, thinking I was a boy, I loved as a comrade. My fellow player Jack and I were stuck at Audley End, well away from plague-haunted London, with a handful of players and poets when Lizzie appeared with Ferdinando Stanley's entourage. With Lizzie making three, Jack and I had a jolly time romping through the estate's expansive grounds. Then she told me she loved me and planted a kiss on my lips. Eventually Lizzie extracted a kiss from me in exchange for telling me secrets important at the time, but I didn't fulfill her hopes of more.

Like Lizzie, Frances had a cheerful nature until this crisis, though not Lizzie's freckles and scatterbrained ways. But treasured friend and confidant as she'd become, never a thought of kisses on either side.

With John Donne it was entirely different. From my first sight of him coming out of the Dolphin the day I arrived in London, I loved him. Little by little we'd made each others' acquaintance, me knowing all the while what I would want, were it possible, and he confused by his mixed feelings toward me, a boy. Eventually, he discovered otherwise, to both our pleasure.

But Lizzie believed me a boy henceforward. She kissed me goodbye and left Audley End on Stanley's wagon, me watching them vanish, bemused. A girl loved me—as a boy. Lizzie was a sweetheart, and I recalled thinking I'd have fancied her were I a boy indeed.

But Frances? She too was a sweetheart, I supposed, but I was now a man, not given to romantic imagining. Yet Frances was the one I must convince to marry me. I felt sad and more than a little angry. Why should I be responsible for Johnny's reckless behavior?

Frances' image came to me, superimposed on Lizzie's and a girl who'd helped Dr. Garnet years ago named Dorcas. All of them petite, energetic, capable, kind, and pretty. All were better women than Kate Collins would have been. I had too much of the boy in me to be sweet. I hadn't wanted to serve any man, not my would-be husband Martin Day, but not John Donne either.

Perhaps, then, I must serve a woman as best I could.

I sighed and turned away from the river, determined. Folks were filling London Bridge as I went on my way, careful not to be struck by a horse or fumbled by a man who fancied a handsome young fellow, especially if he recognized me as an actor.

Inside Frances' shop, scraps of fabric scattered over the floor gave the effect of a brilliant Turkey carpet. Frances sat at the cluttered table, stabbing her needle into peacock blue velvet.

She gave me a tense smile. "What did Johnny say?"

"I'm sorry I have no better report. He went on and on about

Lady Elizabeth Sidney. I couldn't convince him that he owes you an obligation beyond money."

Frances blinked her eyes, holding back tears. "You did your best. Oh, Sander!"

"He actually suggested that *I* marry you."

"He didn't!"

"He did."

"You're a great friend Sander, and I've kept your secret. But we couldn't *marry*."

"I know perfectly well that women don't marry." I too had been repelled at Johnny's suggestion. But for so long I'd lived as a man with never as domestic an arrangement as my occasional suppers with Frances in her upstairs dwelling. If we married, she would be the wife. There would be a baby, a family.

I shook myself.

"Sander? Are you all right? You look strange."

"You need a husband, Frances. The Queen may assume you're married, but here on the Bridge, they'll know better."

"Does that mean I should marry you?"

"Perhaps."

"I can't. It would be against the will of God."

"If I'd taken to heart the teachings of our priest back in Saffron Walden about woman's place, I'd never have dared flee my wedding and assume male identity."

"That was different. You avoided marriage altogether."

"By becoming a boy. Ever since, I've been Alexander Cooke."

"Can you imagine marrying me under false pretenses?"

"I can, for your sake. For friendship."

Her eyes shone with unshed tears. "I appreciate your sense of duty, but surely we needn't do anything so drastic. Johnny may marry me later."

"Are you pinning your hopes on that?"

A tear ran down her cheek.

"How far gone are you?"

"Some two months."

"Don't expect Johnny to change his mind. When he's set on something, that's it. Look at how hard he worked to join me in London and become an actor. Now he's devoted to Lady Elizabeth, certain that her patronage will open every door. Besides, he pities her."

"As he doesn't pity me."

"Apparently not. I've always thought it best a woman be capable, but in this case, your independence works against you. Johnny thinks you'll do just fine on your own. I know better, Frances. I pity you."

"You needn't." She gripped my hand. "I don't see why you'd want to marry me. What good would it do you?"

"I never expected to marry, and certainly not a woman."

"I should think not!"

"Still, I can imagine making a home with you and helping raise your child."

"I can't marry a woman, Sander, even one in doublet and hose."

"Think about it." I stood.

"Wait," Frances put a hand on my arm. "I've never needed a friend as I do now. I have no one to talk to about—about any of this. Will you stay a little?"

I sat. "You're a brave woman."

"No I'm not. I'm desperate. I knew Johnny befriended Lady Elizabeth but never guessed what she meant to him. When I realized I was pregnant, I was certain he'd marry me. He always said how he loved me, how there was no one like me." She attempted a laugh. "Anyone who gets to the ripe age of twenty-one still a virgin lacks wisdom about men. No one ever caught my fancy, but Johnny—" Frances sighed. "He's charming, your brother, and a lot like you, or so I thought. Now I know he won't change his mind, at least not before the baby's born."

"You want to be a mother." It was more statement than question.

"I always expected to be, yes. I'm settled and healthy—and," Frances grimaced, "part way there."

"Part way to a family, all but the father."

"My prentice master Gemma Cooper brought up her son without a father. A fine young man her Robin turned out to be. It's easier in the country, though, especially if a woman is employed in a noble household as Gemma was when Robin was born. I could go home to Leicestershire. My mother would welcome me, but there's no life for me there, nor employment. Nothing like this." Her wave encompassed the shop, the river below, and city beyond.

"You asked what good it would be for me to marry you, Frances. A great deal, when I think about it. I never expected to have my own family, but here's one ready-made, and I like the idea. I can't think of any other woman I'd consider marrying."

"Nor can I." Frances almost smiled.

"You mean, you will consider it?"

"No, no. I meant I'd never thought of marrying any woman. But perhaps I could—consider it, I mean. I don't know, Sander. I really don't know. What about Johnny?"

"He's not part of any decision you make. When he refused you, what did you intend to do?"

"It was only five days ago that we spoke, and I've hardly slept since. Everything you say, except for you and me marrying, of course, has gone through my head. Shame and rage and—" Frances stopped herself. "I pulled myself together. I told myself, dress discreetly and when the time comes, find a way to raise the child alone."

"You cannot do that. Marry me and you'll save your reputation and be a mother with no questions asked. I'll admit, Frances, I'm tired of living in lodgings. We could create a household together."

"A marriage of friends." She spoke in a small voice. "I like you very much, Sander, but I can't see you playing husband."

I rose. "Think about it."

Stepping onto the wet Bridge, I imagined what was going through Frances' mind. Her choice was down to marrying me or no one. Marrying a woman would be better than forging on alone, but could she give up Johnny? Never again yearn for a man's embrace? Much was at stake, the child, her employment, even her safety, but she could she live a lie? For years I'd lived a lie, sacrificing woman's emotions, which now I could share with her.

My heart clutched as I pictured Frances weighing these considerations as she stared into Thames' oblivion. May she decide for self-preservation and feel sufficient affection for me to make our union possible.

LEONATO: *What do you mean, my lord?*
CLAUDIO: *Not to be married.*
MUCH ADO ABOUT NOTHING

CHAPTER V
May 1599

The afternoon sun warmed the wooden planks of The Theatre. From backstage we heard the audience gathering, loud voices fueled by drink and anticipation of the new history by the Lord Chamberlain's Men, *Henry V.*

The flourish sounded, the audience quieted, and the play began with Shakespeare alone on the stage.

> *O for a Muse of fire, that would ascend*
> *The brightest heaven of invention!*
> *A kingdom for a stage, princes to act,*
> *And monarchs to behold the swelling scene!*

My heart pounded with the ring of the words. The audience was utterly silent as if expanding their imaginations to contain the vast fields of France.

As I awaited my entrance, I thought of King Henry VI, my first time on Shakespeare's stage, all those years ago, pious son of this valiant Henry, who lost all his father had won. In those three long-ago plays of *Henry VI*, I played powerful women: Joan de Pucelle, called Joan of Arc, and Queen Margaret, who commanded her weak husband's army herself.

My roles in *Henry V* didn't come close to Joan and Queen

Margaret or to witty Beatrice in our recent comedy, *Much Ado About Nothing*.

But the audience loved every minute, stirring speeches and heroic King Henry turned into lover at the end. Not until we took our bows did I look at them. There sat Frances in the front row of the gallery. In the gown of Princess Katherine, I threw her a kiss, then cast kisses generally to the cheering crowd.

When applause died down, Frances pushed her way to our backstage exit. "You were superb. I didn't know you could speak French."

In the chaos in the doorway, Johnny unwittingly bumped against her. Frances turned to him, eyes flaring. "You well suit the part of Richard of Cambridge, Johnny Cooke! A faithless traitor."

"No one likes a would-be assassin," Johnny replied blithely.

I liked Frances' anger. Before she went on her way, we agreed to meet later.

With a hopeful heart, I joined the hubbub of actors in the tiring room. Earlier in my career I'd have been on edge, changing clothes so near my fellow players. Fortunately, I'd had no enemies in the company since Samuel Gilburne left and the hotheaded Gabriel Spencer met his end in a duel with Ben Jonson. The newer boy players regarded me as the one for the principle women's roles, more concerned with playing their parts well than speculating about me.

Occasionally I made a ritual of shaving my face, as did the other boys as hairs began to sprout. The pretense of blade against my skin gave my cheeks a roughness requiring careful makeup for female roles. Long practice served me well. With my back to the others, I held down my shift when putting on or shedding skirts, keeping my breast bindings well-concealed. This maneuvering I did like a man, experienced and efficient.

Backstage I felt relatively safe, though from long habit vigilant in public. One overly curious eye catching me out, one slip, and I'd be finished. It was no less a crime now for a woman to pass as a man than ever, Moll Frith notwithstanding. I dared admit my sex only to my most trusted friends. Flogging was the least of the dire consequences. Discovery would end my stage acting, the only life I could envision.

Though passing as a husband would be a further danger, the idea of marrying Frances had taken hold of me.

In our own clothes, we headed to the Mermaid, a band of brothers of the non-warlike sort. Most every drinker had seen our show and wanted to buy us cups of ale. Burbage was hailed as a Mars playing King Harry, and the rest of us, even those who'd played the French king and Dauphin, were hailed as a victorious army.

I looked for Shakespeare, who in the midst of revelry faded into the background in his unobtrusive brown clothing, serene and detached. He sat to one side, looking satisfied.

I joined him. "Today I noticed something that surprised me. When you described King Henry's triumphant welcome in London, you said something that could only be about the Earl of Essex. Weren't you comparing King Henry to the Earl of Essex when he returns from Ireland?"

Shakespeare looked amused. "As a loving likelihood, I believe the Chorus says."

"He'll bring 'rebellion breached upon his sword.' I heard that as a threat. Do you think Essex will return from Ireland to rebel against the Queen?"

"It's a play, Sander."

"That's no answer." The noise rose along with the consumption of ale. "Do you think it could happen?"

Shakespeare spoke close to my ear. "Essex is bold and of royal blood. Once the Queen's favorite, he's flaunted his disrespect of Her Majesty and now is at odds with Sir Robert Cecil. So yes, I think it's possible he could foment rebellion."

A terrible feeling came over me. This was not the time to be drinking a cup of ale. "I have to go, but first I'll tell you a secret."

"Please do."

"At least a hint. When Princess Katherine refuses to kiss King Henry, he tells her, 'You and I cannot be confined within the weak lists of a country's fashion.' Even though I'm no king, I found those words encouraging for something daring I plan to do."

"More than this?" He eyed my codpiece as I rose from the bench.

"More even than this." I started to tell him I hoped to marry Frances Field, but the ruckus drowned me out. A wave and I was off.

By the time I reached London Bridge, the day had ended in purple and amber light casting brilliant reflections on the river. Shops were closed, but Frances' door was on the latch. Inside was dark except for a faint light at the top of the stairs. She called down, "Sander? Lock the door and come up."

Her worktable was cleared and covered with a calico cloth. A candle flickered, a low fire burned in the grate, and wine was laid out. I pointed to the rail of partial garments, "I too am all pins and needles. What did you decide?"

"Even while watching your play, Sander, I thought about our marrying. It terrifies me more even than coming to London on my own."

"Can you get past terror?"

"I did back when I was but a girl." Frances took a sip of wine, collecting her courage. "You offer me an escape from my dilemma, but I'd have to make sacred vows knowing you're a woman and sign the church registry as Mistress Alexander Cooke."

"We might live together without marriage, but the child would still be a bastard and your reputation ruined if you cohabited with an actor. You need to be Mistress Cooke."

"Can you pronounce those vows?"

I looked down my male attire with a shrug. "Reading the marriage service gave me pause, but yes, I can do that too."

"Such a marriage would be regarded as the devil's doing."

Moll would call my confident reply male bravado. "We won't be found out."

"And Johnny?"

"You tell me. Can you let him go?"

Frances looked surprised. "I don't think of him that way now. No, I mean, do you trust him?"

"He's selfish. But he's a loyal brother, and this was his idea in the first place. We'd be making things all too easy for him, but that's beside the point."

Wine cups in hand, we sat next to each other facing the fire, a foretaste, I could imagine, of a companionable life together.

"Men suit themselves. I've admired how you do that, Sander, as if you really were male."

"I shouldn't have to tell you, as one who fashions clothes which define clients by status and profession: people base their impressions on how you present yourself, and not just onstage. I've more or less become a man even to myself, and onstage I'm whatever the role demands. With me as husband, you'll have a better marriage than most."

"You're as crazy as Moll Frith."

"She'd marry a woman openly if she wanted to."

"Even Moll daren't go that far."

"I said 'if she wanted to.' She doesn't." I emptied my wine cup. "A crying baby is no asset for a business woman. Marry me, Frances, and we'll be two solving these problems."

As I looked into her doubtful face, I felt a surge of affection. "Dear Frances, we'll carry this off so long as we're united: women together in the man's world of Queen Elizabeth's London. The two of us can create something brand new."

"That would be more daring that anything penned by a playwright. Something brand new." Her eyes seemed bright with possibility.

"You once told me you were hesitant to marry because a husband would have rights over your shop and could control you. You and I would share sovereignty. I'll be husband and you wife, but beneath appearances, you and I are equal."

"Equal." Frances smiled. "I like the sound of that."

"I mean it. Marry me and save your reputation and your livelihood."

"You argue persuasively."

I took that as consent. "Let's drink to it," I said as I refilled our cups. "To the union of Frances Field and Alexander Cooke."

"You must find a priest who'll wed us. Properly."

"Of course."

Frances' face glowed with relief.

Early next morning, I crossed the Bridge to Bankside and searched out the Bear and Staff, down a dark lane in the bowels of Southwark. I'd not before ventured into Moll Frith's territory. She lodged somewhere nearby where her little gang found crannies to sleep. Her boys were mostly orphans, among the many lost souls haunting the poorest parts of London.

To give Moll her due, she made sure they didn't go hungry. She trained them in nipping purses, the only education available for such lads. Sometimes she found one of them a job as a potboy in a tavern or a sweeper of horseshit, a way out of thievery though probably less profitable. Boys did occasionally rise, thanks to luck or aid. I saw one of her lads, clean and sweet-faced, serving as an altar boy at St. Saviour's.

Moll was leaving the tavern as I turned into the filthy lane.

"What are you doing here, Sander Cooke? No place for a stage player!"

"Then come with me to somewhere suitable."

Moll hurried me to brighter streets. "I missed you at the Mermaid after *Henry V*. Wanted to compliment you on that naughty French lesson."

Narrow alleys had given way to the working section of Bankside. Moll had to shout. "Plenty of noise here if you want to be drowned out."

We passed the reeking Bear Garden, where mastiffs barked and snarled loud enough to make a deaf person's ears ache. At a derelict yard by the Rose Theatre, just out of range of the rancid fumes of bear and dog droppings, we paused, shreds of playbills caught in the tufts of weeds at our feet.

Moll took off her hat, her hair greasy in the dull light. She brushed the hat brim absently, caressing the feather and the red paste jewel that held it in place. "I imagine you're here because Frances consented, mercy to her."

I ignored her guffaw. "Time to visit your Father Daniel."

"You are in a hurry." But she started walking at a brisk pace.

The church of St. Alfage looked surprisingly well tended, given its surroundings. Adjoining it was a wasteland taken over by cats and men sleeping rough. Debris and remnants of the house that once stood here had been haphazardly piled to make room for this population, ever-changing, according to Moll. I could only wonder, who would stay here if they could find anything better? I felt for this ragged population, never before realizing that so many in London lived in grim poverty.

Inside the church there was no sign of Father Daniel. Moll walked up the side aisle to a curtain concealing the sacristy and peeked in.

"Oh, it's you, Mary." A small man with a splotchy red face sat in a low chair. His eyes were indeed bleary, but his smile was wide, three teeth missing. He rested his hand on the closed Bible on the table in front of him, as if he'd been absorbing it through his palm. Next to the Bible was a dented pewter cup.

"Good morning, Father. Here's your breakfast."

Moll took a pork pie and a leather flask from the wallet over her shoulder and filled his cup. He drank deep, ignoring the pie.

I glanced round this closet, once meant for the priest to store vestments and prepare for services but now a bare domicile. A narrow cot was pushed against the wall beneath a small stained-glass window depicting St. Jerome, and the cupboard bulged with Father Daniel's shabby worldly goods.

"This is my friend Alexander Cooke. He's to marry on Saturday, and you're the man for the job."

"Good, good." Father Daniel gave me a nod and held out his cup for a refill.

"You'll read the banns tomorrow, right? Alexander Cooke and Frances Field. Three times, at the beginning, middle, and end of the service."

Back in Saffron Walden, the banns were read aloud three consecutive Sundays or holy days. St. Alfage's appeared more flexible.

Father Daniel grinned at me. "In a rush, are you?"

"It's happened before," Moll replied in a jocular tone.

"Many times, many times." The priest removed the largest of the scraps of paper marking pages in his Bible. "Write their names."

I'd never considered whether Moll could write, but here she was, writing out the entire statement in a childish hand, using both sides of the paper. She read it aloud.

"'I hereby publish the banns of marriage between Alexander Cooke of the Parish of Southwark and Frances Field of this Parish. If any of you know a cause why these persons should not be joined together, ye are to declare it.' Be sure to say that this is the first or second or third reading."

"Here, one reading will be enough." Father Daniel took the paper from Moll. "Frances. I've always liked that name."

"We'll be here by eleven on Saturday for the wedding."

"With?" He gestured toward the flask in Moll's hands.

"You can rely on it." She emptied the rest into his cup. "Alexander Cooke and Frances Field."

Father Daniel's voice wasn't the firmest but his smile was wholehearted. "I'll remember. It's been a while since I've blessed a marriage."

Outside the church, Moll promised to send someone on the morrow to hear the banns read. No one who knew Frances or me, of course.

"If Father Daniel does that much, he's likely to follow through on the wedding. Never you fear. I'll drag him out of bed if I have to."

We parted, me in a daze. We had our priest!

I never did repent for doing good,
Nor shall not now.
PORTIA, *THE MERCHANT OF VENICE*

CHAPTER VI
May 1599

The air over the Thames was a miasma, thick and dank. I intended to stop into Frances' shop with the news, but it was filled with women, so I walked on to St. Paul's Yard where booksellers were buzzing.

Pausing to listen to a poet shouting his verse and hawking broadsheets, I saw a familiar dark-clad figure at a stall beyond. The feather in his hat was smaller, his clothing more distinguished than when last I saw him, but that slender grace, that innate beauty, could belong to none other than John Donne.

After all this time, my heart lurched at the sight of him. Occasionally I'd seen Donne in the theatre and heard passing news of him, but this was the closest we'd been in a very long time.

Seeing his long fingers opening a book, his face in profile, eyes intent on the text, my sensations were bittersweet. John Donne was not for me and never could be, but if I let him . . . . My face burned. I stared unseeing at the books on the stall in front of me, overcome with memories, especially the first time we met in person.

At Wilton House where I was playing Rosaline in *Love's Labours' Lost*, we four ladies briefly sat in the audience, me on John's lap— and he discovered the truth about me. Love and chance led us to a hill above the ancient monument of Stonehenge where once transcendent afternoon we'd found fulfillment in each others' arms. A moment out of time, our union remained vivid even now, standing at the edge of Paul's Yard.

I put a cooling hand on my burning cheeks and took a deep breath to calm my racing heart. Perhaps I should leave before John saw me.

His voice stopped me. "If it isn't Princess Katherine of France. I liked how you played at learning those suggestive English words."

"I'm glad you were amused. It's good to see you, John." I lingered over his name, rounding the 'n' into a second syllable. Everyone around me might as well have disappeared. No one but John Donne, tall and immaculate beside me.

"Have you a moment?"

When I nodded, he edged me away from the stalls toward the entrance to St. Paul's cathedral. Often the porch and nave were crowded, but today all action was in the churchyard.

We walked into the stone-smelling church, dull silver light slanting through the open door, and moved away from its glare.

Ill at ease, I said the first thing that came to mind. "I hear you're rising in the Queen's service these days."

"Ah yes. Politics. They do sharpen a man's brain."

"Yours was ever sharp, John Donne."

"Ah, Sander. I'm glad we can be friends."

"You mean we're not enemies. But friends?" I shook my head. "I think friends see rather more of one another than do you and I."

"I disagree. True friends exist in our souls forever."

"That much is true; memories are eternal. I shall never forget you, John. Are you still a bachelor?"

"I am. If I didn't know you better, I'd think you wanted me to say that no woman has ever matched you."

Looking into John's quick black eyes prompted a reckless reply. "I imagine that none has. Aren't you going to ask me if I'm still a bachelor?"

"Bachelor, spinster: I know the answer to that," he replied. "Only unmarried bliss is safe for you."

"Guess again."

He looked stunned. "Surely you don't mean there's a lucky man?"

"Of course not."

"Are you going to tell me you married a woman?"

"I haven't married her yet, but why not? As you see, I'm a man."

"Except that I know differently. I hope this poor girl does too. What in the world are you doing?"

"It's a secret. Saying even this much is indiscreet."

"Do you really intend to marry a woman?"

"It's a risk, but God willing, we shall marry." I stopped. "How can I say 'God willing'? I doubt that's likely, not if one reads the words of the marriage service."

"Yes, matrimony is between one man and one woman. There was a time when I'd gladly have married you." I quaked as his glance took in my entire person. "But you chose to remain in breeches."

"I know how precious is the love between man and woman," I said in an undertone. "For you, John, I dared become woman again." Then, in my best Alexander Cooke voice: "But that was long ago. You can guess the reason I intend to marry now: my bride is pregnant. I shall be father to her child."

"A marriage of honor. I think you're safe to say 'God willing' in this case. A child needs a father."

"Thank you, John. I like 'marriage of honor' better than 'of convenience.' This woman owns a shop and is Silkwoman to Queen Elizabeth. If she gives birth to a bastard, the life she's made in London ends."

"Do you mean Frances Field?"

I nodded.

"I know of her. A gifted seamstress, they say."

"Frances needs me. One day you shall find a woman who needs you, John."

"You didn't need me."

"You know it wasn't that simple, John. My heart did."

"And your body. But not your will." He looked into my eyes, sadness and affection flowing between us. "That's what counted in the end."

"Your and my lives couldn't mesh. Look at you now, John. And look at me, playing bawds and princesses on stage."

"We both sacrificed."

My expression must have reflected the regret my words could not. John lifted my hand to his lips for the briefest touch.

"For Frances, you do not have to renounce your acting." His voice was a whisper. "Does passion play a part?"

I hadn't put it so bluntly. Holding Frances in a love embrace seemed remote at best. "I could say, what couples have between them is private, but to you, John, I'll be honest. At present, passion plays no part whatsoever. Might it ever?" I shrugged. "I can't imagine."

Walking the long aisle under the blue and red stained-glass windows that gave the vast space a purplish tinge, we came to a standstill before the tomb of a knight and his lady, he carved with his shield, dog at his feet, she with a worn, pious face.

"You have an ardent heart, Sander. You're a passionate lover. Men may share that sort of ardor with one another, but I doubt that women do. It would be sad to lose it forever."

Silent, much hanging between us, I was struck by that truth. Of necessity I had closed off my ardent heart. Looking at this man I'd so adored, I felt desire long submerged, a desire I must not allow to the surface. He was what, twenty-six? He would find a woman to love; of that I had no doubt. Likely one who was unsuitable in the world's eyes, as can happen with ardent hearts.

I was just twenty-three, though my troupe thought me a good two years younger. When I married Frances, I would turn my back forever on passion. An inner voice intruded. What did our vows mean if the marriage wasn't consummated? Perhaps Frances did still desire Johnny, despite how badly he'd behaved.

I shook myself, returning my attention to John.

"I don't know if you're right or wrong about women's love for one another. I've had girls fancy me, as a lad. Nothing came of it beyond flirtation. Frances and I share a bond of friendship. Beyond that, I'm as doubtful as you as to what's possible between us." Circling back toward the church door, we avoided the few worshippers. "There's no one else with whom I can speak like this. We're friends indeed."

"Look out for yourself, Sander Cooke."

"You too, John. You've given me much to think about." I laughed. "But perhaps I won't—think about it, I mean. I plan to be wed next Saturday."

"Every blessing on your union." At the doorway he gave my hand a quick squeeze before we headed in opposite directions. "May it be a success."

Seeing John had stirred my sense of loss afresh, but strangely, as I walked back toward London Bridge, I felt hopeful about Frances. Our marriage seemed more real now that I'd told him. We'd even spoken of passion, the deepest mystery.

"We have our priest and our church," I told Frances. "We're set for Saturday morning."

"What sort of priest? He must be very odd, if you needed Moll Frith to find him."

"Father Daniel is ordained and his church well looked after. This will be a real wedding, Frances, ring and all."

She handed me a package wrapped in a length of muslin. "I made this for you."

Momentarily startled that she'd anticipated my news, I unwrapped a beautifully stitched shirt with a lace collar.

"And I've nearly finished sewing my gown."

"We shall be the most handsome of couples."

"Perhaps." Frances paused. "Is Moll to be our witness?"

"She is."

"Won't she prove this wedding a sham?"

That was the least of my concerns at St. Alfage. I shook my head. "You'll like the house I've found us, in Cornhill. I'm sleeping there tonight. The widow who owns it has moved to Mortlake to live with her daughter. She left behind beds, a table, a cook pot, and such."

Frances' face brightened. Our marriage had become real.

Thou art sad; get thee a wife, get thee a wife!
BENEDICK, *MUCH ADO ABOUT NOTHING*

CHAPTER VII
May 1599

Afraid I'd overslept the cool May morning of our wedding, I jumped up from the bed with its fresh sheets and splashed water on my face. Through the restless night, I had lulled myself to the brink of sleep, thinking about what good sense this marriage made, then woke with a start. Perhaps Frances and I were giving up too much. Or we would be discovered and pilloried, or worse.

No. We would face the challenges together, an indivisible two. With that thought, I'd slept peacefully at last.

I dressed in my lace-collared shirt and best doublet and breeches. Out in the street, the rising sun tinged the clouds with gold against an azure sky foretelling a bright day. A blessing, especially after the heavy grey of the past week.

Frances waited outside her shop, a cloak covering her new gown. I couldn't read her expression and wondered if she'd spent the night in prayer.

"Are you all right?"

"When I awoke this morning, I felt blessed. The Virgin Mary wed Joseph of Nazareth, who wasn't the father of her child. No angel Gabriel visited, but I felt the Virgin's protective arms around me. Our marriage is the right thing for the child, Sander, regardless of all else."

Warmed, I took her arm in mine and we set off for London Bridge and the remoter streets of Bankside. Beyond the public amusements, ragged folk in dreary alleyways extended begging hands. One must be generous to the poor on such occasions, and although I could not cast out handfuls of coins as the nobility did, I'd saved a fat bag of pennies.

As I pressed a coin into the hand of a dun-faced woman with an expression that suggested a life of hardship, Moll Frith appeared at my side. "Give her another, Sander. This girl will find a way out of this place. A good one for housework and child-minding, is our Rebecca."

Girl? How could that be? But then I realized, most of Moll's boys had a similar look, and they were children.

I gave Rebecca three pennies. "We may have work for you. Moll will bring you to our house."

Rebecca bobbed a girlish curtsey. Clear green eyes shone out of that grimy face, and her posture gave grace to her painfully slight figure.

"You won't be sorry, Sander. Rebecca's a good girl, but one like her can't stay good for long out here without help."

St. Alfage's was cold and silent, though sun shone through the window, streaking gold and green and vermillion across the floor. Frances removed her cloak to reveal a pale blue bodice and skirt, iridescent as if showered by a dissolving rainbow. The same fabric served as a kerchief around her shoulders, and a blue ribbon was wound through her shiny hair. I'd never seen her so luminous, her face paler than usual, her blue eyes darker.

Moll went ahead to Father Daniel's sacristy. Frances' eyes widened as he staggered out, but she said nothing. He'd hung a clerical stole around his neck at an uneven angle, and his face was splotched even redder than before.

But his smile was welcoming. "I took a little lie-down."

Petite Frances stood eye to eye with the priest as he stood at the altar facing us, with Moll slightly behind like a beneficent angel. Father Daniel waved forward the scattering of locals clustered in the back of the church. After shuffling thorough the *Book of Common Prayer*, he began speaking in a shaky voice:

"Dearly beloved friends, we are gathered in the sight of God to join together this man and this woman in holy matrimony, instituted of God in paradise, signifying unto us the mystical holy estate—" Here he realized he'd missed some of the words and looked down at the prayer book. As he moved his finger uncertainly over the text, I wondered if he'd be able to read the ceremony through.

In a stage whisper, Moll prompted him: "not to be enterprised nor taken in hand unadvisedly, lightly, or wantonly," and Father Daniel stumbled on, skipping chunks of the text.

"Not like brute beasts that have no understanding, but discreetly, duly considering the causes for which matrimony was ordained . . . the procreation of children . . . remedy against sin, and to avoid fornication . . . for the mutual society, help, and comfort in prosperity and adversity: into the which holy estate these two persons present come now to be joined. Therefore, if any man can show any just cause why they may not lawfully be joined together, let him now speak, or else hereafter forever hold his peace."

I held my breath. I recognized not a soul here, but still, a long tense moment.

No voice sounded.

Father Daniel looked from Frances to me and spoke fast: "I require and charge you that if either of you do know any impediment that ye confess it." He rolled right into the next part, his eyes on the text.

"Alexander Cooke, wilt thou have this woman to thy wedded wife, to live together after God's ordinance in the holy estate of matrimony? Wilt thou love her, comfort her, honor and keep her, in sickness, and in health? And forsaking all others, keep thee only to her, so long as you both shall live?"

"I will." The two words resonated differently than those I spoke onstage, yet there was something of the same feeling, that this was a public performance. But these came from the heart, a sacred vow that I intended to keep. I *did* honor Frances; I *would* be true to her.

"Frances Field, wilt thou have this man to thy wedded husband, to live together after God's ordinance in the holy estate of matrimony? Wilt thou obey him and serve him, love, honor, and keep him, in sickness, and in health? And forsaking all others, keep thee only unto him, so long as you both shall live?"

This time, I heard "forsaking all others" in its full force. Could Frances promise never to love a man? I felt a chill of apprehension, but she whispered, "I will," her eyes welling tears.

Father Daniel seemed at a loss, so I said, "I Alexander take thee Frances to be my wedded wife according to God's holy ordinance: And thereto I plight thee my troth."

"I Frances take thee Alexander to be my wedded husband, according to God's holy ordinance: And thereto I give thee my troth."

From the purse at my belt, I took a ring with a tiny blue stone that I'd bought in Cheapside. Father Daniel ought to tell me what to say, but I spared him. Too much had been omitted up to now; this vow I pronounced word for word as I slipped the ring onto Frances' finger: "With this ring I thee wed: with my body I thee worship: and with all my worldly goods I thee endow. In the name of the Father, and of the Son, and of the Holy Ghost. Amen."

The phrase sat strangely on my tongue, "with my body I thee worship." I knew full well the meaning. How could I say any such thing? Only by thinking of my warm affection for Frances, my commitment to the baby she carried.

Father Daniel read the final blessing right through: "O eternal God, creator and preserver of all mankind, giver of all spiritual grace, the author of life everlasting: Send thy blessing upon these thy servants, this man and this woman, whom we bless in thy name, to perform and keep the vow and covenant betwixt them made, whereof this ring given and received and may ever remain in perfect love and peace together, and live according unto thy laws, through Jesus Christ our Lord. Amen."

He looked over the motley congregation, and without a glance at the text spoke in a strong voice. "In the presence of God and these witnesses, I pronounce you, Alexander, and you, Frances, husband and wife. May your marriage be fruitful and may you walk the righteous path together. All blessings upon you, Amen."

He clasped our hands in his. "Those whom God hath joined together, let no man put asunder."

We were married! My doubts transformed into exultation. Yes, all of London with its dangers and suspicions lay outside this sanctuary, but Frances and I would face whatever we must together. I leaned down and kissed my wife lightly on the lips, our first real kiss. A chaste kiss, a holy kiss, a moment outside time.

Moll assured that the registry book was properly signed, gave Father Daniel a generous coin, a bottle of sack and a loaf for his own private communion, and we left St. Alfage's.

I wondered what Frances felt. She smiled when we were pronounced man and wife: relief on her side too. We linked arms like two explorers striding into uncharted wilderness.

"You two must be hungry as bears. I propose a wedding breakfast at the George," Moll said. As we turned in that direction, me striding like a proud husband, we encountered William Shakespeare.

"Where are you off to this fine morning?"

"To breakfast," Moll replied. "Come along."

He looked from Frances to me and back again, noting our unity, our tentative hopefulness. "What's the occasion?"

"Alexander and Frances have tied the knot," Moll said.

I sensed the calculations behind Will's probing brown eyes. He winked. "Setting your own fashion, just like King Henry and Princess Katherine." He slapped me on the back and kissed Frances' cheek. "Let me be the first to drink to your happiness."

In the George we had an alcove to ourselves, its leaded-glass windows open to the sunny innyard. Shakespeare ordered wine, strawberries, and nut cakes, which arrived quickly. I didn't mind if we were recognized as a bridal couple. So would we be henceforth: husband and wife. Frances had shed her cloak and seemed to relish her part as bride as much as if she'd married her truelove. Moll was her genial self, drinking up, ordering more food, keeping the party going.

The landlady returned with a fresh bottle, followed by a cook's assistant carrying a platter of roast capon, green beans and carrots. I carved the capon and handed the first plate to Frances, feeling very much the head of our household.

Shakespeare looked on, bemused. I suspected that he regarded our union as a variation of the old bedtrick in folk tales. In the usual story, one woke up with a person different than he believed he'd slept with and was now committed to that person. In our case: two women appearing otherwise. No doubt he'd guessed that Frances was pregnant.

With wine-enhanced cheer, we left the George. I caught a glimpse of Amelia Bassano Lanyer and her musician cousins sitting in the corner, her curious gaze following us to the door. It was too late to ask her to join us, though I should have thought of telling her earlier, friend that she'd been to me over the years.

In the street Moll and Shakespeare bid us farewell and headed their separate directions.

"Today we take a wherry boat," I told Frances. "No walking across London Bridge after our wedding."

At the dock we were greeted by John Taylor, the waterman I met soon after arriving in London. Once a famed reciter of the poems of Sir Philip Sidney, Taylor now composed his own verse. His youthful muscular body belied his face, weather-beaten as the ocher-colored river and eyes darker yet.

Taylor looked us over with admiration. "Why the finery?"

"We've come from our wedding breakfast. I present my bride, Mistress Frances Cooke." I turned to her. "This is John Taylor, waterman poet of the Thames."

"Congratulations to you both! Step aboard, Mistress Frances."

I pointed at the Bridge above us. "Hers is the shop at the sign of the needle."

"Needlewoman: a worthy profession." Taylor winked at Frances. "Is it wise of you to marry an actor? A man of frivolous amusements?"

"What better in this sweet short life than to be amused?" I said. "Sing us a song, John—one of your own."

"I can't write a love song: leave that to the fancy men."

"Then one of Sir Phillip's."

"That I can do."

As he rowed us through the water against the ebbing tide, Taylor sang, "My true love has my heart and I have his." I'd always found that song surprising, written by a man in the voice of a woman. Frances beamed at being serenaded.

On the northern shore Taylor helped her out with a gallant hand. "Perhaps I shall write a song about the needle and thread that hold us all together." He waved away my coin. "Next time. No charge to newlyweds."

"I like how you describe sewing, Master Taylor," Frances said. "A thread that holds us together applies as well to marriage."

Once indoors, the bride was shy, though she looked around our new home appreciatively. Seeing the room through Frances' eyes, I noted what furniture was missing, but nonetheless the parlor felt welcoming.

I lit the fire and produced the wine I'd purchased along with necessities for our kitchen: flour, eggs, cheese, ale, and two pies from the bakeshop, a sweet and a savory.

Frances, who'd followed me into the kitchen, smiled. "You've thought of everything."

"You'll have to buy soup bones and vegetables and all tomorrow. But we do have plates and cups." I took them from a box on the floor. "We'll have to find a dresser and—"

"There's no hurry."

A table with wooden benches on each side stood near the cooking hearth, backing up to the main fire in the parlor.

I put the leek and onion tart in the warming oven. "Do you want to see upstairs?"

"In a minute. I'm not yet accustomed to these rooms." She glanced at the staircase uneasily.

"Upstairs are two bedchambers." I meant to reassure her, though I couldn't be sure what she thought. So I pulled the settle up to the crackling parlor fire and poured two cups of wine. "To my wife and companion, my confidant and partner."

Frances raised her cup and took a sip, her expression tentative.

"Don't worry Frances. This marriage will be whatever we want it to be."

"And if we disagree?"

"The wife gets the last word in our house."

Frances touched my cheek with her lips. "Does it feel strange to have a wife? I mean, you could be one."

I laughed. "You know me, Frances. I was never cut out to be a wife. The first time I put on my brother's clothes, I felt my true self. The day that happened—" I broke off, feeling those scratchy breeches on my legs more intensely than the finer pair I was actually wearing.

"I've always wondered, Sander. When we first became friends you gave the outlines of your story, I've longed to hear more." She moved closer to me on the settle.

"As I see looking back, it was a day of portent. First thing that morning, I ran to tell Gran my father was marrying me to Martin, twenty-five years old with greedy little eyes." I laughed. "Not that I'd want any husband, but a dull sheep man without even a Bible in the house and ambitions to be a tanner seemed the worst. You and I early learned to read. Can you imagine not having a clue about marks on a page?"

Smiling, she shook her head.

"That day, crossing the Green, I paused at Troytown, a maze cut into the chalk soil. In the center stood a great ash, our wishing tree. I walked the maze path to the ash and leaned my forehead against her, warm and throbbing with life, her leaves whispering secrets into the wind. I didn't actually speak my wish. It came from my entire being as I embraced the tree. My trance ended when a jingling boy somersaulted through the maze like a whirling rainbow."

A baked oniony fragrance filled the room, adding to the homey atmosphere. "Let's eat. We've traveled a great distance since breakfast, into our very own house and life."

"Yes, but do continue your story." Frances took the tart from the warming oven and cut two slices. I broke off a piece, and between savory bites, continued.

"That boy's name was Jack, just arrived with Lord North's Men.

He invited me to their play that afternoon at the Rose and Crown. Gran found two pennies and off we went. I'd seen traveling players before, but this was the best yet, with Jack playing a reluctant maid who kills herself rather than marry her agèd suitor. Afterward I waited in the innyard until Jack came out. He laughed when I said I wanted to join his company: village boys always said that—and worse, I was a girl! When he was called in to supper, he said they'd be practicing the next day's play that evening inside."

"That was the first time you wore Johnny's clothes, right?" She said his name as causally as anyone might, so I simply continued.

"Yes. Gran had made me practice carrying myself like a boy, standing tall, walking with brash confidence. What freedom those breeches gave! I snuck into the Rose and Crown the back way and, hidden in a dark corner, watched them practice."

"So you decided to be an actor."

"Not a stage player, but I did decide to get out of Saffron Walden by acting the boy. I trusted that I'd find my way, once I fled my village marriage. Anyway, the players would leave town before my wedding. I'd have time to plan my escape to the nearest port where I'd join a sailing ship."

"What a dream for a girl!" she laughed. "I know the next part: your father tricked you by pushing the wedding forward. Johnny and one of your Gran's friends saved you, and you left Saffron Walden forever." Ah that name again. I'd have to get used to it, though at the moment, true as the story was, I wished she'd not repeated it. But looking at her eager expectant face, I cared only about telling her the story. I took a sip of wine.

"So I did. My new identity started with a pair of mended breeches and, on the road, when the first person I met took me for a boy. I've had marvelous days since then, but that was the most memorable. Until today. To my wife." I lifted my cup to her and drank the remaining drops, refilling both our cups.

The room darkened around us as we sat in the fire glow. The wine was tasty, the mood communal, and nothing need be said. Then, as if uncomfortable with our intimacy, Frances rose.

"Shall we have the peach pie?"

"Let's save it for tomorrow, Sander. I'm tired."

"Do you want me to come upstairs with you?"

"You've not finished your wine. I can find my way." Frances took one of the candles, stopping at the foot of the steep staircase. "Do you care which room I sleep in?"

"Your choice," I said, saddened at this sudden distance between us and wishing for an embrace such as friends share on parting.

Frances was halfway up the stairs. "Goodnight, Sander."

"Sleep well." I poured myself more wine, feeling chilled despite the fire.

I heard her footsteps stop at the room across from the one where I'd slept the night before, imagining her piling her clothes on the chair and climbing into bed. Then silence.

How did that ring feel on her finger? Did she welcome the reminder that henceforth we were to be each other's chief friend in all the world? It didn't feel so at the moment. I sighed. This marriage was a necessity, a saving grace. We'd make of it what we could. For my part, I hoped this cozy evening together foretold many more.

When the fire burned down, I climbed the narrow staircase. Frances was tossing and turning. I stood in her open doorway.

"Are you asleep?"

"Almost," she murmured. Not another sound or movement.

"Good night." I retired to my chamber. So here's where those hand-me-down breeches took me, to being a solitary husband.

If he were honester
He were much goodlier
DIANA, ALL'S WELL THAT ENDS WELL

CHAPTER VIII
May 1599

At the entrance to The Theatre, the porter handed me a sealed note with *Alexander Cooke* written in a lacy hand on the front. I cracked the seal.

Do find time to visit me this afternoon. ABL

ABL could be no one but my old friend Amelia Bassano Lanyer. When her husband Alfonso accompanied the Earl of Essex to Cadiz, we spent a great deal of time together, but after his return our friendship lapsed. Perhaps Alfonso had gone on another voyage, hoping to come home laden with gold, or was off to Ireland with Essex's troops.

After a rehearsal of my scenes in *Love's Labour's Lost* for our upcoming revival, I walked to Amelia's house in Westminster, a gift from Lord Hunsdon. Lively were the entertainments Amelia had provided for Hunsdon's friends in this charming little house, but all that came to an abrupt end with her pregnancy and Hunsdon's marrying her to Alfonso Lanyer. Court musician and cousin to Amelia by marriage, Alfonso was a convenient husband, no doubt compensated for his acquiescence, but neither was overly thrilled with the arrangement. Still, they'd stuck with it for the sake of baby Harry. Alfonso frequently joined voyages to the New World, and Amelia pursued her music and poetry.

During Alfonso's first voyage, not only did Amelia discover my secret and become my friend; she enchanted William Shakespeare. Their affair long ended, I didn't know if Amelia and Will were even friendly.

When she greeted me at the door, I was struck by her appearance. Though at home with only her son for company, she wore a vibrant red gown that set off her black hair and obsidian eyes, the white lace at the neckline like froth against her olive skin. Kissing Amelia's cheek, I caught the aroma of orange and cinnamon. She still set a standard for beauty, as she had as a girl on Lord Hunsdon's arm.

The back door stood open and sunshine poured in, scented by a flowering apple tree in the kitchen garden. Harry, now a lad of six or seven years, held his recorder, fingers on the stops.

"What tune are you learning now, my boy?"

"One of John Dowland's, Master Cooke." He spoke with the ease of one used to addressing adults.

"I want to talk to my friend, Harry. Go practice the 'King of Denmark's Galliard' and you can play it for us when you're ready."

"Won't he hear me practicing?"

"I shall listen only to your mother. Play in the kitchen and we won't hear a sound."

"I'd rather go outside." Harry dashed out to the kitchen garden, recorder in hand.

Amelia and I sat on the tapestried bench in front of the hearth, the embers flickering. "You didn't invite me."

"Invite you where?"

"To your wedding breakfast at the George. I saw you, and Will Shakespeare as well. My secretive Sandro, you must tell me everything!"

"You're the one with prescience. What do you think?"

"The bride is pregnant. That's the easy part, but who's the father?" Amelia looked into my eyes. "Ah, someone close to you, very close. Don't tell me he's your brother?"

My expression gave her all the answer required.

"So your niece or nephew will have the surname Cooke. Too perfect! But what about that bad boy Johnny? Surely he's in disgrace?"

"Not as much as he should be."

"Because you saved him." Amelia shook her head. "These men. Married or irresponsible or both. Is Johnny betrothed to another?"

"No, it's worse than that. He dances attendance on Lady Elizabeth Sidney Manners."

"The young Countess of Rutland. Do you know her?"

"I've seen her in passing. I must say, I'm curious: she's young and so well-married. How did Johnny make her acquaintance?"

"All I know is, one way or another, men seek their fortune. I imagine he's infatuated with her, but I doubt that the Countess can help him. Of course, I'm pessimistic about aristocrats—and husbands, at least of the male variety." She gave me a friendly nudge. "Wouldn't you know it, that fool Alfonso has left on another expedition on distant seas. Being a royal musician is an honor. I wish he'd accept his lot with grace."

"So should Johnny as a stage player. As Alfonso yearns to be a gentleman of means, Johnny dreams of becoming a playwright with noble connections."

"Silly men! I can't predict about Johnny, but Alfonso won't meet success." Amelia's gaze darkened. "Don't laugh, Sandro: I consulted Simon Forman about my husband's prospects."

"You didn't! Remember my sage friend Dr. Garnet's warnings about Forman? Why would you go see such a man?"

Amelia brought a flagon of wine and two glasses from the dresser, Harry's music floating in from the garden as he worked his way through Dowland's lively tune.

"Dr. Garnet may not respect Simon Forman, but I was curious." She handed me a glass of wine and sat back down beside me. "Women constantly seek his advice."

"Their mistake."

She took a sip, smiling. "True, Forman told me nothing I didn't know. Alfonso will not return wealthy, and I shan't become a fine lady. He didn't even recommend that I pursue my own talents, which would have been good advice. Instead—Dr. Garnet spoke true about Forman—he treated me like a wanton."

"What?" My protective instincts flared. "You—" I stopped when I saw the twinkle in Amelia's eyes. "Don't tell me you led him on."

"Not intentionally, but such a man believes that a woman in a well-fitted bodice has dressed for him. Dr. Forman stared more at my neckline than my face. At the end of our consultation he asked me the silliest question I've ever heard. He asked me to halek with him."

"Halek. Isn't that a salt cod? Oh!" I shuddered. "What a foolish man, to think you want anything to do with his halek." We laughed, our wine sloshing.

"I must confess; I teased him just a little. He deserved it—or, better, a slap across his smug face. He dared to assume I'd actually do it with him." Amelia wrinkled her nose. "He smelled like his leathery old books, overlaid with oil of anise seed, and his beard was flecked with tobacco ash. I leaned toward him, and when he reached for my breast I jumped up. 'Oh Dr. Forman. I couldn't.' Then I ran out the door. He called after me, 'Return on Saturday. I shall give you a more detailed astrological reading. And I have a special surprise for you.' I said I might."

"Did you?"

"Certainly not. I'm well aware of his surprise. His little salt cod, for mercy's sake. Dr. Forman merely repeated what I'd said myself, couched in fancy language."

"He'll be telling quite a tale about you and that halek."

"Who would believe him?"

"Gossip can be more powerful than truth." Sometimes I wished Amelia weren't so self-assured. She could be volatile and suffer dark moods, but thanks to her Italian blood and her past successes, she felt more invulnerable than was prudent. "Tell me you won't call on him again."

"I paid him his coin and that was the end of it. Alfonso always comes home empty-handed. Now, after burning through the gold

Lord Hunsdon gave me, he's off again. When Hunsdon died, his son George, the new Lord Chamberlain, cut off my allowance. Not that I want it, not from him." Amelia refilled our glasses. "Enough of Alfonso. Tell me about this wedding of yours, Sandro. Why did you step in to save Frances? I cannot imagine a marriage between two women."

"That's a worrying phrase, 'marriage between two women.' In the world's eyes I'm the husband, but Frances and I will create our marriage as we go. We're friends with a common purpose. That's all I can say."

"What does Will Shakespeare think about all this?"

"He's amused. No doubt he regards Johnny's behavior as contemptible, but he does enjoy secrets."

"And makes good use of them in his plays."

Harry came in. "I'm ready, Mama."

Our tête a tête was over; time to hear Harry play his spirited rendition of the galliard.

Late that afternoon, Johnny banged on our door. "I came to wish you well on your new life, Sander."

"We're not settled in."

"Perhaps I can be of help."

From the kitchen Frances greeted him with one word: "Well." Without asking him to take a seat, she resumed kneading bread dough.

I glanced around the parlor and into the kitchen with Johnny's eyes, seeing that the plaster walls needed whitewash.

"As I said, Johnny, we're not ready for visitors. No proper chairs or cushions or a dresser to hold these—" I pointed to the dishes stacked on the floor. "We've not yet added much to what the widow left behind."

"What would you like for a wedding gift?"

"We're all right. We have a table, the settle and two beds."

My words seemed to perturb him, either the "we" or the "two

beds." Clearly, Johnny had given little thought to what would follow Frances' wedding.

He glanced around the room, and then, as if inspiration struck, said, "I can find you a chair or two and a cushioned bench along here would serve as either a seat or a bed." He gestured at the empty wall beside the cold parlor hearth. "And perhaps—"

"Perhaps?"

"I could be helpful, you know," he said in a rush. "There's room for me here. I'd more than earn my keep, and would pay my share besides. Just for a short while."

"Wait. Are you suggesting you move in here?"

His face admitted the astounding truth.

"What happened with your Countess? Failed you, did she?"

I went in to the kitchen where Frances was forming the dough into loaves and, standing behind her, put my hands on her shoulders. "It appears Johnny's in trouble."

He followed me, surveying the kitchen. "Nothing like that."

"Then what?"

"As soon as Lady Elizabeth has settled, I shall have rooms."

"What do you mean, when she's settled?"

"After her husband the Earl of Rutland joined Essex in Ireland, Lady Elizabeth moved into Baynard's Castle."

"Yes, I know. So?"

"I thought—"

I interrupted. "Did you give up your lodgings?"

"No, not yet."

"Then you're fine. What do you say, Frances?"

Frances wiped her floury hands on her skirt. "We have much to do to set up this house. Our maid hasn't arrived yet, or a mouser."

"Your maid?"

"Yes, a girl named Rebecca," Frances said. "You're welcome to come to dinner after she arrives."

"I shall bring you two arm chairs."

Frances didn't look at him as he floundered toward the door.

Before it had fully closed Frances turned to me in outrage, "The nerve! Our second day in our house and Johnny comes asking favors. He'll bring a bed and sleep by our fire if we give him half a chance. How dare he!"

Next day I walked into St. Sepulchre's Alley and knocked on Dr. Garnet's door with its brass staff of Asclepius. As he opened the door, his voice sounded less feeble than on my last visit. "Alexander Cooke. Greetings, my friend."

I stepped into the large bookshelf-lined outer room where he sat at his writing table. The hair that showed under his cap was white, as was his beard, but his skin had the freshness of youth. Dr. Garnet reminded me of Gran, the same ageless quality and aura of wisdom.

He'd taken Gran's place in my life as much as anyone could, a wise and kindly elder with exceptional knowledge. But Gran was a healer, while Dr. Garnet was a mathematician and alchemist who had voyaged to the New World. His pale blue eyes held me, watery but alert.

"Did you come to talk about your marriage, Sander? I heard you celebrated your wedding breakfast at the George. The actors Alexander Cooke and William Shakespeare do not go unnoticed. Nor your pretty bride, though I was not told her name."

"She's Frances, Silkwoman to Queen Elizabeth and owner of a dressmaking shop on London Bridge."

"An enterprising young woman. Congratulations to you both! What's your question?"

When I hesitated, he said, "No one would blame you for being troubled, Alexander, no one who knows your secret—which, by the way, my informants about your wedding do not. You're safe in London."

"This wedding is the riskiest thing I've done."

Garnet laughed. "I can think of a few that rate near as high. You do not take the easy way, Alexander Cooke. Tell me what troubles you. Or shall I brew us an herbal drink first?"

"Your brews are always welcome."

As Dr. Garnet poured hot water from the pot hanging over his fire, I thought about my own herbs to stop my female courses, the recipe from Gran: breakstone parsley, raspberry leaves, and tormentil root. Dr. Garnet's blends were meant to clarify the mind. I held the cup, floating with tiny flowers, sticks, and bits of bark, and inhaled the sharp sweetness until cool enough to drink.

"I'm not sure about either Frances or my brother Johnny. Did your informants say anything about him?"

"No, only that you were seen at the George." He paused. "Oh, so Johnny is involved. Then he must be the father of Frances' forthcoming baby."

I nodded.

"You did the right thing, Alexander. I'm sure Frances values you for rescuing her. She'll be a good wife and mother."

"I hear a 'but' coming."

"Angry as she is at your brother for abandoning her—"

I interrupted, driven by my worst fear. "She still loves him?"

"Not so simple. Frances is torn. She made vows to you, but she can't be certain she'll never again want a man."

"Oh." The very thought that darted through my mind at St. Alfage's.

"See her through this pregnancy. I glimpse your future dimly, but this much is clear: your connection to one another is rich and complex."

"Like nothing known before," I said with an ironic smile.

"Nothing known, but perhaps something done before. Private lives can be kept private. You must be the man now, more than ever."

"Frances is independent—"

"Yes, but she's the woman."

"Do you think women are weaker?"

"No. I mean she risks childbirth."

Perhaps it was the drink or the pungent herbal smell in Dr. Garnet's chamber, perhaps memory or something emanating from his books or his voice, but I felt distressed.

Dr. Garnet looked at me closely. "Alexander? Are you all right?

You know, feelings are ambiguous and ever-changing. The future will unfold as fate will have it, so face one thing at a time. Be a good husband, that's my advice."

We finished our drinks in companionable silence. That advice I could follow well enough.

"What do you hear from Mistress Amelia Lanyer?" Garnet asked, seemingly out of nowhere. He smiled at my discomfiture. "She told you about her visit to Dr. Simon Forman?"

I gulped. "Umm—"

"I heard it from the old goat himself. Or young goat, I should say, which is worse. I've no doubt he made up the half of it."

"I can guess which half. That she actually did what he wanted."

"He daren't go that far. He says she teased him mercilessly and denied him at the last moment. That's better for Amelia's reputation, her chastity maintained. But such a tale raises questions about her virtue. He's a wily one, Dr. Forman, vain as a peacock and just as proud. She should stay well clear of him."

"As she discovered for herself."

"Dazed by Amelia's beauty, folk will believe any rumor with no idea what a rare woman she is. So clever, so musical."

I set down my cup, the liquid gone but the herbs and flowers still fragrant. "What shall I bring you next visit?"

"Something baked in your kitchen. By Frances or by yourself."

I laughed. "Oh, it will be by Frances' hand. I'm useless in the kitchen, and besides, we have a theatre to open. You've heard about the Globe?"

"Only that the Burbages played a trick on their landlord and are building a new theatre in Bankside to be called the Globe. A perfect name! The stage encompasses all the world."

"As do we players and our plays. Every sort of person, every sort of story."

"At least in so far as playwrights recognize every sort of person. One day, persons such as I've seen across the sea may appear on stage." He paused. "Or perhaps not. All too many returning explorers' tales are far-fetched. When Martin Frobisher and such captains display captured New World natives in London, folk barely consider them human. Savages, they're called.

"I know differently. Their customs and religion differ from ours, but parents love their children, people work together for each other's good, and they live simply, in harmony with nature. Much can be gained from their example, but I fear I shan't live long enough to see it, on or off stage. Indeed, I often fear the worst." For a moment, Garnet seemed lost in thought, but then brightened. "Go on, go on, Alexander. Tell me about the Globe. Has something to do with the Burbage family, I imagine."

"You know that James Burbage built The Theatre in Shoreditch."

"Indeed. My teacher and the Queen's own astrologer Dr. John Dee helped him design that playhouse." At my surprise, he added, "Oh yes, among Dee's countless skills we must count architecture. As an actor, James Burbage wanted a better performance space than the innyards and sporting rings players used. So with Dr. Dee's help he designed The Theatre."

"I didn't know that." Funny old Garnet, introducing magic to what I had thought was simply cleverness.

"Burbage leased the land from Giles Allen more than 20 years ago, Allen being a Puritan who hates plays." Dr. Garnet chuckled. "Nothing he could do to stop him building it. That was the gossip at the time."

"That explains why, when the lease ran out last year, Allen refused to renew it. By then James Burbage's sons Cuthburt and Richard had inherited his carpentry business."

"Not surprising that Richard Burbage is your lead player. His old dad James performed with Leicester's Men. Talented family."

"You'll appreciate what they did, Dr. Garnet. Although the Burbages had leased the land from Allen, they owned title to the theatre building. At the dead of night they took it down to the foundations, hiding the materials in a warehouse by the Thames. After securing a site for the Globe in Bankside, they ferried the lot across for our new theatre."

"Good story! No doubt Allen tried to have them arrested."

"He took them to court, but in the end his suits failed. The Globe opens soon."

"Their trick on that skinflint Allen does your company credit. Actors to a man—including you. Carry on with your stage-playing, Alexander. Trust Frances and love her."

I embraced him, feeling more easy in myself. Be a good husband. That I could do.

Thou speak'st wiser than thou art ware of.
ROSALIND, *AS YOU LIKE IT*

CHAPTER IX
Late June 1599

I arrived early at the newly built Globe. Odd to see the same boards from The Theatre, the same stage, the same galleries, everything but the former tile roof, now thatched, in a new location, freshly painted. The canopy over the stage was supported by two pillars embellished to look like porphyry marble worthy the Roman senate, setting of our first play here: the Roman forum of *Julius Caesar*.

The finest theatre in London by far! As I glanced up at painted galaxies, a vision of Lord North's Men's wagon came to mind. When I first saw it in Saffron Walden, it seemed the most charmed place imaginable, full of costumes and properties—including a mirror—to create a stage world, a place of drama and imagination. I wanted nothing more than to join that company, walk along with that wagon, and create plays on that moveable plank stage. And eventually I'd succeeded. In our enchanted wagon, I'd dreamt of London, but never of performing in such a grand playhouse.

Shakespeare came up behind me as I stood gazing at the azure heaven spangled with moon and stars.

"What do you think?"

"What a feat to rebuild this so beautifully. The Globe indeed!"

"All the world's a stage—" Shakespeare gestured around the wooden O of the theatre, "and all the men and women merely players."

"A line from a play?"

"My next one, as it happens. After *Julius Caesar* comes a comedy.

First you'll play Brutus' wife Portia. In the new comedy you'll be a clever girl-boy."

"Oh good, a masquerade part." I'd not played one of those since Julia in *Two Gentlemen of Verona*, where she disguises herself as a page to follow her beloved to Milan.

Shakespeare sat on the edge of the stage, legs dangling, and I beside him.

"How does marriage suit you?" During my moment of surprised silence he added, "And how is Johnny taking it, I wonder. I didn't intend to draw Claudio in *Much Ado* so close to life, but the part turned out to reflect him: a callow youth easily taken in by appearances with no understanding of the woman he professes to love. Apparently I was prescient."

I stuttered, "W-What do you mean?"

"Johnny is the father of Frances' child, is he not? He shifted his responsibilities to you and skipped off to ingratiate himself to Lady Elizabeth Sidney. Your brother is fully as shallow and self-centered as Claudio, but his behavior has real consequences. Claudio is but a character in a play that ends more or less happily."

"How did you guess about Johnny?"

"Observation and guesswork. I can't resist noting the peculiar varieties of the human heart."

"What does your dramatic sense tell you happened next?"

"Lady Elizabeth disappointed him."

"Indeed."

"I hear that her husband, the Earl of Rutland, has returned in disgrace from Ireland."

"In disgrace?"

"Yes, he and his wife have moved to Essex House, home of her stepfather, Robert Devereux, Earl of Essex. Essex himself is still in Ireland, but whatever he's been up to there has put him and the noblemen who follow him out of favor with Her Majesty. Johnny's hopes for elevation through Lady Elizabeth's means are dim." Shakespeare looked me in the eye. "Whereas you, Sander, made an honorable choice."

"Now Johnny wants to be part of our life."

Shakespeare's laugh was as hearty as Moll Frith's. "Don't tell me he proposed to move in with you."

"He did indeed. Not a chance."

"Tough lesson. Johnny supposed that between Lady Elizabeth and you, he had delightful options. Are you and Frances happy together?"

The simple answer would be "yes." But I wanted to say more. Will was a friend worthy my confidence. "Every day is a discovery. I've never been close to a woman in such a way, as equals. I know it sounds peculiar: I'm the husband. But I have no more command over Frances than she has over me. Sometimes I wish we'd sleep in the same bed as servant girls do, or cousins. Warm and comforting." I flushed pink at the curiosity in his face, at myself for saying so much, and blurted out, "We're not lovers, to whatever extent women can be."

Chamberlain's Men began to straggle in, shaking the mud off their boots. "They can be," he said softly. "Kisses and tender embraces." He pushed himself to his feet, and I followed.

"We're in the middle of a marsh!" Tom Pope said. "Before we open this Globe, they had better build a walkway."

Heminges laughed. "Play-goers care more about the show than how they reach the playhouse. Besides, that's what pattens and nose-gays are for. Raise your feet above the muck and block out the stench. They're coming to see the tragedy of *Julius Caesar*. Worth a little mud."

I looked over the players, all of them familiar except for Robert Armin, who'd taken over the role of Dogberry after Will Kemp sadly departed our company.

I made sure Armin saw me as an effeminate young man. No broad male shoulders nor full beard but male nonetheless. Gran's herbs had proved efficacious; days went by when I scarcely recalled that I was born female. But a new member of the company made me tense. The most recent new boy, Christopher Beeston, apprenticed to my own one-time prentice master Tom Pope, regarded me as a player to emulate.

Robert Armin appeared more acute. His face was sharp, with

jagged eyebrows, piercing grey-blue eyes, narrow lips, an indented chin and bristly beard. Small and flexible, his body was nervous, ready to pounce, and he was reputed a biting humorist. His mind and demeanor put me on guard.

Johnny strode in, virile and self-assured. The last to arrive, his manner showed nothing apologetic. I hadn't mentioned to Shakespeare my worry that in a secret chamber of her heart, Frances still loved this handsome rogue.

As our parts were distributed, Johnny grumbled that his were too small. "All these marvelous roles and I get Flavius and Trebonius and Cinna the Poet. Not one shines."

"Cinna meets the same bloody fate as Julius Caesar, surely a form of shining," I said. "The rebels kill poetry as well."

Johnny gave me a dismissive glance, but I knew that "shining" meant little in a playing troupe. We must work together so that the play itself shone. Shakespeare wrote each part with its own brilliant moments. My moment came when Portia, Brutus' wife, showed her manly fortitude.

Johnny wouldn't want to play Portia. Mark Antony would be more to his liking, but that part went to Augustine Phillips.

When I returned home that evening, Frances sat at the kitchen table chopping a pile of vegetables with Rebecca beside her. Rebecca little resembled the impoverished girl we met outside St. Alfage's. Grime had aged her and hunger hollowed her cheeks, but now, clean and efficient in her fresh blue skirt and bodice, a white apron tied around her waist, she looked her age, fourteen. Grateful for secure work, Rebecca knew how to make herself invisible. Most nights she slept in the kitchen, though Moll Frith had found her part-time work helping an old woman who lived in a tiny cottage where Rebecca sometimes stayed the night.

"I just returned myself," Frances said. "The shop's busier than ever. I worry about my apprentice. Joan's only sixteen. Will she be able to take over during my confinement?"

"I wager she'll be able to. Isn't this her last year as an apprentice?" I paused. "Did I ever tell you I've met her mother?"

"Her mother?"

"Maud. She and her husband keep the tavern near my old lodgings in Silver Street: the Spread Eagle. Joan's needlework is displayed on the walls there, from her earliest sampler."

"I forgot about that. Yes, Joan came to me well prepared, though I worry about her being scatter-brained. Nothing like Rebecca here." She smiled at the girl. "You'll need to help with the baby for a while, Rebecca, but soon you can begin stitching yourself."

"Thank you, Mistress. There's nothing I'd like more. I don't remember much from my childhood, my mother died when I was so tiny. But I do remember her sitting and sewing."

"I'm sure you'll take to stitchery like you were born to it." Frances turned to me. "I have to trust Joan to rise to what's needed. My prentice master Gemma will check on the shop from time to time. She and her lawyer husband live near by. She'll want to be sure the shop she deeded to me does well in my absence." She tipped the vegetables into the stewpot hanging over the fire. "My shop is my concern. What's yours?"

I felt caught off guard, still not accustomed to the intimacy of marital communication, but did my best. "Only a new play, a new role. Portia, wife of Caesar's friend Brutus, is a warrior at heart. She begs her Brutus to let her into his secrets. She knows he slips from their bed and meets with strange men in the night. Portia suspects a conspiracy and cannot bear that he won't tell her."

"Say one of her speeches."

Without preamble I began, in Portia's commanding voice:

> I grant I am a woman; but withal
> A woman that Lord Brutus took to wife:
> I grant I am a woman; but withal
> A woman well-reputed, Cato's daughter.
> Think you I am no stronger than my sex,
> Being so father'd and so husbanded?

Tell me your counsels, I will not disclose 'em:
I have made strong proof of my constancy,
Giving myself a voluntary wound
Here, in the thigh. Can I bear that with patience.
And not my husband's secrets?

Frances sounded shocked. "She stabs herself in her thigh?"

"That's what a true Roman would do."

"Which shows she's stronger than her sex. You play women who are more than women."

In front of Rebecca, I resisted saying, "As I am myself." Instead: "Like everyone in this play, Portia is an historical personage. Shakespeare makes her even more magnificent than Plutarch does." I sighed. "Not that she has any power in the end."

"Nor does Julius Caesar, if he was murdered."

"That's because he had too much power. The senators fear he aspires to be emperor."

"I hope the play shows that they're wrong to murder him."

"Oh, Will Shakespeare is careful. In the end the conspirators suffer. But I did overhear Heminges and Condell wondering at him choosing that topic, as Queen Elizabeth herself has been threatened with assassination plots."

"I've seen the heads piked at the end of the Bridge."

"Right, they don't get far with those plots. No one will leave thinking we advocate assassination. It's a perfect play to initiate the new Globe: you'll believe you're in Rome!" As Frances stirred the stew, I added, "A new member has joined the company: a quick-witted fellow called Robert Armin. I must befriend him."

"Just be yourself." Yet the expression that flickered over Frances' face seemed to ask just who that self was. Her look stopped me short, and I wondered about her attraction to me. We'd never broached any such topic. It was pleasant to pass the time in conversation with one another, much more difficult to bare our emotions. I occasionally kissed her on the cheek, but always we maintained a gentle restraint.

I glanced at Rebecca, and Frances caught my warning.

"Laugh at Armin's jests; make him feel welcome," was all she said.

That night, I reflected on our marriage. More than a month wed, we'd had no difficulty in society. Most people take one on appearances, as I'd learned early. Neither Tom Pope nor his sister Ruth saw me as anything but a lad. I felt secure as Frances' husband, so far as Rebecca or gossips in our small world were concerned. If Rebecca thought anything about our sleeping in separate rooms, she'd have attributed it to Frances' pregnancy.

My discomfort about Johnny was altogether different. He made me question my relationship to Frances. I knew that she was grateful to me and anticipated legitimate motherhood with relief. That was all I could rightfully expect.

Yet my love for Frances grew each day, and felt unrequited. I wanted a deeper bond and found it difficult to live under the same roof without. Could we not share the warmth of one bed? Kisses and tender embraces: hard to imagine, yet I was filled with vague yearnings.

Easy conversation, caring about each other—these gave a constancy to our days. If only I could be content with her friendship! If only I could trust her love. But all too often I felt like an inadequate stand-in for Johnny.

Frances values you; Frances values you, I repeated again and again until I fell asleep.

Hark, hark! one knocks: Portia, go in awhile;
And by and by thy bosom shall partake
The secrets of my heart.
    BRUTUS, *JULIUS CAESAR*

CHAPTER X
July 1599

"At least there's no plague this year," Johnny said as we entered the Globe for our rehearsal of *Julius Caesar.*

"I'd not mind a summer's tour through the countryside." John Heminges wiped his sweaty face on his sleeve. "Gentle breezes, fragrance of hedgerow and field, and clear running water." He looked down at the brown Thames, redolent of garbage and offal.

This oppressive day I agreed with Heminges. I'd rather be anywhere than London. After all these years I didn't mind the overripe stench, but I was concerned for Frances. The baby had begun to weigh down her small frame, with some four months left of the pregnancy. I wished I could whisk her away to a healthful place.

Most of the company had assembled in the tiring room. Today we were rehearsing the assassination of Julius Caesar. Portia has no part in that hacking, a death utterly unlike what Brutus described to his fellow conspirators as "carving Caesar like a meal fit for the gods." This corpse would be fit for none but curs, were the wounds real.

Robert Armin played small roles: citizens, the soothsayer, and Lepidus. I made sure to be very much the young man around him, but Armin was more intrigued by our marvelous new theatre than curious about me or anyone else in the company. Ever since I spoke

Portia's speech to Frances, my part had resonated with emotions from my own marriage. Portia's feelings were not so different from mine when I doubted Frances.

My favorite speech was when Brutus rose early "in the raw cold morning." Portia feels the rift in his affections and follows him out of their chamber.

> *You've ungently, Brutus,*
> *Stole from my bed: and yesternight, at supper,*
> *You suddenly arose, and walk'd about,*
> *Musing and sighing, with your arms across,*
> *And when I ask'd you what the matter was,*
> *You stared upon me with ungentle looks;*
> *I urged you further; then you scratch'd your head,*
> *And too impatiently stamp'd with your foot;*
> *Yet I insisted, yet you answer'd not,*
> *But, with an angry wafture of your hand,*
> *Gave sign for me to leave you: so I did;*
> *Fearing to strengthen that impatience*
> *Which seem'd too much enkindled, and withal*
> *Hoping it was but an effect of humour,*
> *   . . . Dear my lord,*
> *Make me acquainted with your cause of grief.*

Portia kneels before her husband and, on the strength of their marriage vows, urges him to "unfold to me, yourself, . . . Why you are heavy."

Brutus' secret heaviness is his conspiracy against Julius Caesar. Frances' heaviness came from her pregnancy, but beyond that, I feared, lingering secrets of her heart. Brutus promises to tell Portia all. I could only hope that so too would Frances tell me one day—or better yet, cease having secrets. Then would she be, as Brutus pledges to Portia, my true wife.

The opening performance of *Julius Caesar* was a roaring success, applause echoing from the galleries. Whether the audience rejoiced that the conspirators were defeated or whether their appreciation came from the performances and the splendor of the Globe itself, we couldn't know, but we went home happy. Our new theatre would bring us good fortune.

Next day I walked Frances to the Bridge, left her at her shop door and turned toward the Mermaid. The tavern was dim and quiet, no players yet in sight.

Seeing the familiar form of John Donne at an empty table, I headed in his direction. Our encounter at St. Paul's had relieved my heart and I was determined to regard him equably as a friend.

He greeted me with a friendly smile. Whatever feelings John may have about our long-ago afternoon together did not belong in the Mermaid.

"I was on the edge of my seat as the momentum built toward Caesar's murder. What a relief that it didn't mark the end of the play," he said as the barmaid set a tankard before me.

"Will Shakespeare is too astute for that. But I wonder. Is Brutus meant to represent Essex, or does Casca come closer?"

"Do you regard the Earl of Essex as such an enemy?" He said "enemy" as if weighing the word.

"I'm not saying he's murderous." A long thoughtful pause, while I gazed at John's handsome face. "But he has taken power into his own hands in Ireland, to the Queen's great displeasure. The Earl of Rutland has returned home. Essex, along with Southampton and the rest of his followers, may soon be called back as well."

I knew the Earl of Southampton, at one time the most dashing young courtier in London and the patron to whom Shakespeare dedicated two long poems. One unforgettable night I played golden-gowned Venus at a reading of *Venus and Adonis* in Southampton's London house. He'd seemed frivolous in those days, but some five years had passed and he was no longer simply a pretty, art-loving aristocrat.

"Might they be accused of treason?" I asked.

"They're coming perilously close. I know Essex from my voyage to Cadiz with him, unsuccessful though it was. He's out for his own aggrandizement and may well have almost royal aspirations."

"Almost?"

"From the outset, his Irish campaign seemed more about his ambition than the Queen's: that's why I didn't join. And why I feared Shakespeare agreed with Essex in the first half of your play: Queen Elizabeth's power also extends too far."

"A false analogy."

"So I saw. The conspirators end up fighting with each other and Brutus commits suicide. It's Caesar's man Mark Antony who takes control in the end."

"So Chamberlain's Men did not perform a treacherous play."

"You did not." Donne spoke with judicial solemnity, then smiled. "Though I wager it will not be found in the bookstalls at St. Paul's."

"They murder Cinna the Poet because his name is the same as one of the conspirators."

"Cinna the Poet. I noticed that's one of your brother's roles. I hope he's cautious."

"I doubt he'll be torn limb from limb on the streets of London."

"I've heard he regards himself as some sort of champion to Rutland's wife Lady Elizabeth Sidney. If that extends to sharing Rutland's politics, warn him off."

"Johnny would never be a rebel."

"Perhaps not, but beware of appearing to support Essex. Heads could fall."

"Mercy, John. You're more alarming than Dr. Garnet."

He laughed. "I know that old wizard. He would say the same."

"Players don't get involved in politics."

"No? Think of the playwrights who've fallen foul of the censors: Ben Jonson and Tom Nashe, Tom Kyd and Christopher Marlowe. Prison, their works destroyed, torture, even death. Your Shakespeare is one of the few who's not run into difficulties, wise enough to work by indirection. These are tense times, Sander. Don't be complacent."

He looked to the door as a noisy crew entered. "Here comes the man himself, along with your colleagues." Donne bade me farewell, leaving a sudden empty space at the table.

My fellow players filled the benches. Their conversation was less charged than John Donne's, more about plays than politics, jokes than fears. I said nothing about the political risks Donne alluded to. Even if the play weren't printed, we would perform *Julius Caesar* regularly this summer.

And next came the promised comedy where I played a girl-boy!

If thou remember'st not the slightest folly
That ever love did make thee run into,
Thou hast not loved.
SILVIUS, *AS YOU LIKE IT*

CHAPTER XI
July 1599

All I knew was its title, *As You Like It*, and that I played Rosalind who disguises herself as the boy Ganymede. At the Globe as our parts were handed out, Robert Armin grumbled, "I suppose the play ends with a wedding."

"Four weddings." Shakespeare smiled. "Even the clown Touchstone takes a bride, Armin. You'll get your chance to be a lover."

"That can't come to good."

Shakespeare spoke in the voice of Touchstone. "'We that are true lovers run into strange capers; but as all is mortal in nature, so is all nature in love mortal in folly.'"

"Right enough." Armin grinned. "Touchstone's my man."

Rosalind's part was by far the thickest. I feigned dropping it from its weight and Shakespeare laughed. "The longest I've ever written for a female character."

I glanced at Armin's and Burbage's parts: Touchstone and Orlando had distinctly smaller roles. Occupied with examining their own lines, no one listened as I spoke to Shakespeare.

"I haven't played a girl who masquerades as a boy since *Two Gentlemen of Verona*."

"Rosalind little resembles Julia. She spends most of the play as Ganymede in doublet and hose. She'll likely run away with the show."

"Oh?" No doubt I seemed unappreciative, but I'd seen the worst of actors' envy when Samuel Gilburne was my bitter rival, goaded on by Gabriel Spencer. It had been a glad day when Samuel left the company rather than staying on as a hired man.

"I've had a character like Rosalind in mind since I first saw you in action, Sander. Thomas Lodge's tale *Roslynd: Euphues' Golden Legacie*, gave me the perfect plot, a girl who escapes to the woods as a boy. There she encounters the man she loves who doesn't recognize her. Rosalind takes charge. Just the role for you."

"I'm sure I'll love it." I glanced toward Armin. "But such a big part—" I broke off.

He put his hand on my arm. "Don't worry. Every character has his moment, even the melancholy Jaques."

When Shakespeare handed that part to Augustine Phillips, Phillips had laughed. "My character's name is Jakes? As in a privy? You're the funny one, Will."

"Your best speech begins, 'All the world's a stage.' I trust you to make it sufficiently bleak."

"Well, if I'm to be melancholy and mouth satire, I suppose I should have a satirical sort of name." Phillips scrunched his face into a frown. "Do I look sufficiently sour?"

"You'll improve with practice."

We lingered at the Globe reading over our parts. Early on, Rosalind adopts the doublet and hose of Ganymede and flees her uncle's threatening court along with Touchstone and her cousin Celia, who passes as Ganymede's sister Aliena. The three of us make our way to the Forest of Arden, domain of shepherds and exiles—including Rosalind's own father.

I could see elements of my own life obliquely woven into the role. As a young man, Ganymede displays wit and courage, especially when encountering another refugee from court: Orlando, the youth she fell in love with at first sight.

Orlando takes her for a saucy boy. At first she laments her disguise but quickly makes good use of it, proposing to cure Orlando of his mad infatuation. The scenes where she attempts that cure would be the most delicious. She flirts with Orlando while telling him how willful women can be. Her cousin Celia, who witnesses their game, chides her for decrying her own sex.

Leaving the theatre, I lagged behind with Shakespeare. "Doesn't Orlando ever guess Ganymede's identity? I know disguises aren't usually questioned, but he'd fallen in love with Rosalind."

"Do you remember Rosaline in *Romeo and Juliet*?"

"She's never on stage."

"Nonetheless, she's a presence. Mercutio mocks Romeo for adoring a woman he doesn't know."

"In bawdy lines." I recalled Johnny's pleasure in learning Mercutio's part.

"Mercutio has to bring Romeo down to earth. He's created his passion for Rosaline out of words and imagination. He idealizes her, but the real Rosaline is coy and scornful."

"Do you mean that Orlando risks the same sort of illusions about Rosalind?"

Shakespeare laughed. "Well, he hangs love poems on trees."

"That's no way to treat a tree."

"Exactly. He needs to get to know her, which he couldn't if he courted her in her skirts. Rosalind plays the part of Ganymede so well that a shepherdess falls in love with her."

"Meantime she tells Orlando to pretend that she's his Rosalind and to woo her. I wonder how long can she keep him from suspecting who she is."

"Orlando enjoys Ganymede's company. Likely he never recognizes her as Rosalind until the end, when she appears in her wedding gown. I leave the nuances to you and Burbage."

We were nearing the Anchor. I begged off joining the company for ale and pies; I must get home.

Concerns for Frances had sent me on my way, but something else troubled me. *As You Like It* is a comedy, so no ill would come to Ganymede. But playing such a large and juicy part? I hoped it wouldn't prove a danger. Back when I was on the road with Lord North's Men a jealous actor discovered my true sex and chased me out of Stourbridge Faire—and out of our company of players—with the help of a gang of ruffians. I'd since been accosted more than once by men who discovered me to be a woman and those who believed me a boy. For some time I'd felt safe in my disguise, and in our company even Robert Armin seemed less of a threat. Yet this out-sized role stirred up old memories and fears.

I took refuge from my anxieties on the shadowy porch of St. Michael's and stepped inside the door, unseen by solitary worshippers silhouetted in candlelight. Breathing slowly and deeply in the venerable peace emanating from its stone walls, I collected myself. All that was long past. Ganymede's chief risk is having the shepherdess Phoebe fall in love with her. The Forest of Arden is a woodland refuge, and I too was safe in the Lord Chamberlain's Men.

Taking a final calming breath, I left the church and continued on home to supper with Frances. She greeted me with a smile and ladled bowls of stew as Rebecca set out bread and small beer, all pleasant and familiar in our tidy house fragrant with rosemary and pinks. Even Frances' softly rounded belly had come to seem normal.

I laughed to myself: husband to a pregnant wife was hardly what I'd ever imagined as normal. Yet not only were we so in the world's eyes—wives were expected to produce a child the first year of marriage—but to ourselves as well. Frances and I enjoyed the comfort of a married couple, even of the same sex so long as we kept that secret.

As I sat beside her on the settle after supper, Frances said, "It's moving!"

I put my hand on her belly and felt the ripple of what must have been a tiny arm. How strange is pregnancy. Hers had been a problem to solve, and we solved it. As her belly swelled, I knew that in time a baby would appear, but the process, the reality that Frances' body was home to another being, I'd not fully taken in. There was something awesome about that gentle movement, a child growing within her.

Did I envy Frances? I'd become enough of a man to be relieved not to experience pregnancy, but I was curious. After all, I had all the female parts, hidden and denied though they were. Probably

I couldn't get pregnant if I wanted to, after all these years of Gran's herbs.

"Do say me your favorite speech from your new play, Sander."

"I haven't learned them all, but this one comes early on." I stood in front of the window, one foot on the chair in a masculine pose.

> *Were it not better,*
> *Because that I am more than common tall,*
> *That I did suit me all points like a man?*
> *A gallant curtle-axe upon my thigh,*
> *A boar-spear in my hand; and—in my heart*
> *Lie there what hidden woman's fear there will—*
> *We'll have a swashing and a martial outside,*
> *As many other mannish cowards have*
> *That do outface it with their semblances.*

"What's a curtle-axe?" Frances asked.

"A broad sword. You know: a cutlass."

"You don't actually wear one!"

"Alas no."

"Even without cutlass and boar-spear, Ganymede tells you how to play the part. Keep your woman's fears hid and show 'a swashing and a martial outside.' Even cowards can do that."

"Do you think me a coward, Frances?"

"You're braver than Moll Frith!"

"What a compliment."

"I mean it. Rosalind is more spirited even than Beatrice in *Much Ado About Nothing*."

"Rosalind speaks the epilogue. In her wedding dress."

"Say the speech."

"I will when I have the lines perfectly, but I know the gist." I smiled at Frances. "I conjure the women and the men to find the play pleasing and threaten to kiss all the men who please me."

"Kiss the men?" Frances poked me in the ribs. "You had better not!"

Truth will come to light.
LAUNCELOT, *THE MERCHANT OF VENICE*

CHAPTER XII
July 1599

"Do you think Orlando ever recognizes Ganymede?" I asked Richard Burbage when we met to rehearse our scenes.

"No line suggests so. After all, clothes make the man." Burbage's tone suggested no reference to myself, but I stayed on guard. "He comes close when Celia performs their mock wedding ceremony. What possesses Ganymede to ask Celia to marry them? Seems she's pushing too far."

"Bold of her."

"There's a moment where I felt an unexpected jolt. When I took your hand, it didn't feel like we were playing make-believe."

"You nearly kissed me."

"So very close." He smiled. "We'll keep the audience in suspense. Will Orlando make a sacred vow to a boy?"

"If they kiss after saying the words, they're as good as married."

"When he takes her hand and looks into her eyes, he's promising to marry his supposed belovèd—a boy playing a girl. He doesn't consciously think it's Rosalind."

"There's the mystery," I said. "Orlando loves a boy and a girl."

Blood rushed to my cheeks; I hoped Burbage didn't notice. That's what Frances had with me, a boy and a girl. I lacked what any other boy playing Rosalind would possess. Did some sense of that cause Burbage's jolt?

I spoke with manly self-assurance, "Let the audience make of that moment what they will. Otherwise Rosalind's appearance in her wedding gown will lack the power of magical revelation."

Shakespeare came over to us. "Dinner at the Anchor." We left the Globe together.

Armin and Tom Pope beckoned us to their table. Johnny was among the seated players, the first time in days that I'd seen him off stage. I didn't sit beside him. All seemed fraught between us, not that he gave any hint of feeling the same. Just a bland nod from across the table.

"Who are all these people?" I asked Tom Pope, gesturing at the unusually large crowd in the tavern.

"Volunteer soldiers, farmers and tradesmen in from the country."

"Is there a war?"

"Queen Elizabeth anticipates an invasion from Spain, so she's mustered an army. Have you heard nothing?"

"I've been preoccupied."

"Tied to your wife's apron strings, no doubt," Armin said.

Burbage laughed, then scanned the crowd. "I expect these not-so-willing volunteers will still be in London when our play opens and much in need of merriment."

"We'll have to play As You Like It three days running to accommodate them all," Pope said.

Ben Jonson pressed into the last space at our table. "I doubt there'll be an invasion."

Pope cautioned him to silence.

"I speak no treason. Besides, who can hear anything in this madhouse?"

Not even the barmaid. She was so busy serving other drinkers that she didn't come near our table, farthest from the taproom. Jonson had brought his full cup with him.

"Why do you doubt an invasion?" I asked.

"The Spaniards aren't prepared. Whatever threat they blustered is over. These men want to go home to their crops and their business."

"Then why remain here?"

Now Jonson did lower his voice. "You notice that the Queen has made no public appearance, no rallying of the troops as she did when we were threatened by the Armada. I think it's because we're in no danger of Spanish attack and she cannot pretend. This muster is not popular."

"Why call up so many men?" Phillips persisted.

"Could be she's warning off the Earl of Essex, should he entertain a notion of bringing his troops to London."

Armin waved at the barmaid, who nodded our way. "She may actually serve us," he laughed. "Don't they say Essex is the Queen's sweet Robbie?"

"That was before ambition ran away with him."

"Essex is fighting in Ireland for Her Majesty," Johnny said. "Why would she need to protect herself from him?"

"That from you, of all people." Jonson shook his head. "I thought you were hanging about the Countess of Rutland at Essex House these days."

"You've been her guest as well. So what—"

Jonson cut him off. "Her husband Rutland supports Essex in his assault on the throne."

"Assault?" Johnny looked shocked.

"Not with arms, not yet anyhow, but Essex has created a miniature kingdom for himself in Ireland. He's been knighting his men—"

"As he did after Cadiz; no one complaining."

No one replied to Johnny. Our ale had at last appeared.

When the barmaid left, Jonson continued his argument. "Essex negotiated with the Irish leader Tyrone on his own, not in the Queen's name. That's the report. He's put it about that her powers are failing and she's to blame for our economic woes. According to Essex, England is losing ground and needs a new leader. One assumes he means himself."

"I've heard that Essex has royal blood," I said.

"Yes, as do numerous other nobles."

So had Ferdinando Stanley, Lord Strange, patron of the original company I joined in London. Will Kemp's company, William Shakespeare's company. As soon as he inherited his title Earl of Derby, Stanley was regarded as a challenge to the throne, as supposedly the northern Catholics supported him. He protested, but nonetheless, seven months later he was poisoned. Stanley's death had to have been politically motivated, but who did it? They never discovered.

I couldn't imagine that such a fate would come to the Earl of Essex. But where Stanley was modest with no personal ambition beyond managing his extensive Lancashire estates, Essex commanded an army. Did he truly aspire to the throne? A frightening thought.

Jonson set down his empty tankard. "I expect we'll be seeing armed rebellion. Don't take my word. Listen around."

"Enough, Ben." Shakespeare had the last word and our party soon broke up.

"Hurrying home to the little wife?" Armin asked me as we left the tavern.

"I'm later than I expected."

"I'll tag along with you, whichever way you're going."

"Cornhill." I could think of no one whose company I less desired than Robert Armin's, but no refusing.

"Right. So, Alexander Cooke. I've taken the measure of every man in the company, and you're the enigma."

"Oh?"

"Everyone's an accomplished actor. You're the Lord Chamberlain's Men, after all. There's no mystery to Will Shakespeare except genius: one never knows where that will go. Augustine Phillips possesses the leadership of a minor official, caring about protocol but not always getting it right. Tom Pope has the simplicity of a man large of heart and body who sees life as an entertainment. Heminges and Condell and Sincler and the rest are worker bees one way and another, and your brother's something of a popinjay who may come into his own as a writer, or so my friend Jonson thinks. Richard Burbage is and always will be the star. He's a muse for Shakespeare, ever pushing him to write greater roles."

We dodged a gallant with a beautifully made up, overdressed woman on each arm, a waft of mixed perfumes in their wake.

"You are observant, Master Armin."

"Here's where my funny feeling about you comes in. This Rosalind-Ganymede character of yours made me think that you played some part in her creation."

"As the oldest man to play female roles, you mean? It's a big part for someone like Beeston."

"It is indeed. I understand how our Will works: he writes parts for the players in the company. I took the place of Will Kemp, I understand, because our playwright had a different sort of clown in mind and I fit the bill."

I looked at Armin with startled apprehension. "He told you that?"

"No one needed to tell me. Was there a jig after *Julius Caesar*? Do I get laughs that aren't written into the play?"

"There's no clown in *Julius Caesar*."

"True enough, but can you imagine Will Kemp playing Lepidus? He'd be a comic pantaloon and likely offer a bawdy jig afterwards. I suspect your powers of observation are more dulled than mine because so much of your energy goes elsewhere."

"I'm sorry, but what—"

"Oh, I think you understand me perfectly. Sander Cooke is as much a creation as Caesar, Brutus, or Portia. A husband!" Armin laughed.

I walked with a soldierly stride and spoke in my firmest voice. "Yes, I'm married to Frances, and blessedly so."

"Not so sure about the blessed part."

"My house is just ahead."

"I won't ask to be invited in, though if I were, I've no doubt you'd rise to the occasion, no pun intended. But first I must say: apart from Burbage, you're the best actor in the company, as every moment of your life is an act. I've nothing to gain by telling your secret. Shakespeare is the only one in our company besides your brother who knows, am I right?"

I was taller than Armin and outweighed him, though not by much. I made myself bigger by sheer will. "I respect your powers of observation and your discretion, Master Armin. It's a pleasure to work with you. And now, my wife awaits me."

I am falser than vows made in wine.
ROSALIND, *AS YOU LIKE IT*

CHAPTER XIII
July 1599

At the end of the first performance of *As You Like It*, cheers and applause were so hearty it seemed Rosalind had conjured the audience indeed.

Amelia Bassano Lanyer met me outside the Globe.

"A brilliant play! Everyone laughed at something different. One woman thought Jaques the most entertaining—she giggled all through his 'All the world's a stage'. The man in front of me slapped his friend's shoulder every time Touchstone opened his mouth. I loved your role, but I agree with Celia: Ganymede slanders women mercilessly." We turned toward the Anchor, nearest tavern to the Globe. "Your brother played Silvius. What did he think of that?"

"The lovelorn shepherd?" I took Amelia's arm as two heedless apprentices practically pushed us off the pathway. "You don't mean that he's lovelorn over Lady Elizabeth?" I laughed. "That's not what's going on with him."

"Perhaps not. But I wouldn't put it past Will to have had Johnny in mind when he wrote Silvius. It's him, exaggerated."

"Will plays with us all; we're all in some sort of play in his imagination."

"That's what I mean."

We'd reached the company's favorite room in the Anchor, smoky from spluttering candles and tobacco smokers in adjoining chambers. Two large tables were pushed together in front of a bench extending the length of one wall, upholstered in frieze. Shorter wooden benches and chairs around the modest fire could be pulled up on the other side.

Amelia and I took seats at one end of the table as Moll Frith pulled up the largest of the chairs. "I came to join in singing those songs, the killing of the deer and the lover and his lass. Where are Touchstone and Jaques?"

She made an exaggerated bow to Amelia and sat facing her. "Shakespeare knows more about love than any of us. Don't you agree, Mistress Bassano?"

Amelia's blank look concealed anything from mystification to anger. Moll knew perfectly well about Shakespeare's sonnets to his dark lady, assumed to be Amelia herself, that moved from adoration to lust to harsh regret. I doubted Moll had read them, as they'd merely circulated among the cultured, but she never missed even a hint of gossip. I would know no more of them than she or the rest of our company if I hadn't been Amelia's confidant.

"Ganymede tells Orlando how untrustworthy women are," Moll continued. "Fickle, too witty by half, perfectly willing to take another man to bed and afterward make excuses to their husbands. Sander speaks those words, but they're Shakespeare's. Sander thinks no such thing."

"Nor does Rosalind," I protested. "She's teasing Orlando."

Moll shook her head. "More like wising him up. You're too idealistic."

"Idealistic?" I laughed.

"You're like Orlando. You think that—"

I cut her off. "You have no idea what I think. Keep your opinions to yourself, you bawdy thing. What do you know about love?"

"Not so much as Will Shakespeare, but enough to see its folly. Knaves and sluts fancying each other in a shared bubble of illusion, pricked to nothing."

"Such a tongue you have, Moll Frith." I turned to Amelia. "What shall we do with her?"

"Who ever curbed Moll Frith? You have a colorful way of

expressing yourself, Moll, but I think our playwright shows love as far more complicated than those lines."

"I know, I know. Four marriages at the end of the play, each different." She looked in vain for someone to serve us, but the Anchor with its warren of rooms kept them busy and none were to be seen.

Moll took a pipe from her doublet, packed it with tobacco, and lit it. "I wager I could write a play myself if I put my mind to it."

"About what?"

"Nothing like your Will's, you can be sure. I'd describe city folk I know."

Amelia laughed. "Rogues and thieves."

"My hero would be a character like the melancholy Jaques," Moll said. "A libertine, his skeptical voice gained by experience." Moll spoke in the voice of Duke Senior:

> *Most mischievous foul sin, in chiding sin:*
> *For thou thyself hast been a libertine,*
> *As sensual as the brutish sting itself;*
> *And all the embossed sores and headed evils,*
> *That thou with license of free foot hast caught,*
> *Wouldst thou disgorge into the general world.*

She omitted not a syllable.

Moll grinned at our surprise. "I confess. I overheard Tom Pope practicing that—and Phillips saying Jaques' lines. At the end, he takes himself off to a cave. 'So, to your pleasures: I am for other than for dancing measures.' All that festivity and love require a spoilsport."

"Shakespeare keeps a balance," Amelia said. "I admire him—"

"Who do you admire?" The voice belonged to the man himself, followed by our troupe.

"You, sir." Seeing Will unexpectedly, Amelia's face turned pale, but her voice was serene. "For giving the epilogue to Rosalind."

"I thought you spake of something more personal."

"More personal," Armin raised an eyebrow. "Of what nature?"

"We shan't push a lady to flattery or lies," Tom Pope said.

Armin put on Touchstone's voice. "I durst go no further than the Lie Circumstantial, nor she durst not give me the Lie Direct; and so we measure swords and part."

"You're quite right," Shakespeare said. "Never accuse a lady of even the Lie Circumstantial."

I felt Amelia bristle, but all attention had turned to Moll Frith, playing at measuring swords with Armin. If I didn't know the training of actors was more demanding than that of thieves, I'd worry that Moll would take my part as Ganymede. She couldn't play Rosalind, however, as she claimed never, even as a child, to have worn a skirt.

Moll delivered "All the world's a stage," on her feet.

Phillips laughed at Moll's antic presentation, especially her imitation of the soldier, waving her dagger like a sword.

> Full of strange oaths and bearded like the pard,
> Jealous in honour, sudden and quick in quarrel,
> Seeking the bubble reputation
> Even in the cannon's mouth.

Her histrionics had quieted the room, so Moll finished Jaques' speech in a stage whisper:

> Last scene of all,
> That ends this strange eventful history,
> Is second childishness and mere oblivion,
> Sans teeth, sans eyes, sans taste, sans everything.

Applause erupted, and the barmaids—two had finally appeared laden with jugs and tankards—could scarce keep up with shouted orders from rooms beyond our own. I wondered if I should rescue Amelia from drink-inspired ribaldry, but she seemed content enough beside Shakespeare who'd squeezed in on her other side.

Moll stood and launched into the song, "Who is he that killed the deer?" and the company joined in, some standing with Moll, some pounding their tankards on the table.

Burbage pulled up a chair by me. When ale arrived, he'd ordered a glass of wine for Amelia. Not having played in the hunting scene, he and I skipped the song, more din than music. We edged away from the clamor, Shakespeare and Amelia joining us.

"Orlando reminded me of Adonis," Burbage said. "Remember that time we enacted *Venus and Adonis* at the Earl of Southampton's house in Bloomsbury? You were there too, Mistress Lanyer."

"Such a long time ago." I spoke under the cacophony.

"Innocent days," Amelia said.

"I'd hardly call Venus innocent," Burbage laughed. "What do you say, Will?"

"She's a goddess."

"I remember feeling like a maiden that night," Amelia said. "With Alfonso off on Sir Richard Hawkins' expedition to the wilds of Peru, for one dazzling night I needn't be wife or mother."

Burbage smiled. "You were very young and very beautiful. Oh, you still are beautiful, of course you are. But there was a quality—" his eyes looked dreamy.

"It appears that Adonis was half in love with you, Amelia." I lifted my mug in a jesting toast.

"I wasn't the only one."

Amelia hadn't a blushing complexion, but her skin glowed. "Enough, Master Burbage."

He was not deterred. "You fell the hardest, Will."

Heedless Richard Burbage saw this as little more than gossip, with no sense of the turmoil in Amelia's heart, nor likely in Will's. After Shakespeare's sonnets about his dark-browed mistress shifted from admiration to torment and derision, Amelia let him go. His parting gift was to recite to her his incomparable verse: "Let me not to the marriage of true minds admit impediment." Her husband was due home and their love had run its course, with what feelings on either side I couldn't guess.

Amelia's ire at the amorous hopes and fears in the verses of men determined her to write poems herself on subjects other than love. Subjects of significance to women. She wasn't flattered when I suggested she'd influenced Shakespeare's female characters, dark-haired and sharp-tongued. Whatever she felt for him now, this public meeting ended abruptly. "I promised to be home in time to sup with my boy Harry." A nod, and Amelia vanished.

"Did I offend her?" Burbage asked.

"Mistress Lanyer is unpredictable," Shakespeare replied.

"I could have said more." Burbage took a drink. "I could have said that she was the image of Venus herself."

The chorus led by Robert Armin drowned us out. No choice but to join the best song of the play.

> *And, therefore, take the present time*
> *With a hey, and a ho, and a hey nonino*
> *For love is crowned with the prime*
> *In springtime, the only pretty ring time,*
> *When birds do sing, hey ding a ding a ding,*
> *Sweet lovers love the spring.*

Is love a tender thing? It is too rough,
Too rude, too boisterous, and it pricks like thorn.
ROMEO, *ROMEO AND JULIET*

CHAPTER XIV
Autumn 1599

Shakespeare spoke aright: Johnny's hopes of Lady Elizabeth failed him, yet that made him feel she needed him more than ever. Like her husband Rutland, Essex and Southampton returned from Ireland in disgrace with the Queen. Ostracized from court, the three had little to amuse themselves but plays, and were much seen in the public theatres.

Drinking with Moll Frith one afternoon at the Anchor, I told her how Johnny irritated me, insisting how much Lady Elizabeth needed him, yet taking advantage of our hospitality.

"What does Frances think?"

"She doesn't say. I don't understand him, that's all, and I wish he'd skip these prospective uncle visits."

"Are you jealous?"

I shrugged. I'd not have called what I felt jealousy.

"You needn't be, you know. Frances lives with *you*. Be the man."

"I play that part."

"Inside yourself as well. Men are sure of themselves. If we feel something, we act on it."

"What action do you suggest?" I asked.

"Show Johnny up for the fool he is."

"I married Frances when he refused to."

"In that instance Johnny was worse than a fool."

"You mean I should mock him for doting on Lady Elizabeth Sidney?"

"That's not action."

"I can't throw my weight around at home. What I have to offer Frances is my reliability and companionship."

"No woman wants to be married to a woman. Some may wish their husbands were gentler, but not too gentle. I'll never marry, heaven forbid, but I've loved wenches and no doubt will again."

"Oh?" Moll had never said as much before, though I wasn't surprised. I'd seen the flirtatious looks women gave her, dressed like a man but somehow mocking men or at least displaying an attractive boldness. The looks men gave her blatant woman-man self reflected a confusion of male bonhomie, admiration, scorn, and fear of her audacity.

"Wenches know I'm a woman, but they look to me to be the man. They want someone strong and assertive and a little rough. Believe me, I know what I'm talking about."

Shakespeare once said women could share tender embraces. Moll's embraces would be no such. But what were they? How would a woman play a man in bed?

I felt my cheeks warm. "I don't think of Frances that way. She's expecting a baby."

The serving maid refilled our mugs, giving Moll a coy smile as she took her coin. The last thing I'd want was to be taken for a woman-man! If a girl flirted with me, she thought me a comely male stage player.

Moll drank deep. "Think of Frances as your wife."

"I do, and I wish Johnny would stay away."

"You don't own Frances, and she doesn't own you. But in bed, you must be the husband." Moll emptied her mug and wiped her mouth on her grimy shirtsleeve. "Off to livelier business."

I stayed where I was until the blood stopped pounding in my ears and my flushed cheeks cooled. Perhaps Frances was telling me this very thing when she admired Ganymede's lines about her "swashing and martial outside." I rather doubted it, certainly this late in her pregnancy, though on my way home I assumed a soldier's stride.

Performing *Julius Caesar*, we breathed out our words in misty gusts and the audience, warmly cloaked, huddled even closer together than usual.

I struggled to keep my mind on the play. Heavy-bellied, Frances felt so miserable that I hated to leave her alone with Rebecca. What a relief when Octavius uttered the final words: "So call the field to rest, and let's away, to part the glories of this happy day."

The audience applauded, the dead revived to take their bows, and I dashed offstage before cheers stopped ringing. I'd left Frances alone for more than two hours as fate and fortune turned against everyone except Mark Antony.

Shoving my way through the crowd on London Bridge, I caught a glimpse of Joan tending Frances' shop. At home Frances lay on her side on the woolen rug in front of the hearth with Rebecca kneeling beside her.

"Frances, dearest! Are you all right?"

"I can't do anything for her." Rebecca sounded desperate.

I took her place. "Put a log on the fire and fill the pot with water. And bring clean sheets."

As I cradled Frances' head in my lap, her eyelids fluttered and her voice was hoarse. "The baby's coming." Pain wrenched her. I wished that Gran were here with her healing touch. At least we had Mother Tilda, and Rebecca ran to fetch her.

"Breathe, Frances. Breathe." I stirred the fire under the pot of water, rubbed her back, and waited. It seemed forever—breathe in, breathe out, breathe in, breathe out—before Rebecca returned with the midwife.

Frances moaned with the next contraction.

"We must get her to bed. This is no place to birth a baby!" Mother Tilda and I carried her as tenderly as we could up the stairs,

Frances stifling her cries. We lay her on the bed just before the next pain came.

Holding her hand, I kept my eyes on Frances' face rather than what was happening beneath her lifted skirts. As the pains came faster, her wails rose. She gripped my hand until her fingers were white and mine felt bruised. My heart pounded as I prayed, "Keep her safe. Keep her safe. Keep her safe." The room felt unbearably hot, but I timed my breathing to Frances'. "Slowly, slowly."

Her breaths came as gasps.

After what seemed hours, Frances heaved in a mighty thrust I feared would tear her apart. Mother Tilda sprang into action. In moments, I heard the baby gulp her first breath. She made a soft cry. *She*.

Mother Tilda cut the cord, wiped the baby clean, and wrapped the tiny bundle in linen, then a blanket. She placed her in my arms, and I looked from the infant's face, a bluish shade of pink, to Frances' pale one, her eyes shadowed.

The baby whimpered, no lusty cry but better than silence. I'd have liked to name her Katherine, after Gran, but it was also the name I myself was given at birth. Better to name this baby Marie, after the Countess of Pembroke. She needed every blessing, poor frail thing, Marie Sidney's and holy Mary's as well.

As I rubbed warmth into the tiny hands, Frances stirred and opened her eyes. "The baby—"

"She's fine. Will you hold her?"

I helped Frances to a sitting position, propping the pillow behind her and wrapping a blanket around her shoulders. The infant's eyes were open, her breathing raspy.

"She's so tiny! She seems too small to live."

"Babies are tiny," Mother Tilda said. "Don't worry, we shall help her grow and thrive. How are you, Frances?"

"Exhausted." Frances gazed into her daughter's face. "What a perfect little mouth."

Mother Tilda added a log to the fire. "Offer her your breast."

She turned to Rebecca. "Fetch your mistress a cup of broth. After she nurses the baby, she must sleep."

"Drink up, sweetheart," Frances murmured, tickling the child's cheek.

"Shall we call her Marie?" I asked.

Frances positioned the baby more comfortably, the little mouth grasping. "Yes. Marie."

"She can suck. A good sign," Tilda said. "Not much there for her yet, but your milk soon comes in."

Marie let go of the nipple and inhaled harshly.

Tilda took her from Frances and put her in my arms. Marie's head rested against me so familiarly that I wished my breasts weren't bound. I couldn't nurse the child, but I held her against my heart. My arms knew how to cradle an infant, even one as fragile as Marie. She aroused a different sort of love than I'd known, this fragile bit of flesh growing inside Frances these many months. I saw Frances anew, a Madonna enacting one of the most ancient rituals of humanity. My wife, my child.

"Not every father takes to the little ones," Mother Tilda said. "They prefer them walking and talking. And a sickly one who came three or four weeks early—" She shook her head.

I hated the word "sickly." Few fathers cared to spend their love on a baby who might not survive, but I'd do all I could to love this child into health.

Where love is great, the littlest doubts are fear;
Where little fear grows great, great love grows there.
PLAYER QUEEN, *HAMLET*

CHAPTER XV
November 1599

Frances and I spent much of the next week in bed together, as close as we'd ever been, the baby between us. I loved the sense that we were both comforting her. While I was at the Globe, Rebecca looked after mother and child, and Mother Tilda stopped in daily. For the first time in my life, I didn't want to rehearse or perform. I'd rather spend all day with Marie and Frances.

When I was home, the baby was never far from my arms. Midwives advised swaddling babies tightly and leaving them in their cradles, but I meant to exercise strength into Marie's frail limbs. I would sit in front of the fire with her in my lap, moving her arms and legs gently, repetitiously. Marie often whimpered, but now and then she'd look into my eyes, a valiant expression on her wan little face. But despite our efforts, she wasn't thriving.

We strove to keep Marie alive. She spent little time in her cradle, loving arms ever open to her. After her initial fear that the baby was too delicate to touch, Rebecca took to childcare with devotion. If Marie rejected Frances' nipple, we offered her honey teats. We warmed her little hands and feet, tickled her gently. Anything to keep her connected to us, to life.

From long experience, Mother Tilda must have known how tenuous was that connection, but Frances and I felt it in our hearts. This child seemed made of half earth, half heaven. I couldn't pray but Frances prayed endlessly to the Virgin Mary to save her precious babe.

Marie's struggle lasted three weeks. Mother Tilda called in more frequently as the infant's hold on the slim thread that tied her to us loosened.

Before dawn of the twenty-second day, Marie gave up. In the bed between Frances and me lay a perfect little angel, lifeless, transfigured into something neither of us could fathom. Marie had moved beyond us. We spent the rest of the night keeping her warm, hoping that life would miraculously return.

It did not. When the thin November sun rose, the tiny body remained lifeless.

Frances held Marie to her breast, keening. She collapsed onto the bed, handing the limp child to me. I wrapped her in linen and carried her downstairs. Rebecca, tears running down her face, opened the door to Mother Tilda.

I held out the near-weightless body. "She's left us."

Tilda embraced Marie, her eyes wet. She'd seen this too often, but the loss seemed freshly intense. This baby came into the world with all her potential and gifts, and now she was no more. Tilda's job was to preserve life, yet here again she ministered to its premature ending. She swathed Marie in another layer of linen, this one embroidered, and held her close.

We buried Marie Katherine Cooke in St. Botolph's churchyard on a dreary damp day, November 12, 1599. Joining us at her grave were Rebecca, Mother Tilda, Tom Pope, William Shakespeare, and Amelia and Harry, the boy's eyes red. His mother walked him away when he began weeping. I caught a glimpse of Moll Frith just beyond our circle. She doffed her plumed hat, bowed, and departed. I thought I saw Johnny behind the yew trees, but he didn't appear.

Shakespeare offered to buy us all a warm cup of wine, but Frances and I declined. Closed in our sorrow, we returned to the empty house. Rebecca served us supper in front of the fire, retreating to the kitchen and leaving us to our grief.

Frances went upstairs, and I sat in front of the fire, my heart aching. No baby! I could never be a mother, but fatherhood: fatherhood would compensate for all I'd lost. The worst had been giving up John Donne. Since then, only in playing female roles could I express my womanly emotions. Until marriage. What a precious opportunity, to raise a baby with Frances. Dear Marie. I wept as I never had before. Bitter, bitter loss.

Yet it brought Frances closer to my heart. A shared loss, but at least we had each other.

When the fire burned low, I joined Frances in bed, and she did not resist. It felt natural to me, holding each other after such suffering. I slept lightly, as I supposed, did she. When one of us moved, the other curled against her.

In early morning, after sleep defeated me, I went downstairs. The room was warm and smelled of baking bread. Frances followed sometime later, looking numb. With Rebecca caring for us as best she could, we dragged through a mostly silent day. After supper, Frances rose to go upstairs.

"I'll sleep alone tonight, Sander. My mind is too full for company."

An overwhelming sadness swept over me. Rebecca must have overheard, for she brought me a cup of wine. I drank it, wondering how Frances could refuse my consoling arms. It felt terribly wrong.

In time, sleep overcame me.

I awoke next morning, stiff and unrested, still sitting in my chair, the fire scanty embers. As I stirred them to life, Frances came downstairs, her face haggard, hair hanging loose.

"How are you doing, Frances?"

"I feel empty." She gave me a look I couldn't interpret.

"Rebecca's made breakfast. That should help you feel better."

"I can't eat." She sat on the edge of the chair opposite me. "I've been thinking all the night."

Her tone made me apprehensive about what she'd been thinking. "Oh?"

"It's come to me. With Marie gone, there's no reason for us to be married."

I couldn't believe my ears. "How can you say that, now of all times?"

"Don't you feel it Sander? That we can't go on together?"

"No!" Surely Frances shared my sorrow, but her face was cold, all emotion imprisoned.

"You've been kind to me and willing to make my baby your own. But there's no longer a baby."

"You would be a wonderful mother, Frances, and I looked forward to fatherhood. Losing Marie broke both our hearts. Remember all we've shared? We still have that bond. You and I made vows to each other in front of the priest."

"Lying vows. I wasn't really marrying Alexander Cooke. The groom was Kate Collins."

"You're wrong. You married Alexander Cooke, the only name I shall have so long as I live. You and I are joined for life."

"You mean you want to stay with me?"

"Of course I do. I love you, Frances, and I hope you love me. We've gone through the worst a parent can, losing a child. We must rely on each other now."

"I thought you married me out of generosity."

"Perhaps I did. But I made those promises to you from the depths of my heart. Marie's death doesn't change that."

As Frances stared at me, I hoped that my manly firmness and love touched her, but her blank expression made me fear what was going through her head. Under my clothes I wasn't a man. Was that the issue? Maddened by grief, she'd lost all reason and, apparently, all affection.

"What's prompted this?"

"It would be too strange to live here as your wife, Sander. If you want to remain here, I can go back to living above my shop. Rebecca will look after you."

"Is that what you want to do, Frances? Pretend none of this happened? Marie's death is my loss too."

"I don't want to hurt you, Sander. You'll be fine if—when we part."

"Won't you consider living with me as a friend? As we have?"

"I need to rest. You go on to the theatre." She seemed wracked with silent sobs.

"You're in no state to make such a decision. We should stay here, together. Help each other through this."

"I'm sorry. I need to be alone." She turned toward the stairs.

"That's all?"

Frances did not reply.

Heavy-hearted, I walked slowly down Cornhill. Frances and I lost our daughter. Must we lose each other? All the long night after we buried Marie, I dreamt of the future, Frances and me facing the world together, facing adversity together, sharing companionship. Tenderness, pity, and a desperate yearning surged through me. Living alone did not suit me; living with Frances did. We enhanced each other.

Except, Frances felt otherwise.

Everyone can master a grief except he who has it.
BENEDICK, *MUCH ADO ABOUT NOTHING*

CHAPTER XVI
November 1599

I hurried across London Bridge and past her shop. Once Frances recovered from the depths of her pain, surely she would come round. She must come round! Who would care for her more than I did? Who could love her better? Certainly not Johnny, no longer a prospective uncle who stopped by for an occasional supper.

Just past St. Saviour's, Will Shakespeare caught up to me. "I'm so sorry, Sander."

"I can't get over it. Marie was everything to me."

"Everything. I know. I've lost a child. There's nothing worse."

I'd forgotten about his boy Hamnet, dead some two years.

He took me by the arm. "Come with me." We stepped into St. Saviour's, quiet at this hour, and sat near the back.

"Marie was the reason I—"

"The reason you changed your life and gave yourself to parenthood."

"I feel I've lost all that I valued. It's too much to bear."

"You have Frances."

A tear ran down my cheek.

"Sander?"

"No, that's the worst of it. Frances wants to—" I stopped, then tried again. "She wants to get over the loss of Marie alone. She's over me as well."

Shakespeare looked shocked and put his arm round me. "Can that be? Women's moods change."

"She seemed absolutely firm. I'm to move out. I can't believe it! We were friends for so long before marrying. Does that count for nothing?"

He said nothing, sitting quietly, his arm still draped over my shoulder. It was all I could not to lean on him and weep.

"I like being married, that's the simple truth. 'So long as we both shall live.' I don't want anyone else. I want to share my life with Frances and hers with me, even without Marie. I need Frances, and surely she needs me. I imagined that facing our loss together would bring us closer."

"In plays, magic can prevail. Puck or Hymen to the rescue, blessings all round."

"Yes, in plays. Audiences want the forever promise. So do I, in sickness and in health, for richer and poorer."

As a scattering of worshippers came in, we left the church, opposite in grandeur from modest St. Alphage's where I had so hopefully made those wedding vows.

Outside, Will said, "Give it time. Marriage is a complicated business. I know, in my comedies I gloss over the chanciness of the marriages that end those plays. Real life is far more thorny than happy ever after."

We maneuvered in silence through icy streets filled with grim, bundled-up folk. Near the Globe Will turned to me.

"Remember, Sander: Frances married *you*."

"I may be a kinder version of my brother, but I lack the essential."

"That could be doubted, 'the essential,' as you put it."

When we slowed to a stop, Tom Pope passed us. "Come along. You're late."

"In a moment." Shakespeare waved him on.

"So?"

"I was going to say, to keep Frances, you may have to seduce her."

I had to laugh. What a ridiculous thought! But it shook me out of my gloom. We hurried the last few paces to the Globe, my cheeks flushed from more than the chill air.

When I returned home that afternoon full of ideas, Frances asked me to move that very night to lodgings. I wanted to stay with her, console her—for us to console each other—and consider our future, but she was adamant. "Please go. I need to be alone."

"Are you sure?"

"Just go."

"You don't mean forever?"

Frances looked up, her eyes dark with sorrow, and said nothing.

With the grief in my heart weighing me down more heavily than my handbag of clothes, I made my way to my old street in Shoreditch. Was this what our marriage had come to?

I hated to leave Frances on her own. Rebecca was competent, but too quiet, too young, to be real company. Now Frances faced an empty future. Together we could move forward.

I blinked away the tears. Who'd have thought the loss of an infant could arouse such love? Trying to keep Marie alive had united us in a deeper way than I could have imagined. How could Frances not feel the same?

She didn't want me and that was that. Somehow, we must remain friends. So what if my love counted for nothing to her now, or even our friendship? I couldn't simply erase them.

Rubbing a hand over my wet cheeks I strode forth. Back to lodgings.

Let Virtue be your guide, for she alone
Can lead you right that you can never fall.
AMELIA BASSANO, "TO ALL VIRTUOUS WOMEN IN
GENERAL," *SALVE DEUS REX JUDAEORUM*

CHAPTER XVII
Winter 1600

For the Queen's holiday revels at Richmond Palace, Philip Henslowe's Admiral's Men would perform two plays by Thomas Dekker: *The Shoemaker's Holiday* and one revived especially for the occasion called *The Comedy of Old Fortunatus*. Our company would present *As You Like It* and Ben Jonson's *Every Man Out of His Humour*. I had only a small part in Jonson's play, as Rosalind's role was so long.

Rather than making the trip up the Thames from London each day, actors were housed in Richmond, not far from the palace. It was almost like being an apprentice again, I thought, sharing rooms with Christopher Beeston and our newest player boy, Rafe. In the same house lodged Tom Pope, who shared with Johnny and Robert Armin.

I had little to say to Johnny and no idea what he felt about Marie's death. Not much, I guessed. With her husband out of favor, he must be sorry Lady Elizabeth would not attend festivities at Richmond Palace.

When I'd crossed paths with Frances' apprentice Joan, before the girl ran off in awkward haste, she told me her mistress would spend New Years with the former owner of her shop, Gemma Cooper, and her husband at their house in Throckmorton Street. Despite their generous hospitality, it would be a difficult time for Frances. No child for her during the season of celebrating nativity. I'd sent her the best gift I could think of, a warm hat from the milliner's on the Bridge. No reply.

Here I was spending Yuletide with the players, preparing for a royal audience.

The night after the court performance of *Fortunatus*, we players gathered at the elegant Orange Tree Inn in Richmond for supper. I should have expected that a tavern in the refined atmosphere of Richmond would little resemble those we frequented in London. The walls were lined with linen-fold paneling, the spacious room furnished with dark green plush chairs and benches and tables of dark wood with carved bases. No scratches or sticky remnants of past ale. The hearths at each end of the chamber were framed by stone pilasters topped with chiseled Atlases holding the broad mantel on their shoulders. Hearth fires and wall torches barely smoked, glowing over all.

I was reminded of the stately manors I'd visited the summer I travelled with Lord North's Men. We'd performed in rooms not so different from this, except for their music gallery above and their heraldic decorations. Embroidered tapestries dotted the Orange Tree walls, richly colored but not as artistic as the thickly-flowered ones Joan created for the Spread Eagle. I wished I could share this luxury with Frances.

Instead, I had the lively company of Ben Jonson and Shakespeare and our fellows, talking beneath the clamor around us. Jonson set down his wine cup. "It seems peculiar that after Essex was arrested when he returned from the trouble he caused in Ireland, everyone at court is so merry."

From behind us, someone said, "I agree." I recognized the voice of John Donne.

"I was waiting for the right company, and here I've found it. I'm puzzled as well. It's as though there's a sickness at court which all deny, throwing themselves into holiday festivities. Most peculiar." He turned to me. "I understand we'll be treated to your Rosalind tomorrow. That should spread merriment through the great chamber."

As ever, my heart lurched when I looked into John's eyes, but I smiled, pleased that he'd see me in a court performance.

"You find such merriment false?" Shakespeare refilled his cup and pushed the jug of spiced wine across the table toward Donne.

"Don't you? All this manic jollity. It makes no sense."

"You mean because of the absence of Robert Devereux, Earl of Essex, ever the life of the party?" Shakespeare asked. "The Queen must miss him more than we do, yet she gives no sign."

"She's not seen him in months, not since he burst in on her in her private chamber when she was scarcely decent," Jonson said. "She must have forgiven that appalling breach of protocol, but now Essex remains under house arrest and cannot even see his wife, newly delivered of a child. He's a vainglorious fool. Nonetheless, he should be attending the royal celebrations. He's the last of the old order of knights."

John Donne set down the wine cup he'd been sniffing, the fragrance almost as delicious as the contents. "If so, he's a knight errant. When I served with him in Cadiz, I thought him an alarming mixture of courage and bravado. Yet though he often angered the Queen, she excused him again and again. Now Essex and his glittery train are less noted at court than Lucifer and his angels after being cast from heaven. I'm afraid that Essex has no better chance of returning to royal favor than those fallen bright ones to the divine empyrean."

From across the table, Johnny said, "As I understand, Essex lives in hope."

"I think his spirit wastes away," Donne replied. "Robert Devereux will fall." I saw the worry in Johnny's eyes, but Donne merely smiled at the serving maids. "Ah, dinner."

The maids set down trays loaded with roast fowl and vegetables, knotted loaves of machet bread, and pear tarts, and replaced the empty wine jug with two fresh ones.

Donne spoke in my ear. "One also lives in hope of love. May your marriage have brought you that." Fortunately it wasn't a question. "I've found love myself," he added.

"I've heard rumors."

"Her name is Anne More. Neither her father nor my employer, Sir Thomas Egerton, favors our marriage, but we shall persevere. Strangely, Sander, my love for Anne is in some ways a consequence of yours and mine. I learned something with you that opened a part of my soul never before touched. I hope you take no offense—"

"I too treasure that day, John." I spoke in the same even tone, though my heart whirled. My hand on his knee, my voice was barely above a whisper. "I hope you and Anne may marry soon."

I turned to the feast spread before us and forked half a guinea fowl onto my plate. Nothing would entice me to tell John the sorry state of my own marriage.

Memories of our triumphant court performance of *As You Like It*, cheered me, especially my addressing Rosalind's epilogue directly to the Queen. The gaiety and grandeur at Richmond Palace had gilded everyone's spirits.

But in London, January was cold and bleak. One soggy day, I ran into Rebecca on her way to Aldgate to see the widow she aided. Her cheeks were rosy, her brown eyes bright with good health, her worsted wool cloak fashionable.

"You're looking well, Rebecca."

"I wish I could say the same for my mistress. She's not herself."

"Still mourning Marie?"

Rebecca's voice was timid. "Yes—and perhaps she's sad about asking you to leave. How are you?"

"Busy with plays, as always. Tell me about Frances."

"She comes to the shop when she has to, but prefers to do embroidery at home. Joan and I pretty much run the place, and it was busy before the holidays."

"Good for you, Rebecca. Does that leave you time to help around the house?"

"I have to. Mistress Frances barely keeps the fire burning."

"Can you or Joan talk sense to her?"

"Joan insists that she return to us full time, but Mistress Frances spends many days lost in melancholy."

"Does she speak to you?"

"Not much. One afternoon when I came home, she was talking to herself. It was mostly nonsense, but I picked up a few words before I was able to calm her with a hot drink. She would never be a mother; that much I understood. The rest, about no future and something about your brother and men—I don't know what all. It didn't make sense."

"Can you give her a message?"

"I can, but wouldn't it be better for you to come yourself, sir?"

"No, I don't think so."

"We've tried everything. You must call on her, sir."

"I'm not sure—"

Shakespeare came up behind us. "Of course you'll go, Sander! When I stopped in to see Frances yesterday, she wished it were you. Go on. And do bring her something tasty."

Ever since I moved out of our house, Frances was never far from my mind. Even as I learned the part of Queen Gertrude for our new play *Hamlet*, I worried about her on her own.

I knocked on the familiar door in Cornhill. Frances opened it a crack, looked startled but held it wide.

My words rushed out as I came into the room, colder than it should be this wintry day. "How are you doing?"

"Just fine."

"I'm worried about you." More so than I dared say. Frances made a point of dressing well, her clothes as well fit as a noblewoman's, minus the sumptuous fabrics. Even during pregnancy she'd devised dresses that gave only a hint of her changed figure. But now she wore a long shift and was wrapped in worsted that more resembled a blanket than a shawl, none of it the freshest. Her hair fell in disheveled, lank curls.

She waved me to a seat by the scanty fire and went into the

kitchen. I moved the chairs close to the hearth and added wood, stirring it to flame.

Frances returned with a tray: a piece of dry cheese, a slightly shriveled apple, a jug of beer and two cups. "Not much in the cupboard today."

"I brought something." I set the spinach pie, still warm from the bakers, and a bottle of claret on the hearth.

"How's the shop?" I asked as I passed her a cup of wine.

"I've been letting it go, I'm afraid. Joan and Rebecca are getting impatient. I must get back to work soon."

"I find work a saving grace."

She nodded noncommittedly. "A friend of yours came to call. Joan sent her here after fitting her new gown. Amelia Bassano Lanyer! I'd never actually spoken to her before. What a fascinating woman, so beautiful. And she writes poetry!"

"I'm glad you had a chance to meet her. Yes, Amelia treads new ground. Such women are few."

"You do, Sander Cooke—a minority of one. Moll Frith goes about as a man-woman, but you have taken on male identity altogether."

"But not well enough to be your husband?"

"That's not what I meant."

"Isn't that the reason you asked me to leave?"

"Our marriage seemed pointless, that's all."

I took a sip of wine to cover my distress. "We should have faced the loss of baby Marie together. Grief torments the mind and heart. Did Amelia tell you of her daughter Odelia's death?"

"Our losses bonded us."

A tear spilled down Frances' cheek. I pulled her to her feet and folded her into my arms. She leaned into me, weeping soundlessly.

When her body stopped trembling, I held her at arm's length and wiped her tears away with a finger. "Are you all right?"

She straightened herself and sat back down. "Of course."

"I thought of you at Richmond. I wished you'd been there. If only we'd needed a seamstress!"

Frances managed a smile and lifted her untasted cup to her lips.

"I'm sorry you still suffer melancholy. At the Globe, everyone escapes to another realm for a couple of hours. You should come to opening night of our next play. It's called *Hamlet*, a tragedy such as you've never seen."

"A tragedy? Now?"

"Tragedy has its place in the darkest time of the year."

The pie was so fresh it crumbled as Frances served it. I took a bite and brushed the crumbs from my chin. "Remember that spring day you and I went to Richmond Palace, back when we were becoming friends? You had a gown to deliver to Her Majesty. The palace kitchen gave you milk and sweet buns, and we picnicked under a flowering horse chestnut tree."

"Of course I remember."

"That was the day I felt I knew you."

"Because I told you about my girlhood?"

"That, of course," I said, "and your secret about being raised in the Old Faith. But you said something even more significant."

"Oh?"

"You told me that your heart had never been tainted by love. Not in those words—they're spoken by Princess Margaret of Anjou in *Henry VI*. That's how she says she's a virgin. Her heart has never been tainted by love. You said that if you wanted to marry, you would have to be choosy. You were to inherit Gemma Cooper's shop, and a husband could interfere with your business."

"Did I say that? Well, it's true. What's mine would become his, and I wanted no man telling me what to do."

"Nor has one." I saw a flicker of awareness in her eyes. "You also said that you were armed against love because for you, desire was balanced by fear. We ended the conversation talking about your ambitions to be Silkwoman to the Queen. As it's turned out, we've both fulfilled the dreams we spoke of that day. In my case, beyond imagining."

After a long pause, Frances asked, "What's your role in *Hamlet*?"

"I'm Queen Gertrude, mother to the prince."

"A mother?" She laughed. "You're too young!"

"Now that I'm a hired man I'm grateful to play a woman at all. Anyway, Gertrude was practically a child bride. When the play opens, her husband has died. Her marriage to his brother Claudius and their coronation follow soon after."

"I doubt Prince Hamlet is happy about that."

"No, and it gets worse."

"You said the play's a tragedy. I remember from *Romeo and Juliet* that tragedies always get worse."

"*Hamlet* has little to do with love. He suffers alone, but Ophelia, the girl he loves, is worse off than he is. Beeston plays that part, and Johnny plays Hamlet's one true friend, Horatio."

"Does he now."

"Though Horatio is Hamlet's only true friend, he's rarely there when most needed."

"I don't find that the least surprising."

"It's a role, Frances."

"I know, but roles are cast to type, are they not? Like your Rosalind? You've said that Shakespeare writes parts for the men in the company."

"As actors."

"I doubt Johnny can be a true friend to either of us."

"He and I work together agreeably enough. Offstage he mumbles a word or two and keeps his distance."

"I've not seen him since Marie's funeral—if that was him hiding behind the yew trees."

That was as close as Frances came to speaking of our daughter. When I rose to leave, I opened my arms to her and we shared a strained embrace.

Love sought is good, but given unsought is better.
OLIVIA, *TWELFTH NIGHT*

CHAPTER XVIII
Winter 1600

Chamberlain's Men opened *Hamlet* at the Cross Keys Inn, and I saved Frances a seat in the sheltered gallery, protected from Mother Nature in her whimsical winter mode. Earlier, Tom Kyd wrote a version of *Hamlet*, heavy on revenge and light on humor. Shakespeare's was brand new, and the Cross Keys rippled with anticipation.

The play begins with soldiers on the battlements, deathly frightened after the ghost of Hamlet's father appears to them in full armor. Then the soldier Marcellus speaks the most lovely Christmas speech I'd ever heard. Telling Horatio about the ghost's visitation, Marcellus says,

> *It faded on the crowing of the cock.*
> *Some say that ever 'gainst that season comes*
> *Wherein our Saviour's birth is celebrated,*
> *The bird of dawning singeth all night long.*
> *And then, they say, no spirit dare stir abroad.*
> *The nights are wholesome. Then no planets strike,*
> *No fairy takes, nor witch hath power to charm,*
> *So hallowed and so gracious is that time.*

The words touched me as I waited backstage for my entrance: "So hallowed and so gracious." What a speech for a terrified soldier on a freezing Danish night after being visited by a ghost!

I entered as Gertrude on the arm of King Claudius, celebrating our wedding and his coronation, while Hamlet lurked gloomily in the shadows.

Frances looked awed, her eyes upon me. I kept my attention on Claudius as he spoke, but could feel Frances' intensity.

> *Therefore our sometime sister, now our queen,*
> *The imperial jointress to this warlike state,*
> *Have we, as 'twere with a defeated joy,*
> *With an auspicious and a dropping eye,*
> *With mirth in funeral and with dirge in marriage,*
> *In equal scale weighing delight and dole,*
> *Taken to wife.*

I stood regal beside him in ermine and satin, a sufficiently warm costume for such a chilly day. My blond wig was elegantly coiffed under a bejeweled crown: the queen who inadvertently prompted Claudius to commit murder.

Not that Gertrude or the audience knew that. Not until the next scene does the ghost of his father tell Hamlet that Claudius murdered him in his garden for his crown and his queen. Hamlet can't be certain whether the ghost speaks truth or demonic deception. If true, how can he avenge his father's murder?

From my first reading of my part, I'd felt Shakespeare gave Gertrude too few lines. The audience must learn her feelings from my expressions and silences. I must personify Gertrude's divided affections and her helplessness, a woman of heart while those around her, particularly her husband and son, are driven by other forces.

When Hamlet, Richard Burbage, comes accusingly into my chamber, he mistakes Polonius for Claudius and stabs the old man through a curtain.

As Polonius' body fell into the chamber I cried, "O what a rash and bloody deed is this!"

"A bloody deed!" Hamlet echoed. "Almost as bad, good mother, As kill a king, and marry with his brother."

My short reply had to carry all Gertrude's shock and dismay, "As kill a king!"

Until this moment Gertrude was unaware of Hamlet's anguished suspicion that Claudius murdered his father, but at least I had a chance to tell him off: "What have I done, that thou darest wag thy tongue in noise so rude against me?"

I couldn't stop him, and by the time Hamlet finished his tirade against me and all women, I was broken. "O, speak to me no more; These words, like daggers, enter in mine ears. No more, sweet Hamlet!"

It was too much even for the ghost of Hamlet's father, who, visible only to his son, told him to look to me. "O step between your mother and her fighting soul."

With all my being I had to embody despair, fear for my son's sanity, conflicted love, and guilt.

"O, Hamlet, thou hast cleft my heart in twain."

I couldn't save him from his internal torture, nor could I save Ophelia from her father Polonius and her brother Laertes' failure to credit the love Hamlet had felt for her. I, Gertrude, was the only one who truly loved Ophelia, hoping she would become Hamlet's wife. Because of obtuse men, Ophelia went mad, abandoned by Hamlet, her father murdered, her brother no help at all.

I was the one to describe Ophelia's death, my best speech in the play.

> There is a willow grows aslant a brook,
> That shows his hoar leaves in the glassy stream;
> There with fantastic garlands did she come
> Of crow-flowers, nettles, daisies, and long purples.
> There, on the pendent boughs her coronet weeds
> Clambering to hang, an envious sliver broke;
> When down her weedy trophies and herself
> Fell in the weeping brook. Her clothes spread wide;
> And, mermaid-like, awhile they bore her up:
> Which time she chanted snatches of old tunes;

> *As one incapable of her own distress,*
> *Or like a creature native and indued*
> *Unto that element.*

I lingered over every word, so that the audience saw Ophelia falling into the brook in slow motion. By accident? By intent?

She floated, a tragic mermaid in her element.

> *But long it could not be*
> *Till that her garments, heavy with their drink,*
> *Pull'd the poor wretch from her melodious lay*
> *To muddy death.*

Tears ran down my cheeks. Hamlet should have looked beyond his own suffering to Ophelia's while he had the chance.

Gertrude lives for love and dies for love. During the final fencing match between Hamlet and Laertes, I watched Claudius drop a pearl into the wine he offered Hamlet between rounds. I recognized the drink as poisoned and lifted the cup myself to carouse to Hamlet's success. As soon as I drained it, I collapsed, warning Hamlet, "The drink, the drink," before I died, my death a sacrifice for my son and proof of Claudius' villainy. This was consequence of men's pursuit of revenge: the death of the woman who loved them.

From the stage where I'd fallen, I saw Laertes cut Hamlet's arm with sword unbated and poisoned. When Hamlet managed to exchange swords with him during their fight, Laertes fell dead, his plot turned against him.

Horatio sent Hamlet off: "Let flights of angels sing thee to thy rest," and Hamlet spoke his last. "The rest is silence."

As Fortinbras of Norway strode onstage, we corpses lay in a bloody tableau.

"Take up the bodies," Fortinbras said. "Such a sight as this Becomes the field but here shows much amiss. Go, bid the soldiers shoot."

A martial salute rang from backstage, but still we did not move.

Then applause rang out and Burbage pulled me to my feet, tears streaming onstage and off. In the gallery above, Frances' tear-stained face was transformed by a strange vitality.

After the performance our company went to the Anchor, relieved that we had our own private chamber. Hamlet, as well as Ophelia, Laertes, Claudius, Polonius, the ghost of Hamlet's father and Gertrude, preferred not to be surrounded by well-wishers after our harrowing performance.

I followed Shakespeare and Burbage into the warm room where a woman sat on the settle to one side of the fire. Before I caught a close look, I heard Shakespeare say "Frances! I didn't realize it was you. Did you see *Hamlet*?"

"I did. You made a scary ghost."

"I hope so; I drive Hamlet to the brink of madness. What did you think of Gertrude?" Shakespeare put an arm around my shoulders and propelled me in Frances' direction.

Tom Pope answered the question as he came to our table with the serving maid, both loaded down with cups and jugs of hot spiced wine. "Queen Gertrude needs more lines."

"Lines don't make the part," Shakespeare replied.

"But audiences come to hear a play."

Armin laughed. "This play has plenty of words!"

"And Gertrude is much on stage," Shakespeare added. "We feel for her—"

"Yes, but we don't always know what to feel about her," Pope persisted.

"Our Sander solved that." Shakespeare lifted his cup to me. "He made us see Gertrude as a tragic, outmaneuvered woman in treacherous Elsinore. We feel that in her expressions, her bearing."

His compliments warmed me more than the wine.

"What did you feel, Frances?" he asked.

"Pity." She didn't look at me, though I sensed she felt much more.

"As she deserves." Shakespeare joined the table of drinkers, and I sat beside Frances on the settle, room for two to sit snugly side by side.

"You were wonderful, Sander, but Hamlet exhausted me, all his arguments with himself. He thinks too much. Gertrude isn't like that."

"You mean she doesn't think?"

"I mean she's ruled by emotion, which is not enough in Elsinore. I agree with Master Shakespeare: your performance was moving. At first Gertrude was a mystery to me, marrying Claudius when her husband was barely cold in his grave, but your depiction shows her powerlessness. What else could she do?" Frances gazed at the fire and then into my eyes. "I'd like to hear you say her speech describing Ophelia's death, just for me. Oh Sander, we could discuss this play all night long."

"I'd like that very much."

I took her hand, and she didn't pull away.

"Did you enjoy playing Gertrude?"

"Tom Pope is right. She could use more lines. But yes, I very much enjoyed playing her. I felt her dilemma."

"You made me feel it too, to my heart. But most of your other roles have seemed more like the Sander I know, especially Rosalind dressed as a boy. Onstage I think of you as a man playing women's roles."

"But not a man in bed," I said quietly. "That's the naked truth."

We laughed, a moment of embarrassed intimacy in the noisy tavern.

"I've missed you, Sander. I think of all the things I'd like to talk about with you. You're my best friend."

I couldn't reply. Surely Frances knew I would prefer to live with her, daily companions.

We sipped our cinnamon-scented wine, our free hands touching as they rested on my thigh.

"It's pleasant sitting here with you, Frances, but—"

"But you want to carouse with your friends."

"I'm not sure 'carouse' is the word. That's what Gertrude says she's doing when she drinks the poisoned cup meant for Hamlet. Are you offering me poison?"

"I don't know that I'm offering you anything."

"I thought not." I withdrew my hand.

"Wait." Frances pressed my thigh as if to restrain me. "We can talk more freely in all this clamor."

"About what?"

"The play. Well, not exactly. My feelings while I watched the play. They're difficult to put into words. Hamlet's dilemma didn't touch me as Gertrude and Ophelia's did. Ophelia broke my heart. Her father spied on her with Hamlet, and no one took her side. Seeing how Gertrude's loving heart was betrayed, I ached. It felt like the tragedy of helpless women."

"Neither you nor I face their plights. We've been fortunate."

"We've had our narrow escapes, Sander. You could be a huswife in Saffron Walden now, under the thumb of a brutal husband."

I grimaced.

"Seeing you so poignant as Gertrude made me wish you and I could—could—" she trailed off.

The wine, the fire, and Frances beside me made me churn with uncertainty. I suppressed the urge to kiss her.

"Will you walk me home?" She rose and threw on her cloak. None of the boisterous actors seemed to notice as we slipped through the door into evening's chill fog.

Still warmly wrapped, Frances embraced me as soon as we were inside our house. It was cold and smelled of ash, but our own heat consumed us. I held her tight and kissed her. My heart pounded, my mind was confused—and my body yearned.

She pushed me away, speaking breathlessly. "Slow down. Is this something we can do?"

"All I know is I want you to be close to me and me to you. As close as you wish."

Frances stirred the embers, added logs, and stood in front of the fledgling blaze until warm enough to remove her cloak. From behind her, I wrapped my arms around her waist. I wanted to protect her. I wanted her to see that we could end our loss and grief through love.

"I cherish you," I whispered in her ear. "I'll do anything you wish."

She turned to face me, leaning against my well-bound breasts. "Kiss me."

I leaned down and found her lips. She looked into my eyes, then closed hers and let herself go. Our arms moved on each other's backs, caressing, closer, tighter. As far I knew no one had touched Frances so except Johnny. In her freely expressed desire, I rejoiced that perhaps she felt less shy with me than she would with a man.

"I love kissing you," I said, "—and I love you."

"I know."

"I want you, Frances. You."

She answered with a kiss. In that moment no one existed except the two of us, pressed together by the lonely ache that had built within us through our long solitary nights. I felt her heart open to me.

Frances picked up her cloak from where she let it fall and spread it in front of the fire. We knelt on top of the cloak, face to face, and I drew her into my arms. Unlaced, her bodice slipped off her shoulders and then her shift, as, with the help of her dexterous fingers, did my shirt and constraining band.

What a relief! My breasts could never be free in ordinary life. At night as I unbound them, I'd lost the habit of even looking down. My reality long had been the band of linen Frances so easily threw aside. Now this was reality, embracing breast to breast. We kissed.

I loosened her skirt and my hand slipped to the front. She turned to allow access to the placket, and her skirt fell off. She stood, naked in the fire glow.

"Your turn," she said as she poured two cups of wine from the jug on the hearth. I watched her with admiring eyes.

"I'm happy to gaze on you." I felt shy, awestruck, disbelieving

Frances looked closely at my breasts, then touched my breeches. "May I?"

I nodded, almost laughing aloud. Frances would never ask a man such a thing!

She untied the points and gave a quick jerk downward. When I lifted myself in order to slip the breeches over knees and feet, my padded codpiece fell to the floor. Laughing at its silly exaggeration, Frances rose to her feet as well. We looked long at each other, both naked, skin glowing in the soft firelight.

"You're so beautiful!" I said.

"And you. What a secret self you have!" We tipped our wine cups to each other and emptied them, our eyes sparking each other's.

"And you. Oh Sander, I never thought of you like this—I—I—" I stopped her with a kiss.

As we embraced in front of the fire, I felt that Frances' body, once so tender from nursing Marie and hollowed out from childbirth, had become strong again. She lifted her lips to mine, a kiss that said all that words could not.

Then we were lying face to face on her cloak, hands and mouths free and inspired, exploring, responding: the gift of touch, savoring, discovering a new world that felt wondrous to me, miraculous. I followed instinct into this unknown realm.

Much later, the fire low and our bodies alive with exhausted satisfaction, we climbed the stairs to our shared bed. Holding each other close, we drifted into the peaceful sleep of lovers fulfilled.

My last waking sense was elation. Frances and I had created our own magical secret this dark night in the dead of winter, a love to sustain us until spring and beyond.

On waking, my first thought: Frances and I were married anew. My second: without a child to make us a family, could this last?

Perhaps we'd not repeat last night, or perhaps we'd refine those pleasures. What counted: we were fast friends, each the other's chief comrade. If Frances wanted Johnny, she'd had time. She hadn't trusted him with her grief, nor had he been her comforter.

So I could afford to be generous. If Johnny wanted to visit us, he was welcome. Apart from his irresponsibility, he could be entertaining, and after all, he was my brother.

Later that morning walking to the Globe, I encountered Shakespeare. He grinned. "Something changed in you, Sander. Something big."

Blood rose to my cheeks. "What sort of change?"

"You look like a satisfied man."

Cheered by his use of "man," I said, "Frances took me back."

"I guessed as much when I saw you two slip out of the Anchor last night. Happiness to you."

I appreciated that he didn't repeat the accustomed wish to married couples, "happiness to your sheets," but felt uneasy. "It's nothing to be spoken of—"

He interrupted me. "All part of the delicious comedy of our lives. Don't worry. I keep my counsel."

O gentle son,
Upon the heat and flame of thy distemper
Sprinkle cool patience.
GERTRUDE, *HAMLET*

CHAPTER XIX
February 1600

After Queen Elizabeth heard of our performance at the Cross Keys, she summoned us to Whitehall Palace to so she could see *Hamlet* for herself. Frances would be our costume mistress. Robert Cecil had suggested that as the play concerned the royal family of Denmark, we might find appropriate costumes in a palace storage chest and Frances was invited to come have a look.

The day before our performance, she left for Whitehall in an early morning dusting of snow. During the long chill hours Frances was gone, I looked over Gertrude's lines and idled away the hours until her return. Finally she breezed through the door, brushing snow from her cloak.

While Rebecca rattled around in the kitchen finishing our delayed midday meal, Frances sat beside me and began talking, as if her frosty walk home had enlivened her tongue. Or the Queen herself, as it turned out.

"Moments after I arrived I was taken to an anteroom. Who should be standing in the doorway, attended by three of her ladies, but Her Majesty. I fell into a deep curtsey, my eyes on her royal face. Many would long for a private audience, but even though I'd fitted her in the Royal Wardrobe, I was terrified. Then I'd been doing my job, disregarded. Now she looked straight at me, her eyes penetrating against her white makeup. I couldn't return her gaze, so let my eyes take in her whole being. Her hair was darker than when I'd last seen her, a wig of auburn curls around her face, her diadem decorated with pearl and topaz."

"That seems like a lot of jewelry to receive a Silkwoman."

Frances laughed. "It certainly wasn't for my benefit. The Queen dressed to receive petitioners in the Privy Chamber. But she did speak informally to me. I reassured myself: after all, I'd once secured the bands of russet-orange across that very satin bodice and created embroidery on the skirt. But I'd not born the full power of those eyes. The Queen agreed that for *Hamlet*, nothing but noble castoff clothes would suffice."

"I shall wear something of the Queen's?" My secret dream come true.

"She only said 'noble,' so I imagined she meant clothing worn by ladies and courtiers. Two of her ladies I recognized from my shop, her cousins Lady Katherine, the Countess of Nottingham, and Lady Philadelphia Scrope. Lady Katherine told me I could choose from the chest behind me and to be sure all alterations were removed before I returned the clothes, as even the slimmest boy actor wouldn't likely have a woman's waist." She reached over and measured mine between her two hands. "You're slim enough under that jerkin, Sander. Oh, and Lady Katherine trusted that the players would be careful."

"Careful! I hope you told her most all the characters die in the end."

Frances smiled. "Yes. I promised to remind you not to tear your costumes. The Queen laughed a dry little laugh, saying that she doubted I could promise any such thing. All she asked was that I mend rips so no one would suspect them. So mind your clothes, Sander."

"What did you choose for me?"

"Be patient. First, the youngest attendant, Lady Isabel, stared at me with her disconcerting blue eyes. Unlike the Queen's dignified cousins, she had a teasing sparkle, her bodice lower and hair more youthfully styled with frosty blond strands curling free. I hadn't expected anything like what she asked, Was it true that I'd married a player?"

My whole body tensed. "How did you answer?"

"I nodded as agreeably as I could. I felt the Queen's attention, but kept my eyes down, all too aware that she'd once guessed your true identity. Why did Lady Isabel have to intrude? I'd have thought the Queen and her cousins would have swept out, but they seemed in no hurry. So I opened the chest and lifted out an embossed purple skirt.

"Her Majesty asked her cousin why it was there, that she'd worn it not two years before. I retrieved a matching bodice and offered them to her. Lady Katherine pointed out that the skirt had a faded streak and waved the pieces away. 'Let no one but Denmark's queen wear this purple.' That will be you, Sander—and it's not noticeably faded."

"So I shall wear a garment of Queen Elizabeth!"

"You shall, my dear. Royal purple."

"That's the best part of the story, Frances. I'm thrilled."

"Maybe not so thrilled at the gossip, though. The elder three left Lady Isabel and a maid behind while I chose garments for Claudius, Hamlet, Polonius, and Laertes. Christopher Beeston won't wear anything regal, as poor Ophelia never gets that far in her life.

"While I was handing pieces to the maid to hang on the clothes rail, Isabel went on and on about how wonderful to live with a player, that you never know who you're waking up with or whose words he speaks. Was my husband handsome Richard Burbage? I smiled, saying that if Burbage marries, half the hearts in London will break."

"But she didn't let you off that easily."

"Of course not. Isabel forced me to say your name. At 'Cooke,' she replied, one of the Cooke brothers. Must be Alexander. The other one serves Lady Elizabeth Sidney Manners."

"Mercy! Johnny is food for gossip in palace corridors."

"Lady Elizabeth would be food for gossip no matter what, more the fool Johnny. As you can imagine I was feeling more awkward by the minute. Saucy Isabel couldn't contain herself. 'Wait until the

Queen hears! She admires Alexander Cooke in his women's roles. Even now, when he's more man than boy. I wager he plays the Danish queen. Quite the catch, Mistress Frances.'"

"What an insolent young woman."

"I simply laughed and said I doubted Her Majesty cares about her servants' marriages. Isabel replied that players are more than servants, as are Silkwomen, and the Queen can be whimsical about what or whom she cares about. I knew such a prying girl wouldn't keep any of this to herself. All I could do was refuse her request to be present for the actors' fittings. After I'd made my selections, she got in the last word. She plans to greet you players when you arrive. I discouraged her from that. No fawning over Burbage—nor you!"

"We can easily avoid her."

Rebecca called to us from the kitchen that the soup was ready. I stood and spoke softly. "All we can do, Frances, is carry on, you as costume mistress and me as Queen Gertrude, with as little notice as possible."

"You'll have all eyes upon you in your purple gown."

"I shall play Gertrude as Johnny would and hope the Queen has forgotten or believes she'd guessed wrong."

The table was set and we sat down to the savory pottage.

Frances and I walked together to Whitehall next day, players joining us as we went. On this freezing day, ice had collected around the stanchions of London Bridge.

Down the chilly corridors of Whitehall, we found the tiring room with hearth aglow and our costumes hung neatly on a rail. While the audience chattered in the great chamber beyond, Frances helped with our lacings and buttonings.

In the first scene Johnny, as Horatio, appeared on the battlements where the soldiers had seen the ghost of old Hamlet. How I wished I were playing Prince Hamlet's friend today rather than his mother! I knew his lines, few as they were.

Adjusting my crown, I waited for my entrance on King

Claudius' arm. I took a deep breath and said my lines over, *sotto voce*. Shakespeare, awaiting his entrance as the ghost of Hamlet's father, murmured, "No need to worry."

"I have reason. Queen Elizabeth knows."

"About you and Frances? Don't give it another thought."

John Heminges, newly crowned as Claudius, escorted me onstage while Hamlet hid from us behind a pillar in the viewers' plain sight. My smile took in the entire audience as if they were the Danish court celebrating our marriage and coronation—including Queen Elizabeth in her chair of state like a celebrant herself.

I threw myself into Gertrude's role, keeping my voice low and making some effort to suggest a slightly inept boy actor. My biggest challenge was how to die. Ordinarily I slipped to the floor with feminine grace. When the moment came, I couldn't let manly awkwardness mar it. The Queen could think what she would about the person playing Gertrude, but I must fulfill her tragedy.

"The drink, Hamlet, the drink," I gasped in a hoarse whisper, then collapsed. The final fight I watched through shuttered eyes, minimizing my breathing and holding my face still as death. Fortinbras' cannons sounded, followed by eerie silence as the tableau of death made a final impression.

Applause erupted. Burbage helped me to my feet. As at the Globe, tears stung my eyes. Indeed every eye was bright, including the Queen's.

I was safe. Tonight had been such a triumph that no thought would be wasted on something so trivial as my marriage. Queen Elizabeth loved plays, and she'd never seen one as intense as *Hamlet*. Tonight we actors were invulnerable.

Tomorrow? I sighed as applause died down and we retreated to the tiring room. Perhaps all would blow over in her press of royal duties.

O spirit of love! . . .
So full of shapes is fancy
That it alone is high fantastical.
COUNT ORSINO, *TWELFTH NIGHT*

CHAPTER XX
March 1600

Frances and I had settled into a peaceful routine until one bright March morning when the company met at the Globe.

Shakespeare hushed the buzz of conversation. "Queen Elizabeth was so delighted with *Hamlet* that she has requested a special performance."

"A new play?" Burbage looked hopeful.

"It's mostly done," Shakespeare replied. "We're to present it to Her Majesty on the Spring Equinox."

Pope's voice rose in agitation. "In three days?"

"Her Majesty doesn't want a staged performance. She regrets that the public saw *Hamlet* before she did and has requested a private reading."

"Of something not finished." Armin shook his head.

"Almost finished. You'll like your role: a singing clown called Feste."

"We never read a play to anyone before it's ready, let alone to Queen Elizabeth!" Tom Pope said. "Have the roles been copied out?"

"I've finished a draft, and the scribe is making a master now. You can copy out your own parts."

"How could you have committed us? We'll shame—" Pope was silenced by Shakespeare's firm voice.

"The Queen requested it. Sir Robert Cecil promises only a small audience. Her Majesty desires to see what she calls a work in process. She knows the play isn't in its final form. Her whim is to hear something newer than a first-night performance."

"Wonderful," Armin said. "She wants to see us at our worst, reading a half-finished work with no preparation."

"No such thing," Shakespeare said. "It's as good as finished. None of us shamed—indeed, you'll be as entertained as she is. We meet here at eight tomorrow morning to hear the plot. You'll have plenty of time to copy your parts."

Armin sighed. "You're mad, Will Shakespeare."

"No, he's brilliant," Burbage said. "At the least we'll receive a gold sovereign each."

I didn't relish the idea of sitting close to Queen Elizabeth's scrutiny. No doubt Shakespeare would cast me as a woman.

So he did, but a most curious woman. Except for the first scene where I appeared as Viola, I remained "Cesario" in boy's disguise for the entire play, even at the end after Viola's female identity is revealed. Olivia and Maria would wear skirts; the other players their best doublet and hose and leave the rest to imagination.

The story of the play was more curious yet. No doubt Shakespeare got it from some old tale as was his wont, but it struck close to home. At one point in his telling of the plot, when Viola as Cesario laments the evils of disguise, I was sure Will winked at me. I'd never met a more theatrically untrustworthy man. Anything could fuel his imagination.

This play, *Twelfth Night, or What You Will*, seemed a twisted version of the relations between Frances, Johnny, and me. Here, Johnny and I play twins rather than simply brother and sister, and Countess Olivia falls in love with me in my boy's disguise. Then Viola's long-lost brother Sebastian appears in Illyria, unaware that Viola dwells there as a young man. With none of Cesario's reluctance to be loved, Sebastian allows Olivia to rush him to church for a formal betrothal.

The complications and confusions suited Twelfth Night revelry.

Countess Olivia's pompous steward Malvolio, her maid Maria, her drunken uncle Sir Toby Belch, and the gull Aguecheek added to the play's madness.

To me, the most telling line comes when Olivia first sees Viola and her twin Sebastian side by side: "Most wonderful!" The line, read by Beeston, gave me chills, as if Shakespeare intuited Frances' muddled feelings. Did Frances love both me and my brother?

Shakespeare described the ending: Viola will marry Duke Orsino whom she'd served and loved in vain, and, when she resumes her female garb, they would celebrate their wedding together with Olivia and Sebastian.

I shuddered. This is the play we would read for the Queen?

"It's as fresh as a play can be," Shakespeare said.

"With every chance for mishap," Armin grumbled. "Your part as the sea captain Antonio is short, I notice. And you want me to sing!"

"You can sing any song I write, Robert Armin, with gusto. Just wait. You've never had such a delightful time. Not a line to learn, not a movement to master—"

"Would Philip Henslowe do this to his men?"

"He would, " Burbage said, "and be thrilled at the opportunity. Ben Jonson and Ned Alleyn will turn green with envy."

"Of course I'm happy to sing your songs, Will," Armin said, "but I don't make up tunes on the spot."

"Walk with me to the Nag's Head. We'll make them together."

Armin sighed resignedly.

"Where are we doing this reading?" Pope asked. "Not in the great chamber, surely."

"No, in the royal library. A play reading in the Queen's shelf-lined room." Shakespeare looked pleased.

"Have you seen her library?" Pope asked.

When Shakespeare shook his head, Augustine Phillips said, "A lot of books and not much space, is my guess. The Queen and her guests will sit in a half circle and we'll stand. Think of it as an entertainment in a great house."

Most of the company took off for the Nag's Head. I threw on my cloak and hurried into the snow-flurried street where I fell into step with Johnny. He reached out his hand.

"I'm so sorry about Marie. I know how much you loved her. You and Frances did all you could."

I was surprised: he'd never before alluded to our loss. If it weren't for his grip on my arm, I'd have stumbled on the icy path. "You—you—"

"I know, Sander. I made no effort to help you. I had no idea what to do, and now it's been months. So very sad."

We walked on in silence, until approaching the Thames I said, "Here we are on stage, brother, playing twins loved by the same woman."

"What a good story! Trust clever Will Shakespeare."

"Think again, Johnny. It's not a clever a plot for you or for me." His expression was blank. "I suppose spending time with Lady Elizabeth has dulled your wits."

"What are you talking about?"

"The Queen knows about my marriage."

"You seem happy since Frances let you move back in."

"That's not the point." I heard my old annoyance with Johnny when he seemed particularly dim. "Queen Elizabeth more than suspects I'm a woman. Women do not marry women. I dread reading this play to her in close quarters, and so should you."

"You imagine the worst. The Queen wants to hear a brand new play, mistakes and all."

I rolled my eyes. Fortunately we were joined by Tom Pope, who played Sir Toby Belch. He was more than ready to laugh about his unruly character and offered better company than my brother. I couldn't be as carefree as Johnny Cooke, but next best: appear so.

Queen Elizabeth came to the reading accompanied by none but her ladies of the bedchamber and maids of honor. She was always surrounded by men, but for this special treat, like her rumored evening lute-playing on the Thames, she preferred the company of women.

I saw a young blond woman, likely snoopy Lady Isabel, but she sat in the row behind the Queen's. We could relax. This was no state occasion.

The library was pleasantly informal, with its glass-encased shelves, Turkey carpets, and a fire at each end beneath magnificently carved mantle pieces. Not even hunchbacked Sir Robert Cecil was present. Shakespeare must have known. He'd not have been so cavalier if more were at stake.

The Queen appeared unusually at ease in a gown less bejeweled than those she wore at Court, her auburn wig wreathed under a simple coronet.

We bowed and took our places while two serving men offered the ladies wine and cakes.

When silence reigned, Shakespeare spoke. "We beg your forgiveness, Your Royal Highness, for any slips of tongue or wording. The ink is scarce dry on these pages."

"As we wish it, playwright."

"I gave this reading a title especially for you: *What You Will*, as it is named. I'll describe the scene; after that, we rely on your imagination."

We bowed as he introduced each of us by our parts. "Alexander Cooke, who plays the maiden Viola, shipwrecked in Illyria when her brother is lost at sea. Viola disguises herself as Cesario and becomes page to Duke Orsino," he indicated Phillips, "desperately in love with Countess Olivia." Beeston curtseyed.

Shakespeare described the rest of Olivia's household and Orsino's much smaller one, the doubling of roles to be indicated by a change of jerkin. Fat candles shone near us and slanted across the Queen in her cushioned chair. When not in a scene, we stepped into the shadows.

Our scripts resting on music stands, we began our presentation. Armin played a love song on his lute, and Count Orsino said, "If music be the food of love, play on." The scene shifted as I entered as Viola, skirt over my breeches, shipwrecked on Illyria and mourning the loss of my brother at sea.

After an early scene with Captain Antonio, Johnny spent the rest of the play as foppish Sir Andrew Aguecheek until Sebastian's surprise appearance at the end. As Sebastian, Johnny wore a fawn colored doublet identical to Cesario's; as Sir Andrew, bright red.

I avoided the Queen's eyes when I said, "Conceal me what I am." Cesario possesses little of Ganymede's fearlessness in *As You Like It*, but surely Her Majesty recognized that the same actor played both. I felt Cesario's line throughout my performance, "Disguise, I see thou art a wickedness." Luckily I had my part before me, for fear would likely have dried my words.

Having survived the shipwreck thanks to Captain Antonio, Viola's brother Sebastian arrives in Illyria. Antonio, played by Shakespeare himself, loves Sebastian, but Sebastian, as if in a dream, succumbs to Lady Olivia's spell and goes to church with her to plight their troth.

In the final scene, I saw the Queen glance from one Cooke to the other. When Sebastian and Cesario questioned each other's parentage and discovered that we were siblings, I feared what she might be thinking.

Orsino pledges his love to Cesario, now revealed as female. "And since you called me master for so long, here is my hand; you shall be from this time, your master's mistress." Olivia smiles at Cesario, whom until now she'd regarded as male. "A sister, you are she."

Feste sang his last song: "But that's all one, our play is done, and we'll try to please you every day."

"I'm the first to hear this, the very first!" the Queen said. "Thank you, my men. Come, sup with us. You, Master Shakespeare—or should I say Captain Antonio. Escort me." She took his arm as we walked to the adjoining chamber, fire-warm and intimate. Platters of food were laid out, four serving men, no other pomp.

"Your fetching twins shall sit close by us," Her Majesty said, gesturing to Johnny and me.

Our proximity made me feel more challenged than reading those unfamiliar lines. That was within the demands of my profession, but this self-presentation required a different sort of creativity. Johnny smiled, as if to be so singled out was the rarest of treats.

Will Shakespeare sat nearby with the rest of the company. I saw him listening in.

Through the laughter and chatting of the Queen's ladies, I saw the speculative expression in those imperious eyes as she said, "When I look at the two of you I see twins. Boy and girl twins. Countess Olivia was rightfully confused—and delighted. She gained not only a husband but a sister as well."

Shakespeare spoke up. "A Twelfth Night carnival of misrule, Your Majesty. I am gratified that you enjoyed it. I see much to improve upon, however, especially with Malvolio. He'll be more amusing when you see the play fully staged."

Thankfully the Queen addressed him. "Malvolio amuses me as he is, but you artists are never satisfied."

"Actually, Will tends to be well satisfied," Heminges said. "No sooner have these characters burst out of his head onto the page than new ones are clamoring for their own play. I wish he'd write more lines for the sea captain who rescues Viola, but chances are he won't. He's already thinking about the next play."

The Queen laughed. "You're my man, William Shakespeare."

The repast was modest—oysters and machet bread, comfits and cakes. The Queen sipped madeira but ate scarcely a bite.

Conversation had been general, nothing more directed to Johnny or me. But when we rose at her departure, the Queen stepped between us, linking an arm through each of ours.

"I love a secret," she said in a low voice, "and I have suspicions about yours. I'd like to hear it from your lips. Come along." She turned to her ladies. "I shall have a quick word with these young men. Thank you again, Master Shakespeare and your splendid company. I look forward to seeing a full production soon in the Great Chamber."

Waves of fever and chills raged through me as I followed down the corridor to a private waiting room. Disguise was indeed a wickedness, but all I could do was maintain mine, walking straight and tall. My whole life was a lie, but never had I felt it so intensely, not even pronouncing vows at St. Alfage's. I would be caught, exposed—my thoughts raced.

Lady Isabel walked behind us.

"You wait here," the Queen told her.

She shut the door behind us, no doubt disappointed.

There was no fire, but Her Majesty seemed not to notice. She looked Johnny in the eye.

"This marriage between Alexander and my Silkwoman Frances: does it have anything to do with you? The story of the Countess Olivia and the twins seems to resemble your own."

"I—I don't understand," he stammered.

"Try a little harder. Does Mistress Frances Cooke love you?"

"I should think not, Your Highness."

"We have heard that you attend on Lady Elizabeth Sidney Manners. You have no time for a Silkwoman, am I right? Tell me the whole story. Why did Frances marry you, Alexander?"

"I love her, Your Majesty. We are making a life together."

"But my dear, I have descried your secret." When she paused, I wiped all reaction from my face. "I can let that go," she continued, "unprecedented as it is. You're a fine actor and I've been intrigued to see what Master Shakespeare does with your gifts. However, I do not understand this marriage of yours."

"Their marriage was solemnized by the priest of St. Alfage," Johnny offered.

I could have throttled him! Why name the church? He wasn't even there.

"Worse yet," she said. "Explain."

"Frances was pregnant," I said, barely a whisper. "The baby died."

"Who was the father?" The Queen glared at Johnny.

His face was pale. "I was, Your Majesty."

"Why did you not marry her yourself?"

Only now did Johnny's voice falter. "I—I couldn't."

"Couldn't!" she said scornfully. "I have a mind to send all three of you to the Tower. As I listened to this play, however, I thought the better. First I want to know the whole truth, and then I shall decide what action to take."

I took a deep breath. "Long before Johnny caught her eye, I was friend to Frances Field."

"Rather like the Countess Olivia and Cesario." The Queen's smile was encouraging.

"In a way. Frances discovered my secret long ago and kept it to herself."

"Secrets can be a bond—or a conspiracy."

"We intended no conspiracy, Your Majesty. But when Frances fell in love with Johnny, well, she acted like Olivia upon meeting Sebastian. She embraced him like a husband."

"Without a betrothal. I'd have thought her a more sensible young woman."

"In matters of the heart—" I broke off.

"In matters of the heart one often acts foolishly. We do not need Master Shakespeare to tell us so." The Queen looked at Johnny. "Frances embraced you, 'like a husband' as Alexander so quaintly expressed it, and fell pregnant. I repeat, Johnny. Why did you not marry her? There is no shame in that; you're of a class and Frances is worthy—and, I'll wager, a virgin when she met you. Your shame lies in refusing her."

Johnny clenched his jaw.

"Answer my question!"

"It seemed like a good idea for Alexander to marry her."

"You mean after you refused to. That's reprehensible!"

"Yes, Your Highness."

"You are an insubordinate young man. I should have you carried off to the Tower this minute. You make a young woman pregnant and refuse to marry her, I'm guessing because you're enamored of Lady Elizabeth Sidney and hope to console her for that disgraceful husband of hers."

"There's nothing improper between myself and Lady Elizabeth."

"I did not say there was, only that she is your lady." The Queen rose to her full majesty. "I am the lady of all my courtiers. You should read what they write to me! I adore every word of it, flatterers all. So too Lady Elizabeth must enjoy your courtesies to her. Poor Mistress Frances is quite outside that cozy arrangement." Her flashing eyes pierced Johnny with royal contempt.

I had regarded the Queen as a man's woman since I first saw her surrounded by her advisors, her ladies fluttering off at a distance. Now I recognized something deeper: pride that she was the leader of men, a prince in her own right, superior and sovereign.

She turned to me. "So, Alexander. You stepped in where your brother failed. I commend that, but nonetheless."

"The priest believed what he saw, Your Majesty. I was married as a man."

"Lying before God!" Then her stern face softened. "Now there is no baby. You needn't remain married. Go on as before. The priest of St. Alfage's can strike your names from the church register. Your secrecy in this matter is to your benefit."

I replied with all the grace I could muster, "I humbly thank you, Your Majesty."

"If anyone marries Frances, it should be your brother. Unfortunately he's proven himself unworthy."

Johnny nodded, insufferably relieved.

"Don't think you shall get off so lightly, young man. I shan't punish Frances or Alexander, nor shall I call further attention to this strange business. But as for you, John Cooke, you will give up your position with the Countess of Rutland, whatever that may be, and your place with the Lord Chamberlain's Men for one year, until next Eastertide. Sir Robert Cecil needs a secretary who can read and write with flair. You shall spend a year in his service, living at his London house in the servants' quarters. You shall do exactly as Cecil says and make no effort to contact Lady Elizabeth or your acting company without his permission. That includes your brother Alexander, and of course, Mistress Frances."

Your brother! I almost smiled. Johnny could make use of the year with Cecil: the Queen was giving him a rare opportunity, however humbling his servant status, however much he had to give up. I wanted to throw myself at her feet, beg to be allowed to live with

Frances, but restrained myself. She hadn't said in so many words that I could not.

Queen Elizabeth looked at me as if intuiting my thoughts. "I need to think about this marriage of yours, Alexander. Few know the truth, is that correct?"

"Very few."

"I can guess one who knows: Moll Frith. That woman!" The Queen laughed. "We allow her to walk free. I've heard they call her Cutpurse, but we know better. As for her boys, we do have to keep them in line. Moll commits no capital crime, except of course, dressing as a man."

Was I to think I'd joined the invulnerable company of Moll Frith? I held my breath.

"I may change my mind tomorrow, but for now, thanks in part to your Master Shakespeare's *What You Will* that I enjoyed so thoroughly this afternoon, I shall turn a blind eye to your domestic arrangements. You are discreet."

I could scarcely believe my ears. Was it possible that Frances and I might continue as we were with an oblique blessing from the Queen herself?

"I warn you; I may change my mind. That is the royal prerogative. Now be gone, the two of you. I have much to attend to. I shall tell Robert Cecil to expect you tomorrow, John Cooke."

We bowed out of the room, two actors dismissed by the Queen with our skins intact and our spirits chastened.

"So. Secretary to Sir Robert Cecil. I shall be on the inside of the political circle," Johnny said. "It could be worse."

"Will you tell him why you've been sent to him?"

Johnny grinned. "No, brother, and from what I hear about him, I doubt he'll ask. It's the Queen's will, after all. I shall give good service as a secretary—"

"And leave his service the wiser." I gave him a slap on the back. "Consider ourselves fortunate."

PART TWO

MOORS, SEDITION,
AND THE PAINS OF LOVE

Mislike me not for my complexion,
The shadow'd livery of the burnish'd sun,
To whom I am a neighbour and near bred.
     PRINCE OF MOROCCO, *THE MERCHANT OF VENICE*

CHAPTER XXI
September 1600

"Have you seen them?" Amelia's son Harry burst into the house, followed by his mother. "They're like princes from some faraway place."

Every time I saw him, I admired how handsome a child Harry was, the self-assurance of his father Lord Hunsdon combined with probing black eyes of his mother and a mop of golden hair that could be credited to neither.

"Harry means the Moorish ambassadors," Amelia said.

"I'm sorry Frances isn't here. She loves to hear your stories, Harry. You'll have to tell her all over again."

Harry took a seedcake from the plate on the table, crumbs flying as he spoke. "They have the most beautiful sword cases, covered in gold and jewels. I want one like that when I grow up. And you won't believe what they wear! Long white robes and their heads wrapped in turbans. That's what Mama says their hats are called. Their faces are so brown that the whites of their eyes flash. They scare my friends but not me, only their big black guards with fierce marks on their faces. If ever I need a guard, I'll choose a man like that."

"You shan't be needing any guard, my pet. They're the ambassador's men at arms. They won't hurt a soul."

"Oh they would, they would, if someone attacked their beautiful Moors."

"No one will attack them," I said.

Harry reached down to pet Hero. "I wish I could have a kitten myself, but Mama says it would scratch the carpets."

"You can play with Hero any time you like. We haven't a carpet worth the scratching."

"I like your house, Master Cooke."

"Yours better suits you—all those musical instruments. Better than a kitten."

He ignored me, trying to coax Hero onto his lap.

Besides being so loveable and gifted with musical talent, Harry had quenchless curiosity. Amelia told me she never imagined a child could be such good company, far better than preoccupied Alfonso Lanyer, his father in name. I wondered whether Harry would ever learn of his kinship to the Queen or if she knew about him. Hunsdon was her first cousin through her mother's sister Mary Boleyn; some even said the Queen's half-brother.

If Harry knew, what good would it do him? For such a child, noble and royal through Hunsdon, Italian and Jewish through his mother and, through Alfonso, in the class of court musician, nothing was certain. Male aristocratic by-blows might be recognized by their fathers, and given a boost in the world, but that wouldn't happen to Harry, as Lord Hunsdon died some four years ago. The boy must make his way in the world as a Lanyer.

Harry trailed a string across the floor for Hero who scratched him as she jumped for it. His only reaction was to laugh, so we laughed, too, that little fur ball showing her baby claws.

"Have you heard?" I asked Amelia. "We're performing *Much Ado About Nothing* at Nonsuch Palace."

"Yes, I know. I shall play my lute with the Lupo consort."

Amelia in livery? "It came to no good the last time you tried such a caper."

"Lord Hunsdon was alive then, Henry Wriothesley a flirtatious young man—and I was much younger."

"It's still risky."

She shrugged. "Don't worry. I'll conceal my hair in a cap, and no one will guess I'm a woman."

"Not even a discerning Moor?"

Amelia glanced at Harry, preoccupied with Hero, then said softly, "You run the same risk."

"I suppose if you stay in the musicians' gallery, you'll be all right."

"Besides, Innocent Lanyer has taken Harry under his wing, so he too will play with us."

"A child will definitely be noticed."

"He'll pass for an apprentice. As soon as he turns seven, he'll be one officially." Amelia looked up as the door opened. "Frances!"

"Hallo Harry. Hallo Amelia." Frances swept into the room, bright-eyed from the brisk September evening. She took off her cloak to reveal a bodice and skirt I'd not seen before, autumnal shades of golden orange linen with delicate russet and leaf green embroidery at the neck, sleeves, and hem. The shirt she wore today had full sleeves with ruffles at the wrist. The whole effect, setting off her fair rosy skin and the appealing roundness of her form, touched me and roused in me a protective pride toward her, a desirable woman in her prime.

Frances sat and stretched her feet toward the low-burning fire, and I fetched a jug of cider and settled in beside her.

"What a day it's been with all the ladies who want gowns for the royal celebration of the Moorish delegation! Three of them chose the same green satin. I have enough for just one. Do you think I could talk any out of their choice? No such luck. Apparently it's the color of the season."

"You would know," Amelia said.

"As far as I'm concerned, there is no color of the season. What do they think, that I order bales of silk in the same shade? You can imagine what a nightmare it's been to secure more. And of course, each has to be in an entirely different style."

"You always manage," I said.

"Oh, I shall, I shall. But they don't make it easy."

"I remember the competitiveness over Court fashion." Amelia's tone was wistful. "Who are these ladies?"

"The young Lady Anne Clifford, Lady Helena Snakenborg Gorges, and Lady Lucy Bedford. Each of them is much admired, and each sets a different tone. That's my challenge."

"Another reason for me to be in the musicians' gallery, to see how you resolve that," Amelia said.

"You, in the musicians' gallery?" Frances laughed.

"Indeed. I shall play the lute with my cousins' consort for *Much Ado About Nothing*."

"You're a daring woman. What do you mean, 'another reason'?"

"Besides playing music and observing the entertainments from above, I can see who among the ladies I might solicit as a patron." At Frances' puzzled look, Amelia added, "You know I've found it difficult to be banned from Court since Lord Hunsdon—" she trailed off gazing into the fire as I poured cups of cider. "Thinking about my poetry, I remembered how the Countess of Kent mentored me when I was a girl. I shall seek such women now, noble patrons such as male poets have. Even a lady without independent means could champion me."

"A woman champion! What would the knights say?" I lifted my cup. "To female poets, female patrons, and female champions."

Over supper of cold roast capon, pippins, and the last of the seed cakes, Harry described the Moors to Frances. She smiled to hear his animated account.

I hoped coming home to Amelia and Harry in our parlor gave her more pleasure than envy. Midway through every month, Frances was possessed by the desire for a child of her own. Much can be said for others' children—no tantrums, no fevers, no sleepless nights— but likely Frances disagreed. Her longing for motherhood saddened me. I would give her anything, but a baby was beyond my power.

Harry added to the liveliness of our supper. Whether or not the legendary King Henry VIII was his grandfather, Harry had a robust spirit and commanding Tudor demeanor. Better for women if King Henry's wayward blood did not pulse in this lad!

Frances' approving smile to the boy extended to me across the table. At her shop when she saw clients' possessive husbands or the drunken knaves ladies of the night had to contend with, she appreciated her marriage to an actor in the Lord Chamberlain's Men, despite that actor's sex. That much I was sure of, but when my mind jumped to Johnny, I was less confident.

No doubt Sir Robert Cecil told him of the performance at Nonsuch, as he wouldn't be allowed to attend. Although Cecil and his head scrivener kept a sharp eye on Johnny's movements and worked him hard, evidently no one locked up the writing paper. An under footman would, for a penny, deliver letters anywhere in London and collect letters that awaited Johnny, so I received his occasional missive and read them to Frances. I learned too much and too little in these, and would have liked to see those to Lady Elizabeth, including more details that to us he merely alluded to.

Apparently, he sent her imagined dialogues based on misbehaving court and gentry. When meeting Cecil's visitors, he incorporated them into his dialogues with fictitious names. Thus was Johnny serving his apprenticeship as a playwright. But Lady Elizabeth never forwarded his writings to Ben Jonson, and recently Jonson had introduced Francis Beaumont into her circle, a law student at the Inner Temple still in his teens. Johnny had begun writing satirical dialogues mocking this upstart.

But it was his sporadic correspondence with Lady Elizabeth's stepfather Robert Devereux, the Earl of Essex, that worried me. Although Essex was no longer under house arrest and could attend the public theatre, he was shunned by all but a few firebrands.

Johnny's audacity in writing to him shocked me. Sir Robert Cecil was Essex's enemy. Letters coming in and out of Cecil's house were subject to censorship. Dangerous for him to smuggle out that sort of correspondence. The messenger who brought my letters had told me, who else might he mention it to? Still, despite my mixed feelings, I appreciated the occasional dialogue Johnny sent. Frances was scandalized, but better he write satires in private letters than emulate Essex's rebellious spirit.

Sigh no more, ladies, sigh no more;
Men were deceivers ever;
One foot in sea and one on shore,
To one thing constant never;
Then sigh not so,
But let them go,
And be you blithe and bonny;
Converting all your sounds of woe
Into Hey nonny, nonny.
BALTHASAR, (SONG) MUCH ADO ABOUT NOTHING

CHAPTER XXII
Late September 1600

Autumn crisped the air as we rode south toward Nonsuch. If I were a leaf, this cool breeze would be my hint to start changing colors, heralding the brilliant blaze before winter. On such an invigorating day, I found it more agreeable to sit on a cushion in our company's wagon than in a closed coach.

What would the Moorish embassy make of *Much Ado About Nothing*? No doubt in Barbary as well, returning soldiers sought congenial society and love. But what form did social pleasures take in those distant Afric lands, and what form did love take? Moors must have scorners like Beatrice and Benedick, easily deceived men like Claudio, betrayed women like Hero, envious villains like Don John, and incompetent constables like Dogberry. In Shakespeare's comedy, all combined into a happy ending. Unless their society had utterly different notions of entertainment, the Moors would surely enjoy it.

I'd love to talk to one of them. I could imagine how striking

Moorish women must be, with that intense bronze coloring and long-lashed black eyes, but there were no women in the Moors' entourage. Mostly the turbaned group walked about London taking in the sights, escorted by their threatening guards, or remained in their lodgings. No one reported them near the stews or taverns of Bankside.

"Do the Moors speak English?" I asked Shakespeare.

"I understand that in their counsels with the Queen, they'll speak Spanish. The learnèd man of languages, Sir Lewes Lewknor, will translate."

"Do you think they'll understand our play?"

"Many foreign visitors understand more English than they speak. The Queen's master of revels suggested we play *Much Ado* because the action is clear even to those with limited skill in our language."

Armin scowled. "I hadn't considered that they might not understand us. Will they miss my jokes?"

"Just call on your gift of mime, Robert. Or one of them can explain."

"So they'll be whispering throughout."

Shakespeare laughed. "No worse than the noise of hazelnuts being cracked in the Globe."

Midafternoon we arrived at Nonsuch Palace, built by King Henry VIII as a hunting lodge, but on a grand scale. Of golden stone with lacy turrets, it was said to be Queen Elizabeth's favorite place of recreation. The setting and structures were more welcoming than formidable, unlike Richmond Palace or the imposing brick edifice of Hampton Court, built by Cardinal Wolsey. Beyond Nonsuch stretched the deer park, but the lack of a river, we were told, made this palace less desirable as a dwelling. I wouldn't have guessed, with its flowery terraced garden around a spouting fountain.

We followed the servants carrying our costume chest through dark back passages to the tiring room, which had a window overlooking an inner courtyard, its stone walls decorated with elaborate carvings. Beyond I glimpsed a diminutive herd of roe deer grazing.

In the chamber adjoining the musicians' gallery above, the

consort unpacked their instruments. I'd caught a glimpse of Amelia's
son Harry following their procession up the stairs. When Amelia
played with the consort before, she'd been horrified when called
upon to sing. Fortunately, today the singing fell to Don Pedro's
attendant Balthasar.

A royal page came to the door of the tiring room. "The Queen
sends an urgent request. Her Moorish guests desire to hear a few of
our English ballads and to perform some of their own songs. After
our play, Moors skilled in the Arabic flute and stringed oud will join
you for an impromptu concert."

"You've come to the wrong place," Phillips said. "The consort is
upstairs."

The page climbed the stairs two at a time.

"Highly unusual," Tom Pope said.

"They won't even have time to practice together!"

Thomas Lupo's voice floated down from above. "They do not
know our music nor we theirs."

The page: "The Queen and Ambassador Ben Messaoud desire
you play together."

"Surely we know some of the same melodies," said a musician.

Lupo's voice: "We'll improvise on one of John Johnson's, which
the Moors should be able to join with ease."

"After the marriage dance at the end of the play, your consort is
to join the Moorish musicians onstage," the page said.

"To it, men. We must prepare."

I wondered how Amelia was taking all this. Perhaps she'd have
to sing after all.

No extra preparation for us, as we'd played *Much Ado* recently.
The afternoon was ours to explore and refresh ourselves.

I loved my part as Beatrice, sharp tongued and mocking. Besides
the garbled language of Dogberry the constable, Beatrice's battle
of wits with Benedick brought the laughs. Before he went to war,
Benedick had jilted her, and from the moment they meet again, they
spar relentlessly.

Neither reveals their love to the other, but their friends eavesdrop on them confessing in private. The play turns dark when Claudio denounces his bride, Beatrice's cousin Hero, at the altar. Instead of following his friend Claudio off stage, Benedick stays behind with Beatrice and Hero, who appears dead from shock. When he asks what he can do to prove his love for her, Beatrice replies with my favorite line: "Kill Claudio!"

Johnny's role of Claudio was played by John Sincler, shallow Claudio who has no faith in his bride. Dogberry's officers overheard the villains describing how they faked Hero's betrayal of Claudio but Dogberry reports it too confusingly to be understood. Eventually Hero's innocence is proven, the villains punished, Claudio repents, and the play ends with the celebration of not just Hero and Claudio's marriage but also Beatrice and Benedick's.

At Nonsuch we performed the story more physically than at the Globe. There, audiences came to the theatre chiefly to hear a play. Here we exaggerated our acting to help the Moors follow the story, hoping that most of them knew at least a little English. They payed close attention, laughing at Dogberry and his deputies, sober-faced during Claudio's obsequies at Hero's supposed tomb. By the end, I was exhausted. Beatrice's character shines in her witty lines, and it had been hard work to make myself understood.

After the wedding dance, we moved to the side of the stage and the consort descended from their gallery, led by Innocent Lanyer and Harry. As she passed me, I patted Amelia's back, man to man. Though she looked tense, her step was confident.

The Moorish musicians joined them onstage. Their eyes were deep-set and as black as Amelia's, and compared to the smiling Lupo consort in their red and gold livery, the Moors looked severe. Their robes were of fine white linen, their heads swathed in turbans of shot silk, but they'd shed their ceremonial swords. There were three of them, the oud and flute players and a lithe young man with a tambourine.

The tambourine player turned out to be the stellar addition. I wanted to take up the instrument myself, so spirited did it make the music. Once they began to play, the musicians watched each other, playing improvisations as if they'd been doing so for years for their own pleasure.

Amelia and the oud player harmonized imaginative flourishes while her Bassano uncle carried the steady *discantor*. Among a rich selection of music, the most recognizable English song was "There was a lover and his lass." Lupo's consort bellowed it out, the Moors joined in the second round with garbled words a little off key, with Amelia's voice swallowed into the musical chaos.

A sprightly tune with haunting overtones ended the concert, combining both musical styles. The audience burst into applause, and as Lupo's musicians embraced their newfound fellows, Amelia clutched her lute in front of her.

We players moved into the audience. Though still in costume, we'd finished our official duties. The consort had not. They gathered behind the banqueting table and begin playing, Amelia anonymous in livery.

Dressed in Beatrice's gown, I was not anonymous, but I dearly wanted to speak to the Moors, inscrutable as figures in a portrait. What did they think of a boy actor playing a woman? Perhaps they did the same in their land, since Arabic women were likely more sheltered than English. If only I could ask.

To my delight, the most youthful of the Moorish delegation tapped me on the shoulder: the tambourine player, now without his tambourine.

"Pardon," he said in accented English. "Our leader wishes to speak with you."

I followed him to the small circle of turbaned guests. As we approached, the most distinguished stepped forward. Stiffly, with pauses between each word, the young man presented me to Ambassador Abd el-Ouahed ben Messaoud. They exchanged a few words in Arabic, then the young man turned to me, his eyes lined in kohl. He was a slender version of his elder except for the rich black fabric draped over ben Messaoud's shoulder.

"Our noble ambassador is pleased to make your acquaintance," he said. "I, his nephew, shall speak for him. He wishes to tell you he has never seen such a portrayal of a woman onstage. Boys are also entertainers in our land, but do not play roles like yours."

"Tell His Grace that in London boys are apprenticed as stage-players and trained to play women's roles. In Italy, however, a woman could play Beatrice. Do women perform in your land?"

The nephew laughed. "Never," before he translated my question. Ben Messaoud smiled and replied in rapid syllables that took his nephew longer to translate.

"We have different customs in Barbary and no plays that resemble this one. Thank your Master Shakespeare for us." The other Moors drifted off like burnished angels in their swaying white robes, but the ambassador spoke a few more words, translated by his nephew.

"Abd el-Ouahed ben Messaoud thanks you for conversing with him and hopes to see you again on stage whilst he is in London."

I curtseyed and backed away. The ambassador joined his men, but his nephew remained with me.

"Is my English sufficient?" he asked shyly.

"More than sufficient, my friend." Feeling odd in my woman's dress but not playing a woman's role, I maintained a manly stance.

"You are my first friend in London. My name is Ibrahim. The rest of it is too long for an Englishman to learn."

"I am called Alexander Cooke. Excuse my clothing."

"You are an actor, Master Cooke. I am happy to meet you. We have had little chance to converse with local men."

"Will you attend the official conferences with Queen Elizabeth?"

"In silence. I shall not interpret."

"I hear that your ambassadors will speak in Spanish."

"Some of us know many languages. As does your Queen, we are told."

"She may even know some Arabic."

"It is a beautiful language. When written, a work of art. My uncle has brought a precious book in Arabic script as a gift to your Queen." The more Ibrahim spoke, the more easily his words flowed.

"I should like to see it."

Ibrahim glanced toward his countrymen, now being served from a platter of candied fruit, weighing whether to join them. Apparently he decided not, for he reached into a pocket in his robe for a small scroll.

"This is not as rare as the gift for your Queen, but shows our writing." He unrolled it to reveal a graceful script.

"What does it say?"

"It is my favorite poem, by the poet Füzuli. I know it 'by heart,' as you English say. I carry it with me always, for luck."

"Please say it to me."

Ibrahim spoke the verse softly, musically, without looking at the roll. Of all poems I'd heard spoken, this was the most moving, even though I understood not a word. Amelia Bassano and William Shakespeare would envy me.

Ibrahim ended on a plaintive note.

"What does it mean?"

"My English is not adequate to say. It is about the pain of love."

"We must find the translator Lewknor who serves at your conferences."

"I believe he is not present tonight."

"Someone must translate the poem into English. You and I could be friends, Ibrahim. I know poets who would enjoy hearing you speak these verses."

"I would be honored. Poetry, music, and story-telling are highly regarded in Arabic countries. But as my uncle said, we have no such theatre as yours. I hope to see you again onstage, Alexander Cooke. You play a woman well."

Ibrahim bowed, touched his forehead, and rejoined his companions.

Shakespeare was hurrying my way. "I tried to reach you before he took his leave. A remarkable sight, Beatrice speaking to a Moorish tambourine player."

"His name is Ibrahim, nephew of the ambassador. He said a poem to me in Arabic, a melodious language. You must hear it."

"I hope I may."

The Queen and her ladies departed, the Moors quick on their heels. Servants began snuffing out the candles. I followed Shakespeare and our fellows, my mind full of those exotic Arabic syllables.

In the corridor by the tiring room, I caught up to Thomas Lupo's consort. "You were a great success with the Moors."

"They wish to play music with us again," Lupo said.

Amelia gave me a boyish wave, but her movements were hurried. Going out the door, she put a protective arm around Harry's shoulder.

I tell thee, lady, this aspect of mine
Hath fear'd the valiant: by my love I swear
The best-regarded virgins of our clime
Have loved it too: I would not change this hue,
Except to steal your thoughts, my gentle queen
PRINCE OF MOROCCO, *THE MERCHANT OF VENICE*

CHAPTER XXIII
Late September 1600

We dismounted from our carriages at the Globe, shadowy and dull after the splendor of Nonsuch. As actors headed off their separate ways and musicians unloaded their instruments, Shakespeare leaned down to Amelia in her livery.

I was close enough to hear him say, "Boy's attire suits you."

Amelia looked startled, and, holding Harry's hand, hurried after her cousins.

Shakespeare smiled at me. "It does suit her."

"You're a rogue, Will Shakespeare, disconcerting the poor lady."

"Quite the contrary. She was flattered. A beautiful woman convincingly dressed as a young man—most enticing." He winked. "Not that I think of you that way."

"Lucky I'm not beautiful."

He slapped me on the back. "True enough, in your doublet and hose."

At home, I told Frances that only Shakespeare had recognized Amelia.

"I wish she wouldn't play boy musician!"

"Risk or not, she enjoyed herself. Me too: I spoke to the Moor's tambourine player—Ibrahim, the ambassador's nephew. He read me a poem in Arabic."

"Were you dressed like that?" she indicated my breeches.

"No, I was the fetching Beatrice, boy actor."

"Oh Sander, the chances you take!" Laughing, we went to bed.

The next afternoon I browsed through the stalls in St. Paul's churchyard looking for quartos of plays. No *Julius Caesar*, though several of *Hamlet*.

"Sander!" Moll Frith stood beside me. "I'll stand you a drink if you tell me about your visit to Nonsuch. That's one palace I've never seen."

"You've seen the others?"

"All those in easy range of London. My cousin Dick—remember Dick Frith?"

"Of course. I came near to apprenticing at his smithy when I arrived in London."

"Can't see you as a blacksmith, you lightweight. Any road, Dick sent me to Greenwich to deliver a spring jack he'd made for the royal kitchens, and later, one of my boys who'd found work in the stables at Whitehall showed me round."

"Around palace kitchens and stables."

"Oh, much more. As the Queen wasn't in residence, we had ourselves a thorough look-round. And I've seen Hampton Court and Richmond Palace."

"Nonsuch is prettier than the others, more delicate though no less grand in its way. But the chief attraction was the visiting Moorish embassy. Perhaps you've seen them around town?"

Moll laughed. "I doubt we frequent the same places."

As we walked out of the busy booksellers' yard, I was surprised to see the Moorish delegation approaching: Ambassador ben Messaoud, his nephew and fellow emissaries, and their fierce guards.

"So those are your noble Moors," Moll said. "Impressive."

Ibrahim stepped toward me, drawing a scroll from his robe. "Open it later," he murmured and dashed back.

"What in bloody hell are you up to, Sander Cooke? Secret messages from a Moor? You?"

"I'm no spy, if that's what you mean." I waved the roll. "Aren't you curious?"

"He said 'Open it later.' This is late enough."

Moll snatched it and stepped into an alcove. Untying the narrow red ribbon, she thrust the scroll into my hand. I read it aloud.

> *God, let me know the pain of love*
> *Do not for a second separate me from it*
> *Do not diminish your aid to the afflicted*
> *But rather, make me a lovesick one among them.*

Moll looked bewildered. "A Moor sent you a love poem!"

"Don't be ridiculous. It's not writ to me. Listen." I read it again.

"I don't understand. 'God' and 'afflicted' and 'lovesick.' What's he talking about?"

"Ibrahim read it to me in Arabic. It's by a famous poet. The 'pain of love' is not romance. It's a different sort of—" I searched for the word "—of yearning."

"That makes no sense."

"After hearing the verse in Arabic, I asked Ibrahim what it meant in English, and here's the translation."

"For what it's worth."

Moll walked off toward the Strand.

I tucked the poem in my wallet and chased after her. Better a drink than a literary discussion with Moll, but the word "yearning" lingered in the back of my mind.

In the Nag's Head, Will Shakespeare and Ben Jonson called us to their table.

"I thought I'd found myself one actor to sup with," Moll said, "and what do I find but a gang of bawdy theatre men." She pushed in beside Jonson, and Shakespeare made room for me.

Jonson laughed. "Who are you to talk about bawdy?"

"I don't write lines for actors to speak. My words vanish the minute I say them."

"Not so, Moll. You are much quoted."

"Me?" Moll chortled. "Nothing I say is fit to print, let alone remember."

"How about 'An overflow of good converts to bad.' Your self-justification, is it not?"

"I can't take credit for that way of putting it. Your Master Shakespeare writ it in a play about one of his kings. Or stole it. You never know with you clever ones." Moll punched Shakespeare's arm.

Jonson said, "And then there's 'A fool thinks himself to be wise, but a wise man knows himself to be a fool.'"

"Talking about me?"

Robert Armin, small as he was, could not squeeze in on either side of the table, so he pulled up a chair at the head. "Am I a fool or a wise man?"

"Definitely a wise man," Shakespeare said. "Do you not know yourself to be a fool?"

"I do indeed." Armin gave his cap a fool's flourish as the maid poured his ale.

"My favorite is 'And oftentimes excusing of a fault doth make the fault the worse by the excuse,'" I said, holding out an empty tankard to be filled. "I've never heard Moll apologize for anything. No excuses."

"Altogether the best way," she said.

"Ben was asking about the Barbary delegation at Nonsuch. I told him you, Sander, were the only one to speak to any of them."

Moll leered. "Sander says the fellow wanted to try out his English on an actor, but it was more." I kicked her shin under the table, and she responded with a dramatic "Ouch!"

"His name is Ibrahim, and he's the soul of courtesy," I said. "His English improved as he spoke."

"I'd wager that most of them don't let on how much English they know," Jonson said.

"I suppose that for official talks, Spanish or Italian gives proper distance," Shakespeare said, "but the more English those Moors understand, the better they'll enjoy our plays."

Jonson shook his head. "Apparently not enough English for mine. Sir Robert Cecil refused a performance of *Every Man Out of His Humor* at Nonsuch."

"So what?" Shakespeare said. "The Moors can see it at the Globe if they like."

"Or your *Merchant of Venice*, if they like." Jonson mocked the last three words. "That's not a play to entertain Arabic visitors."

"Why not?" Moll asked. "It's a comedy."

"At the Jew's expense."

Shakespeare looked surprised. "Is that what you think?"

"At the end Antonio forces Shylock to convert to Christianity. I almost pity him."

"Exactly what's happened to Jews and Moors since Queen Isabella and King Ferdinand of Spain," Shakespeare said. "Convert or get out. No pound of flesh involved."

"Amelia Bassano told me Venetian Jews were called 'Marrannos,'" I said. "It means pigs."

Armin thumped down his tankard. "Your Venice play is simply a story. The crowd will laugh at Launcelot Gobbo. That's what matters. I've seen those fancy swords the Moors carry, but I doubt they'll use them if they don't get the jokes. In London no one throws onions at me, let alone a scimitar." He emptied his drink and headed off for other company. I thought Moll might follow, but she stayed put.

"Conversos, whether Jewish or Muslim, had no an easy time of it in Spain—or anywhere else—until they arrived in Italy," Shakespeare said. "The Italians welcomed them even if they didn't convert. England was not so kind. Only conversos allowed."

"Including King Henry VIII's musical Bassano family," Jonson said.

Shakespeare remained unruffled. If Ben meant to bait him about Amelia Bassano, he failed.

"Shylock's insisting on the pound of flesh is his downfall," Shakespeare said. "Antonio spits on him in the Rialto, and the Christians Solanio and Salerio taunt him. The Christians are no moral exemplars, though they do know how to enjoy their money.

Too much so, in Bassanio's case. Shylock is impoverished in every way except his store of ducats. But his Jewish friend Tubal little resembles him"

"You're right that Tubal isn't as vengeful as Shylock," Jonson said, "but watching your play, I was reminded of Marlowe's *Jew of Malta.*"

I couldn't let that pass. "Come now, Jonson! I've seen the play. The Jew Barabbas is a monster. With Marlowe, it's horrified laughter all the way."

"What do you think, Moll?" Shakespeare asked. "Will our Moorish visitors be entertained by *The Merchant of Venice?*"

"Of course. They have law courts and moneylenders and merchants."

"Exactly. The Moors may have come here about an alliance against Spain, but I understand their meetings with the Queen and Council chiefly concern trade."

"Nonetheless, they'd be better pleased with a more flattering play," Jonson said. "Be glad there's no performance of *Titus Andronicus* while they're here. Your Aaron is anything but a noble Moor. In *Merchant of Venice* Portia rejects the Prince of Morocco, but at least he's regal."

Perhaps, I thought, Shakespeare could write a play showing a Moor in a more flattering light, not that even he could finish it before this delegation left in London. Ambassador ben Messaoud was unquestionably noble.

"But don't forget what Portia says when the Prince of Morocco guesses the wrong casket," Jonson added. "'A gentle riddance. Draw the curtains, go. Let all of his complexion choose me so.'"

"I'll have to think about that," Shakespeare replied. "Such a line might not be politic with Moors in the audience."

The barmaid set down bowls of mutton stew. Ned Alleyn, lead actor for Henslowe's Admiral's Men, following behind her, ordered a bowl for himself and sat in Armin's empty chair.

What a curious table! Moll Frith was the most elaborately garbed, her doublet vividly striped and the green paste jewel on her hat larger than usual. Ned Alleyn's beard was trimmed into a neat point, his doublet well cut, and his white linen gleaming, a vivid contrast to Ben Jonson, whose unkempt hair and dress suggested that he'd just come in from the brickyards. Shakespeare and I vied for the least noticeable, though his brown doublet was more finely tailored than mine.

Alleyn started talking about the theatre that he and Phillip Henslowe were building in Cripplegate, to be called the Fortune. Jonson seemed particularly interested, perhaps because he sold his work wherever he could. I expect he tried the Lord Chamberlain's Men first, but he'd had works performed by the Boys of Chapel Royal as well as the Lord Admiral's Men at the Rose, with its faded glory.

Moll gulped down her meal and stood. "I'll leave you to it."

In her absence, I moved closer to Shakespeare, leaving the other two to talk on, and spoke in his ear. "Your *Merchant* play reminds me of Amelia Bassano Lanyer."

"Oh?" he glanced at Alleyn and Jonson, deep in conversation.

"Not just Portia's suitor being called Bassanio. Amelia mentioned that you used stories she once told you."

"Did she now."

"They were Italian tales, the test of the three caskets for Portia's hand and the pound-of-flesh bond that Shylock makes with Antonio. And the disguised lawyer as well, I believe."

"Mistress Bassano was full of stories in those days," he replied before Ned Alleyn seized his attention.

"Guess what, Will? Admiral's Men intend to revive the jig at the end of plays."

"I hope the playwright has some say about it," Jonson grumbled.

"The jig was Will Kemp's forte, developing his performances *ex tempore*," Shakespeare said. "If Admiral's give their clown half a chance, he'll do the same."

"Is that why Chamberlain's Men stopped the old style of jigs at the Globe? Because Kemp left?"

"Last spring Kemp danced his way from London to Norwich where he likely found refuge in the arms of a warm-hearted widow.

His book about that adventure is due at the booksellers' any day now: *Kemp's Nine-Days Wonder*. Will Kemp was the best jig-maker ever to appear on the London stage."

That was the first I'd heard about Kemp's book, but I was more impressed with how adroitly Shakespeare avoided Alleyn's question.

"Jigs, masques, clowning: theatre crowds have catholic tastes," Alleyn said.

"Including hanging, drawing, and quartering as a spectator event and bear-baiting as a pleasure worth paying for. I can't say that pleasing the crowd is our first requirement."

"We know your tricks, Will. You want to train them to like what pleases you."

"It's worked with the Queen. Why not with Londoners?"

"Will is always Will," Jonson said, "and a crowd-pleaser, whether he admits it or not."

All that glisters is not gold.
PRINCE OF MOROCCO, *THE MERCHANT OF VENICE*

CHAPTER XXIV
October 1600

One sparkling October afternoon, Frances and Amelia went together to *The Merchant of Venice* at the Globe. They sat in a gallery opposite the Moors, who looked distant and superior as ever. Only Ibrahim seemed amused by the melee in the pit below: drinking and shouting, shoving to get closer to the stage, soliciting and purse-nipping.

The fanfare sounded, the crowd quieted, and Shakespeare, as the merchant Antonio, entered with Salerio and Solanio, speaking of his melancholy. In came the loudmouth Gratiano, shallow and ever ready with a wisecrack—a part Shakespeare surely wrote for Johnny.

As I awaited my entrance as Portia, I noticed that John Sincler, playing the Prince of Morocco, wore a lighter shade of makeup than in previous productions. In Belmont, where selecting the correct casket which would grant the winner Portia's hand in marriage, he promptly refuses the one made of lead: "A golden mind stoops not to shows of dross."

Without ever knowing a Moroccan, so far as I knew, Shakespeare had captured their grandeur. I could well believe they possessed golden minds. Their skin appeared gilded in the late afternoon light, their sword cases burnished, and their gold-shot silk turbans gleamed.

The Prince refuses the silver casket as well, choosing gold as the only one worthy of Portia. "Never so rich a gem was set in worse than gold." But when he opens it, instead of finding the image of the lady of Belmont, a death's head confronts him with the note: "Gilded tombs do worms enfold."

That ends the Prince of Morocco's suit. I hoped that no offense passed over the stoical faces of the Moors as I depicted Portia's relief that he'd failed to win her, but I'd made sure to turn my head away from their gallery.

The story moves rapidly. Shylock's daughter Jessica runs away from her sequestered home with the Christian Lorenzo, dressed in boy's clothes and carrying her father's chest of ducats and jewels. The Prince of Aragon wrongly chooses the silver casket, and Bassanio the correct one: lead. But before his and Portia's marriage can be consummated, and her attendant Nerissa's to Gratiano, Antonio's ships are lost at sea. He will forfeit the bond. Shylock goes to court for the pound of flesh Antonio agreed to.

I attend the trial disguised as the lawyer Balthazar and Nerissa as my clerk, urging Shylock to show mercy and accept Antonio's payment times two, times ten. When he persists in his refusal, I agree: the pound of flesh is Shylock's right by the terms of the bond. The law allows him his pound from Antonio's breast. But no more and no less than a pound, nor may he shed any blood. The bond does not allow it. Shylock is defeated. Playing Portia disguised as a lawyer was my most enjoyable masquerade part in many ways. Nothing to do with love games, only expertise in a profession that, in Italy or England, no woman could imagine.

Still, aware of the Moors, I felt ashamed that Portia didn't exhibit the quality of mercy she advocates, agreeing with Antonio that Shylock must become a Christian. True, she gives him a chance to repent of his cruel bond, but I understood Ben Jonson's point. Shylock is denied the faith of his Jewish forbears and left with next to nothing.

The final scenes at Belmont are lighthearted, even though Bassanio and Gratiano gave away their bridal rings to the young lawyer and his clerk. Back home and wearing our pretty gowns, Nerissa and I confront our husbands about the lost rings and tease them mercilessly before revealing our deception.

In the end, despite Bassanio and Gratiano's frailties, we four celebrate our nuptials along with Lorenzo and Jessica, who will inherit
her father Shylock's wealth.

Like Shylock, Antonio is left alone, as melancholic at the end of
the play as he was at the beginning. His friendship with Bassanio,
so strong that he wagered a pound of his own flesh to secure him a
loan, comes second to Bassanio's duty to his wife. Perhaps that's why
the play is called *The Merchant of Venice*, though Armin joked that it
was no doubt because our playwright played the merchant Antonio.

In his last line, Antonio addresses me as Portia: "Sweet lady, you
have given me life and living." Not only did I save him in the court-
room as Balthazar, but I'm the one to report that his ships landed
safely. Yet the expression on Shakespeare's face reflected Antonio's
loss. Henceforth his realm would be the Rialto with its buying
and selling, not musical Belmont where Bassanio would dwell
as husband and lord. But the applause was hearty and the music
joyous: a wedding dance to send everyone home happy.

After the performance, we players were invited to Bedford House,
unusual following a public show. Lady Lucy Russell, Countess of
Bedford, was an unusual woman, Frances told me, well-educated and
strong-willed. Her husband Edward, Earl of Bedford, had returned
from Ireland and, like numerous others who served with Essex,
found himself out of favor with Queen Elizabeth.

If they couldn't participate in Court revels, what better than
gather together players and poets themselves? That was Will
Shakespeare's explanation for the Russells' banquet. I'd not been
inside Bedford house nor its neighbor Essex House, where Johnny
spent time before being confined with Cecil. The Nag's Head was
my haven on the Strand.

The Moorish delegation had been invited as well. Their Ethiop
guards, who'd stood sentinel at the back of the gentlemen's gallery
during the play, encircled them as they entered Bedford House.
Their leather jerkins were similar to those worn by Londoners but
tooled in gold, and their shirts of such fine linen we could see their
muscular arms beneath. I was as awed as Harry Lanyer seeing those

guards up close. The Moors had come to the banquet without their ceremonial swords, but their guards wore sheathed daggers at their waists.

The doorman looked shocked. "I was told to welcome ambassadors from Barbary, but nothing was said about black-skinned guards. If they must attend you, Ambassador, they must do so from the outer porch."

The guards' expressionless faces suggested they neither knew they were being addressed nor what was said. Ibrahim stepped forward. "Our men cannot be sent outside. They shall stand at the back of the hall."

"Don't tell me they expect you to be attacked?"

"Your nobles and ladies too have attendants."

"Not fierce black men!"

At that moment Ben Jonson appeared at the open door, accompanied by Michael Drayton, Samuel Daniel, and John Donne. Frances had mentioned Lady Lucy's fondness for poetry, but I'd not imagined seeing Donne here.

"What's the problem?" Jonson asked. By now the entry was full with our company, the Moorish delegation, the poets.

Ibrahim turned to Jonson. "The keeper of the door refuses entry to our attendants."

"Now Alf," Jonson clapped the doorman on the shoulder, "this embassy is made all the more notable by such magnificent men. I guarantee the Earl and his lady will welcome them and that their behavior will meet every standard of decorum within these doors."

"How can you guarantee the behavior of four wild men?" Alf said under his breath.

"Trust me, Alf." He nodded to Ibrahim. "Come along." They walked into the great hall together, the rest of us trailing after, including the guards.

I'd heard mutterings on the street about blackamoors parading around London, but no one at this banquet would say so, even *sotto voce*. How Lady Lucy had persuaded the Moorish delegation to come I had no idea, but their presence added to the rarity of the evening.

The banquet table overflowed with sweet breads, cheeses, cakes, and confits. We were offered wine, the Moors orange cordial. After a show I rarely had much appetite, so chose only soft cheese and a knotted bread roll to go with the fine Spanish wine. I stood not far from the guards, who were being offered a platter of dates, procured no doubt from Barbary.

More interested in watching others than making myself noticed, I'd worn my best dark blue doublet and hose, nondescript amidst the vibrant guests. But when I saw that the Moor's group now included William Shakespeare, I moved closer. Ambassador ben Messaoud's Italian wafted toward me, with Dr. Giovanni Florio as translator. How Amelia would enjoy the opportunity to mix with Lady Lucy and her poets and to speak Italian!

"One needs moneylenders," ben Messaoud said. "How else would we have trade? Your Barbary Trading company borrows money in order to set sail. We hope that no ships are lost at sea like your Antonio's." He waited for Florio to translate. "In Morocco we would never permit a bond of flesh—nor of course would you in England. In Venice?" He shrugged.

"I think only in a play set in Venice," Shakespeare said. "An old story."

"Nor do women train in the law, though a woman disguised as a man: it is not impossible," one of ben Messaoud's men said.

"Do you have stories of disguise?" Drayton asked.

Ben Messaoud smiled as Florio put the question to him. "Our *Thousand and One Nights* includes many tales of disguise and deception. Scheherazade tells the Sultan a story night after night to save her life. A woman of superior wit and imagination."

I saw a hungry look in Shakespeare's eyes. Before the Moors departed, no doubt he'd try to obtain a copy of Scherazade's storybook of the thousand and one nights. Had it been translated, I wondered? It would be a sight to behold in Arabic, judging by the poem Ibrahim showed me, but utterly unreadable to anyone we knew.

Ibrahim spoke English but did not write it. The poem he'd

translated from Arabic consisted of four lines. Nothing like a thousand and one tales, nor even a few. If Will wanted those stories, he'd have to find his own Scheherazade. In grey London, Amelia Bassano with her old Italian tales came the closest.

Lady Lucy, delighted to host a room full of actors, circulated among us with warm greetings to each. Then she focused all her attention on John Donne. He shot me a friendly glance, but I didn't intrude on their conversation. He hoped to marry Anne More, but every poet benefits from a patron, and one well-born, well-married, young, and beautiful would be all the better.

The thought jolted me. That's what Johnny hoped for with Lady Elizabeth, Countess of Rutland. She must be here, as they were neighbors and both women's husbands had served with Essex.

I looked around the glittering hall, decorated in pale green and gold with torches down the walls between ancestral portraits, and candelabra spaced throughout. On an intricately carved chair speaking to a nobleman sat Lady Elizabeth herself, in a bejeweled forest green gown that, while not as grand as Frances' finest creations, evoked wealth and privilege.

Envy bubbled up in me. Except when I used to envy Johnny his easy stride in breeches when we were children, it was an unfamiliar feeling. Fear yes, anxiety yes, but who would I envy? My life held more than ever I'd dreamed. Amelia's house was handsomer than ours and great halls and palaces far beyond me, but I felt blessed to live with Frances in Cornhill. My visits to the houses and estates of Marie, the Countess of Pembroke, aroused only gratitude for our friendship.

So why would Lady Elizabeth Sidney Manners arouse envy? I'd no more seek her favors, nor Lady Lucy's, than I coveted their finery. Yet tonight I felt a gulf, as if we players, and even the Moors, were curiosities on display to our superiors.

Amelia likely could help me articulate this strange emotion. She concealed her resentments, but as her longtime friend I'd sensed them beneath her words. When she spoke of women patrons, she must have envied their status. Once Amelia moved freely among them at Court. They had that right by birth and upbringing, she by association, harshly ended at the wish of Lord Hunsdon. Amelia wanted to sit in the musician's gallery at Whitehall for the joy of playing music in public, but also to gaze at the glamour below. The closest she could come to her former life was as hired musician in boy's disguise.

In Saffron Walden, as in all of England, we were raised to accept our place in life. I'd rebelled against my own, a girl sentenced to obedience, service, and silence, to wifehood, motherhood. Instead of envying boys I became one—of my same class. What could a village boy do to escape the confines imposed on him by his village but run away to sea? I'd intended to follow the course of such a boy.

A door existed that could raise the status of a clever village boy, as I discovered in Cambridge with Lord North's Men. With a strong intellect and someone to help him gain entrance to the University, he could matriculate by serving as a sizar, serving meals to his fellow students. Though his humble origins wouldn't be ignored, with determination he might become a scholar, teacher, or churchman.

Otherwise, labor was his destiny, land-owning his biggest dream. Even after my summer as a traveling player with Lord North's Men, when I arrived in London I had to support myself as assistant in Dick Frith's smithy.

When Will Kemp helped me join Lord Strange's Men as an apprentice player, my future was set. I'd always rejoiced in my freedom and my membership in a company who, apart from Shakespeare, perhaps Kemp, and now Armin, saw me as male. I'd been fortunate.

So why, looking at Lady Lucy and Lady Elizabeth, did envy fill my heart? Did I sense their condescension? With a courtly lady, a talented young man need only admire her, offer her his poems or music or art, and in return gain whatever benefits were hers to dispense. I understood why Amelia sought women patrons for her poetry, yet beneath that wish must dwell envy. She would have to flatter and charm them. She would never be their equal.

My eyes shifted to the Moors. I doubted that ben Messaoud

envied Queen Elizabeth or her courtiers. His proud bearing reflected the confidence of a leader. As for the Ethiop guards, were they slaves? What was their situation in Barbary and how had they come to serve the Moors? In London, dark-skinned persons were rare and often suffered for it. The villain in our play *Titus Andronicus* was a Moor, his only virtue his love for his baby. Whether the child would survive after Aaron's execution wasn't made clear in the script. Our productions of the play gave him a chance; no vengeful child-murder. Africans numbered among the Roman troops, so perhaps a mixed blood baby could thrive back then.

I had no idea about ancient Rome, but I did know that in this creamy-skinned society, even Amelia, with olive skin and dark hair, had been called black. For a brief time her exotic beauty, as Shakespeare wrote in one of his sonnets, set a new standard. Amelia had every advantage a young woman could gain, tutored by a countess in her youth, mistress of a close relative of the Queen—until she was cast off and married to a husband of her own class.

Envy and loss must dog her in the haunting hours before dawn: loss of aristocratic company, loss of the passion between herself and Shakespeare, regret for all that could never be. What drove her to consult Dr. Forman had been her hope he'd foretell a rise in her status. With Alfonso Lanyer as her only means, the answer was no, spiced by Forman's impertinence and disrespect. Amelia must stifle her jealousy, persist with her poetry, and seek noble patronage.

How easily might envy lead to hatred! I could regard the noblemen making their fortunes from Barbary and the New World as despicable in their assumptions and superiority. Another feeling to stifle.

Lady Elizabeth and her husband, a fair, slight man dressed in peacock blue that clashed with her green, rose from their seats. On the strength of two glasses of wine, or perhaps three, I was tempted to speak to them. But the party had wound down as I'd been staring at the guests, lost in thought. Just as well Tom Pope waved me over to join him. I doubted I could have maintained Portia's dignity in such a conversation.

Vaguely angry, I followed Pope and our company out the door, continuing on to Cornhill.

Frances sat stitching in front of the fire in a flower-sprigged house dress and pink apron. "You should look happier after playing Portia so brilliantly—and then a banquet at Bedford House."

"I wish you'd been there."

She laughed. "I've touched Lady Lucy's ribcage but will never see where she lives, nor would I expect to."

"But why—"

"Don't waste a thought on that, Sander. We've come remarkably far from our villages. I've visited Richmond and Whitehall palaces. Much to be grateful for."

That stopped me. As a player and a man, I had more opportunities than Frances did, yet I was the one feeling envious.

"I'm sorry, Frances. The play was a success, and the party at Bedford house entertaining. Somehow it left me agitated, that's all."

"Don't worry. Next time you play *Merchant of Venice*, there'll be no Moors and no banquet. Just the play itself, and afterward a round of drinks at the Anchor."

"Ah, life as usual." We embraced.

God, let me know the pain of love
FÜZULI, *DÂSTÂN-1 LEYLÎ VÜ MECNUN*
(*THE EPIC OF LAYLA AND MANJUN*)

CHAPTER XXV
Midwinter 1600

One chill December afternoon Richard Burbage arranged for us to use Blackfriars indoor playhouse, intimate and lit by candles, for a concert by the Moorish musicians playing with Thomas Lupo's royal consort. No doubt Queen Elizabeth would have loved to attend, but this gathering was more for musicians than audience. Among the handful of aficionados I saw John Donne, the Earl of Southampton, Countess Marie and her eldest son William Herbert, and the Earls of Bedford and Rutland with their wives. Lady Elizabeth Sidney wore the same green gown as at Bedford House, a ribbon of gold lace added at the neckline.

Again Amelia played lute, taking greater pains to conceal her sex than at Nonsuch Palace. As an extra precaution, Harry didn't hold her hand, determinedly acting like his uncle Innocent's apprentice. She wore black hose, a well-tailored doublet of fine wool in a rich blue, and a matching blue cap. Her fellow musicians were similarly garbed, but Amelia with her arresting black eyes was the most attractive. The Italian men in Lupo's consort were lean and dark browed and John Johnson pink-skinned and somewhat thick around the middle. Among them Amelia's beauty seemed ill-disguised.

The stage, without a pit, was broad but more shallow than in outdoor playhouses. To one side a table held a basket of candied fruit brought by the Moors and jugs of wine brought by our men.

Ibrahim again accompanied the Moorish oud and flute players on his tambourine. This time the musicians mingled in a diverting array. The severe man on the oud stood tall between Amelia and Antonio Bassano, the flautist with his lustrous moustache beside Innocent Lanyer and Harry. In his youthful grace, Ibrahim stood slightly apart, facing the others. The Blackfriars audience was silent, captivated by the unparalleled scene before them.

After playing Spanish airs, the musicians began a back-and-forth of harmonies and solos. When they moved to a vocal song, they hummed the words. To my ears, Amelia's contralto came through loudest. But the musicians paid no attention, nor to us listening, caught up in their shared creations. Even the sober Moors smiled at a particularly fluent passage or startling discord.

Blackfriars that day embraced the most exceptional musical performance heard in London, unrehearsed and inspired. None of us would ever forget it. Surely Shakespeare recognized Amelia, though her single-minded attention to her fingers made her fade into her fellows, equally involved.

After the last note sounded, we joined the musicians onstage, enjoying wine and fruit. The Moors declined wine but otherwise enjoyed the repast. Speaking Italian, Spanish, and a little English, we managed to communicate.

Candied grapes in hand, I approached Ibrahim and Amelia talking together to the side of the stage.

"Thank you for the poem, Ibrahim," I said. "It is beautiful in English as well."

"I can recite it in English."

"Please," Amelia said. His eyes remained upon her as he spoke:

> God, let me know the pain of love
> Do not for a second separate me from it
> Do not diminish your aid to the afflicted
> But rather, make me a lovesick one among them.

I'd regarded the poem as metaphor for divine love, but Ibrahim's expression as he spoke to Amelia suggested otherwise. If ever a face could be described as lovesick, it was his.

The passion in Ibrahim's eyes reminded me of the long-ago summer when, with a handful of players and poets, I fled the plague in London to the country estate Audley End. There I saw a more worldly version of that emotion in the eyes of Christopher Marlowe when he gazed at me, believing me a boy. The panic I felt then swept over me now for Amelia.

On that occasion I saved myself from much more than a kiss. In our second encounter, Kit Marlowe discovered my true sex, to his disappointment. We ended as friends, but a dangerously close call. I hoped Amelia could guard herself better now than I had with Marlowe.

But I was disconcerted by her expression. Her eyes, wide open like an innocent boy's, gave a compelling sense of vulnerability. Ibrahim looked utterly smitten. Did Amelia think he was another Dr. Simon Forman to tease? I scanned the stage for someone to come to her rescue—or to Ibrahim's. The Lupo consort chatted with others, and Ibrahim's uncle was deep in conversation with Shakespeare and the translator Sir Lewes Lewknor.

"The poet seeks the pain of love," Amelia said to Ibrahim. "Why is that?"

"Thus does the soul truly know God."

"Allah?"

"Yes, Allah."

"The divinity in this poem sounds more like Venus to me. Do they tell the old Greek stories in your land?"

Ibrahim shook his head.

Amelia took a step closer to him, ignoring me hovering nearby, and spoke like a precocious boy.

"Venus is the goddess of love, who blesses us through pain. Her son is called Cupid."

"I have heard of Cupid." Ibrahim gave her a melting look. "You, boy musician. You are his very image."

His accent was endearing, and the way he addressed Amelia as "boy musician." Amelia glowed. Did she not sense the risk? She held herself like a boy and sounded like one.

"Tell me your name, pretty boy."

"Emilio."

"May I see you, Emilio—away from here?"

I could not hold my tongue. Looking at Ibrahim I said sternly: "What would your uncle think of that?"

"What?" Ibrahim looked at me as if coming out of a fog.

"Do you not owe your uncle—"

Ibrahim interrupted. "My uncle does not object to love."

"Or its pain?" Amelia gave him a coy smile.

"That is my—" Ibrahim paused, struggling for a word.

"Your concern?" I took his arm, man to man. "You cannot imagine the danger, my friend. Emilio cannot meet you in private."

"No?" Ibrahim drew himself to his full height, looking down on me, a good three inches shorter, and Amelia, two inches shorter yet. "He may if he wishes. Do you wish it?" His gaze rested on Amelia.

"Very much."

I had to stop this reckless game. "Not today."

"Not today." Amelia laughed. "No, I suppose not. You may kiss me, Ibrahim." She offered her cheek.

He took her face between his hands and kissed her—on the lips. "Until next time."

Amelia allowed me to lead her away.

"How could you be so foolish?"

"That is the most beautiful love that has been made to me in ages, Sandro. You would deny me?"

"You mustn't see him again."

Amelia sighed. "Ibrahim wants to be lovesick. I did him a favor."

The Moorish delegation was leaving, Ibrahim last. He bowed to Amelia and threw her a kiss. I hid my surprise. Was that an Arabic custom? Amelia gave Ibrahim her most enticing smile, boy and temptress both.

That poor young man, I thought, but Amelia's expression

surprised me. She too looked forlorn. Evidently yearning cut both ways.

The Moors departed, Ibrahim no doubt nursing pangs of lovesickness for lost Emilio.

Winter settled in, bringing a troubling atmosphere heavier than the sooty clouds hanging over London. I walked to the Mermaid earlier than the agreed-on time, as Shakespeare often did the same. I hoped we might talk about the weightiness I sensed, somehow related to the Earl of Essex. But sitting with him by the fire, I didn't get a chance.

"I've been thinking about the Moors. I don't blame their young musician for loving Amelia. His is hardly the first heart she's captured. But she seemed entranced by him as well."

"You saw?" Silly question; of course Shakespeare watched them. His heart was one Amelia had captured.

"Likely they'll never see each other again, but they did start me wondering. What if a Moor and an Italian loved each other?"

"Impossible in England. Might Italy be different?"

"Perhaps it's different in many places. After all, Tamora loves Aaron the Moor."

"In *Titus Andronicus*, set in ancient Rome. And she's a Goth from a remoter place yet."

"I needn't tell you about the complications of the human heart, Sander. A seemingly disparate couple can love each other. Society disapproves; that's all." He gave me a speculative look that made my cheeks flush.

"Don't compare that to me and Frances. No tragic outcome so long as I pass for male. A Moor can but be who he is."

"And the pale-skinned can be cruel. A tale of a noble Moor who loved an Italian woman, even if she loved him in return, could only end in tragedy."

Burbage, Armin, and a handful of others arrived, ale all round.

"You've heard?" Shakespeare asked. "Sir Robert Cecil requests

A Midsummer's Dream for the Queen's Twelfth Night revels at
Whitehall. 'Celebrate midsummer in midwinter,' as he put it."

"I didn't enjoy last year's revels at Richmond," Armin said. "False
gaiety gets on the nerves."

"Which is why the Court loved *As You Like It*. Nothing like
a woodland comedy," Phillips said. "And *Dream* is even better. Not
only confusions of love but faeries and magic. We played it first for
Frances Howard's wedding with the Earl of Kildare at Whitehall,
remember?"

"Wasn't there," Armin said.

"You've been playing Bottom at the Globe, so now's your chance
to make the Queen laugh."

An expression that could only be regret glanced across
Shakespeare's face. He wrote the part of Bottom the Weaver for
Will Kemp, and Armin, for all his gifts, was not that sort of clown.
Bottom's braggadocio was hilarious. Armin carried it off well enough,
for those who'd never seen Will Kemp.

After playing Hippolyta in the first scene, Queen of the Amazons
and Theseus' reluctant bride, I became Titania, Queen of the Faeries.
When clouded by Puck's magical drops, Titania falls in love with
Bottom wearing the ass's head Puck gave him. The scene played
nothing like it had with Kemp. Still, I leashed Armin with a garland
of flowers and made much of him, and he brayed his words amusingly.

"Cecil also promised us access to a storage chest of clothing,"
Shakespeare said, "as we returned the Queen's purple in good condition after *Hamlet*."

That meant Frances would again be costume mistress. Lately
she'd seemed restless and edgy, and all I'd thought of was inviting
Amelia and Harry to visit from time to time. That had worked, more
or less. On days when I came in to the fragrance of Rebecca's baking
and found Amelia and Frances stitching together while Harry played
with the ginger cat Hero or trilled on his flute, our house felt almost
joyful. These cold nights Frances and I shared a bed for warmth, for
comfort, and, especially if Amelia and Harry's visit had lightened the
mood, for mutual pleasure.

Yet each of Frances' kisses felt like a singular delight, as if it were the last. Nothing she did or said confirmed my fears, but even in our domestic amiability, I sensed disquiet in her heart.

Over supper that night, I told Frances and Amelia about performing in the Grand Chamber at Whitehall.

"Did I tell you I played with my cousin's consort for the first performance of *Midsummer Night's Dream* at the palace?" Amelia asked Frances. "Thomas asked me at the last minute, so I had time only to learn the music—which I loved, but it all turned out worse than I'd expected."

"You were discovered?"

"By Lord Hunsdon! But that was long ago, and everything has changed. Still," Amelia winked, "I had the opportunity to play music with the Moors. The best of all!"

"Sander told me."

"I'd give anything to be at Whitehall with you. Last year, with Essex missing, Sander reported how strange the revels felt, and the political situation has only worsened since then." Amelia sighed. "Ah well, I'll rely on you three for a full report. Who would imagine that a seven-year old boy has access to Court and his mother does not?"

"I'll describe everything I see," Harry said.

"I know, pet. But keep your eye on your uncles and your fingers. Music comes first."

To George Carey, Lord Hunsdon's successor to the title and now Queen's Lord Chamberlain, Amelia didn't exist. With her Italian temperament, as the only one of us missing these revels she must feel murderous envy.

I did my best to reassure her. She'd seen the same cast at the Globe except for a new boy as Hermia. Burbage would again play Theseus and Oberon, the faery king, and Will Shakespeare Hermia's harsh father Egeus in the first and last scenes.

"In between is the part you'll like best, Harry. Master Shakespeare is Peter Quince, play-master for the tradesmen who put together a crazy play for the wedding celebration. Your mother will tell you the story. *Midsummer Night's Dream* is full of chases through the woods and all sorts of silliness."

The week before the performance, Frances and Augustine Philips went to Whitehall together, as he was the closest our company had to a manager. Frances reported that as before, Lady Isabel offered anything in the clothing chest in what would be our tiring room, so long as she returned each piece mended.

Among those that would need repairs before we could use them was mine as Hippolyta: a gown with a bodice that resembled armor. Perhaps it was the very one Queen Elizabeth wore years ago to encourage the departing navy facing the Spanish Armada. We'd bring our own costumes for the tradesmen and the faeries. As Titania I'd wear gossamer and flowers, with a flannel shift beneath.

Frances made everything look new and brought the most valuable pieces wrapped in linen on performance day. She hung our costumes on the rail and remained in the tiring room to help with costume changes and watch through the gap in the curtained doorway where we awaited our entrances.

Whitehall emanated a sense of privilege and anticipation that lifted our spirits. Onstage, trees bedecked with glittery flowers suggested an enchanted woods, its magic enhanced by candlelight. As we put on our costumes we sipped the wine set out for us on a side table, but the atmosphere was more intoxicating.

Condell played a flute fanfare. I entered on the arm of Theseus, and the play began.

When Titania falls asleep onstage, I scanned the audience through half-shut eyes. The performance had the effect of a living dream, as if Puck's drops dazzled every eye. There sat Johnny with Sir Robert Cecil. Now that was a surprise! I wondered if he envied Sincler playing Lysander.

We rolled through my love scene with Bottom in ass ears, the sorting of the four lovers misled by Puck's magic drops, then the tradesmen's farcical tragedy of Pyramus and Thisby, Armin doing almost as hilarious a death scene as Will Kemp had.

Puck's final words released the audience from the spell.

> *If we shadows have offended,*
> *Think but this, and all is mended.*
> *That you have but slumbered here*
> *While these visions did appear.*
> *And this weak and idle theme,*
> *No more yielding than a dream . . .*

The stage filled with faeries, not only players who'd been woodland sprites but all the company, outer layers shed to their shirts, now drifting with iridescent gauze for a spectacular dance, soon joined by courtiers and ladies. As I spun through the steps, I caught a glimpse of the Queen masked in white facepaint, her eyes glistening with unshed tears, perhaps because Robert Devereux had been her last dancing partner, and now she had none.

As a banquet of sweets and wine was laid out, I found Frances, released from her duties in the tiring room. Johnny appeared out of nowhere and embraced us both at once. Frances twisted away.

"Look who's here," I said. "How do you like serving Sir Robert Cecil?"

"He's a tough taskmaster who despises the Earl of Essex."

"Shhh," I put a finger on my lips. "Not a welcome name here."

"No one's listening. Cecil's attitude makes it difficult for me, I must say. And all the secrecy!"

I took two glasses of wine from a serving man and gave one to Frances. As Johnny helped himself to a glass, Richard Burbage slapped him on the back. "We miss you, you naughty fellow. We'd rather you played your bad-boy parts onstage."

Neither Burbage nor the rest of the company knew exactly why the Queen had sentenced Johnny to Cecil's service. Shakespeare said only that it could have been worse. Amidst the current tensions, no one pried.

"Oh, I don't mind," Johnny said. "I'm practicing to be a playwright."

Burbage laughed. "You could never mount a play about what you're witnessing at Cecil's! You know the prohibition against politics on stage."

"Power and folly are universal themes," Johnny said. "I know what's safe."

"Your situation suggests otherwise. You should have learned your lesson well by the time you return to us."

Johnny punched Burbage's shoulder affectionately and kissed Frances' cheek. "I must join my esteemed master. Till next time."

"Johnny's saucy as ever," Frances said to me.

"It can't be much fun for him to be cooped up with Cecil week after week."

Without ceremony, Queen Elizabeth left the room, and the evening came to a premature halt. Though her bearing was regal as ever, Her Majesty looked tired and her courtiers disappointed. She'd not even greeted our company personally, something she usually did as much for herself as for us.

Was tonight a formality she'd suffered through? That was the question backstage as we removed our costumes.

"I think she was delighted to escape into the woods with us," I said.

"She needed the break," Pope folded his costume as Philostrate. "But now—no more faery dust. Blessings to her."

As we left Whitehall, I thought about how Frances and I were better off than the Queen of England, our warm house welcoming and ours to control.

With mine own tears I wash away my balm,
With mine own hands I give away my crown
KING RICHARD, *RICHARD II*

CHAPTER XXVI
February 1601

Entering the Globe for a company meeting, I was surprised to see men I recognized as friends of the Earl of Essex in intense conversation with Shakespeare, Burbage, Condell, and Phillips. I made myself inconspicuous, ears attuned. Though I caught only the occasional word, Phillips, Condell, and Burbage seemed animated. The one face I could see, Shakespeare's, looked guarded. A few words more and Essex's men vanished into the vaper.

Once Moll Frith and I saw the Earl of Essex in Bankside. Despite lines of age and loss, he and his companions exuded bravado, swords bright and strides brash. Essex reminded me of Juliet's cousin Tybalt in *Romeo and Juliet*, spoiling for a fight. In the theatre today, however, Essex's friends had conducted themselves with reserve. No swords in sight.

When the company assembled, Augustine Phillips addressed us. "We'd intended to revive *Henry V*, which drew the crowds last summer. Instead we'll be performing *Richard II* on Saturday."

"That old play?" Pope asked. "*Henry V* is the better choice. More rousing."

"Yes, that old play," Phillips said. "We've been paid in advance, forty shillings, besides our paying audience."

Pope muttered, "Very irregular, very irregular."

"Speak up, Tom," Phillips said.

He shrugged resignedly. "It will be profitable, I suppose."

"That's the point, men. Here are your parts."

My roles in *Richard II* included the Duchess of York, the only woman of action in a play where women lament and grieve. The Duchess' final scene was entertaining, but I'd much rather play Hostess of the Boar's Head and Princess Katherine in *Henry V*.

"I don't like it," Pope said as a few of us left the Globe together. "Who commissioned this performance?"

"I can tell you," John Sincler said. "Sir Charles Percy and Lord Monteagle and two or three more."

Pope looked stricken. "Essex men! Why did Phillips and Shakespeare agree?"

Sincler winked. "Good for the coffers."

"Doesn't feel right."

I wished I could question Shakespeare, but he left the theatre by himself. Well did I remember the sad story of King Richard II. He banishes his cousin, Henry Bullingbrook, and confiscates Bullingbrook's rightful inheritance from his father, John of Gaunt, played by Shakespeare. Richard continually abuses his kingly power, albeit in beautiful language.

Bullingbrook returns from banishment with an army and deposes Richard. Parted from his wife and left with only his sorrows, Richard is sent to Pomfret Castle, where he's murdered. Henry Bullingbrook interrupted the line of succession. No wonder the women in the play were grieving. Richard's Queen Isabel would not mother the next king. The royal line was broken.

Like Bullingbrook, Essex had traces of royal blood, and like Bullingbrook, he was not in the line of succession—though Bullingbrook had more claim to the English throne than the Earl of Essex.

But Queen Elizabeth was nothing like King Richard II. It was ridiculous to think that Essex's friends would want to perform a play because they thought Essex was another Bullingbrook set to depose our ruler. More likely this was a whim of those theatre-loving comrades of his, Southampton and Rutland. They loved fine clothes and fine poetry, which abound in this play.

The next day I found Tom Pope alone in our favorite room in the Anchor.

"Expecting anyone else?"

"A few, yes. No harm if you stay." He filled my tankard from the jug on the table.

"You object to this special performance of *Richard II*."

"I wouldn't if it were a shareholders' decision. We planned on *Henry V* and now it's *Richard II*. No discussion among us."

"Phillips says it's simply good business, a fee in addition to the house box."

"So he says." Pope emptied his ale and called to the serving girl for another jug. She bobbed her head and turned, nearly colliding with Phillips and Shakespeare coming in the door, Burbage and Armin behind.

Phillips gave me a slantwise look that made me question my welcome, but I didn't leave. Greetings were passed around, ale poured, and when we had the room to ourselves, Phillips said to Pope, "You want to talk about *Richard II*."

"I don't see why it requires discussion," Burbage said. "We know our parts."

"That's not the issue," Pope said. "If the Earl of Essex has anything to do with it, this commission is dangerous."

Burbage lifted his full cup. "Too late to back out; we've taken their money."

"We can return it to Lord Monteagle. Until the handbills are posted, it's not too late."

"You would rather do *Henry V* than this 'old play'." Phillips spoke as he would to an irritating uncle. "*Richard II* is every bit as good onstage."

"Think about it. When the quarto went on sale at the

booksellers, the scene where Richard surrenders his crown to Henry Bullingbrook was censored, and it's never been printed since."

"We always include that scene in performance with no complaints from the Master of Revels."

"Enough arguing you two," Burbage said. "*Richard II* is full of wonderfully poetic language, especially King Richard's."

"Which is your part," Pope grumbled.

"Let me remind you that Burbage plays King Henry V as well," Phillips said. "What do you think, Will?"

Shakespeare had been worrying a snagged thumbnail, which was now bleeding. He tucked the thumb into his fist.

"I agree, it's odd that Essex's friends paid us to perform this particular play. That poetry you praise, Burbage, is Richard's flaw. He's a man of words, not action. He loves his royal title and the idea of kingship, the crown and all its symbolism, but as monarch he's capricious, vain, and short-sighted."

"And cruel," Burbage added with a grin. "Richard is ever an actor. Even when alone, he speaks as if onstage. You give him grand lines, Will. When Richard relinquishes the crown, he asks for a mirror so he can see how the loss registers on his face—and describe it."

"True enough." Phillips laughed. "Henry Bullingbrook is the man of action."

"You two love your own roles," Armin said. "So what? We agree that it's a well-wrought play. The issue isn't its merit but the fact that the monarch is deposed. What if Essex sees himself as a Bullingbrook, saving the country from—"

"Watch your tongue." Burbage glanced toward the doorway.

"Why are we here if we can't talk about the perils of this play?" Armin had lowered his voice, but was no less angry, muttering half to himself, "I must play Sir Pierce of Exton, murderer of King Richard."

"We're a theatre company, Armin," Phillips' tone was condescending. "We perform plays the audience wants to see. You and Pope exaggerate the risks."

"Hear, hear," Burbage raised his cup. "This performance will be no different than any other, except that it was commissioned. So are the plays we perform in a manor or at Court."

"Those who attend private performances do not pay an admission fee," Pope retorted.

The serving girl brought a fresh jug. Burbage, Philips and I held out our cups for refills. Shakespeare hesitated, then offered his as well. Armin did not, but made no move to leave.

Tom Pope rose from the table. "So that's it?" No one contradicted him. "Then I shall do my best in *Richard II*. I hope we don't live to rue it."

Pope's departure left us in silence until Burbage began to speak lines of Richard's, pretending to look into a mirror.

> *O flatt'ring glass,*
> *Like to my followers in prosperity,*
> *Thou dost beguile me! Was this face the face*
> *That like the sun, did make beholders wink?*
> *Is this the face which fac'd so many follies*
> *That was at last outfac'd by Bullingbrook?*
> *A brittle glory shineth in this face,*
> *As brittle as the glory is the face—*

Burbage hurled the imaginary mirror to the floor with a violence that would shatter it were it real. How I would love to play that role!

> *For there it is, crack'd in an hundred shivers.*
> *Mark, silent king, the moral of this sport,*
> *How soon my sorrow hath destroy'd my face.*

Burbage bowed; the table applauded.

Walking home, I wondered about Pope and Armin's worries. Did anyone believe Queen Elizabeth should be deposed? Given the strained atmosphere in London, that question was more difficult to answer than it should have been.

Frances greeted me. "You look glum."

When I told her about the meeting, she tut-tutted. "William

Shakespeare is a cautious man. He wouldn't have written a seditious play."

"Did you ever see *Richard II*?"

"I did," Frances said. "King Richard was more pompous than any as could rule today."

"Do you remember what happens to him in the end?"

"No one deserves to be murdered, but Richard wasn't a good king. He had no conscience."

"Is that what the audience thought?"

"I expect so."

"The murder of King Richard was regicide. A frightening precedent."

"Oh Sander, it's an old story. Nothing to do with our Queen."

Not until the day before the performance were playbills posted: *The Tragedy of King Richard the Second* at the Globe, February 7, 1601. When I reached the theatre that morning, I saw folk waiting for it to open, queuing much earlier than usual, their voices crackling with curiosity.

Backstage, the players, including Tom Pope as Northumberland, put on costumes in silence. I sensed an unspoken agreement that we perform the play as historical pageant. My roles were small, the Duchess of Gloucester early on and the Duchess of York at the end. Beeston spoke the poignant lines of Richard's Queen Isabel.

Burbage set an almost whimsical tone in his opening scene, as King Richard conducts the trial between Thomas Mowbray and Henry Bullingbrook. The fatal complications begin with Richard's banishment of Bullingbrook.

Later, when Richard sees that he is defeated, he speaks as no Tudor ruler would:

> *What must the King do now? Must he submit?*
> *The King shall do it. Must he be depos'd?*

The King shall be content. Must he lose
The name of king? A' God's name let it go.
I'll give my jewels for a set of beads,
My gorgeous palace for a hermitage . . .
And my large kingdom for a little grave . . .

Even when summoned to give Henry Bullingbrook his crown, Richard plays a role.

Now mark me how I will undo myself:
I give this heavy weight from off my head,
And this unwieldy scepter from my hand,
The pride of kingly sway from out my heart;
With mine own tears I wash away my balm,
With mine own hands I give away my crown . . .
God save King Henry, unking'd Richard says,
And send him many years of sunshine days!

Awaiting my entrance as the Duchess of York, I felt a hush in the theatre. True, King Richard brought his defeat upon himself, but it was shocking to see a king deposed.

The play sped to Richard's death, with a humorous interlude where the Duchess of York pleads successfully to save her son's life, even though his father testifies against him. At the end, Sir Pierce Exton laments, "Oh would the deed were good! For now the devil that told me I did well says that this deed is chronicled in hell."

The applause was polite, and the audience made a hasty exit.

Backstage, Burbage gave Tom Pope's shoulder a friendly slap. "Feel better now? The play came off without a catch."

"I'm glad I was wrong." Pope pulled on his hat. "But I'm going straight home."

"Please yourself." Burbage turned to the rest of us. "I'm for the Mermaid: anyone care to join me?"

The "ayes" followed him out the door, but I was among those who turned toward home.

And as in the common course of all treasons, we
still see them reveal themselves, till they attain
to their abhorred ends, so he that in this action
contrives against his own nobility, in his proper
stream o'erflows himself.

A LORD, *ALL'S WELL THAT ENDS WELL*

CHAPTER XXVII
February 1601

On our walk southward to St. Saviour's next morning, Frances and I heard a rising din. Ben Jonson stopped us.

"You two should go home. Avoid St. Paul's. That's where the rebels are."

"What rebels?" We spoke in unison.

"The Earl of Essex's men. That's the rumor. I'm to the Mermaid for the latest news. You two had better stay indoors."

I would have dearly loved to accompany Jonson, but one look at Frances' face and I turned around to spend a quiet day with my wife while dire deeds swirled. Could Essex really be mounting a rebellion? How I wished I could see for myself!

Back home, the two of us alone, as Rebecca was staying with the widow, Frances began stitching. I opened *The Arcadia* Marie Sidney Herbert had given me, hoping that her brother Philip's pastoral poetry would distract me from the distant turmoil.

When she became bored of stitchery and confinement behind shuttered windows, Frances began to prepare a meal of all the food we had on hand: guinea fowl, carrots and beetroot for a mélange, ingredients for bread and an apple pie. Her flurry in the kitchen lasted until late afternoon when she put the pie in the oven.

Perhaps the tasty aromas summoned our guest: it was not long until William Shakespeare knocked at the door with a flagon of wine.

"This is not a night for drinking in a tavern. Anything could happen."

"Like what?" I asked. "Ben Jonson told us to stay indoors. We've been in suspense all day."

Shakespeare sat beside the fire. "It started with an uproar last night at Essex House."

"Essex House?" Frances repeated.

"Yes, where Johnny's been such a familiar. Lucky for him he's now with Sir Robert Cecil. Apparently, members of the Privy Council went to summon Essex to testify, gathering a crowd along the way. When they arrived at his house, the mob pursued them up the stairs. The story goes that Essex locked the counselors in his library under guard and left. He and some 300 armed followers poured toward the City shouting 'Murder! For the Queen. For plots with Spain.'"

"For the Queen?" Frances said in a stunned voice.

"To save her or to capture her; opinions differ. Essex's supporters say he meant to save Queen Elizabeth from the Spaniards."

"Are Spaniards coming?" she asked.

"No evidence. I wish I could tell you more definitely what followed. They say that instead of armor, Essex wore his finest court clothes. Yet he stopped at the home of Sheriff Smythe to gather more men, presumably according to a prior plan. When Essex reached Ludgate, he found it locked, and all the other city gates as well. Thus was the Earl of Essex defeated without a battle. That's all I can tell you. I don't know what happened to Essex's men or to the counselors imprisoned at his house, or whether he himself was arrested. Rumor has it that Essex took a wherry boat home."

"I'm glad you came to us," Frances said.

"I thought: where can I go to escape the madness and have a good meal? My nose guided me here."

"You're very welcome. Roast guinea fowl and vegetables—we have more than enough."

"That's fortunate. Ben Jonson saw me coming this way. I expect he'll be along soon."

"I don't understand why Essex would refuse a summons to the Privy Council," I said. "When they summoned Christopher Marlowe, didn't they simply require him to report back daily?"

"Marlowe was never imprisoned, yet he ended up stabbed to death under questionable circumstances. Kit Marlowe may have played at espionage, but he was harmless compared to the Earl of Essex. Evidently Essex assumed that the men who fought with him in Ireland would join his rebellion and that Sheriff Smythe could raise all the discontented of London, gentlemen and commoners alike, to his cause. Essex is a threat to the throne."

"Which Marlowe never was." I heard the anger in my voice: I never understood why the wild, brilliant Kit Marlowe was murdered.

"No, Marlowe was no threat. A couple of scoundrels caught up with him in Deptford; we'll never know for sure who ordered them to kill him. Essex's case is altogether different. He challenged the Queen, or at least gave every appearance of doing so. He'll be accused of nothing less than treason."

I poured out three cups of wine. "Do you know what's happened to my brother?"

"Johnny's in no danger so long as he remains with Cecil." Will raised his cup. "His sympathies may lie with Essex and Rutland, but I trust Johnny is not such a fool as to join them."

"He can be foolish, but he's not an idiot. His offense—" Frances stopped.

"His offense was abandoning you most shamefully," I finished, taking her hand. "That's treason enough, but not against the throne."

Will ignored the interruption. "Cecil has spies, and he'll not let anyone wander in or out of his household, especially not Johnny."

Frances jumped as a heavy fist rattled the door. I motioned her to stay where she was and opened the door a crack—to Ben Jonson.

"Just in time, Ben," Shakespeare said. "You're invited to a feast of Mistress Cooke's best devising."

Jonson kissed Frances' hand and accepted a cup of wine.

I found it odd to have this burly man sitting by our fire. Ben Jonson had never before visited us, nor had he discovered the secret I'd hidden all these years. I'd performed in his plays and sat many a time at his table in this or that tavern with not so much as a suspicious glance. Either it was a tribute to my acting or Jonson's lack of observation—or perhaps he didn't care. He simply treated me as a young man.

"You said you wouldn't come until you had the latest news," Will said. "So?"

"I have news all right. Last you heard, Essex returned home by boat from his failed venture."

"That's what I told Sander and Frances."

"When he arrived at Essex House, he discovered that the captive counselors had been freed to return to Whitehall. The story goes, Essex began burning his papers. His house was soon surrounded by Lord Nottingham's forces, armed with cannon. Essex refused to surrender, climbing to his roof and shouting, sword aloft, 'I would sooner fly to heaven.'"

Shakespeare shook his head. "Did he think he was in a play?"

"This whole affair has been a poorly conceived drama, with an ignominious ending. When Nottingham threatened to blow up his house, Essex surrendered his sword. He's in custody, and the Tower is full of his followers. Sheriff Smythe and a number of gentlemen were arrested immediately, including the Earl of Rutland, his brothers, and the Earls of Southampton and Bedford."

"Oh dear," Frances said.

"I'd beware of a tender heart," Jonson's glance took in Shakespeare as well as Frances. "They're traitors, however dashing their manner or splendid their finery."

I knew that the Earl of Southampton, Henry Wriothesley, had been Shakespeare's patron and friend. Readers of Shakespeare's sonnets imagined that the young man he described was none other than Southampton. Shakespeare's face, however, gave nothing away.

"I look forward to this supper, Mistress Cooke," Jonson said, "but first, the most serious news. It's whispered that your performance of *Richard II* was part of Essex's plot."

"What?" I lowered my voice. "Who's whispering?"

"Some say that Essex's followers hoped to recruit all of London to overthrow the Queen by commissioning a play where Henry Bullingbrook deposes King Richard. They expected your performance to result in a spontaneous uprising to put Essex on the throne."

"Ridiculous!" Frances said. "The audience was mannerly, and there was no demonstration of any sort. You were actors doing your job."

"I appreciate loyalty in a woman." Jonson raised his cup. "To Frances Cooke."

"May the Privy Council agree with you, Frances," Shakespeare said. "None of us wants part of any rebellion or counter-rebellion."

"Here's to the Queen's safety." I lifted mine.

Shakespeare did the same. "It's a pleasure to be among like-minded friends."

We sat down to our feast. Outside, London was unusually silent. The rebellion must have come to nothing, and Queen Elizabeth remained secure on her throne. Or so we hoped.

After dinner, Shakespeare and Jonson slipped into the foggy, deserted street. I heard Jonson's voice as I closed the door behind them. "What a pleasant household. All they need is a child or two running around."

I couldn't sleep. Will didn't seem concerned about our production of *Richard II*, but I felt uneasy. My worry wasn't for Shakespeare as John of Gaunt, nor myself as the Duchesses—but Henry Bullingbrook? Augustine Phillips, the very person who accepted the commission from Essex's men, had played King Richard's usurper.

Jonson's presence reminded me that playwrights could be at risk. A fine line between theatre and politics, so that even a suspicion of seditious intent onstage was dangerous. Ben had survived his imprisonments, I thought, falling to sleep curled against Frances' warm back. Might we face nothing like!

Next morning I joined the subdued crowd walking toward St. Paul's. So far, some eighty-five followers of Essex had been arrested. No one cried the news in the churchyard, but speculations flew. Ruffians laid odds on whether those arrested would be hanged or lose their heads. Lawyers from the Middle Temple argued that not all were equally guilty but could not agree about how to determine degrees of guilt.

A group of well-dressed men stood together discussing the fates of Southampton, Bedford, and Rutland, husband of Johnny's sometime patron Lady Elizabeth. Some were certain that they would share Essex's doom; others disagreed. Those so-called rebels were aristocrats, and look at all they'd done for the Queen in Ireland!

I moved near the church steps where a handful of priests and the quieter sort of citizens gathered. They agreed Her Majesty must be grateful that her enemies were so quickly imprisoned. A young priest with a carrying voice said how dreadful that the chief of those enemies was the Earl of Essex, the Queen's favorite, a young man she'd regarded like a son.

"All the worse that he turned on her so brutally," another said. "The Queen has been hard served by foolish, rebellious young men. A sorry day for London."

A sorry day for the Lord Chamberlain's Men as well, I soon learned. As I left Paul's Yard, Tom Pope stopped me. "Come along to the Globe. We've been summoned by the Lord Chamberlain himself."

"Haven't plays been suspended?"

"I'm afraid this is another matter."

As we crossed the Bridge, our fellows joined us, grumbling at the unprecedented summons. The Lord Chamberlain attended most all our plays, but never had he come backstage, let alone called a meeting there. By the appointed hour, we were assembled in the tiring room, whispering uncomfortably among ourselves. When the Lord Chamberlain, old Lord Hunsdon's eldest son George, came through the door, we became a tableau.

He spoke with sonorous formality. "I have come on the order of the Privy Council. You men were incautious in the extreme to accept a commission from Percy and Monteagle. Your performance of *Richard II* was seditious."

"Never!"

"No such thing."

"We meant no harm."

"It's only a play!"

"And an old one."

Hunsdon held up his hand for silence. "They offered you the commission for a reason. As King Richard was deposed and disgraced, so would be Her Majesty. As Bullingbrook was welcomed to London as a hero, so would be the Earl of Essex. That is what Sir Robert Cecil believes. Essex's men intended your play to raise the audience to rebellion. They expected the mob to join them raging through the streets. You accepted the commission with full knowledge of and collusion with their purpose."

Shakespeare stepped forward. "Surely you do not believe that, my lord."

Lord Hunsdon looked at him long and hard, as if just now considering what he himself believed. Shakespeare added quietly, "There was no rebellion in the streets after the play."

"You are right, Master Shakespeare, there was none then. But you know what happened subsequently. I am displeased that you men played even a minor role in that treacherous debacle."

"Did you not defend us to the Privy Council?" Shakespeare persisted.

"I was told to speak to you, and so I have. You must explain yourselves. These are troubled times, and Essex's offenses to the Queen are notorious. One of you must appear before the Council tomorrow at ten o'clock. I assume that means you, Master Phillips. You are the one, they say, who took the money from Percy and Monteagle."

Hunsdon turned abruptly, his cloak swirling around him, and walked out the door.

"We can expect no help from him," Burbage said. "Some patron!"

Tom Pope gave Burbage and Phillips a reproachful look.

"We must all go home," Shakespeare said. "In this atmosphere even drinking together could appear to be a plot. 'Conspire,' you know, means 'breathe together.' Walk along with me, Augustine."

I was tempted to follow them, but Shakespeare took Phillips by the arm and led him away quickly, speaking in his ear. Disappointed that we couldn't discuss this together, we headed our separate ways in a haze of doubt and dread.

At home, Frances' immediate response was "You're innocent. Don't worry. You and your men did nothing wrong."

I didn't bother to state the obvious. Many have been imprisoned, even executed, who did nothing wrong. Appearances counted, and in light of Essex's ensuing behavior, our performance of *Richard II* looked bad indeed.

After testifying before the Privy Council, Augustine Phillips came directly to the Mermaid, where we awaited the verdict. Apparently his actor's skill—and the truth—enhanced his plea. He'd protested that the Lord Chamberlain's Men had no treasonous intent. We deeply regretted that we didn't realize such an old and much-performed play as *Richard II* could cause offense.

"No more than a reprimand, my fellows. We're to be cautious in future."

"Too close a call," Pope said. "Think about the mobs in *Julius Caesar*. Their affections resemble a feather on a wave, isn't that how you say it, Will? Ever bobbing to and fro. We must thank our lucky stars that the Earl of Essex was not as successful as Henry Bullingbrook."

In that case, we'd have been on the winner's side, I thought, but kept that to myself. Civil war and the defeat of Queen Elizabeth was too horrifying a possibility.

Frances went daily to her shop despite the foul weather and unsettled mood in London, but along with the rest of the Lord Chamberlain's Men, I lay low after our reprimand, and the theatres remained closed.

At home, I practiced my singing and read the tragedies of Seneca, neither of which put my mind at ease. Johnny was incommunicado but safe at Sir Robert Cecil's house; that much I'd discovered. But news was scarce. London taverns were losing business and Paul's Yard was empty, not even news criers. Much as folks loved gossip and rumor, fear kept conferences private.

There is no remedy; I must cony-catch; I must shift.
FALSTAFF, *THE MERRY WIVES OF WINDSOR*

CHAPTER XXVIII
February 1601

On February 19, 1601, Essex and Southampton were tried and found guilty of high treason. On February 20, Queen Elizabeth signed the death warrant for thirty-four–year old Robert Devereux, Earl of Essex. He was to be beheaded, a traitor's death.

We'd barely absorbed the news when, to our astonishment, the Queen requested the Lord Chamberlain's Men to play *The Merry Wives of Windsor* at Court that very night, the eve of Essex's execution.

"We've been forgiven!" Augustine Phillips crowed after he read the message from Cecil.

"It makes no sense," Tom Pope said, "A bizarre request, at ridiculously short notice."

"We played it at the Globe not three months ago, Tom," Phillips said. "You remember Falstaff's lines perfectly well."

Pope gave him a withering look. "That's not what I mean."

The Queen had moved quickly to sign Essex's death warrant, though surely it cost her dear. But for her to choose such a frivolous play on the eve of his execution? A statement, no question, but what sort?

I thought of all the times she had forgiven him. Perhaps he'd felt invulnerable. But raising a rebellion was worse than bursting in on her before she was dressed and wigged. Distressed as she was then, she forgave her Robbie.

Shakespeare was certain that Essex's refusal to humble himself before the Queen after his arrest, his failure to beg for mercy on bended knee, had been the deepest offense—and grief—she'd suffered. She had no choice but to sign that death warrant—and now, apparently, to make light of it with this jesting play.

After our run-through of *Merry Wives*, I caught Shakespeare alone. "What do you think about this play, tonight of all times?"

"The Queen is said to delight in *Merry Wives*. But why tonight?" Shakespeare lowered his voice. "Yes, she's forgiven us, but this is more an act of defiance to Essex. He'll spend the night praying and contemplating his death, while the Queen laughs at the antics of Sir John Falstaff."

"Grim humor."

"Indeed. Her greatest test in a royal life based on performance."

I reported this interchange to Frances.

"Queen Elizabeth has a heart beneath her bodice, held in as tightly as is her body in its corset," she said. "I feel for her."

"And Essex? I can't say I pity him."

"Another willful man who thought he could get away with anything. I do not pity the Earl of Essex, not one bit." Her last words were spoken so harshly that I suspected they encompassed the Earl's relatives and cohorts, including Johnny Cooke.

As I practiced the lines of Mistress Alice Ford, another idea occurred as to why Queen Elizabeth would choose *The Merry Wives of Windsor*. I'd never have thought stout Sir John Falstaff, full of lust and folly, an Earl of Essex sort of man, yet there was an odd link between them. The play is set in Windsor, but it doesn't feel historical, not like Shakespeare's earlier histories, where Falstaff is Prince Hal's drinking pal before Hal becomes King Henry V.

Although Falstaff is a knight, *Merry Wives* doesn't take place amidst royalty and nobility. The citizens of Windsor are ordinary English folk. Falstaff does his best to disrupt town life by seducing not one but two married women, who triumph over him again and again. After his final defeat, the folk of Windsor carry on as before, only happier. Everyone goes home laughing, even Falstaff.

"Our job is to please the Queen," Pope said on our way to Whitehall Palace, determined to get every possible laugh as Sir John Falstaff.

Looking through the curtain into the Great Chamber, I watched the royal party enter. Queen Elizabeth was dressed in a black gown spangled with gold, the one she wore for the portrait where she holds a live ermine. In a glittering regal way, she'd dressed in mourning tonight, as had Essex when last he appeared at Court in black filigreed with silver.

Through our performance, the Queen's mask of mild amusement never slipped. We kept up a merry pace as the wives duped Falstaff. There was no lack of laughter, though subdued.

In the tiring room after we'd taken our bows to light applause, Augustine Phillips said, "We acquitted ourselves well." Murmured responses. By the time we were out of our costumes, all but an occasional torch in the corridors had been snuffed, a single servant remaining to shut the back palace door behind us.

Frances and I did not attend the execution of the Earl of Essex on Tower Hill, but Shakespeare stopped by our house afterward with a report. Essex had removed his doublet to reveal a red waistcoat, and, horribly, the executioner needed three strokes.

"Essex spoke bravely and humbly, confessing his pride and vanity and asking forgiveness of Queen and God," Shakespeare said. "He should have had the sense to beg Her Majesty's forgiveness when he had the chance."

"Like a character in Greek tragedy," I said. "Hubris, isn't that what it's called?"

"Yes, hubris."

"The ladies in my shop say that the Queen loved him dearly," Frances said.

"So she did, but after his early gallantry, Essex, ever spoiled and willful, failed to revere her. And yet—" Shakespeare paused. "In many ways, Essex was the last knight of old, full of zeal and a

heightened sense of honor. There'll never again be his like; he out-
lived his time by a good century. The man for today is more a Sir
Robert Cecil, pragmatic and clever. What difference that Cecil is
crippled? Essex, of course, possessed a magnificent manly bearing."
He sighed. "There are sure to be virile, vain young men in times to
come, but they'll have no real power and their manners will offer no
threat. The Queen couldn't be deceived by such a man as Essex; she
endlessly rebuked him. Yet she loved him, vainglorious as he was.
A charming, elegant rogue."

Shakespeare's words so resembled a eulogy that we remained
silent. Frances was the first to speak.

"When a woman makes a decisive action, she often comes to
regret it, even in much lesser matters than a queen issuing a death
warrant."

Shakespeare looked up. "Oh?"

"Women tell me stories as I fit their gowns. Most often they
regret discouraging a suitor. Or speaking maliciously. They wish
they'd better known their hearts or controlled their anger."

"Rash behavior in love is of a different order than a death sentence," Shakespeare said. "Queen Elizabeth will always lament the
loss of Robert Devereux. Yet in the end she had no choice."

Queen Elizabeth had gained command and respect by her
prompt dealing with Essex, despite her private grief. Never again
would a young man court her, flatter her, or warm her heart and
body as Essex did. No more embraces or tender touches.

Henry Wriothesley, the Earl of Southampton, beautiful as he
once was, never aroused the Queen's affections. After Essex's execution, however, urged by Southampton's mother and the argument
that his crime was lesser, Queen Elizabeth commuted his death
sentence to life imprisonment in the Tower.

More zealous in her monarchical duties than ever, she expressed
no desire for players and entertainments. Her ladies whispered that
the Queen suffered a malaise her doctors could not diagnose. "An
illness of the heart," was their verdict.

Meeting me in Paul's Yard, Moll Frith was skeptical. "Do you really believe that there's a heart inside the Queen's rich garments?"

"One full of courage."

"She should have ordered a fine-bladed French sword, as was used to dispatch her mother Anne Boleyn. Hacking Essex's neck again and again—rotten Englishmen to delight in such spectacle."

"I'd not expect that from you, Moll. Aren't you an Englishman yourself?"

"I play the man for my own reasons. I can best those blood-lusty toughs who relished Essex's gory end, but I needn't join them. True, I live as I choose, but I'm not a rotten Englishman, whatever mad reputation I may have. I know what I'm about, same as you."

"You roar through London."

"So we must, keeping our wits about us. I'm off to see *The Shoemaker's Holiday*. Come along!"

"May as well. Only comedies onstage these days, but the Queen's having none of them. William Shakespeare says we must shake her out of her melancholy."

"Good luck with that. Have you heard? She's released your brother Johnny from Cecil's service."

"His year's not up."

"No, but she relented, and Cecil was happy to see the back of him. He suspected that Johnny maintained his ties to Lady Elizabeth Sidney and didn't want any friend of the Essex faction under his roof."

"Do you know where he's gone?"

"Probably to Belvoir Castle, Rutland's country estate. That's where Lady Elizabeth went when Essex was arrested. Her husband got off easy, if you regard a fine of thirty thousand pounds easy, living under house arrest along with his two rebel brothers at their uncle's in some even more remote place."

"Whatever will Johnny will do at Belvoir Castle?"

"Walk in the snow and write whatever it is he likes to write— satires, is it?" Moll looked amused. "As dangerous as depicting the fall of rulers."

"Johnny should know enough to be cautious."

Moll looked dubious. "In any case, he'll have company. Most of those who sided with Essex fled to country estates where they dine well and wander around idle. I wouldn't last a day in such a place. No excitement, no action, no surprises."

"They've probably had their fill of excitement and action."

"Let's go, Sander. *The Shoemaker's Holiday* beckons."

We linked arms, two roaring boys off for a bit of fun. Thinking of Johnny in exile at snowy Belvoir Castle heightened my zest to celebrate the joys of London.

PART THREE

SUNS SETTING
AND SUNS RISING

Who knows himself a braggart
Let him fear this, for it will come to pass
That every braggart shall be found an ass.
PAROLLES, *ALL'S WELL THAT ENDS WELL*

CHAPTER XXIX
September 1601

Autumn came early. Leaves touched with red, birds flying south, the sticky summer thankfully over. Savoring the breeze wafting upriver, I was one of the last to arrive at the Globe.

"Robert Cecil has sent a request," Phillips said as I walked through the door. "We're to mount a private performance of *All's Well that Ends Well* in the Queen's Presence Chamber at Whitehall day after tomorrow."

"How did he hear about it?" Armin asked. "*All's Well* isn't booked at the Globe until after the new year."

"The Lord Chamberlain must have mentioned it to Her Majesty," Phillips said. "This sounds like one of her whims."

"After the gloomy news from the palace, I'm glad she has such a whim," Burbage said. "Short notice, though."

"At least we've learned our parts." I looked at Johnny, who nodded. Returned from Belvoir Castle, he'd been reinstated with the Lord Chamberlain's Men and would play Parolles.

"I've never heard of actors playing in the Queen's Presence Chamber," Armin said.

"Just us and a handful of her closest," Burbage said. "What do you think, Will?"

"We couldn't ask for a better opportunity. Reply that we'll bring our costume chest and arrive early to assess the playing space."

I wasn't so sure. True, Johnny had completed his enforced service to Cecil, and Moll reported that no one had removed the record of our marriage from the register at St. Alfage's. All danger seemed past. This prospect of close royal scrutiny shook me out of complacency.

Walking home I fell into step with Shakespeare. He picked up a drifting playbill for a show at the Fortune and smiled. Ours was the company called upon to lighten the Queen's grief, not Admiral's.

"Should I be uneasy, Will?"

"Certainly not. This performance is even better than opening *All's Well* at the Globe. Ben Jonson will eat his heart out when he hears, along with every player in London."

A pie seller balancing her tray on her head called to us, "Fresh pork pie. A penny for a pie."

Shakespeare squeezed past. "No thank you, dear."

"I mean, I'll be playing Helena practically under Her Majesty's nose. Helena argues with Parolles about the value of virginity, for mercy's sake."

"I thought you liked that part, Sander. Helena's virginity has an almost magical force. Besides her father's secret medicine, it helps her cure the King of France. When she loses her virginity, it's by her own choice."

"I don't mind that Helena sleeps with her husband under false pretenses. But I'm afraid that Queen Elizabeth will be watching me as a woman. A married woman."

"As she did when you played Gertrude and—"

"Those were in huge halls. The Queen might not recognize Parolles onstage, but here she'll see him as my brother Johnny, the man she punished. She may wonder if Frances and I live together still. Why remind her?" I stepped over a streaming gutter, holding my nose. "I imagine you had Johnny in mind when you wrote the part of Bertram, that shallow selfish fellow. *All's Well* seems like a version of our own lives held up for the Queen's examination."

"Not at all. Burbage, not Johnny, plays Bertram, and the bedtrick in the play involves one woman replacing another in Bertram's bed. That's not your story."

"Not directly, no. But Queen Elizabeth has as subtle a mind and as leaping an imagination as you yourself. She understands complex allusions. This *feels* like our story."

"Don't you want to play Helena?"

I swallowed my doubts. "Of course I do."

"The Queen is suffering too greatly to wonder about your marriage. Our play will vanquish her sorrows for a couple of hours. She'll especially enjoy wise Countess Roussillon and the clowns." As we navigated the pathway amidst pedestrians and beggars, he added, "I'll confess, bedtrick stories began to interest me around the time of your marriage, not that I'd put your version on stage. The old stories don't fault a woman for gaining a husband through such a deception. Once he embraced her in bed, even if he'd believed her to be someone else, he married her. In fact, I have another plot in mind, another bedtrick. This one, I think, will involve a holy sister."

I shook my head. "You're incorrigible!"

"Oh, it gets better: you'll play a novitiate in a holy order."

I couldn't imagine such a story or such a role in Anglican England. But why not? Another new woman for the Queen's delectation. Should she live so long, but I kept that worry to myself.

The rest of the way home, I reflected on the peculiarities of my role as Helena. Though a physician's daughter with little status, she possesses sufficient confidence to offer to heal the King of France. Bertram's mother the Countess of Roussillon loves her, but Bertram himself feels only scorn. When compelled to marry Helena, Bertram publicly disgraces her, but the King of France insists. After they marry, Bertram leaves immediately for the wars in Italy, sending a letter to Helena saying she cannot call him husband until she gets the ring from his finger that he never removes and his child is begotten in her body—which will be never. Yet Helena pursues him to Italy disguised as a pilgrim and finds a way to do the impossible: substitute herself for the woman he lusts after, obtain the ring, and conceive the child.

I recalled how Burbage played Bertram our first time through
the play, disgruntled after Helena wins him back by means of the
bedtrick. Shakespeare looked disapproving, but before he could say
anything, Robert Armin spoke up.

"You've got it wrong, Richard. Helena healed the king's fistula
of the body and now heals Bertram's illness of the heart. That's the
point."

When Shakespeare nodded agreement, Burbage looked doubtful
and sighed. "All right. I'll play it that way." I too had doubts. Can such
a man ever love Helena dearly?

The Countess' clown Lavatch and Bertram's friend Parolles will
certainly make the Queen laugh. Late in the play, after he's exposed
as a bragging coward, Parolles ends up a clown in the noble Lafew's
household, where he can make good use of his folly.

Not so different from Johnny, I thought. After his return from
Belvoir, he'd come to sup with us. Frances' attitude to him alternated
between aloof and irritated, but she laughed when she heard us
rehearse Parolles and Helena's conversation about virginity. Like
Parolles, Johnny could clown his way out of most anything.

Nonetheless, I'd prefer no royal eyes observing the similarities
of Bertram's treatment of Helena to Johnny's of Frances. May
Shakespeare be right that the Queen's mind was too preoccupied
to care.

The day of our performance, we stood in costume outside the
Presence Chamber, all but Robert Armin, who played Lavatch.
Shakespeare secured permission for him to enter by way of the
Queen's private entrance, partly, he laughed, because the Her
Majesty had fallen half in love with Armin. "He'll leave some of his
wit behind for her benefit."

From the side door we could see the chamber transformed into
an intimate theatre lit by torches. I'd imagined the Queen would
arrive with pomp, but she was already seated, wearing a gown of
deep purple velvet. Around her fluttered her ladies, as close to us

as groundlings in the pit. A quick glance showed her eyes fever-bright and alert, but no amount of facepaint could cover the hollows beneath them, nor the lines creasing her brow. As she coughed, one of her ladies patted her gently.

The wall's white panels gleamed in the flickering golden light, the alternating black panels shadowed into nothingness, and the relief sculptures on the wall appeared grotesque. Candles lined the front of the stage, a raised platform extending the breadth of the room. Would our faces look as eerie in this light as the sculptures did?

I would focus on making Helena's plight touch the Queen's heart. Augustine Phillips, in a rare female role, played Bertram's mother, the Countess of Roussillon, made up with Her Majesty's white facepaint. The Countess and Helena, along with kindly old Lafew and Shakespeare as the King of France, should do much to engage royal sympathies.

Henry Condell blew a muted fanfare on his recorder, and the small audience sat quietly as we entered dressed in black: Bertram and his mother, with Lafew and me following discreetly behind, all in black. A scene of mourning is perfect beginning for a comedy. Things can only get better.

Queen Elizabeth, reputed to have not smiled in months, nearly choked on laughter when Parolles' fellow soldiers capture and blind-fold him and, speaking in an invented language, frighten him not only into speaking ill of them but revealing military secrets. When they remove the blindfold, Parolles is shamed to recognize his interrogators, but his humiliation is brief. The war has been settled by treaty; his treachery cost the men nothing.

Parolles' exposure causes him no anguish. "If my heart were great, would burst at this. . . . Simply the thing I am shall make me live."

But then Parolles, now serving as Lafew's jester, reveals to the King of France Bertram's tryst with the young woman Diana. As Parolles was publicly unmasked, so is Bertram. He discovers that the woman who met him in the dark chamber was not Diana but the wife he rejected. Helena has fulfilled his seemingly impossible terms: she wears Bertram's ring and carries his child.

Bertram addresses the King, but his eyes were on me, seeing Helena anew. "If she, my liege, can make me know this clearly, I'll love her dearly, ever, ever dearly." Burbage spoke the lines with warm affection and a sense of revelation. A happy ending of sorts.

As we bowed, the Queen's eyes shone with tears, and Sir Robert Cecil pressed a heavy coin into each of our hands.

I heard Lady Isabel ask the Queen what she thought of the marriage of Bertram and Helena. "The title tells us. All's well so far as can be in this imperfect world."

After queen and guests departed, we moved silently across the half-lit corridor to our tiring room where a flagon of wine sat, encircled with Venetian glasses.

Burbage lifted his. "To the Queen's health and to fortune!"

Fortune was whimsical in this play, I thought as I sipped the nectar-sweet wine. We'd made the right choice for this performance, but the ending could be played differently. We packed away our costumes and set out for the Mermaid.

Walking down the long back hallway, Johnny said, "We'll gather friends as we go."

Shakespeare laughed. "To boast, no doubt. You are a Parolles indeed, Johnny Cooke!"

We pushed through the side gate of the palace yard and through Westminster like a gang of Italian braggadocios, arms linked and voices loud.

Rumor had brought out theatre-lovers of all sorts. Even the most envious actor was curious about our unprecedented royal summons: the Royal Presence Chamber, of all places! Frances met us along the way and walked between Johnny and me. We entered the Mermaid like conquering heroes.

As exuberance rose, I remained in a reflective mood, intensified by another cup of wine. Frances and Johnny were laughing together. They seemed to be in a bubble of their own. But of course they would be, I told myself. It's noisy in here! Still, I hesitated joining them.

"They say you captivated the Queen tonight." Moll Frith's hearty voice interrupted my reverie. "Why are you moping?"

"I'm thinking."

Moll followed my eyes to Frances and Johnny. "You know there's nothing you can do. You'd best leave them to it."

"To what?"

"To a little amusement. You can't own that woman, wife or no. Enjoy your triumph. My friends will buy you all you can drink for telling us about your performance. Come along, and do be more jolly!"

Moll took my arm and I allowed myself to be dragged off. I caught a glimpse of Frances and Johnny joining an impromptu jig in the main room. The crowd increased so that I could barely see the two of them when I joined Moll's rowdies.

But love is blind, and lovers cannot see
The pretty follies that themselves commit;
For, if they could, Cupid himself would blush.
JESSICA, *THE MERCHANT OF VENICE*

CHAPTER XXX
September 1601

I fell into a deep sleep after stumbling up to bed, not bothering to eat anything. No doubt I drank a cup too many with Moll's companions.

Some time later I awoke feeling ill. My first thought was that the house was haunted. I reached for Frances, but her place was empty. I held myself in silent suspense: what was amiss? I could identify no specific sound, yet surely something was wrong. Perhaps bats were nesting in the rafters?

I rolled out of bed and opened the bedroom door. The shadows had an orange tinge, as if the fire burned low, and the house echoed silence. "Frances?" I called. "Are you home?"

Her voice came faintly from the adjoining bedroom. "Good night, Sander."

"Good night." I returned to bed and slept uneasily, waking before dawn, my face wet, unable to recall the dream that caused my tears. Had I been curled into Frances' warmth through the night, I'd not have wept for any reason.

Disinclined to rise so early in the cold house, I pulled the bedding close. But my thoughts were troubling, and I couldn't lie in the dark another moment. Quietly I opened the door to the other bedroom.

Frances' head was on her pillow, her breathing even. I tiptoed down the narrow staircase and coaxed flames from the embers.

A sentence came to me as if spoken by an inner voice. *You cannot be what she wants.*

With that, memories of the previous night flooded me, Frances and Johnny laughing together, Shakespeare glancing at them with a speculative look and then at me, the two of them dancing in rollicking good humor. Then I'd gone off with Moll and her boisterous friends—foolishly, it now seemed.

I looked around the fire-brightened room as if it were an alien space. A blanket was thrown across the near chair. Frances must have sat there last night. Beside the hearth: bread, a wine jug, and crumbs of pork pie. I pictured Frances making her supper here alone, but other images intruded.

The house oppressed me. I dressed quickly, buttoned up my warmest doublet, and gently closed the door behind me. I headed to Smithfield Market, sure to be busy and bloody in the dawn as London's meat supply was hung and hacked. Nothing like butchering reality to clear the indistinct images tumbling about in my head.

But when I came upon the small church of St. Sepulchre, I turned down the alleyway to the small brass staff of Asclepius marking the door of Dr. Simon Garnet's house. The old doctor claimed never to sleep, catching naps through the day and night like a cat.

He opened the door and took my hand. "Come in, come in, Alexander," he said in his distinctive sing-song. "It has been too lo-ong." Too long indeed: I'd not visited him since just after my marriage, when he'd said the connection between Frances and me was rich with possibility—and complicated. Still, he was sure to have heard about the death of our baby Marie.

Dr. Garnet's outer chamber was the same as ever. Whitewashed walls, bunches of herbs hanging from the rafters, and a stack of books piled on the writing table, where he'd been working. He blew out the candle, led me to the inner chamber, and lighted an old metal lamp that appeared to have come from a crumbling church.

Although Dr. Simon Garnet was more astrologer and mathematician than alchemist, I noticed new urns, beakers, and burner on a table in the dim corner.

Garnet sat on his neat white bed, which appeared not to have been slept in, and I pulled up a chair.

"Never have you called on me at such an hour. What troubles you, my child?"

"I'm scarcely a child. I feel the burden of years."

Garnet laughed. "All twenty-three of them. But the young suffer more than we who have known every joy and seen every evil. A time comes when one can no longer suffer, only sigh or smile as the occasion demands, and carry on for another sweet short day."

"You haven't changed, Dr. Garnet. I cannot tell you how that heartens me."

"Long ago I survived plague. How could anything destroy my peace after that?"

"I need some of your peace."

"Then you must learn the lesson of the agèd. It's not impossible for a young person to grasp, but most uncommon. Youth are consumed by flames of emotion and impulse. Can you step back and coolly observe?"

His words brought William Shakespeare to mind. He did just that, stand back and observe. Garnet was waiting, his eyes distant as if his sight extended beyond this room.

"Is there a particular reason?"

"I see something coming that could fill you with anger or sorrow. The only way to inner peace is to eschew those emotions. Observe. Sympathize. I could say forgive, but better that you feel no need to."

"Shall I be wronged?"

Garnet took a deep breath. "No, Alexander. You will not be wronged. You will be given a gift, but only if you forgo rage and fear will you discover how precious."

"You speak in riddles."

"My wisdom is not obscure to one with open eyes. Or more important, an open heart, an open soul. When you feel the urge to fury or grief, remember my words. Step back and observe. Cultivate patience."

My laugh was harsh. "I don't even know what my worst fears are, and you say they will happen."

"I speak of what I sense might happen."

"I'll remember. Cultivate patience." I imitated his manner of speaking, stretching out "pa-atience." I began pacing the small room. "You're maddening, Dr. Garnet. I know, I'm not to yield to anger. You hint at all sorts of terrible things but tell me nothing useful."

"Sit beside me."

I perched on the edge of his bed.

"Look me in the eye. No matter what happens, you must silence your judgments and maintain a clear and loving heart."

"Do I need to watch my step or be on guard?"

"You already do that, am I right?" I nodded at the obvious. "All I'm saying is, whatever happens, Alexander, view it as a boon."

"Like Johnny's sentence to serve Robert Cecil you mean? He gained from the loss of stage-playing."

"Always the wisest course. Now, shall we breakfast? You have eaten nothing today."

Drinking Dr. Garnet's fragrant herbal brew and eating the dark bread with fresh butter, I felt the wise man's peace creep over me.

Outside in the foggy morning, workers came out of their dwellings with bleary eyes. Instead of going home, I walked to London Bridge, where shops were not yet open. The Thames below displayed its eternal movement, tides ebbing, tides flowing. I saw no face I recognized. No John Taylor on the river, no player or familiar tradesman crossing the Bridge.

At length, the person I encountered was my brother Johnny, coming toward me. He looked disheveled, as if he'd slept in a cranny like one of Moll's boys.

"Where have you been?" I asked. "Aren't your lodgings in the opposite direction?"

"Yes, but it was too late last night to disturb the landlady."

"Why late?"

"Oh you know. Too much celebrating after our performance at Whitehall. I should have kept my eye on the time."

"You don't look so good," I said.

"I ended up at an inn sharing a bed with a couple of restless wayfarers. I don't recommend it."

I laughed. "I'll avoid any such. You could have stayed at Westminster Abbey. Isn't there some sort of hospital there?"

"I think so, but I didn't want to bother the priests."

"You must have been very late," I said.

"Afraid so. Better go clean myself up."

Johnny enjoyed a jolly time with all and sundry, but had never been a big drinker. I attributed that to our father's destructive drinking: neither of us would go that way.

The image of Johnny dancing with Frances came back to me. He made a point of treating her like a sister, affectionate but deferring to me as her husband. Since returning from Belvoir, Johnny seemed even less interested in our situation, no overstaying his welcome, nothing more than family friendship. Yet there was a clutching at my heart, the old familiar doubt: Where do Frances' affections lie?

Sitting on the wherry dock, I watched the busy river until it was near time for rehearsal of our upcoming *Hamlet*.

Stay calm. Cultivate patience.

Love is merely a madness. . . . Yet I profess curing it by counsel.
ROSALIND, *AS YOU LIKE IT*

CHAPTER XXXI
December 1601

December kept us busy at the Globe, revivals of play after play. And Frances' shop grew more hectic by the day, holiday finery in demand. She and I found little time for private conversation, tired at the end of the day and glad of a respite of warmth and good food, prepared by Rebecca earlier and left on the hob when she went to the widow's.

One night when we sat alone, Frances, who'd been swirling her spoon through her bowl of mutton stew without taking a bite, leaned forward and said in a quiet voice: "I have something to tell you, Sander."

A piece of carrot lodged in my throat and I coughed it free.

She reached across the table for my hand. "I hope you'll be happy. It's news that affects you too."

"Oh?" I tried to look encouraging, but trepidation filled my heart. "Go ahead, Frances. Let's hear it."

In a whisper she said, "I'm expecting a baby."

"Say that again."

"You heard me. I am pregnant." She closed her eyes.

My apprehensions flooded in, blood rushing to my cheeks and blows hammering my heart. Surprise. Anger. Shock.

When I managed to speak, my voice was flat. "How did that happen?"

Frances said nothing.

"Is Johnny the father?"

A faint nod. "I didn't do it to hurt you."

"That I believe—you didn't think of me at all!"

"I'm thinking of you now. Oh, Sander, I hope you can be happy. We'll have a family."

"Why didn't you tell me that you're seeing Johnny? Or better, before hand. You just—you just did it."

She answered in a small voice. "Only the once, unplanned. The night after you played *All's Well* for Queen Elizabeth."

"I knew something had happened. That night I thought how much Johnny resembled Bertram, and then he proved it. Callow and thoughtless and driven by—" I swallowed the word "lust." "I'm sorry Frances. I should have seen this coming. I'm going out for a walk."

"It's raining."

"I'll wear a cloak."

"Don't go. I hope you see what a blessing a child will be. We loved Marie so much! It nearly destroyed us to lose her. Since I've suspected that I'm pregnant, I keep thinking about her. This baby will make up for that loss."

I heard Dr. Garnet's voice in my head and suppressed my angry words, replying as calmly as I could. "I mourned Marie's death as much as you did. But this is a different sort of challenge." A long silence. "What about Johnny?"

"I haven't told him. You're the father."

"Please, Frances. Don't. I am not the father."

"So far as anyone knows you are. You're my husband."

"That's a sham."

"Now Sander—"

"You love my brother."

"I don't. Not the way I love you."

"You mean you do not love me the way you love him." I rose. "I have to think about this. Alone."

"Do stay—"

"I'll return."

I closed the door behind me and stepped into the wet twilight, rain a mere drizzle. Light glimmered inside houses, perhaps false warmth as in our house, a glowing window and inside, pregnant Frances.

I inhaled the damp, smoke-filled air. Dr. Garnet's words tumbled together: gift—silence judgment—maintain a clear and loving heart—gift. Cultivate patience.

As if that were easy.

I passed noisy taverns, groups heading toward the river and Bankside entertainments. The occasional watchman paid me no heed.

Walking, walking, walking, I found myself on the steps of St. Botolph's where baby Marie was buried. The churchyard was dark but the church itself gleamed with candlelight. Inside, evensong had begun. I stood shadowed at the back, listening to the music and stilling my thoughts.

The church was old, with a carved Madonna and child in a niche near me. The serene face of Virgin Mary, chubby baby Jesus. Our Marie was never such an infant, though Frances resembled Mary when gazing at her dear, sickly child.

I took a deep breath. We had another blessed chance at parenthood. That's the boon Dr. Garnet meant.

Joseph was not the father of Jesus. Frances' pregnancy was no immaculate conception, but she conceived the only way she could. Johnny would be no more a father to this child than he had been to Marie.

I stood quiet until the benediction, my mind clear on what I must do, difficult as it would be. I hurried home through dim streets.

Frances sat by the fire, which cast a glow on her troubled face. I put a hand on her shoulder.

"I love you, Frances. You can rely on me."

We sat together, a fresh log leaping into flame.

"I know this is hard news," Frances said. "Johnny and I lost ourselves that night. I haven't seen him since and don't plan to."

"So what was that night about? I don't understand."

Her eyes were large and moist, and I felt tears in my own. Then Dr. Garnet's words echoed, and Moll's, too.

"Perhaps I do understand," I said, feeling my way forward. "You don't need to explain yourself. It's easy to think the worst of Johnny, but I don't own you, and I shall try to see this as a gift for us both."

"I hope you can, Sander. With all my heart I hope you can. I wanted a child so badly. I cannot but regard this as divine providence."

My heart softened. Frances had kept to herself her distress, her fears, her hope. No, she needn't explain.

We leaned toward each other into an embrace. The only sound was the spit and crackle of the logs and our breathing.

I felt Frances' heartbeat and held her more tightly.

"You're the one I married," she whispered in my ear. "I love you."

After long minutes we released each other and gazed, eye to eye.

"I suppose I've been thinking like a man." I attempted a laugh. "Wanting you all to myself. But I'm not—"

Frances put a finger on my lips. "Shhh. We're partners. Johnny is no more than this child's uncle."

"Does that grieve you?"

"He and I will never be together. I know that."

"Would you want more with him if he were willing?"

"No," Frances said firmly. "My pregnancy feels like more than the result of a moment's whim. It feels right." She smiled. "This is how our marriage began, Sander. I shall be a mother!"

"I want you to be a mother," I said, thinking, if only I could have been the father. Aloud I added, "A child will be a joy in the house."

Gran had honored a divine force she called Bounteous Nature. If ever Bounteous Nature had played a part in my life, it was now.

"I'm happy for you, Frances. I'm happy for us."

I wanted more than anything to mean it.

Next morning I walked to Amelia's. The day more resembled autumn than winter. After the rains, a fresh breeze blew in from the open fields to the north, carrying the few remaining fallen leaves in a dancing drift.

In her parlor Amelia sat with Harry, bent over a book.

"Look at this, Master Cooke." Harry held up the book. "I'm learning to read!"

"Good for you!"

"Mama says a boy who can read goes far in the world. I do like stories!"

"Me too, Harry. Me too."

Amelia glanced up and, seeing my expression, said, "Can you carry on by yourself for a few minutes, Harry?"

"Or you could go practice a song on your flute," I said to the boy. "You can play it for us, and then show me what you're reading."

As Harry went to the kitchen, Amelia spoke quietly. "What is it, Sandro? You look distraught."

"Strange to say, I feel almost happy."

"Yet uneasy. Let's have a cup of cider."

As Amelia glided across the room, I admired her slow grace in the heavy blue skirt. Alfonso must be off on another of his voyages. In his absence Amelia became sufficient unto herself. Amelia's pristine beauty, olive skin against bright white linen, was restful to my tumultuous heart. This woman could arouse men's deepest passions, but within herself dwelt a calm I'd never so appreciated as today.

In the kitchen Harry played an unfamiliar tune, repeating passages until he got them right. The side window was open a crack, blackbirds pecking beneath the bare maple.

Amelia put a cup of warm cider, fragrant with cinnamon, in my hands and sat on the bench beside me. "Tell me."

I took a deep breath. "Frances is pregnant."

"Oh!" Amelia started, and a few drops of cider splashed onto her skirt. She brushed it away. "Are you angry?"

"No, more in a tumult. I could be happy: a child! But . . ." I trailed off.

Amelia finished the thought. "The father."

"My brother, of course."

"Oh dear. The three of you do stay bound together."

"I don't want to share parenthood with Johnny."

"I doubt you'll do that. He hasn't changed. Johnny didn't want to be a father before, and if anything, is less inclined now. You're the father—and something of a mother as well."

"Frances said as much."

"Your woman's heart will be warmed by this child. The world will see you as father, but you may have any relation to the baby that you wish."

"If it lives."

"I'm certain this one will do better than poor little Marie. How far along is Frances?"

"Some two months."

"This baby will be strong. Welcome it with joy."

"That's more or less what Dr. Garnet told me, but I didn't realize he was talking about a baby. Regard a complicated event as a gift, he said. No doubt I shall, but it's a long way from here to there."

"Seven months?" Amelia smiled.

"That's not what I mean. Time goes fast or slow, depending."

"As you say playing Ganymede."

"'Time travels in divers paces with divers persons.' No, what I mean is, we shall go from Alexander Cooke, husband, and Frances, wife, to whom no one pays any particular notice, to Alexander and Frances Cooke as parents. I'd rather not receive that attention."

"You handled it fine before. Friends who know you're not the man you appear will keep the secret."

"People gossip, even friends, and our closest friends will guess Johnny's part. This puts him in a bad light. And me."

Amelia laughed. "You can't be a cuckold!"

"No?"

"I was teasing, but don't give anyone's reactions half a thought. Think of the baby as a blessing, and let the rest go."

I sipped my cider.

"You know I'm right." She called out to Harry. "That sounds good. Come play for us."

When his song ended, the boy said, "This is my book, Master Cooke. It's a fairy tale about a brave boy called Jack."

"Read it to me next time I call, Harry. I'm due at the theatre now. Promise."

"I promise," he said solemnly.

Telling Amelia about Frances' pregnancy prepared me for Moll Frith. When I saw her on my way to the Globe, I slapped her back.

"Congratulate me, Moll. I'm to be a father!"

"Well, well. You've outdone me again, Alexander Cooke. Good work."

Moll asked me nothing! I felt like a proud father indeed.

He loved her, sir, and loved her not.
PAROLLES ABOUT BERTRAM

As thou art a knave, and no knave.
What an equivocal companion is this!
KING OF FRANCE, *ALL'S WELL THAT ENDS WELL*

CHAPTER XXXII
Winter 1601–1602

On Christmas Eve I encountered Johnny at Cheapside. "Come have a cup of holiday cheer!"

"Sorry, Sander. I'm on my way to meet Lady Elizabeth and her guests at Westminster. We're celebrating her husband Rutland's return to London. Maybe tomorrow."

I grabbed his arm. "You have time for a quick cup. We have a surprise for you."

"It had better be good—and quick." He followed me with an impatient stride.

Frances sat by the fire, seeming aglow from more than the heat. She wore a new green dress which caught the hazel gleam in her eyes, a shirt ruffled at neck and cuffs, and a pale green calico kerchief around her shoulders. She'd arranged her hair and dressed so prettily for me, with no idea I'd be bringing my brother home. My heart lifted, any worry about Johnny as a rival blotted out. "Johnny came along to pay homage to our very own Madonna."

Johnny stopped mid step. "What?"

Frances flushed pink and blurted it out. "My baby is due in early summer."

"Who—I—I—who—"

Frances took my hand. "*Our* baby, I should have said."

"Your—your—" Johnny's blithe confidence guttered out like a faulty candlewick.

As I handed round three brimming cups, he rallied. "To the baby. To my nephew."

"Or niece," Frances said.

He looked stunned. By all appearances he'd forgotten that impulsive night with Frances. Ever since he'd been circling around Lady Elizabeth like a drone around the queen bee, no thought of Frances or me. When he and I met at the Globe, it was all business.

I didn't delight in his discomfort, though I found his rapid shifts of expression amusing.

"I must say, I didn't expect this." Johnny gulped down his wine. "What do you want me to—"

"Oh, we don't want a thing," I said.

"That makes it all a lot easier."

"What do you mean, 'it all'?" I asked.

"That you're happy to father this baby, God preserve him. Or her."

"Amen." Frances voice was chilling.

"I must be off to Westminster. You have much to celebrate. Happy Christmas!"

Frances shut the door on Johnny's finely dressed self and scowled at me. "You should have asked me first. I hated how relieved he was that we expect nothing of him. Mercy, mercy." That was as close as Frances came to swearing. Then she sighed. "I suppose it's just as well. You didn't consult me before confiding in Amelia and Moll."

"Nothing to be ashamed of, nothing to forgive. And it's Christmas Eve."

She gave me a kiss. "I appreciate your generosity, Sander, truly I do."

"We're married."

I followed her into the kitchen where Rebecca had been making a racket with the pots and pans.

"Did you hear us talking?" I asked her. "Catch a word or two?"

Rebecca's grey eyes looked from Frances to me. "A little."

"Then you know we're having a baby."

"I love babies!"

"It's due in June," Frances said. "I planned to apprentice you in the shop when Joan becomes a fully qualified seamstress, but I'll need you here till then."

"Thank you." Rebecca took Frances' hand in her floury one. "When the baby comes, you can count on me."

"You may as well tell our guests tonight, Sander," Frances said.

I imagined she felt an anxious twinge at the thought of going public, a carry-over from her shame over her first pregnancy. But who would look askance? We were married, and tonight our only guests would be Joan and Will Shakespeare.

Dinner turned out to be a celebration of baby Cooke. Joan bubbled with excitement, and Shakespeare seemed entertained at the prospect. Joan didn't imagine that anyone other than me had fathered the child, nor, so far as I knew, did Rebecca. Shakespeare likely suspected who did. I could see his imagination sparking.

"We hope you'll be godfather, Will," I said.

"With pleasure, if you trust me to provide the spiritual education I think fit."

"Words and music, stagecraft and poetry. The very reason we ask you."

In our production of *Twelfth Night* at the Middle Temple in February, again I played Viola, disguised as the page Cesario. This production out-frolicked our long-ago reading of the play for Queen Elizabeth. Nothing better pleased law students than cross-dressing and a carnival of misrule!

Between the antics of Sir Toby Belch and Malvolio, Feste, Sir Andrew Aguecheek, and Maria, laughter reigned, and our company rose to the ribald occasion, exaggerating throughout. Robert Armin even added jokes *ex tempore* as Will Kemp used to do. In his gown and wig as the Lady Olivia, Christopher Beeston, ordinarily no flirt, couldn't avoid attentions of the bawdy students.

Cesario would likely receive even more, but I fled the minute the play ended. From the courtyard, the noise pouring out the windows made me smile: I'd escaped with my identity intact, no random hand touching bound breasts beneath my jerkin. In that melee Burbage and Armin would look out for Beeston, a vulnerable boy, but I was a hired man responsible for myself.

As I hurried home, I started to worry. I'd tried to maintain the patience Dr. Garnet counseled, but at the moment I felt like a woman who must put up with her husband's bad behavior. Mine was role of constant spouse and Frances the wandering one, yet the world regarded me as devoted husband to a dutiful and loving wife.

I had to be cuckolded to become a parent. A jarring thought, but perhaps not so rare. Should Lady Elizabeth Sidney become pregnant, the child would not be her husband's, if one believed the gossip. Yet the Earl of Rutland would have an heir. He might even rejoice.

Take but degree away, untune that string,
And hark what discord follows.
ULYSSES, *TROILUS AND CRESSIDA*

CHAPTER XXXIII
February 1602

One bleak wintry day, I came upon Shakespeare as he ducked away from a chamber pot being dumped from a second story window.

"Close call." He laughed. "I shouldn't be surprised at piss falling from heaven. It didn't splash you?"

"Only a drop on my shoes."

"Not so easy to dodge the other filth in the air. Essex's blood didn't wash us clean, that's for certain."

"Don't tell me you expect another revolt."

"No, the rebels were severely punished. The shadow I sense isn't treachery. Honor lost, virtue outdated. London itself seems diseased, and I wouldn't be surprised if plague strikes again."

"Plague? God a mercy, no."

"Cases of sweating sickness have been reported."

"That doesn't necessarily mean plague will follow. You're too pessimistic."

Will chuckled dryly. "I daresay."

We crossed London Bridge in silence. The heads of Thomas Lee and the other conspirators had withered to dried husks on their pikes. Now it was the crowd that seemed ominous. Grim faces, shabby clothes, a sense of dereliction, expressions of anger and despair. Many of the shops on the Bridge were shuttered, perhaps due to foul weather. Frances had not opened hers.

South of London Bridge we picked up our pace.

"Tell me about your new play," I said. "A comedy?"

"A sort of history, I suppose, comic and tragic both."

"Tragical-historical, tragical-comical-historical-pastoral." I quoted Polonius with a smile.

"An apt description, minus the pastoral."

"Which history?"

"Homer's, actually, with some Geoffrey Chaucer mixed in."

I laughed. "A play for our times."

"You jest, but in a sense, that's what it is. The play is called *Troilus and Cressida*, full of chaos and moral confusion."

"What's my role?"

"Helen of Troy, among others."

"Helen!"

"Don't get too excited. A small part and, beautiful as you will look in a golden wig, you won't exactly be the face that launched a thousand ships, as our late lamented Kit Marlowe described her. Your Helen is rather a bawd."

"That's one way to tell the story."

I recalled the *Iliad* vaguely from Johnny's lessons back in Saffron Walden. Helen was married to the Spartan king Menelaus. Handsome Prince Paris visited Sparta and stole Queen Helen off to Troy. All the Greek armies joined together to fight for her return. Thus was Helen blamed for the losses the Greeks suffered in the Trojan War and the destruction of Troy itself. Nonetheless, I would not have called Helen a bawd.

We'd reached the Anchor, close enough to the Globe to serve as refuge for players when theatres were too cold for rehearsal. In our favorite private room, Chamberlain's Men looked jolly, thanks to the fire and their mugs of beer. As Shakespeare read the plot of *Troilus and Cressida*, their expressions shifted to puzzlement.

Robert Armin's role was Thersites, blunt and scurrilous critic of the Greek troops and of Troilus and Cressida's romance. "Lechery, lechery, still wars and lechery, nothing else holds fashion," was his byword.

Tom Pope played Pandarus, dirty-minded voyeur and pander between Trojan Prince Troilus and Cressida, a Trojan priest's daughter. Johnny played Troilus and Beeston Cressida. Lovers in Chaucer's version, here it came to no more than lust between them. So too the love of Paris for Helen.

By Pandarus' final speech, honor and love and nobility had been ravaged. Yet as betrayals and iniquities and murders compounded, I sensed a change in the emotions in the room from bewilderment to dark delight. Shakespeare twisted the old stories into something newer and, in their very perversions, more truthful. Audiences might enjoy this mockery of the heroics of love and war, but Queen Elizabeth's protective advisor Sir Robert Cecil wasn't likely to invite us to perform it for Her Majesty.

He handed me Helen's role and those for the prophetess Cassandra and the Prologue.

"You'll also play the Trojan warrior Antenor," he said. "He's frequently on stage though he has no lines—he's the hostage the Greeks exchange for Cressida. I picture you in the same wig for all your roles. As Prologue, you appear as Antenor, hair pulled back, helmet in hand. Helen will wear a coronet, Cassandra a black veil, and in later scenes Antenor's hair will straggle out beneath his helmet. It's well that the audience sees the same actor play all those parts."

True, I'd be playing both women and a man, which I'd only done before in *Henry V*. But perhaps Shakespeare saw the roles as three intriguing contrasts, the fatal beauty, the disregarded prophet, the captive warrior who sets the scene.

I didn't ask, merely replying, "A seductive voice for Helen, wailing for Cassandra, and a rugged warrior's for Antenor's Prologue."

Armin had been laughing as he read over his part as Thersites, and now said a line aloud: "'Here's Agamemnon, an honest fellow enough and one that loves quails, but he has not so much brains as ear-wax.' I can think of more than a few fellows who deserve that description!"

Laughter carried us out the door. I heard footsteps behind me.

"Sander!" Johnny said. "Is everything all right? You left in such a hurry."

"Frances wasn't feeling well this morning. I must check on her."

"Let me come along. I want to talk to you." Not waiting for a reply, Johnny trotted alongside me through the drizzle. He was like a piece of flotsam caught in an eddy of the swirling river below. I didn't want to hear about his latest mess, but Johnny radiated self-assurance walking beside me to Cornhill.

Frances sat by the fire, embroidering with Joan and Rebecca. "We moved our business here for the day—" She broke off when she saw Johnny. "This is a surprise."

"I just—"

"Sit down."

Johnny glanced at Frances as if he'd never been intimately alone with her in front of this very fire. Her expression was severe as she rested her needle.

"What brings you here, Johnny?"

"I have something I want to ask you."

He looked uncomfortably toward Joan and Rebecca.

"Go ahead and ask. I don't imagine it's anything they mayn't hear."

Joan looked at Johnny with girlish admiration, the stage bad boy so dashing up close!

"My lodging was only temporary, and now I must move out. Lady Elizabeth has had no room to house me since Essex's title was forfeit and Essex House taken from the family. They hope that in time all will be returned, but for now they're crowded into Savoy House."

"You mean all will be returned when—" I didn't finishing the sentence, "the Queen dies." I grimaced and said merely, "You certainly have attached yourself to some questionable characters."

"The Earl of Rutland wasn't the only nobleman who supported Essex."

"They're lucky to still have their heads." I sighed, restrained by

Joan's presence from saying all that I'd like to. "What is it that you want to ask us?" But I'd guessed.

"May I stay here with you? Until we see how the wind blows? Lady Elizabeth and her husband hope to move to larger accommodations soon."

"What!"

Frances' embroidery fell to the floor.

I spoke calmly. "You cannot find other lodgings?"

"I've tried."

"What do you say, Frances?"

Her voice was even, though her cheeks had turned pink. "We need to talk about it. Is there any urgency?"

"The truth is, I have to move today. You're my family, Sander. Please let me stay here a night or two."

My expression blank, I turned to Frances, who looked resentful as if to say, why must I decide?

Rebecca glanced from one to the other, curious, and Frances nodded at her to set out ale, a mutton pie, hard rolls and a wedge of cheese. "We're about to sit down to dinner, Johnny. Join us."

As we ate, Frances weighed the situation. Johnny's presumption annoyed her, but her maternal side responded to his desperation. Dining together wasn't uncomfortable; indeed it was convivial. It would be scant inconvenience if he slept on the cushioned bench. Her face reflected no desire for him. Somehow pregnancy and perhaps my affection had put an end to that.

"I won't disturb you, I promise. I've not always—" Johnny glanced at Joan and Rebecca, "done my share, but I'll help any way you ask. And stay out from underfoot."

Frances sighed. "For a few nights, then," she said at last. "What do you say, Sander?"

"I don't mind if you don't."

Johnny grabbed my hand. "You're the best brother a man could wish!"

HECTOR: *Art thou of blood and honor?*
THERSITES: *No, no, I am a rascal, a scurvy railing knave, a very filthy rogue.*
TROILUS AND CRESSIDA

CHAPTER XXXIV
March 1602

A month later Johnny was still sleeping downstairs and frequently returned home late. Meals together were few. As he played Patroclus, I shared no important scenes with him in *Troilus and Cressida* and rarely saw him at the Globe. Nonetheless, his presence became increasingly awkward. Frances not only was short with him when he did appear, but so too with me.

I was set to give him an ultimatum when, in his blithe way, Johnny came up to me after rehearsal. "I'll be moving out today. Be sure to tell Frances good bye and thank you." That was all. I didn't know if Lady Elizabeth found a closet for him to lay his head or he'd secured lodgings to suit him, nor did I care.

Frances felt well enough to spend long days at her shop and came home exhausted. I was happy to serve supper for our quiet evenings, relieved to have our house to ourselves. When we sat companionably by the fire and she felt the baby move, I put my hand on Frances' belly. This infant was almost too active!

On the day of the vernal equinox, Shakespeare paid us a call.

"It's been a long time, Master Shakespeare," Frances said. "Do stay and dine with us."

"Did you come to give me more lines for Helen of Troy?"

"No, I stopped in to see how you're doing. I hear your brother lodges here."

"Not any more, though as it happens, we're expecting him for dinner, along with Ben Jonson." Frances touched the rounded front of her skirt. "I'm feeling perfectly fit, despite all his kicking. We're certain it's 'he,' and a merry one."

"My wife Anne tells me Susannah kicked her more than Hamnet and Judith both. Of course they were crowded together."

Shakespeare rarely spoke the name of his son Hamnet, dead now nearly five years. I heard him tell Burbage that the name Hamlet in his play came from the old Danish tale of Prince Amlet. Though Hamlet echoed his son's name, otherwise he kept his loss to himself. The only sister and brother twins in his plays were Viola and Sebastian, and although Viola gives Sebastian up for drowned, at the end of *Twelfth Night* she discovers he survived.

"Twins!" Frances said. "Your poor wife."

"They were bonny children." Sorrow crossed Shakespeare's face. "May yours be bonny as well."

The door burst open to admit Johnny and Ben Jonson.

"Ben!" Shakespeare said. "Watch out for this fellow, Johnny. He's dangerous."

"Just dangerous enough," Johnny replied with a smile.

I was always surprised at Ben Jonson's appearance, sturdy, coarse, and mildly threatening. Yet he'd educated himself beyond the level of most University graduates. Appearances deceived—to a point.

"You and Dekker and Marston have kept things lively in London lately, Ben," Will said. "A sorely needed diversion."

"Ben started a satiric war," Johnny said to Frances. "Did you hear about it? His *Poetaster* mocked Dekker and Marston, so Dekker came back with *Satiromastix*, mocking him."

"Sander told me. I never saw the plays."

"The Children of the Chapel performed mine. Everyone expects satire or foolery from boys," Jonson said. "Then Dekker talked your company into doing his."

"You didn't expect us to miss out on the fun." Shakespeare pummeled Ben's arm.

"More like, to capitalize on the fun," Jonson replied. "I don't mind being made to look a fool. We all know better."

"Better indeed." Shakespeare winked. "And here you are."

"To pay my respects to Mistress Frances." Jonson opened the large leather wallet he'd set on the floor beside him and presented her with two punnets of strawberries and a tub of soft cheese. "Springtime blessings on your house." He lifted the cup of wine I handed him. "To these satiric days."

"And to being wary," Will added.

"You needn't remind me. I spent more than a month in Marshalsea for the *Isle of Dogs*, and worse, they destroyed every copy. You came off better with that *Richard II* caper, Will. Did you really have no suspicions as to why Essex's men commissioned you?"

"It's not as if we hadn't played it recently," I said. "The story is history."

"No need to defend us, Sander," Will said. "We knew it was a play about regicide, even if it doesn't advocate it."

"Your plays never advocate anything much," Jonson said.

"Is that a fault?" Will smiled. "Everyone gets to have a say."

"You're expert at evasion, Will Shakespeare, or should I say equivocation. Long may you persist so."

"Equivocation?" Shakespeare raised an eyebrow. "Perhaps you're right. I'm no rebel. My interest lies in King Richard's character that led to his deposition and murder."

"You don't see any parallels to—" Jonson looked around the room as if for spies, "to our current rule?"

"No, I do not. Nor did anyone else for more than twenty performances over the years, even recently."

"You don't know what goes on in audiences' heads."

"One could argue that's to my credit. I don't tell them what to think, so I have no idea what they actually do."

Jonson laughed. "I cannot best you in an argument."

"Is this an argument? Sometimes I worry for you, Ben. I'd have thought spending time in prison—twice!—would be sufficient warning."

"You've never been imprisoned, I grant you that. If writing what I think lands me there, so be it."

"True." Shakespeare said. "But the second time you were jailed was for murder."

"Self-defense," Jonson muttered.

"Murder!" echoed Frances, who'd been only half attending to their exchange.

"You didn't know? Jonson killed that brazen Gabriel Spencer."

"I'm impressed, Master Jonson," she said. "You're as daring as Moll Frith."

"I beg your pardon, Mistress, but *Moll Cutpurse?*" Jonson laughed, but I wasn't amused. Their conversation made me uneasy. Gabriel Spencer had been my enemy, and good riddance to him. Moll—I would never call her Cutpurse—was my friend, never mind her outlaw activities. But she was a woman in man's clothing! Ben Jonson hadn't guessed that I was, and I preferred to keep it that way.

Just be the man of the house, I told myself as I poured another round.

Over supper Jonson said, "Johnny's been telling me about your *Troilus and Cressida.* Too bad I've given up acting and you have that clever Robert Armin. Otherwise I'd play Thersites with relish."

"You would, eh?" Shakespeare laughed. "What do you know about the part?"

"Oh I've heard a bit. I know that Thersites has a foul mouth and sees through the sham of warrior's honor."

"I'd rather you played Pandarus," Shakespeare said.

"I'm no pox-ridden pander! A faithful husband, surely you know that."

We opened *Troilus and Cressida* one gusty afternoon late in March. The encircling walls of the Globe offered protection to theatregoers, particularly those in the galleries, but making our way to the theatre, actors and patrons alike were wind-whipped. Besides stirring up the stench of the marshes and intense barking from the dogs at the Bear Gardens, such a wind carried uneasiness, restlessness—a sense of dis-ease, suiting the mood of the play.

The fanfare sounded. Armed as Antenor and holding his helmet, I stood alone on the stage to speak the prologue, Shakespeare's echo of Homer's epic beginning.

> *In Troy, there lies the scene. From isles of Greece*
> *The princes orgulous, their high blood chafed,*
> *Have to the port of Athens sent their ships,*
> *Fraught with the ministers and instruments*
> *Of cruel war: sixty and nine, that wore*
> *Their crownets regal, from the Athenian bay*
> *Put forth toward Phrygia; and their vow is made*
> *To ransack Troy, within whose strong immures*
> *The ravish'd Helen, Menelaus' queen,*
> *With wanton Paris sleeps; and that's the quarrel.*
> *To Tenedos they come;*
> *And the deep-drawing barks do there disgorge*
> *Their warlike fraughtage: now on Dardan plains*
> *The fresh and yet unbruised Greeks do pitch*
> *Their brave pavilions and*
> *Spur up the sons of Troy.*

As I spoke, leaders of the two sides came onstage, the Greeks to my right, the Trojans to my left. Several actors doubled roles on both sides, but here each side was even: touches of silver-gray on the Greeks' costumes and bronze on the Trojans. They glared at each other as I continued:

> *Now expectation, tickling skittish spirits,*
> *On one and other side, Trojan and Greek,*
> *Sets all on hazard.*

At this point I scanned the audience:

> *And hither am I come*
> *A prologue arm'd, but not in confidence*
> *Of author's pen or actor's voice, but suited*
> *In like conditions as our argument,*
> *To tell you, fair beholders, that our play*
> *Leaps o'er the vaunt and firstlings of those broils,*
> *Beginning in the middle, starting thence away*
> *To what may be digested in a play.*
> *Like or find fault; do as your pleasures are:*
> *Now good or bad, 'tis but the chance of war.*

I put on my helmet and joined the Greek soldiers as their captive.

The audience was unusually attentive, apart from murmurs of surprise and discomfort. There was no one onstage to cheer for, no love to warm the heart. Troilus yearned, Cressida withheld. After she yielded to him, all turned sour between them, just as she'd feared.

The warrior Achilles stayed in his tent in defiance of Agamemnon, as in Homer, but in our play spent his time dallying with Patroclus. When Achilles returned to battle, he didn't fight the Trojan prince Hector man to man but instead sent his Myrmidons to murder him, unarmed.

Was Hector truly the greatest of the Trojans, or Ulysses the wisest of the Greeks? Neither lived by his words. Hector argued that Helen should be sent back to the Greeks, that she was not worth one of the Trojan warriors whose blood was shed on her account—then unaccountably went along with Paris and Troilus who argued they must keep her. Hector ended up treacherously stabbed to death, and Ulysses' wisdom proved shallow.

How different this war from King Henry V's in Agincourt; how different the women. There, I delivered Falstaff's elegy and later played a sweet love scene in broken English with the king. Here I could but rave my foreknowledge of Troy's destruction unheeded and bandy flirtatious words with Pandarus and Paris.

I sensed that the audience, whether familiar with Homer or not, were disconcerted by Shakespeare's bold, often repellent, version of the story. These were folk who flocked to public executions and bearbaiting, but they also loved chivalric show. Here chivalry lost to brutality, love to lust, and the cynical words of Thersites and Pandarus carried the day.

As I made my way through Cheapside, I heard the voice of Amelia Bassano Lanyer, bright as the sunshine of her ancestral Italy on this chill March day.

"Ah, Sandro. I saw *Troilus and Cressida* yesterday. Your Shakespeare dosed us with his pessimism."

We stepped into to a quiet tavern and took a table by the window. In the shadows, a couple leaned close and spoke in whispers and an old man drank alone. No other customers.

"I'm sure you recall that sonnet he wrote ages ago," Amelia said. "'The expense of spirit in a waste of shame is lust in action' and so forth. Thersites and Pandarus say worse on stage, which I would have thought impossible."

"What a poem!"

"You and I have a confederacy," Amelia added, *sotto voce*. "We know each other's secrets."

"Shhh."

I gave her a conspiratorial smile as the serving girl set two cups of sweet wine and a loaf of knotted machet bread on the table, suiting midday repast for a lady like Amelia.

"I'd have thought Will Shakespeare would have moved on by now," she said. "Instead we get Paris, that notable inamorato, with his 'hot blood begets hot thoughts, and hot thoughts beget hot deeds, and hot deeds is love.'"

"So that's the line you remember? Hot blood, hot thoughts, and hot deeds?"

"I also remember Pandarus' retort. 'Those are vipers. Is love a generation of vipers?' I think Shakespeare needs to sweeten his imagination." Amelia tore off a piece of bread as if she were attacking the loaf.

"What do you think of Helen of Troy?" I asked her.

"Beautiful and corrupt. At least she's blonde—dark women aren't the only vixens. I noticed that Cassandra too is blonde, and Antenor. They're all cut from the same cloth, Helen the velvet, Cassandra the backing, and Antenor a scrap—to use a metaphor Frances would like."

Amelia offered me a ragged chunk of bread. I took a bite before replying, "You say I play three blondes who make no pretense of being angelic. Not true of Cassandra, but who listens to her?"

"Exactly. Even though Cassandra is a priestess, the Trojans show her no reverence."

"Reverence!" I lowered my voice. "Everything is debased in this play. It's a fallen world."

"And a pagan one, not that men's vile notions about women have changed much since ancient days." Amelia leaned close. "Nor have they stopped us."

"You and I get away with a good deal." I tipped my glass to her and drank the last of my wine. The serving girl came to our table carrying a delicate lusterware pitcher, its iridescence gleaming in the thin afternoon light.

"I'm tame these days, Sandro, apart from writing poetry," Amelia said as the girl filled our glasses. "A pursuit that must be concealed."

"Can't a woman write with impunity?"

"I don't hide the fact that I write. Alfonso assumes I'm composing songs, which occasionally I do. But he'd be surprised at what else."

"I look forward to reading your poems."

"In due time. They're ambitious. Perhaps shocking."

"Why don't you read them to select friends? I recall those coteries you used to host. The next one should focus on you. That would make a sensation: a woman poet holding forth to men."

"And women. I write for women. But so far my poems are still works in progress." Amelia dipped a morsel of bread into her wine and savored it on her tongue. "I have to say, watching *Troilus and Cressida*, I laughed along with everyone else—and was horrified."

"Tom Pope says he can feel the audience recoil when he speaks Pandarus' final lines, as if he sprayed them with filth."

Amelia glanced around the tavern, now filling. A well-dressed young man gave us a curious look, perhaps recognizing me from the stage, but did not sit close enough to overhear. Still, she spoke quietly. "Pandarus *is* spraying us, Sandro. He's bequeathing us his diseases."

"Tom Pope's an actor who's not infected."

"Of course, but words on stage create a powerful reality. No wonder you wanted to be an actor. You magnify your effect by transforming yourself. I see why plays were once religious. *Troilus and Cressida* is a rant against evil. Even though some of his sonnets are brutal, Will speaks more harshly yet through Thersites and Pandarus."

"I imagine he's seen their like in Bankside."

Amelia twisted her wineglass in her fingers. "No doubt, but this play suggests he has an abhorrence of sex. Is love really no more than lust?"

"Not in *Troilus and Cressida*, but it's hardly Will's final word on the topic."

"Perhaps not, but it does leave a bad taste in the mouth. The Trojan War was fought over a strumpet, and victory goes to the Greeks because Achilles violates the code of honor. What does Thersites say? 'The argument of the war is a whore and a cuckold.'"

"So Shakespeare doesn't think much of military glory. Is that so surprising?"

"If he and I were closer, I'd worry about Will. He wants us to go home after *Troilus and Cressida* feeling ashamed of ourselves, men and women alike."

"You shouldn't be saying this to me, a member of the cast."

"I wouldn't worry. It's not likely that your *Troilus and Cressida* will have many more performances."

"I don't know about that, but I do know we'll not play it for Her Majesty."

"Wise. Too close to the spirit of the times, too disturbing. As far as I'm concerned, it goes beyond satire's mocking of folly."

"Don't say that to Will Shakespeare." I paused. "Do you ever see him?"

"Not intimately, no."

I couldn't read Amelia's expression. Sadness? regret?

"Never mind." She smiled. "I gained much from that brilliant, ferocious man."

Ferocious, I repeated to myself as I walked home. Not a word I'd use for Will Shakespeare, but given the lines he wrote for Thersites, perhaps fitting. Amelia would know.

Now bless thyself. Thou met'st with things dying,
I with things newborn.

SHEPHERD, *THE WINTER'S TALE*

CHAPTER XXXV
June 1602

Frances' pains began one showery afternoon at the time the sun would be setting if not covered in thick black clouds. Judging by her first childbirth, Frances must have feared that she was in for a hard night.

When I returned from the theatre I found her lying on the downstairs bed by the fire, holding a blanket closely around her belly as if protecting herself. I closed the door so quietly that she didn't hear me enter. "Tonight, is it? I was hoping the baby would be born on my birthday—a week to go."

Frances looked up, dazed. "Tonight." She reached out a hand to me and whispered, "I'm glad you're home."

I sat on the edge of the bed, one hand on Frances' belly. Contractions were coming fast and hard. She moaned into the pillow. Where was Rebecca when we needed her?

"I'll fetch Mother Tilda," I said. "This little one is in a hurry."

"Don't leave me!"

Beside the bed was a cooled herbal drink, left there by Mother Tilda. I moistened Frances' lips with the fragrant liquid though she seemed unaware, her brow knotted in pain.

I looked around frantically. What would Mother Tilda do? Frances' moans became a wail, broken by gasping breaths. With furious speed, I took the folded sheet that lay in readiness, unfolded it partway, lifted Frances' arcing body and slipped it under her hips.

She lurched forward, pressing the bed with her feet and pushing with all her might. My urge was to support her back, but the contractions were so mighty that I hovered above her knees. The next thrust and the baby's head was visible. I received it into my hands, followed by his red little body.

His. A son. Frances fell back onto the pillows as the afterbirth gushed out.

Laying the infant on Frances' belly, I thought oh no, this too. But I had to cut the cord. No Mother Tilda to my rescue. I took a deep breath and did it, holding the knife steady by sheer force of will. Not only was I husband, but midwife as well. I kissed her sweaty cheek, wiped the baby clean with a damp cloth, and put him in his mother's arms. Through it all he was shrieking his lungs out.

"He's perfect," I laughed. "With the voice of an actor."

"Big of voice and body." Frances' eyes shone upon the noisy red face.

Compared with Marie, this child was large. He would thrive. I sent a grateful prayer to Bounteous Nature.

June was colder than usual and we kept the fire burning. Baby Francis, for so we named him—Francis William Cooke—was as loved and active as a newborn could be from his first day in the world.

When Johnny came to see him, he called him Billy Boy, and the nickname stuck. Johnny was brother to both Frances and me, uncle to this baby: relationships of innocent clarity. During her pregnancy Frances gave him no looks of longing nor complicity, and Johnny showed none for this maternal young woman so doted on by her husband. Indeed, his only emotion seemed to be relief.

"Billy Boy," Shakespeare said with a laugh when he presented his godfather gift, a beautiful edition of Mary Sidney Herbert's translation of the Psalms. "My name is William, but I never was Billy."

"It fits him, does it not?" I asked.

"Francis is his christening name and no doubt what he'll go by when he leaves home—unless he chooses William," Frances said with a smile. "Billy Boy for now."

"I wonder what he'll do when he leaves home?" I asked.

"Whatever he chooses. A new century, a new era," Shakespeare said. "Teach him all you know and he could attend Oxford or Cambridge."

"Or go on stage or be a tailor," Frances added.

"Tailor to the new monarch—whosoever that may be. It's hard to imagine anyone but Queen Elizabeth on the throne."

Frances bounced the baby. "What's the news from the palace?"

"The Queen carries on valiantly, but she isn't well."

"I've not heard what ails her," I said.

"Nothing and everything. Her doctors find no disease of heart nor body. I believe her soul is troubled—an organ not susceptible to physicians' ministrations, nor priests', nor even musicians'."

"Nor actors'? Might we amuse her again? One doesn't die of a wound to the soul," I said.

"What would best amuse her? Perhaps a tragedy, so she might weep at another's woes. But weeping is risky." Shakespeare sighed. "A comedy?"

"What about the play you once mentioned, with the holy sister and a bedtrick?"

"I've not had time for it."

"Everyone likes a good story."

"The story of the moment is Frances and the baby," Shakespeare said. "Here's to health and happiness!"

We ate and drank watching Billy Boy, whose gurgle resembled a laugh.

I am not well in health, and that is all.
BRUTUS, *JULIUS CAESAR*

CHAPTER XXXVI
July 1602

I pushed through the crowd in the Anchor looking for my fellow players. Moll Frith's broad form blocked the way.

"When were you going to tell me? You're a father!"

"I— I—"

"I'll drink to the baby—and to the miracle that produced him."

Moll pulled me onto a bench by a window, open to allow a breath of air into the overwarm tavern. Emptying the dregs from her pipe onto the floor, she tucked it into her doublet and waved over the serving girl.

I grinned. "Aren't you proud of me, Moll? You can't do the like."

"Nor would I want to. No squalling brats for me. Or does your little marvel sleep like an angel?"

"He has a lusty pair of lungs, but I wouldn't call him a squalling brat."

Moll leaned forward confidentially. "So tell me."

"How we managed? It's none of your business."

"Idle curiosity of a friend. I won't be spreading it around. You can trust me."

"What's your guess?"

"I'd not be surprised if that ne'er-do-well brother of yours slipped between your sheets."

I shrugged. "I'm not a jealous husband."

"Truly? Well, here's to the paragon of men, Alexander Cooke."

I inhaled the breeze that wafted in from the street, aromas of the nearby bakeshop blanketing the pungent smell of spilled ale and tobacco smoke. "Francis William Cooke. I love this boy."

"You don't mind Johnny's part in the business?"

"What's the point? Frances wants to be a mother. Now she is and I'm a father. We call him Billy Boy."

"Billy Boy. Sounds like one of my lads."

"He will not be one of your lads, Moll Frith!"

Moll lifted her cup again. "Here's to your son, may he prosper."

Wiping her mouth on her dirty lace cuff, she said, "You've outshone me yet again, Sander. Good work."

Back home I found Frances at her sewing, Amelia cooing over the baby, and Harry making him a doll from a bit of wood and strands of bright-colored yarn.

Amelia looked up. "At long last, Sandro. I've been waiting for you to tell my news. Guess who befriended me? Lady Margaret, the Countess of Cumberland! When I told her about my poetry, she was most encouraging. I shall write poems of dedication at the beginning of my book to her and other noble women."

I hung my doublet on a hook by the door. "I hear that the Countess of Cumberland is intimate with the Queen's chief ladies in waiting. Does she tell you what's going on at Whitehall?"

"I know that Queen Elizabeth's health is worse than most people realize. She performs convincingly, but suffers constant pain in her hip."

"Chamberlain's Men want to cheer her with a private entertainment."

"Is that a good idea? She won't bear up under much ceremony."

"It's all we can do for her."

Frances set down her handiwork. "I made a strawberry tart. Will you have some?"

"Yes!" Harry answered for us all.

The baby began to cry. Harry rocked the cradle with one foot and looked into Billy Boy's face, scrunched up for another wail.

"Look what I made you, baby." He held out the yarn-wrapped doll.

"Did you tie it securely?" Amelia asked. "We don't want him to choke."

"I know that," Harry said with a nine-year-old's air of authority. As he waved the little toy above him, Billy stopped crying.

Frances spooned triangles of tart into blue and white patterned bowls, red glaze sheening the fragrant berries, and laid out a jug of cream as I poured three tiny glasses of Madeira.

"A toast to the cook." Amelia said. "I've not seen such a voluptuous pastry in a long time."

"What's 'voluptuous'?" Harry asked.

"Rich and bountiful and gorgeous," Amelia replied as she splashed cream over her serving.

I couldn't restrain a smile: so might one describe Amelia Bassano herself, dressed in a dark rose linen gown with strawberry-colored edging against the white lace at the neckline.

"What private entertainment do you have in mind for the Queen?" Frances asked.

"We might stage a reading of Shakespeare's next play."

"Like your *What You Will* in the royal library?" Amelia asked.

"Perhaps. It depends on Sir Robert Cecil."

We focused on the delicate pastry and fat strawberries, which would turn all our mouths as red as Harry's if not for our more refined table manners.

"Heavenly," Amelia said as she set her spoon beside her empty bowl. "You're blessed to have such an excellent cook for a wife, along with all Frances' other virtues."

"I don't feel good." Harry pushed himself away from the table. His brow was hot, and although the room was cool and the door to the garden wide open, he'd broken out in a sweat.

Frances whisked the baby into the kitchen.

"I'm dizzy." Harry sat heavily on the chair nearest the door.

Amelia wiped his brow with the corner of her kerchief.

"Did this just start? You seemed fine a moment ago."

"Has he eaten strawberries before?" I asked. "Sometimes they disagree with children."

"Have you, Harry?"

The boy, white-faced and looking miserable, murmured, "Not this summer."

"Last year?" I pressed him.

"Yes, lots." He bolted from his chair and out the door. I followed, to find him vomiting into the bushes.

"Better?"

He nodded and came back inside, and Amelia helped him to the cushioned bench.

I brought her a damp cloth. "I know someone who can help."

"What do you think it is?" Frances whispered to me in the kitchen. "Should we be worried?"

"I hope not." I recalled Shakespeare's mention of the sweating sickness. "We'll take Harry to Dr. Garnet. He'll know what to do."

"Good idea. Bring back some of his herbs to brew a drink for the baby," Frances said. "We don't want Billy catching anything."

Harry was trying to stand up.

"Do you think you can walk if your mother and I help you?" I asked him.

"I'll try."

He leaned against Amelia and I took his other side, carrying most of his weight between us.

Before I lifted the knocker, Dr. Garnet opened the door. He led us to his inner chamber where Harry sat on the neatly made bed. The room was light as ever, scented with pungent lavender and bay. With surprising agility for a man his age, Garnet knelt in front of the boy and examined his face. Harry's eyelids fluttered.

"You mustn't fall asleep." Dr. Garnet pressed Harry's throat and laid his ear against his chest.

"Lean back, Harry," he said, pushing himself to his feet, "and keep your eyes open."

Amelia and I moved to the window, where Dr. Garnet spoke quietly. "We must be very careful, in case this is sweating sickness.

There hasn't been an epidemic in fifty years, just the occasional case and those not a contagious variety. Here are some herbs that will help." He assembled valerian, sage, and others that I didn't recognize.

"Are these preventative?" I asked. "Frances wants me to bring home herbs to protect the baby."

"I'll make a different blend for him," Garnet said. "Your son should recover completely, Mistress Lanyer. If he drinks a cup brewed from these herbs three more times before bed tonight and feels himself again, he may sleep. But if he doesn't improve, keep him awake and send your maid to me first thing tomorrow. I'd have to prepare more intense remedies. But these should suffice."

He put a heaping spoon of the mixture into a cup and added hot water from the pot on his hearth. After stirring it for three long minutes, he said to Harry: "This tastes pleasant. Drink it slowly. Your mother will sit with you, and when you feel up to it, she'll walk you home."

Dr. Garnet gestured for me to follow him into the outer chamber.

"I think the boy will soon recover, and I doubt that you and Frances need worry about the baby. Do not take him outside if the air is heavy, and be sure to avoid crowds. London is suffering from a kind of disease herself. Perhaps plague is threatening, but I feel it's more a matter of the spirit. Within this twelvemonth, the Queen will die, and times of transition can be dangerous."

I was surprised at his certainty. "Dangerous because of treason?" I asked. "Essex's rebels have been dealt with."

"There won't be another rebellion. The trouble is, Her Majesty hasn't named her heir. She's been wise not to, but now . . ." he trailed off.

"What?"

"I believe that Sir Robert Cecil has selected her successor."

"Shakespeare thinks Cecil favors King James of Scotland."

"Perhaps, but the Queen hasn't made it official. The times require serenity and caution.

"What if we approach Cecil to present a play for the Queen?"

Garnet laughed. "He'll refuse to allow it. You must address Queen Elizabeth herself."

"Easy to say."

"You can do it."

Garnet made up two small parcels. "These are for you, Alexander, and these for Harry. See the lad and his mother home. Mistress Lanyer has the gift of second sight, which in my opinion she uses too rarely. You should remind her to be alert in all her senses."

We returned to the inner chamber where Harry listened to his mother reciting nursery rhymes, a treat for an ill child, even one of his relatively advanced years.

"You look much better, Harry," Dr. Garnet said. "You may go home."

"Will you say more rhymes at home?"

"Of course." Amelia extended her hand, but Harry stood by himself.

"I like your house," he said to Dr. Garnet. "Some day will you show me how those things work?" He waved toward the alchemical equipment.

"Indeed! Come visit when you feel well."

"Your special drink helped me, Doctor."

"Be sure to drink three more cups between now and bedtime."

Harry waved goodbye to Dr. Garnet and walked between his mother and me, holding our hands and moving slowly. We reached Amelia's house in Westminster after only two stops.

"Sit here," Amelia pointed Harry to the large chair and put a wooden puzzle on the table beside him. "Remember, Harry. You're not to fall asleep. We'll tickle your feet if you close your eyes."

Harry laughed and set to work on the puzzle. Amelia and I sat on the tapestried bench across from him.

"Harry will recover, Amelia. You needn't worry." I paused. "It's occurred to me that perhaps you can help us. Our playing company, I mean. We need one of the Queen's waiting women to ask Her Majesty if she'd enjoy hearing a new play by Shakespeare."

"Lady Margaret might be willing."

"Will you see her soon?"

"I shall. What else was Dr. Garnet whispering to you about?"

"You must remember your gift of second sight. Pay attention."

"I believe I've used that with Lady Margaret," she said. "And shall again."

Let us not wrangle.
BRUTUS, *JULIUS CAESAR*

CHAPTER XXXVII
Late July 1602

On Frances' and my first outing with Billy Boy, we stopped in at her shop, where Joan sat intent on her stitching and Rebecca tatted a strip of lace.

We paused in the doorway before either of them noticed us.

"I'm glad to see you hard at work without me," she said. "Your apprentice days have ended, Joan. I've signed the papers. As of today, you are a full-fledged seamstress. And you, Rebecca, will officially become an apprentice."

"Thank you! Thank you!" they chorused.

Joan eyed the bundle in Frances' arms. "Your baby! We want to see him."

Frances folded back the blanket to show Billy's pink face, eyelashes ruffling over his cheeks in sleep.

As they were admiring him, who but Lady Elizabeth Sidney should walk in the door. I'd never been introduced to her and doubted that Frances had.

Joan curtseyed. "Your gown is almost ready, my lady."

Lady Elizabeth peeked at Billy. "How sweet!" She glanced from Frances to me. "You're Johnny Cooke's brother."

"That's right."

"Is this his nephew? I've heard about him."

Frances scrutinized the elegant lady, her curls fashionably coifed under a summer hat.

"I wanted to surprise you, Mistress," Joan said. "This is Lady Elizabeth Sidney Manners. While you were at home, I made a skirt and bodice for her." She turned to Lady Elizabeth. "Frances owns this shop, and of course she'll do the finishing touches. I'll fetch them." She skipped up the stairs.

"Congratulations Mistress Cooke," Lady Elizabeth said. "Your shop has been in good hands."

Frances held the baby close, her smile formal. "I hope you're satisfied with my assistant's work, your ladyship."

"She's industrious and careful. I'm sure I'll be delighted."

Joan stood at the bottom of the stairs, the azure linen in her arms—a piece of fabric Frances had purchased for Lady Lucy, the Countess of Bedford, now cut and sewn.

Lady Elizabeth's eyes, however, were on me rather than her new gown. "I've long wanted to meet you, Master Cooke. Your brother often speaks of you."

I felt a chill. "Nothing too bad, I hope."

"Quite the contrary. He says you are an exemplary brother, husband, and father."

Lady Elizabeth looked at me so closely that I turned away, extending my arms to Frances. "I'll take him." I held the infant in the awkward fashion of a man.

Frances and Lady Elizabeth examined the blue gown, Joan beaming with pride at their murmured approval. Keeping my eyes on Billy, I sensed Frances' displeasure with the Countess, even as she praised Joan's needlework.

Although I'd seen her in the theatre audience from time to time, I'd never been close enough to realize how much Lady Elizabeth resembled her aunt Marie. Not just a physical resemblance, although she too had the Sidney red-blond hair, heart-shaped face and cinnamon-brown eyes. The strongest similarity was her lively expression. Long ago Marie guessed my secret, and I feared that Lady Elizabeth possessed the wit to do so likewise.

Billy let out a wail and Frances retrieved him. "I'll have the gown ready for you Friday afternoon, Lady Elizabeth."

"Next time I hope I shall be ordering clothes for court." Lady Elizabeth sighed. "At present, it's unlikely I shall be invited, not unless I accompany my aunt." Moving toward the door, she paused. "I'm delighted to have seen your baby, Mistress Frances, and to speak to you in person, Master Cooke. My aunt thinks very highly of you, as does Ben Jonson. I should quite like to become better acquainted with you myself."

I kept my head down until she'd left the shop. I had no desire to join that intimate circle, not with her, not with Johnny, not with Ben Jonson.

Frances didn't speak as we walked home, protecting the baby from the crowds on London Bridge and walking fast. I couldn't say anything about Lady Elizabeth if I'd wanted to. I'd felt wary of her, but up till now she'd been a spectre of Johnny's bad judgment. Now I saw her as little more than an out-of-favor idle noble woman, though more intelligent than many.

The minute the door shut behind us, Frances' words burst out as if they'd simmered the entire way.

"You like her! A few words of flattery from a young noble woman and you're smitten. You're as bad as your brother!"

I resisted the urge to laugh. Smitten? Frances sounded jealous.

"You will not join her coterie, Sander. Promise me that. Don't you dare tell me that Lady Elizabeth could advance your career."

"I can assure you I don't plan to join any coterie. Don't be unreasonable—"

"Unreasonable!" Billy jumped at the unfamiliar shrillness in his mother's voice.

"Frances, my dear—"

"Don't you 'my dear' me. You'll do whatever you want to do. If you want to converse with Lady Elizabeth you shall."

"I just told you that I would not."

"Why should I trust you?"

"Because I've always been trustworthy. Because I am not Johnny Cooke."

Her eyes sparked with fury, as if she'd not heard a word. "Do

what you please." She rocked the crying baby in his cradle vehe-
mently enough to stun him into silence.

"Frances, listen to me. I won't say you're in the wrong—"

"You'll only think it. Enough. Think as you like. I have nothing
more to say to you."

"If you won't be kind to me, at least be gentle with Billy."

"Oh, so you're going to tell me how to be a mother. You who
know all."

I gazed at her kneeling beside the cradle in a rage. It took all my
will to stifle the words I wanted to throw at her. So much I'd kept
to myself! But it would come out in an angry tumble and do naught
but harm.

"I'll take a walk while you calm down." I buttoned my doublet.

"Me? I'm perfectly calm." Frances slowed her rocking movements,
her body rigid with the effort.

I pulled on my cap and closed the door softly behind me, the
urge to slam it propelling me down the street. Blood pounded in my
head. I could have reminded Frances that I'd married her, cared for
her through the loss of Marie—even stood by faithfully after she
conceived a child by my brother. Well, I wouldn't say any of it now.

Would we get past this fight? Billy's parentage was a fact. We
must deal with it sensibly, and for the most part we did. But tension
bubbled under the surface as this absurd eruption proved, making
the fabric of our life together seem fragile as gossamer. Was our
marriage based on delusion and wishful thinking? Was I merely an
inadequate stand-in for my brother? Perhaps my sacrifices for her
sake were meaningless. I wondered if Frances knew—or cared—
who I was myself. My indignation so blinded me that I had to jump
out of the path of a wagon along the Strand.

When I found myself at the Mermaid, Shakespeare and Richard
Burbage sat alone. Nothing like their society and a mug of ale for a
dose of cheer.

Shakespeare filled a tankard from the jug on the table and set it
in front of me. "We're talking about *Measure for Measure*, Sander.
Wait till you see what Isabella does. She's the holy sister."

Mention of the theatre and my quarrel with Frances faded. "The one who arranges for another woman to take her place in a secret tryst?" I asked.

"Yes, a bedtrick. Much happens after that."

"Is this the story you want to present to the Queen?"

"She'll be more entertained than shocked. But Sir Robert Cecil acts like a snarling bulldog. No one can come near her."

"Perhaps he thinks he's preserving Her Majesty's energy for important duties," Burbage said.

"He's right." Shakespeare smiled. "In the grand scale of politics and power, plays are frivolous."

"Frivolity can be health giving," I said, thinking how much healthier my own mood was, thanks simply to being with fellow players.

"We want our audiences to feel more life in two hours than in a month of ordinary days," Burbage said. "Laughter and tears."

Robert Armin joined us. "Which will this new play of yours bring forth?"

"Laughter, I hope," Shakespeare replied. "Sir Robert Cecil with his twitching nose will not sniff out any treason, that I can promise."

Augustine Phillips stood beside our table. "There's a lady outside who wishes to talk to you, Sander."

"Send her in," Burbage said.

"She's not the sort of woman who takes her child to taverns." Phillips sent me out.

Amelia held Harry's hand. "We stopped in at your house. Frances said I'd find you here."

"You're looking well, Harry."

"I'm all better. Dr. Garnet's special drink worked. He's very clever, and we're going to be friends. Mama promises to take me to visit him."

"And so I shall, Harry."

"What sort of state was Frances in?" I asked Amelia.

"Upset, rocking Billy and on the verge of weeping."

"Did she seem angry?"

"No." Amelia frowned. "Perhaps the sadness that follows anger?"

"Could be." I took a deep breath and regretted it, the stench of the gutter overwhelming. "Why did you want to see me, Amelia? Richard Burbage says I should bring you inside."

"Is Shakespeare here?"

I nodded.

"Lady Margaret, the Countess of Cumberland, made sure his play was mentioned to Queen Elizabeth, and she hopes to hear it one day soon." Amelia paused. "But I shouldn't be the one to tell your players."

"Why not? It's your doing."

"Not the place for Harry."

William Shakespeare poked his head out the door. "If the person who wanted to see you were Moll Frith with one of her boys, she'd have walked right in. I supposed that your friend was a lady who didn't frequent the Mermaid." Shakespeare looked down at Harry. "A musician in the making. Good work, lad. What's your errand, Mistress Bassano?"

"Queen Elizabeth wants to hear your newest play."

"She told you so?"

"No, one of her ladies suggested it to her," Amelia said. "Her hip pains her, but the thought of your play made her smile. The Queen will overrule any 'no' from Sir Robert Cecil."

"Did you prompt this, Mistress?" Shakespeare asked.

Amelia's olive cheeks showed a tinge of pink. "I dropped a word or two."

"May I ask how you gained access to the Queen's ladies?"

Amelia heard condescension in his tone and made no reply.

"The Countess of Cumberland enjoys poetry and poets," I said. "She's befriended Amelia."

Amelia turned away, gripping Harry's hand. "Expect a royal summons."

I felt heartened to have something cheering to report to Frances.

We cannot weigh our brother with ourself
ISABELLA, *MEASURE FOR MEASURE*

CHAPTER XXXVIII
September 1602

Reportedly, the Queen's moods were up and down. No sooner did she say, "I should love to hear that new play of William Shakespeare's," than she was laid low by a new pain.

With the unseasonable sultry weather and fear of sweating sickness, we played revivals at the Globe. No new plays for the time being.

Shakespeare had outlined the plot of *Measure for Measure*, which begins with the Duke of Vienna supposedly leaving town. After putting his deputy Angelo in charge, he disguises himself as a priest and remains in Vienna to watch what transpires. The Duke failed to enforce the laws of Vienna, so it's up to Angelo to clean up the bawdy houses and put an end to public disorder.

However, the first victims of Angelo's new regime are Claudio and Juliet, a betrothed pair who plan to wed as soon as her dowry is settled. But Juliet has fallen pregnant. Angelo orders her imprisoned and sentences Claudio to death.

Johnny would play Claudio, the irony of his own shortcomings in that regard apparently lost on him. I played Claudio's sister Isabella, a novitiate yet to take her holy vows. Again the righteous sister.

Urged by Claudio's irreverent friend Lucio to plead my brother's case to Angelo, I would leave the convent. But my virtue and strong arguments arouse a desperate lust in Angelo. He of the severe Puritanical demeanor promises me that if I yield him my virginity, he will spare Claudio. That's where the bedtrick enters the story, a means to save my virtue while doing a good deed for Mariana, once betrothed to Angelo, who still loves him despite his abandoning her long before. When I said it sounded sordid, Shakespeare laughed.

"Not at all. True, it's not the usual sort of comedy, but no one dies and the play ends with marriages."

"I've never played such a role. You're no doubt right, Will. It should distract Her Majesty."

"Exactly. Wait till you read your part."

Although the play was not yet scheduled at the Globe, we learned our lines in hopes of a royal performance. We'd not said our lines aloud to each other. I hoped doing so would resolve my questions about Isabella.

One warm autumn day, Queen Elizabeth awoke without a pain or worry, summoned Sir Robert Cecil, and demanded that he invite us to her private dining room. She wanted *Measure for Measure* on the morrow.

Cecil sent Augustine Phillips a message post haste, which he read to us at the Anchor. "Perhaps the tireless Cecil needs a break as well," Phillips said as he folded the note. "He must be up to his neck scheming."

Tom Pope scowled. "I'd feel better if we'd rehearsed."

"We have tonight," Phillips said.

"The Queen's private dining room will be our smallest playing space yet," Armin said. "Smaller than the library, I believe."

"Then the Queen can be part of the action." Burbage laughed. "Perhaps she should play your role, Will, wise old Escalus."

"Too bad there'll insufficient space to portray riotous Vienna as the play opens," Armin said. "Lucio and Pompey and Mistress Overdone could create a carnival of misbehavior and encourage the groundlings to join in. Alas, we'll have to save that for the Globe."

"Yes, the dining room will limit action," Phillips said.

I doubted he'd ever had occasion to see that for himself, but at least Tom Pope was relieved. "So it will be like a reading, only without scripts."

Such rehearsal as we had that night didn't do much to ease my concerns. We'd have to let the lines carry us.

Next day as we waited in the service passage, servants passed us carrying what remained of the Her Majesty's dinner, half a dozen platters that looked untouched. We heard furniture being moved and the rustle of our audience.

Sir Robert Cecil came to the door. "The Queen wishes Master Shakespeare to enter first."

I crowded into the open doorway with the rest of our company to watch him approach Her Majesty. The room was hung with tapestries depicting Biblical subjects, and above the hearth stretched an intricately carved mantelpiece depicting the Virtues. The dining table had been moved to the back of the room, with the ladies' chairs arranged in a half circle to each side of the royal chair of state. A bare space before them would be our stage.

Shakespeare knelt before Queen Elizabeth, her peacock-blue gown draining the color from her face. Her makeup was more masklike than ever, and her wig under the simple diadem seemed carelessly arranged. "Rise, my man, and tell me about this play," she said.

"Today we bring you *Measure for Measure*. Set in Vienna under the rule of Duke Vincentio, it's a tale of justice gone wrong and justice restored."

"Well chosen, Master Shakespeare." The hint of a smile cracked her mask.

We entered single file, each kneeling before Her Majesty and taking our places to the side of the room, the Duke and Escalus remaining in front for the opening scene. I looked forward to not only watching the entire play but observing the Queen as well. We stood in the shadows, coming forward for our scenes, where the spoken word counted for everything.

Henry Condell's opening speeches as Duke Vincentio transformed the dining chamber into a council room in Vienna. He spoke to his deputy Angelo: "Your scope is as mine own, so to enforce or qualify the laws as to your own soul seems good."

Angelo, Richard Burbage in another unusual role, appeared more Puritan than courtier in his severe black garb. A flicker of interest brightened the Queen's eyes as the Duke outlined his plan. Angelo would undergo the fearsome test of power. Then she winced from a sudden stab of pain, subtly shifting her weight in the chair.

Nonetheless, she smiled at Robert Armin as Lucio, flamboyantly dressed in mustard gold and carmine. Lucio was Angelo's opposite, comic where Angelo was stern, lewd and frank where Angelo was self-righteous and hypocritical.

The privacy of the chamber lent intimacy to the scenes, making us eavesdroppers as the Duke confided to Friar Peter that he wished to remain in Vienna disguised as Friar Lodowick to see Angelo in action.

The Queen enjoyed Duke Vincentio's parting lines: "Lord Angelo is precise, . . . scarce confesses that his blood flows or that his appetite is more to bread than stone. Hence shall we see, if power change purpose, what our seemers be."

I imagined that Her Majesty would like to play spy herself, to see what people said behind her back. I probably knew more than she of gossip about the succession.

Her attention focused on Lucio, speaking without mockery to me as Isabella: "I hold you as a thing enskied and sainted, by your renouncement an immortal spirit, and to be talked with sincerity as with a saint."

During my audience with Angelo on behalf of my condemned brother, Lucio urges me on. I base my arguments for leniency on the Biblical text, "Judge not lest ye be judged." Angelo remains unmoved, insisting that he never had nor ever would commit a sin like Claudio's. Ironically, my passionate words, rather than convincing Angelo to be merciful to my brother, arouse his desire.

Angelo delays Claudio's execution, telling me to return on the morrow, alone. When I do, he is blunt: "I shall pose you quickly. Which would you rather, that the most just law now take your brother's life, or, to redeem him give up your body to such sweet uncleanness as she that he hath stained?"

I appeared not to follow his meaning. "I had rather give my body than my soul." I played to the Queen, as if Isabella understood but was trying to return the conversation to Claudio. So Angelo puts it directly: Isabella must "lay down the treasures of her body" or else Claudio dies.

I protested. "Lawful mercy is nothing kin to foul redemption," holding on to the hope that Angelo is testing me. When he assures me he's serious, I threaten to proclaim him publicly.

Who will believe me? he taunts. I'll only bring calumny upon myself, and my refusal will draw out my brother's death. Angelo gives me a day to decide. His parting words move me to despair. "Say what you can, my false outweighs your true."

Isabella hoped that her voice, fired by virtue and justice, could prevail. Clearly not, in the face of man's infamy and power. I wondered how that set with the Queen.

Out of Isabella's hearing, but only a few feet away from me awaiting my next scene, Angelo questions himself.

"Dost thou desire her foully for those things that make her good?" He has no thought of marrying Isabella, only of fulfilling his desire. "Never could the strumpet with all her double vigor, art, and nature once stir my temper. But this virtuous maid subdues me quite."

The disguised Duke, now Friar Lodowick, will have to labor mightily behind the scenes to remedy this imbalance. He counsels Claudio to accept his death sentence with equanimity and tells Isabella about Mariana. Angelo broke their engagement when her dowry was lost, but she loves him still. Lodowick proposes that Isabella agree to meet Angelo in the dark, but it will be Mariana who keeps the rendezvous.

After Mariana reveals that she embraced Angelo in the garden cottage, he must marry her. If all goes according to plan, Claudio will be saved, Isabella's chastity preserved, Mariana advantaged, and Angelo's corruption weighed in the scales of justice.

Queen Elizabeth registered no concern at this plot development but laughed aloud at Pompey the bawd. Perhaps even she could recognize him as a familiar of Bankside, just as Bankside women ran houses like Mistress Overdone's. She seemed to agree with wise old Escalus: keep the bawds and whores in the suburbs and control the worst excesses. As Lucio says about Angelo: "A little more lenity to lechery would do no harm in him: something too crabbed that way." Frances and I may have benefitted from the Queen's lenity to lechery.

Her response changed after Lucio slanders the absent Duke, whom he claims he knows well, accusing him of drunkenness and lewdness: "a very superficial, ignorant, unweighing fellow."

Friar Lodowick replies, "Either this is envy in you, folly, or mistaking. . . . Let the Duke be testimonied in his own bringings-forth, and he shall appear to the envious a scholar, a statesman, and a soldier." Whatever Lucio thinks about the Duke's character, Lodowick adds, "is much darkened in your malice." So does Lucio doom himself.

I caught the Queen's eye and saw a tear brimming. Perhaps Lucio's slander reminded her of her own vulnerability to gossip. She pursed her lips together, and I looked away.

Essex's betrayals had brought home the fading of her glory and invincible zest and certainty. Friar Lodowick's words reverberated: "No might nor greatness in mortality can censure scape. Back-wounding calumny the whitest virtue strikes. What king so strong can tie the gall up in a slanderous tongue?"

When I glanced back at the Queen, she was gasping for breath and wavering in her chair. Her eyes fluttered shut and she slumped over.

We froze.

Lady Scrope rushed to her, and one of her ladies produced smelling salts from her sleeve. In a few moments she came to and leaned against Lady Scrope. Sir Robert Cecil brought two strong serving men to help her out, her eyes half open.

At the door the Queen turned back toward our stunned faces.

In a voice we strained to hear, she said, "Another day, my friends, another day."

The royal party followed her out, only her household comptroller Sir Edward Wotton left behind. "You will make no mention of this incident. We shall send word when the play may continue."

Silently we changed out of our costumes and returned them to the chest in the tiring room. Eerie stillness lay heavy in the passageway. Royal palaces usually a buzzed with activity from distant chambers, the clamor of downstairs kitchens, hurrying servants, courtiers on every sort of errand. Now barely a murmur drifted from above like the whisper of angels. No one spoke until we were outside the palace gates.

"Did she actually faint?" Tom Pope asked.

"So it appeared," Armin replied, "but she left the room on her own two feet."

"With help," Pope said.

Armin turned to Condell. "We didn't get to finish our scene."

"Do you think the Queen took offense?"

"She laughed until the last moment," Shakespeare said. "We'll begin with that scene next time."

"You expect to return?" Phillips sounded incredulous.

"Of course! She would want a play if she were on her deathbed." Armin crossed himself. "May that be long from now." He turned into the Nag's Head and we followed.

At our large table, Pope grumbled, "I didn't get to say Elbow's best lines."

"Nor did most of us say our best. The Queen knows it. I'm sure we'll finish the play soon." Shakespeare raised his cup. "To Her Majesty's recovery."

Armin lifted his. "May she be quaffing a fine claret right this minute."

"Amen."

At home I described to Frances the calamity at Whitehall. "God save the Queen! Folks whisper that she has declined, but can you imagine this country without her?"

"I dread thinking about it. Playwrights and actors thrive because Queen Elizabeth loves theatre. Otherwise puritans would have shut down the play houses long ago."

The day after our aborted performance at Whitehall, Johnny was the last to join the company at the Anchor. He addressed Shakespeare, who sat nearest the door. "You'll need to find someone else to play Claudio."

In the midst of drinkers' uproar, our table went still. The serving girl with her jug hovered for a moment, then set it down, took a coin from Burbage, and retreated.

"Don't tell us that you're sentenced to serve Robert Cecil again." Burbage said. "Shame on you."

"Nothing of the sort. I must accompany Lady Elizabeth to Belvoir Castle."

"Hasn't she a steward and horsemen for such duties?" Phillips asked. "You can't come and go at will."

"I'm not a share-holder in Chamberlain's Men, nor do I expect to be. As a hired man, I may decline employment."

Too late to put my hand over Johnny's mouth, much as I wished to.

Phillips sounded unusually stern. "You're perfectly free to 'decline employment,' as you put it. Do not assume it shall again be offered."

Johnny dropped his bravado. "I don't mean to let you down. I owe you all a great deal—for my roles, your friendship, and you, Master Pope, for apprenticing me. This isn't an easy choice or a whim."

Shakespeare put down his cup with a bang, sloshing the contents. "Yet you're willing to leave your profession."

"Lady Elizabeth's husband won't provide for her unless she goes to Belvoir Castle."

"And you've volunteered to be the lady's entertainment?" Armin's words dripped scorn, which Johnny ignored.

"Only for the present. She's so desolate I cannot refuse."

Everyone looked at him as if he were mad. Tom Pope broke the silence.

"If you must go, practice your own writing. Make use of the library. Gain something besides Lady Elizabeth's undying gratitude and sinecure, which I suspect will be small."

"I shall return to London at the soonest opportunity."

"Do as you must," Phillips said. "We make you no promises."

Johnny grinned. "Perhaps Chamberlain's Men will perform at Belvoir."

Burbage gave him a withering look. "You'll be back here before that happens."

Rutland was unlikely to return to Queen Elizabeth's good graces, not with his close friend the Earl of Southampton condemned to the Tower for life. Johnny would be miles from us for the foreseeable future.

I covered my tankard with my hand when the girl appeared with refills. No more drink for me. I couldn't believe Johnny didn't tell me his plan privately.

"We wish you well, Johnny," Pope said. "Do say goodbye to my sister Ruth. No doubt she'll fill your pack with her good cooking."

Johnny gave me such a beseeching look that I walked out with him into the musty afternoon. The day was as dreary as Johnny's news. I felt as I had so often, that I didn't understand this brother of mine. Could he really think Lady Elizabeth offered him what he sought? Was he in love with her?

I spoke brusquely. "When do you leave?"

"Tomorrow. First, I'd like to come kiss Billy Boy goodbye."

Pushing my way through the crowds around Cheapside shops I asked, "And Frances?"

"Oh Sander, you know there's nothing between us. I love Billy Boy like a nephew and Frances like a sister. I'll come with you now." He headed toward our house without my encouragement.

My row with Frances over Lady Elizabeth still rankled. Ever since, we'd treated each other with cool courtesy. Johnny's visit felt unwise.

I let him enter first. Neither of us called out to Frances, bustling about in the kitchen. Johnny went to the cradle and lifted Billy over his head, which set them both laughing. He pulled the baby close to his chest. "I'll miss you, Nipperkins. You'll be chattering by the time I return."

Frances stood in the kitchen doorway. "Where are you going?"

"I'm off to Belvoir Castle. Wish me good fortune."

"I'll see what we have for a celebration." Frances disappeared into the kitchen, reappearing momentarily with a bowl of gooseberry fool.

This was not the reaction I'd expected.

"These berries looked so perfect, I made this in hopes we'd have a guest." Frances smiled at me rather than Johnny. "Otherwise thou wouldst have had to eat it all."

My heart was warmed by "thou."

Johnny looked chastened. "So I'm the lucky guest."

"You are." That was the extent of Frances' response to his news.

I poured out three cups of wine, and we sat around the table. Conversation was friendly, with no underlying currents. Frances entertained us with Billy's latest attempts at words, treating Johnny's mention of his journey north and the extent of Rutland's library as no more than passing news.

Billy lurched forward and grabbed a handful of the pudding. He licked it, ending up with cream all over face and hands. Laughing, Johnny stood up. "Boy after my own heart." He kissed Billy, getting a smudge of cream on his face.

At the door, Frances and I pulled Johnny into a three-way embrace with the baby in the center.

When he'd gone, Frances put Billy on her shoulder and embraced me, kissing me soundly on the lips. "I'm sorry for getting angry with you, Sander. Let's put this tired baby to bed, and then come sleep with me. It's been too long."

Dear Isabel,
I have a motion much imports your good,
Whereto if you'll a willing ear incline,
What's mine is yours, and what is yours is mine.
DUKE VINCENTIO'S FINAL WORDS TO ISABELLA,
MEASURE FOR MEASURE

CHAPTER XXXIX
January 1603

Measure for Measure opened at the Globe before a return invitation came from Whitehall Palace. The raucous behavior in Vienna was a huge hit with the groundlings, two or three jumping onstage and joining in. Burbage outdid himself as the puritanical Angelo, and George Bryan played Claudio with more humility than Johnny had. At the end, order restored and the Duke seeking Isabella's hand in marriage, she makes no reply. I gave him an equivocal look. Would Isabella marry Duke Vincentio? For the Queen, the answer would be yes, but here, I left it ambiguous.

The next day, I was hopeful when Amelia and Harry visited us at Cornhill. Maybe she could tell us what she'd heard from Whitehall now that she had a friend close to the Queen.

When Harry asked if he could play with the baby, Frances showed how to hold Billy by both hands so he could walk a few shaky steps. When he plopped down on the rug, Harry pulled out his flute and played a jingly tune he'd made up himself.

While Harry entertained Billy, Amelia answered our questions about the Queen's health. Though often infirm, she'd recovered from the spell that ended our private performance. "Lady Margaret says her will is so strong that in public no one imagines she's ailing. The Queen will reign until a warrior goddess sweeps her up to heaven."

Frances began to protest that Her Majesty was no pagan, but I laughed. "I can just picture it, the Queen and Boudicca ascending to heaven, cloaks flying, in a bronze chariot pulled by winged horses."

"I like that," Harry said. "Winged horses!" He returned to Billy Boy, sharing with him one of the cakes Frances had set out.

Amelia accepted a glass of wine. "I saw *Measure for Measure* yesterday at the Globe. I don't understand the ending."

"What about it?"

"Condell reappears in the last scene, again Duke Vincentio, and uses what he learned spying as Friar Lodowick to trap Lucio and Angelo in their vices."

"Surely you don't object?"

"No, but I was distressed about Isabella. Must she marry the Duke?"

Frances gave Harry another cake and passed the plate to us. "I saw the play too. All I can say is, Isabella would be marrying a Duke. Wouldn't that be an honor? Mariana marries faithless Angelo. Evidently she wants him, but what sort of husband will he be? And Lucio will marry Kate Keepdown. Poor Kate is stuck with a rudesby for a husband."

Amelia took a delicate bite. "Isabella didn't intend to marry anyone. She was on her way to become a holy sister."

"Exactly what I told Shakespeare," I said. "I can't see how the Duke's proposal is so very different from Angelo's. They both want to subdue Isabella's virtue to their own desires."

"I'd like to know what he said to that!" Amelia's eyes flashed.

"He said I should think about how she's changed since the beginning."

"The way you played that last moment, Sandro, I wasn't sure. You didn't take the Duke's hand."

"Nor did I turn away. I left it open on purpose. Let the audience decide." I sighed. "I'm fairly certain this will be the end of

Shakespeare's romantic comedies. Two plays that require bedtricks for the marriages."

"True," Frances said, "but Isabella and Mariana end up marrying the men they want."

I squeezed her hand. "If you say so."

"When the Roman faith was practiced in England," she said, "women who preferred study and good works to marriage and motherhood could retreat to convents. An Abbess or Prioress had authority. Maybe Isabella would be a Prioress some day, but at the end of this play I think she's seen too much of the real world to want to return to the convent."

"Or so much as to be well and truly finished with it," I said.

"If Isabella were a Prioress, would she have as much potency as a Duchess?" Amelia asked.

Frances laughed. "Well, we don't have Prioresses these days. But I still say Isabella willingly accepts the Duke. He's been her friend since he was Friar Lodowick. He respects her and honors her."

"Then you believe marriage is the right choice for a woman?" I asked.

"In most cases, yes. I'm happily married myself."

I kissed her cheek. "Me too."

No Twelfth Night revels at Whitehall Palace this year. Soon after Epiphany, rumors began to fly. Evidently the royal household was packing up to move to Richmond, the Queen's warm box of a palace. The silvery January day I heard the news, I walked sadly to the Anchor. Likely I'd never again see Her Royal Highness.

As we sat around the fire in our cozy chamber drinking ale, Phillips came in, rosy from the cold. "Tomorrow we play *Measure for Measure* in the Queen's Presence Chamber!"

"Are you certain?" Tom Pope stopped midstream filling a cup for Phillips.

"Right here in black and white." He waved a message. "Before she leaves for Richmond, Her Majesty wants to see the play from the beginning in a larger space than her dining room."

Pope glanced at the paper. "Is that in the message?"

"No, but that's what the page who delivered it told me. The Queen plans to return to Whitehall by early summer. This is her temporary farewell, and we're to provide the festivities."

"Richmond is smaller and more comfortable," Pope said "The change will do her good."

Shakespeare moved down the bench to make room for Phillips. "I doubt Cecil puts it that way to the Queen. She's not to be treated like an old lady."

"Or a dying one," Armin murmured.

Shakespeare gave him a pointed look. "Gloriana always rallies."

"I hope she rallies sufficiently to see the play to its end."

"She'll want Lucio to get his just desserts, Armin," Phillips said, "—before a large audience. We should expect her Council, Archbishop Whitgift, courtiers, ladies, and notable visitors. Her Majesty will preside as in healthier days."

"Besides," Burbage set down his tankard, "the play ends with a hearing of grievances. The Presence Chamber is just the place for that scene."

"The Duke conducts his hearing in the open street, not in a hall of grotesques." No doubt Armin meant the sculptures on the wall in the black and white chamber, grotesqueries all.

We ran through the play with manic energy, drawing on all our vitality for the Queen's benefit.

On the day of the performance we walked through the back passages of Whitehall, hung with the least valuable of the royal tapestries and no warmer for that. We would have to exert a great deal of effort against the weight of chill and gloom that permeated these walls. At least the tiring room had a blazing fire, and as we put on our costumes, we heard a buzz of conversation beyond. The Queen was seated.

Applause accompanied our entrance. The room was full, torches burning in their stanchions along the walls and candles fronting the stage.

Stiff on her chair of state, Queen Elizabeth resembled one of the relief sculptures decorating the walls. Her ladies had done something to her face to fill out the hollow cheeks, perhaps with linen padding, a thicker layer of makeup than ever holding it together. Her lips were carmine against the white mask of her face, and her wig blazed red under a pearl coronet.

I'd thought of the Queen's face as a mask because of how she concealed her emotions behind a serene visage. Now her eyes burned darkly out of the white paint as if she wore a carnival mask. This woman was fiercely alive, however gaunt her body beneath the velvet and brocade, however exaggerated her visage.

Those brilliant Tudor eyes examined the cast kneeling before her. When they rested on me, I felt a jolt pass between us. Understanding? On my part, sympathy for a noble, suffering woman. I poured all my warmth toward those piercing eyes.

The beginning of the play was somber, as befit the setting. Duke Vincentio handed over his power to his deputy Angelo in formal terms. But as soon as Lucio entered, followed by Mistress Overdone, the mood became bawdy, arousing laughter in even the elder of the ladies. Although the play was set in Vienna and the characters had Italian names, these scenes brought Bankside into the sedate chamber—a holiday into the wild suburbs.

We performed as if at a country faire, coming forth from the sidelines for our scenes. In between, we stood motionless, faces impassive, eyes observant. The Queen moved no more than we waiting players did, her corsets enforcing a regal posture.

Of course she could not acknowledge that age had caught up with her, that her powers waned. For now, we all pretended otherwise. Perhaps because of the bittersweet air of this performance, we avoided ambiguity at the end of the play. Not only did I, as Isabella, reach out a hand to the Duke, delighted to marry him, but Angelo put his arm around Mariana and Lucio embraced Kate Keepdown, a part with no lines played by our newest boy. The couples danced together as if happy marriages were in store for all. Betrothed Claudio and Juliet had been united at last, and the Duke and Isabella would rule Vienna in prosperity and joy.

I know I have but the body of a weak and feeble
woman, but I have the heart and stomach of a king,
and of a king of England too.
QUEEN ELIZABETH I

CHAPTER XL
February 1603

The Queen and all her household moved to Richmond Palace, none too soon. Sooty rain poured over London, tainting the city and its inhabitants.

Two days later as we finished breakfast, Frances received a message from her friend Lucy Hyde Osborn, the royal chamberer.

"I must go to Richmond immediately. The Queen is furious about her wardrobe. She intends to hold court, and they brought only one royal gown, her white taffeta. I'm to meet Lucy Hyde at the Royal Wardrobe to fill a chest with her finest."

Our voices had set Billy wailing, and I lifted him from the crib. "You'll have to spend the night in Richmond."

"More than one night, I fear." She sighed. "You know I've only been feeding him at night, and using the wet nurse Mother Tilda found less and less during the day. Billy's ahead of himself and happily takes the mash Rebecca makes him." Frances turned to the girl who was putting on her cloak. "We'll need your help, Rebecca."

"I can take him to the wet nurse after I finish at the shop."

I must have shown my distress. I'd never had the boy all to myself.

"Joan can spare you at the shop," Frances said. "Go tell her what's happened. She won't be happy to be there alone, but it's good training. Most everyone has enough winter clothes by now, and I'll be home well before the weather changes."

I pulled myself together. It might even be fun to be in charge of Billy. "I can make the mash and whatever you tell me, Rebecca. You don't have to be here all the time."

Rebecca gave me the tolerant look I'd seen on women's faces when dealing with men's domestic limitations. She assured me that she knew I was busy, that she'd be there as much as she could—and yes, she'd teach me how to feed him. "It can't just be bits of cheese, bread, and cakes. So don't worry, Mistress Frances. All will be in good hands here."

"I'm sorry to have to leave so suddenly. Lucy Osborne says the Queen is determined to receive embassies dressed in her finest. No sickbed for her. The Venetian ambassador arrives tomorrow."

I was as upset as Billy at her sudden departure, but jollying him out of his temper, I could only echo Rebecca's reassurances.

Frances squeezed my hand. "Who knows? Perhaps I'll see Her Majesty. No Silkwoman has been near her since the Earl of Essex died."

"At least you'll find out the truth. Rumor has her on her death-bed or working harder than ever. She's irascible and refuses company, or she dances the galliard till dawn. What's really going on?"

"I'll find out from gossip in the corridors, if nothing else."

"We'll miss you. I'm sorry you won't see *Hamlet* tomorrow at the Globe."

"Me too. You make a wonderful Gertrude."

I smiled, recalling how playing Gertrude brought Frances back to me.

She pulled away. "I'll return as soon as possible." While she went with Rebecca into the kitchen, I laid Billy in his cradle and rocked him gently.

"I'll go now, Mistress," Rebecca said. "After the shop I'll get what we need." She tucked away the purse Frances had given her and bid us farewell.

Frances went upstairs to gather her belongings. Sensing

something, Billy began whimpering. I bounced him on my knees until she reappeared.

With him between us, we embraced. Frances leaned down to kiss his forehead, then a longer kiss on my lips.

"I'll miss you both. You'll be in my heart." She retrieved her cloak warming by the fire, gave me a last embrace, and stepped into the wet morning.

I paced the floor, holding Billy close and crooning Hamlet's lines like a lullaby.

> *There are more things in heaven and earth, Horatio,*
> *Than are dreamt of in your philosophy. But come; . . .*
> *How strange or odd soe'er I bear myself,*
> *As I perchance hereafter shall think meet*
> *To put an antic disposition on . . .*

My own disposition must be stoic in Frances' absence. For how long? Instead of wondering when next we'd see her, I imagined myself in her shoes.

We'd visited the Royal Wardrobe in St. Andrews, a short walk from Cornhill, so I could easily picture Lucy meeting her there amidst the cedar cupboards smelling of lavender and rosemary, with a sharp undertone of wormwood to keep moths from invading the domain of robes worn by monarchs time out of mind.

Now the Wardrobe housed Queen Elizabeth's most opulent clothing and some thousand more pieces, including gowns presented to her as gifts. Frances had been in charge of keeping Her Majesty abreast of French fashion, adding and subtracting to the rich garments she already possessed. I pictured Frances and Lucy sorting through neatly folded gowns protected by linen, reminiscing about when they were worn or for what portrait. Though the Queen had grown thinner, her clothes still fit, or Frances would make sure that they did. It was imperative that she regard herself as perpetually young, Gloriana beloved by all of England. The majority of her subjects had known no other ruler. No wonder rumor was rife. Her decline, if we dared call it that, was a frightening prospect.

But one should not underestimate Her Majesty. She might live for many months. I'd heard that a sense of power oft surged through a person nearing their end, the swan singing her heart out before darkness falls. Her courtiers and ladies were wise to be cautious.

"It's better playing with a lion's whelp than an old one dying," as Shakespeare had remarked. As soon as he said this, he'd clapped his hand over his mouth: it was forbidden to say "dying" or "death" in relation to the Queen.

Leaving the Royal Wardrobe, Frances and Lucy would take the clothing chest to Blackfriars Dock and go upriver on the royal barge under black clouds. Perhaps my poet waterman friend John Taylor would convey them to Richmond. Recently he'd recited to me the poem he wrote for Frances, "To the Needle," and would take the opportunity to say it to her.

> To all dispersed sorts of arts and trades
> I write the needle's prayse (that never fades).
> So long as children shall be got or borne,
> So long as garments shall be made or worne,
> So long as hemp or flax, or sheep shall bear
> Their linen woollen fleeces yeare by yeare,
> So long as silk-wormes, with exhausted spoile,
> Of their own entrails for man's gaine shall toyle,
> Yea till the world be quite dissolv'd and past,
> So long at least, the needle's use shall last.

Frances would love hearing how Taylor made her work significant and eternal.

When I'd asked him if he wrote down his spontaneous songs for the Queen, Taylor laughed. "I'll leave that to the fancy boys with their silk slippers."

Today, the river would be brown and thick as pease porridge under dense grey clouds. A peel of thunder interrupted my reverie, followed by a flash of lightning. May Frances be safe!

Since we'd reconciled, she and I hadn't spent a night apart. Not always in the same bed, but ever under the same roof. Though

Frances could write, we'd had no occasion to exchange letters. Now that's all we would have.

Before I could write to her about our performance of *Hamlet*, I received a message that she and Lucy arrived safely in Richmond. The Queen had spent the night at the sickbed of the dearest of her ladies, the Countess of Nottingham: Lady Katherine Howard, one of her Boleyn cousins.

"They fear the sweating sickness. The Queen is too distraught to think about fashion, but we are to remain here, in cold, crowded quarters. We hope the Countess recovers. Otherwise we'll be making mourning clothes. My best news is that Lady Helena Snakenborg Gorges has taken me under her wing. I miss you and Billy! Your loving wife, Frances."

Next day another message arrived. "The Countess of Nottingham died. The Queen has retired to her rooms, attended by Lady Helena and Lady Scrope. No official mourning for a Queen's lady, even one of royal blood, so bells ring only in the private chapel. Black thread and black fabric require much light these short dim days."

In a way, I was glad there was no public mourning for the Countess. It would only feed rumor, already rampant. The Queen was too grieved to rule and civil war would soon wrack the nation. Or, as she'd named no successor, England would end up ruled by Sir Robert Cecil. Flood, fire, disease would be loosed. The end was near.

I didn't take such dire prophecies seriously. Folks had worried that the dawning of the year 1600 would bring disaster, which it had not. But the unsettled situation could delay Frances' return home indefinitely.

My letters assured her that I spent much time with Billy and Rebecca capably ran the house. London stages remained lively, and on stormy days, the Red Bull and Cross Keys inns served as playhouses. For brief winter's days, companies generally chose short plays, but the Lord Chamberlain's Men expected to perform *Hamlet* again before the end of February. I hoped Frances would be home by then.

When Lucy Hyde Osborn came to Whitehall on a royal errand,

she brought Frances' latest letter and a fuller report. The morning's showers had turned into full rain and she accepted my offer to stay through the worst of the storm, even though I felt awkward, entertaining a member of the Queen's intimate circle in our house, which surely appeared humble to her. Still, talking with someone so close to Frances made up for my misgivings.

When Rebecca brought us wine and cakes, she gazed at Lucy with admiration. Not simply because she was the royal chamberer, but so young and pretty, her pale yellow hair coiled in an elegant plait like a crown.

"This is Rebecca, Frances' new apprentice and Billy's big sister these two long weeks."

Lucy extended her hand. "Mistress Frances gives you high praise, Rebecca. With your permission, Master Cooke, she may stay to listen to a strange story from Richmond. Frances said if you're home, I could tell you about the meeting between Queen and le Compte de Beaumont, the French ambassador. As you're both outside the palace circle, I'm sure you'll keep this to yourselves."

We promised.

"It's a sad event that troubled Frances and me and all the Queen's ladies." Lucy took a deep breath, as if, now that she'd started, she wished she hadn't. I wouldn't have minded, but Rebecca's bright-eyed anticipation must have encouraged her to continue.

"As I'm sure you both know, appearance has always been central to Her Majesty. Lately, alas, she's lost interest. After her cousin Katherine Howard died, her black mourning dress made her face look ghostly and her eyes haunted. Even when she gave up mourning, her looks didn't improve. She would wear two large pearls dangling from her ears or a gold chain to her waist, but the rest was careless despite our best efforts."

Lucy nibbled a cake, looking absently at Rebecca as if thinking of how best to tell the story or perhaps debating whether to continue. Decisively, she brushed the crumbs from her lap. "It used to be that the palace revolved around the Queen's authority and commands. Her air of power began to lessen after the execution of Robert

Devereux, but she rallied as she always does. Her loss of her cousin Lady Katherine has evidently been too much.

"A few days ago the Queen called for a mirror. Twenty years had passed since she last looked into one. When she saw her face reflected, she exploded with rage. 'Liars, they are all liars. My council and courtiers flatter me, but in truth I'm old and ugly. Men are ever false, not a one of them to be trusted!'"

Rebecca looked aghast. "How terrible!"

"To a large degree, the Queen had believed in her invincible beauty. Her anger was terrifying. Her advisors had betrayed her! You can imagine our worries about her receiving the French ambassador in that state. We could only hope her regal vitality would prevail."

"Regal vitality," Rebecca repeated. "What pretty words!"

"On the day of Her Majesty's audience with the ambassador, Frances and I carried her two best gowns to the Queen's private chamber where she sat with Lady Helena, Lady Scrope, and the Countess of Warwickshire. She agreed to a paneled skirt embroidered with seed pearls and gold but could not be talked out of a bodice with a low pointed stomacher and ribbon fasteners down the front—definitely not one of those we'd selected. I tried to attach a wide ruff to the neckline, but the Queen would have none of it. 'Only strings of pearls.'

"The ribbons were difficult to secure. The overall effect was not becoming and would be worse if the ties loosened. Her ladies did their best with her facepaint, continuing the white over her bosom, as the bodice was cut low. We tried to make up for the deficiencies of the Queen's costume with an elaborate wig and crown.

"Frances and I were dismayed. The Countess of Warwick accompanied Her Majesty to the Privy Chamber, while the other two ladies remained behind with us. Lady Scrope feared how the fashionable le Compte de Beaumont might exaggerate the Queen's ill dress in his report. When Her Majesty returned, seemingly satisfied with her meeting with le Compte, she looked even worse than Lady Scrope feared. Disheveled, with loose ribbons revealing her shift." Lucy sighed. "That's the last official audience for now. Her Majesty contracted a cold immediately afterward and has retreated to her private rooms."

"Is her condition serious?" Rebecca asked.

"That woman has a remarkably strong constitution! She's always kept her illnesses to herself, more of them than you'd guess. She simply retires until they pass. Her doctors aren't worried, but her throat hurts so she's particularly irritable."

"Will Frances return home soon?"

"She said to give you her love, Master Cooke. She'll leave Richmond as soon as possible." Lucy looked out the front window. "Ah, the rain is clearing." She took up her cloak, but stopped at the cradle where Billy was stirring. "Let's see that darling baby of yours."

That we shall die we know; 'tis but the time
And drawing days out, that men stand upon.
BRUTUS, *JULIUS CAESAR*

CHAPTER XLI
Late February–March 1603

R umors of the Queen's indisposition spread, but on Bankside, plays and revelry continued.

As we rehearsed for a revival of *Julius Caesar*, the lines sounded freshly ominous, even before Caesar's murder in the Senate. Describing Caesar's weakness, Cassius could have been describing Queen Elizabeth.

> *He had a fever when he was in Spain*
> *And when the fit was on him, I did mark*
> *How he did shake; 'tis true, this god did shake.*
> *His coward lips did from their color fly,*
> *And that same eye, whose bend doth awe the world,*
> *Did lose his lustre.*

Audiences at the Globe loved the play, but though the Queen had nothing remotely like coward lips, backstage we were ill at ease.

Frances didn't return in time for that show. She wrote that the Queen's condition had improved sufficiently for her to meet with Lord Cecil and her council, but she isolated herself from her ladies, all but Lady Helena, Lady Scrope, and Lady Anne Russell, the Countess of Warwick. Her letter ended: "The Queen has more than enough gowns in good repair for the demands on her life, fit to be treasures of the state. I shall soon be released from Richmond."

The next day I learned that a barge had been booked for Frances'
return to Blackfriars Dock. After the tide turned, I made my way
through icy slush to await her there.

Frances, warmly bundled, her nose red, practically jumped out of
the boat and rushed into my arms.

"Welcome home! I'd almost forgotten what you look like, wife."

She laughed. "You can scarcely see me under this hood." We
walked home, our well-clad shoulders touching.

Inside, she swooped Billy into her arms and nuzzled his
sweet-smelling neck.

After a startled wail, he gurgled with delight.

"My dearest boy."

Rebecca waved from the kitchen. "Dinner is almost ready."

"Thank you for all you've done, Rebecca. Lucy Osborne called
you Billy's big sister."

"We did our best, Mistress, but it's a relief you're home."

"And besides," I said. "You're in time to see *Hamlet* tomorrow," I
said as we settled in front of the fire, Billy curled in against his mother.

"Has Master Shakespeare given Gertrude more lines?"

"Not a one. But never mind that. *Hamlet* could be about the
present time. I know. It's set in long ago Denmark, but Elsinore feels
strangely like England. Elsie's land."

Frances looked puzzled.

"Elsie, as in Elizabeth," I said. "That's what Ben Jonson said."

No wonder Frances was bewildered: few referred to Queen
Elizabeth as Elsie or Liz or any homely nickname. Once in a while
Good Queen Bess.

"There's no murdering usurping brother in England."

"True, but think about it, Frances. We have chaos and confusion
regarding the succession and the Queen's health. There's a sense of
decay, similar to what Hamlet feels in Elsinore, ruled by his uncle
and mother. He may be pretending madness, but it is a maddening
situation. No one to trust, no clear action. Hamlet is paralyzed, and
when he does act, he mistakenly stabs Polonius."

"I see little similarity to today, and I've just been with the

Queen." She sounded irritated. "She may not be well, but she's hardly decaying!"

"You're right. We'd rather think of Good Queen Bess as the marvel she's been all these years." I rose when Rebecca called us to dinner, a stew rich with mutton and a special wine I'd saved. She filled our bowls and I our wine glasses while Frances tied Billy into his chair with a towel as he waved his spoon happily. Over our meal, I asked Frances to tell us about her time in Richmond.

"First tell me the London gossip, Sander. No doubt it's raced ahead of anything I know."

"You're the one who's been near the Queen's heart."

"Not so very near. Since Lady Katherine died, only her three best-loved ladies were in her confidence. I can tell you how the royal apartments smell, with bowls of orange rind and lavender to keep them fragrant. No hint of illness, although her bedchamber was surprisingly dark, no candles lit, only one open window."

Rebecca looked at her with amazement. "You were in the Queen's private bedchamber?"

"I was as surprised as you. Even though the Queen hates fare-wells, Lady Helena Snakenborg suggested I look in on her before I left. Her Majesty, fully gowned and corseted, stood gazing out the window over the trees of Richmond Park. When she realized we knelt at the door, she invited us to enter. It was uncanny. As she stepped into a band of sunlight, she fairly shone. She looked at me and said the most peculiar thing."

Rebecca's spoon stopped partway to her mouth.

"Queen Elizabeth asked me what I had to add. I must have looked confused, for she said, 'Dr. John Dee just left. He tells me if I have another severe attack I should not go to bed. What do you say?' All I could reply was that Dr. Dee is a wise man, but bedrest can be healing. She scoffed. 'Nonsense. You are as bad as my ladies.'

"I curtseyed and wished her good health, but my voice seemed swallowed by darkness. She dismissed me even more surprisingly. 'My health is fine. You go on home to your shop and your husband.' And then she actually smiled."

Rebecca echoed, "The Queen smiled at you!" but royal mention of Frances' husband was what startled me.

"Yes, she actually smiled. I'm sure you've heard how rare is her smile, because of her teeth, it is whispered. Indeed, they're yellowish brown and two are missing, but the smile brightened her face and her eyes sparkled. 'You and Alexander are a remarkable pair. Long may you prosper.'"

No doubt "a remarkable pair" went over Rebecca's head, but I was touched.

"After Lady Helena and I backed out of the room, she said, 'That's more spirit than Her Majesty has shown in days. Perhaps Dr. Dee's visit did her good, crusty old wizard that he is.' If the Queen can smile at a Silkwoman, there's hope for her recovery. Her cold is minor compared to the loss of her zest for life. I'd feared that this would be my last sight of her, but her condition seems hopeful."

I added a generous splash to our wine glasses. "As hopeful as that ray of sunshine in her gloomy chamber."

"The Queen is still herself."

When Rebecca rose to clear the table, Frances said, "The Queen's heart is troubled over more than the loss of Lady Katherine. Her doctor had to cut her coronation ring off her finger. They say she begged him not to, even though it was digging into her flesh so painfully that her finger turned blue."

"A terrible omen."

"Yes, that's how Her Majesty regards it. She's become obsessed by omens. Lady Helena says the doctor believes that she suffers from what the Greeks called *paranoia*, a mania of suspicion and dread."

"She has reason," I said.

"True. She isn't mad to imagine whispers and plots. Her corridors buzz with them."

"That's part of why Shakespeare says we're living in Elsinore. The omens are real. Hamlet is haunted by the ghost of his father. Does the ghost speak true or is he a deceiver in the service of the devil? Neither answer reassures."

"You once said that I'm not of a metaphorical mind. You're right,

Sander, but I understand what you mean about doubts and omens. Everyone believes that Sir Robert Cecil has secret schemes."

"Such as?"

"That I cannot say, and I couldn't remain at Richmond to find out. A sad, uncertain place, and I missed you and Billy. I know this much. Queen Elizabeth will not depart quietly."

"The passing of great ones," I mused. "Tragic for her, tragic for the country. Some folk believe her time has ended and we're ready for a fresh new era, a fresh new ruler. But what if that person should be a royal relative like Arbella Stuart or Katherine Grey?"

"No one at Richmond mentions either of them. Lady Helena told me that long ago the Queen remarked that the son of her cousin Mary Stuart would be a good king, as James already rules Scotland. But Helena says she's not mentioned King James lately."

"Putting off decisions was her mode of diplomacy, but sometimes that's impossible. All in all, Queen Elizabeth has been an extraordinary ruler." I glanced around our comfortable house. "We owe most of this to her. Her love of plays kept the public theatres open, and her love of fine clothes kept you in work. Our future under another ruler is doubtful. As is everyone's."

"We pray for her health."

Rebecca had cleared the table and retreated to sleep, the fire had burned down, and I lit a candle. "I've missed you, Frances. Let's to bed."

Later, warm in her arms, I was surprised that I hadn't fallen immediately to sleep. Her breathing was even, mine ragged.

Queen Elizabeth worried less about her advisors' deception or the future of England than about death, I suspected. I'd rarely given a thought to my own, though I'd feared for Frances in childbed. Perhaps it's not death one dreads so much as the final reckoning. May God forgive Her Majesty for any missteps. In all, she acted for the good of England as she saw it.

I sighed and gently extricated myself from Frances' embrace. With a degree of trickery, we'd been married in the eyes of God. Frances, in her youth an ardent believer in the Old Faith, agreed so as to give her child legitimacy and a family. I could argue the same. My taking the part of the groom was for poor little Marie, and now for precious Billy. But Frances and I were lovers as well as parents. In the eyes of Father Jaggard, the preacher of my youth, I committed the greater sin, for I played the man.

I shook myself. So too did I in taking on boy's clothing and person. So too on stage, a male actor playing female roles. These disguises had caused me little spiritual concern.

Was there such a thing as a final reckoning? Do we not owe our first duty to our fellow men and women on earth? If so, the Queen brilliantly served the nation. She need not fear judgment. Nor, I hoped, need I worry for my own soul.

After all, in the new Protestant order, Purgatory and the fiery hell of the Old Faith no longer filled us with terror. Perhaps the Greeks were right. None but those who sin against the gods, like blasphemous Tantalus and Sisyphus, suffered eternal punishment. At death, heroes went to the Elysian Fields and all other souls into darkness. Hades lacked sun and sea and the joys of life. For the Greeks, all souls suffered that loss, the only punishment after death. Of any in our world, the spirit of Queen Elizabeth deserved the Elysian Fields.

I found my own peace curled around Frances. My wearied mind released on the thought: I love Frances. I love Billy. All is well.

All is well.

Thou know'st 'tis common; all that lives must die,
Passing through nature to eternity.
GERTRUDE, *HAMLET*

CHAPTER XLII
Spring 1603

On March 23, 1603, not a bell rang in London. In a city usually alive with bells, the silence was eerie. When a great one was dying, clappers were muted so that all could pray. But now, no sound. In Queen Elizabeth's forty-five years on the throne, no preparation had been made for her mortal illness or death. Perhaps the Queen still lived. If she lay on her deathbed, surely every bell from Richmond to Greenwich would be softly tolling.

The suspense sent Londoners into their houses, hiding their valuables and putting their affairs in order, some preparing to flee the city. The worst was upon us, the future dark.

By nightfall, we heard Queen Elizabeth had taken to her bed and Archbishop Whitgift prayed her into the next world on aching knees. Near the end she made a sign to Sir Robert Cecil acknowledging King James of Scotland as her chosen heir. Emissaries galloped to Holyrood Palace in Edinburgh with the news.

"The Queen loved us, and we never forsook her," was on every tongue.

Those close to the court whispered that melancholy had seized her and speculated that she could have been cured, had she the will. When Frances heard this, she said, "Queen Elizabeth had had enough. She'd done all she could for England, and her fighting spirit abandoned her."

Sir Robert Cecil, who anticipated—or engineered—the Queen's endorsement of Scottish King James, wasted no time broadcasting the news. On the morning of March 24, he led a procession of counselors and justices to the High Cross at Cheapside where as much of London as could fit there stood waiting. I stood with my fellow players, leaving Frances home with Billy.

When the procession came to a stop, so did all whispering. Looking down at us, Cecil read out a proclamation that ended: "the High and Mighty Prince, James VI King of Scotland is now by the death of our late sovereign, Queen of England of famous memory, become also our only, lawful, lineal, and rightful Liege James the First, King of England, France, and Ireland, defender of the faith."

After prolonged silence, a few cried, "God save the King." Others joined in flat voices, and we dispersed in silence. Looking at the stunned faces, I remarked to Shakespeare, "Never in London have I seen such a dull crowd."

"Look more closely." He nodded his head toward the rapidly departing men and women. "They're in a state of shock. For all our lives we've cried 'God save the Queen.' We can't imagine what it will mean to have a Scotsman on the throne of England, nor what will happen until he arrives."

No tumult broke out in the streets. In fact we heard an occasional church bell. As folk quietly made their way home, I sensed unease. What lay ahead?

Gossip made its way from Scotland long before the new ruler did, as his trip from Edinburgh was like one of Queen Elizabeth's progresses. Noblemen entertained King James VI of Scotland as he went, satisfying his rumored penurious means and taste for good food. As he rode south, with English folk lining his route, we heard that James was married to Anne of Denmark and had a brood of healthy children. Reportedly he had bad table manners, a love of hunting, a strange manner of speaking, a peculiar fascination with witches, and a tendency to kiss handsome young men on the mouth.

Conjecture outran rumor. Who will be our allies and enemies?

Can Scotland and England be united? Will Scots run the Privy Council? Who will advance and who fall? How will James treat Catholics? What about Queen Elizabeth's jewels?

And: what will happen to the Lord Chamberlain's Men? That was our biggest question. What will become of Alexander Cooke, actor, and Frances Cooke, Silkwoman?

On April 28, while James still traveled to London, Queen Elizabeth's magnificent funeral procession moved from Whitehall Palace to Westminster Abbey where she was to be buried.

Surrounded by actors and theatre folk, Frances and I watched the procession from near its beginning. Lines of black-clad mourners passed, ranks of poor women, officers and gentlemen bearing standards and arms, gentlemen and children of the Chapel singing mournfully. The crowd moaned, and when the hearse passed by, wept openly.

Upon the coffin lay a wax effigy of the Queen, her face and hands painted to look lifelike, her robes red velvet and ermine. On her head a crown, in her hands a ball and scepter: Gloriana, become immortal.

As weeping intensified, Thomas Dekker, playwright friend of Shakespeare, said, "This hearse swims in water." Following the hearse came the chief mourners, Elizabeth's ladies and maids of honor, and bringing up the rear, Sir Walter Ralegh and the Guard, their halberds facing downward.

"Queen Elizabeth's long peaceful reign seems a blessing never to return," Frances said as she and I pushed our way toward Westminster in the somber crowd.

"We have come to the end of a glorious, exuberant era."

A week later, King James arrived at Theobalds, Cecil's grand house in Hertfordshire, some twelve miles from London. Crowds had begun thronging to London for his arrival, and many gathered outside

Theobalds House to watch the parade of finely caparisoned English lords and the less elegant Scots.

Shakespeare and Burbage made the journey to see his arrival. Burbage reported that outside Theobalds petitions were presented to the king "just like those to the Duke at the end of *Measure for Measure.*"

"But King James made no public pronouncements," Shakespeare said. "He was quick to escape to his private chambers. We didn't get a good look at him, just a broad chest and surprisingly bandy legs. He holds himself well on a horse."

When the new king entered London five days later, it was only as far as the Charterhouse in Islington, north of the city proper. London was more crowded than ever I'd seen it. The promise of streets hung with gold and business for every sort of tradesmen drew countrymen and villagers from afar.

Frances returned from a busy day at her shop with the news that plague deaths had risen since the Queen's funeral.

Housing was always short in London, and we appreciated our dwelling in Cornhill. Narrow houses crowded inside the city walls as well as illegal sheds and tenements outside with stinking ditches of waste where chance of disease was compounded. Now plague as well? Possibly, as days grew warmer.

"If there's a danger of infection, Frances, shouldn't you stay at home?"

"Business is brisk, very brisk."

"What good are your profits if you're stricken ill? Close the shop if there's even one case of plague near the Bridge. Please, Frances, for Billy's sake."

Plague deaths had further increased by the time King James arrived for his tour of the Tower. Londoners tried to keep it secret from the authorities to avoid houses of sufferers being marked with red crosses and shut up, imprisoning sick and healthy alike. The truth would curtail public assemblies and city life would come to a standstill.

"Everyone wants a grand royal show," Richard Burbage said one evening when he and Shakespeare dined on Frances' savory pottage. "None wish the coronation to be cancelled."

"Is pageantry worth dying for?"

When the new king made his way to Whitehall Palace in May, no grand entry procession greeted him. Plague had been officially acknowledged. The Royal Arch being built for James' entry was hastily dismantled, to be erected when deemed safe. Nonetheless, King James began his royal business immediately, knighting his followers, choosing his officers.

On May 19, he named the company formerly known as the Lord Chamberlain's Men as his own! We were now the King's Men, though amidst the current uncertainties we couldn't imagine what that would mean.

News leaked out of the Palace, none of it of concern to us except the possible closing of theatres. We heard that the coronation would be in July, but by then who knew where we'd be if theatres were shuttered? Our number had been reduced by one: dear Thomas Pope, my prentice master of the big heart and robust humor, died. Not of plague. Nature simply caught up with him.

"So," Robert Armin said, "we're the King's Men who can't perform in a royal palace."

"Don't be so gloomy, man," Augustine Phillips said. "We're alive, all save Tom Pope, may he rest in peace."

"Good old Pope," Burbage said. "A man of integrity and strong opinions."

"The most generous householder in Southwark," Shakespeare added.

"And best prentice-master." I felt Pope's loss to the heart, the man who fostered my talents and never penetrated my disguise, who welcomed Johnny when he arrived at our door. Tom Pope was ever kind and generous and a gifted comic actor. He never did enjoy going on the road. At least he'd been spared that.

Our company prepared to leave London, all except those who

went to their home villages or other retreats. Johnny traveled to Belvoir Castle, Shakespeare to Stratford-upon-Avon, Condell to East Anglia, Heminges to Worcestershire. Amelia planned to visit Cookeham in Berkshire, the home of Margaret, Countess of Cumberland, and her daughter Lady Anne Clifford. I'd travel with the players, while Rebecca and Joan accompanied Frances and Billy Boy to Rosa Frith's house in Stevenage.

My rowdy friend Moll, Rosa Frith's niece, refused to leave London: "I fled Stevenage as soon as I could and have no desire to return. Plague won't dare strike me!"

Do you not know I am a woman? When I think,
I must speak.
      ROSALIND, *AS YOU LIKE IT*

CHAPTER XLIII
August 1603

We travelled the countryside for some two months, the king's coat of arms on our wagon making us welcome in towns too far north to be hit by plague, though occasionally we were turned away or asked to perform in a field or on the grounds of great estates. It felt like my long-ago summer on the road with Lord North's Men before I came to London, carefree and innovative as each playing situation changed. Our wagon and camaraderie were the only constants, and for the most part, sufficient coins came our way to make it worth our time.

Phillips had chosen shortened versions of several plays to alternate, though *A Midsummer Night's Dream* was a favorite. Not only did I play Titania and Hippolyta, but also one of Peter Quince's mechanicals. Phillips took care of every detail. "Our very own Henslowe," Burbage laughed, but I doubt Henslowe's Admiral's Men could have done as well.

Unless put up at an inn or manor, we slept under the stars. Sometimes our proximity worried me, but part of traveling together was mutual respect. I went into the bushes alone and changed my clothes and bathed carefully. Johnny would have looked out for me, but I didn't need him.

At last the long-awaited invitation came, not from King James himself but from William Herbert, the new Earl of Pembroke, summoning us to Wilton House to perform for the king. Our costumes too threadbare for royalty, we detoured to London for our best, securely stored at the Globe. Phillips sent out message to our far-flung members to meet us there.

As our wagon approached the city through Bishopsgate, plump clouds and a hazy blue sky gave no hint that in shadowy streets and lanes beyond, red crosses marked many a door and carts carried the night's dead to Finsbury Fields. Shops on Cheapside and London Bridge were shut tight. Markets were closed, but ramshackle stalls selling food and a few bakeshops were open. Otherwise the city felt dead. Bankside was more lively, taverns and brothels welcoming customers. Though the plague had begun in the suburbs south of the Thames, the more crowded north had been harder hit.

"We could stop at Stevenage and collect Frances," I said to Shakespeare as we checked the Globe storage room to be sure we'd remembered everything. "It's on the way to Wiltshire."

"Don't tell me you want the baby to come as well."

"Rosa Frith will tend him—and," I indicated the stack of tattered attire, "we could use a costume mistress."

"I suppose you're right. I doubt anyone will object."

Even Armin agreed. Frances had proven herself useful in the past. With a smile in my heart, I sent word ahead to Stevenage. I'd see Billy at least briefly, and Frances would visit Wilton House, the prettiest manor in southwest England.

As our coach and wagon rattled out of London, I thought back on the very different person I'd been when last I saw Wilton. Alexander Cooke, a boy actor enamored of John Donne. Who would guess I'd return with a wife of my own? Donne was now married too, but less easily, I'd heard, as he and Anne More married clandestinely because her family opposed their union.

No one had opposed Frances and mine. Being a player with no known family helped, and Frances' widowed mother dwelt far off in Leicestershire. London freed us to marry. Despite all the rules and strictures, we had created our own haven in Cornhill, which would welcome us back after plague passed.

Now the open road beckoned our reassembled company, including Johnny who'd had quite enough solitude at Belvoir. Hedgerows bloomed with hawthorn and bramble, birds warbled, bees hovered noisily, ponds sparkled through the trees as we dashed by. The bonny English countryside on a hot August day.

Outside the Frith's door, Frances and Rosa waved a welcome. With the help of Joan and Rebecca, they'd set up a long trestle table in the garden laden with pies, cheese, bread, bowls of late cherries, and jugs of ale.

After a quick splash from the well bucket to rinse off road dust, we took our places on benches down each side of the table. Billy greeted me with "Da, da." Johnny showed only an uncle's curiosity about the child. Frances squeezed onto the bench next to me and Armin opened his arms to the baby, bouncing him on his knee and feeding him bits of cheese.

We might have been on holiday, wind rustling the trees above and calves lowing in the field, but the urgency to reach Wiltshire brought an end to our festive meal. Leaving the pleasant yard, we waved goodbye to Rebecca, Joan, and Billy in Rosa Frith's arms, his little face puckered into tears.

Wilton House was even more beautiful than I recalled. Trees had grown, flower borders blossomed in radiant color, and the house shone in its full glory. To me, it resembled a lady, iron pipework on the brick front like panels on a skirt and windows gleaming in feminine rainbow swirls. Yet despite its delicate elegance and the expanded pavilion above the vast back lawns, the manor would soon be a relic, if it stood at all. From what we'd heard, King James overflowed with new ideas for architecture and plantings, and William Herbert was one of his chief courtiers.

We came in the side entrance near the stable yard, where Herbert's mother the Countess of Pembroke, my old friend Marie, welcomed us. Serving girls offered damp towels and led us to the dining hall. One wall consisted almost entirely of tall windows opening to the terraces, lawns, and woods beyond, and the other walls were covered with linenfold paneling hung with portraits of Pembroke ancestors.

The family's supper had ended, but wine, plates of roast sausages and vegetables, fruit, breads, and sweets were laid out for us. Marie presided at the head, Shakespeare on her right and Burbage on her left, the rest of us seating ourselves down each side.

"My sons have ridden out to escort the king." She lifted her glass. "Do begin."

"We're delighted to play for King James at last," Phillips said.

"His Majesty appreciates the chance to leave Hampton Court Palace. According to my son William, he's been feeling like he's under house arrest. No sooner did he arrive in London than plague chased him out of Whitehall Palace. The king will have only a small retinue of Scots attending him, as most English lords have fled to their country houses."

"And Queen Anne?" asked Phillips.

"She's off somewhere with their children, but she should be here soon. King James hopes to go hunting in our woods, but he says you players are even more attractive than the deer."

Shakespeare smiled. "Because we have two legs?"

"Two good legs each and a playscript worth the speaking."

"We've been the King's Men since May," Phillips said, "and all we have to show for it till now are liveries and a travelling fund. Thank you for inviting us."

"Our very great pleasure. You'll be lodged on the second floor. The maid will show you your rooms. As William mentioned in his note, he and I think *As You Like It* is the perfect choice. We have our very own Forest of Arden and it's a good English comedy, with shepherds and exiles and," she smiled at me, "a fetching young Ganymede." Marie turned to Frances. "I'm happy to meet you at last, Mistress Cooke. You're most welcome." She gave me a quick glance. "Your husband stays with the players. You shall room with my chief housekeeper."

I would share with Johnny and Henry Condell, who played Duke Senior. Johnny had seemed distracted, I thought perhaps because he played only Oliver at the beginning and end of the play and one of Duke Senior's merry men in the Greenwood, the forester who sings, "What shall he have who killed the deer?" Or was it Lady Elizabeth who preoccupied him, here in the house of her aunt and cousins?

By the time we finished our meal, the sky beyond the glass doors had turned amethyst. We followed Marie to the windows.

"You'll be playing just there." She indicated a broad terrace outside the door. "The audience will sit on the lower level. That private withdrawing chamber," she pointed to a door to one side of the room, "is your tiring room, which also opens onto the stage."

Shakespeare smiled. "We couldn't ask for a better setting than your gardens, Countess."

As we climbed the stairs to our bedchamber, I asked Johnny why he'd seemed so glum today.

"I'm not glum at all when I think about my play."

"Trouble with the ending?"

"No—it's done. But now what?"

"You finished it?"

Condell pushed open the door to our chamber. "Don't sound so surprised, Sander. You knew he would one day."

Though I'd not been so sure, I slapped Johnny on the back. "Congratulations!"

"Surely you've told Ben Jonson. He knows how to sell a play."

Condell set his travel wallet on one of the three beds, nearly as good as those we had at home. Saved for attendants accompanying noble guests, not for household servants, I supposed. Where did we sleep here those years ago? I'd been so dazzled by Wilton House and shaken by all that followed that I couldn't recall. Though still Sander Cooke, player, I was now a different person.

After breakfast next morning, King James and his retinue arrived, without his queen. Standing with the household behind Marie and her two sons, I caught my first sight of His Majesty.

No doubt, as Shakespeare reported, he would look noble on

horseback, his upper body broad-shouldered, his face distinguished enough, though no one would call him handsome. But walking with his men, his legs indeed looked thin and weak. Of course, these were mostly Scotsmen, large of stature and rough to an eye used to English courtiers. Compared to them, the king's delicacy appeared more refined as were his clothes, to a degree.

William Herbert dismissed us and escorted King James into Wilton House. Burbage and Armin's faces fell in disappointment, but I was pleased for the chance to wander freely. Even in our brief time here, I sensed how Wilton House had changed.

Now we had Stuart rulers and a new configuration of the Sidney-Herbert family. Until William married, Marie remained Countess of Pembroke, but Wilton was now her son's domain. I'd heard she planned soon to visit the warm waters of Bath, famous for soothing aches and pains.

Her chemists and her poets, Samuel Daniel, John Donne and the rest, were nowhere to be seen. From what I'd gathered, William Herbert, his brother Philip, and their fellow English courtiers were young, enterprising, ambitious, and desirous of pleasing King James. It was rumored they'd be sending fleets of trading ships to the New World in this new era.

I felt nostalgic for Wilton House when it belonged to Marie and her aging husband the Earl. But time moves on. We were to perform for King James. Progress was in the air.

Trees were farther apart in the woods than they appeared from the terrace. Through a thicket of fading rhododendron, I reached a grassy riverbank and sat, out of sight of the house. Somewhere along this riverbank, Marie's brother Sir Philip Sidney wrote his *Arcadia*, a pastoral romance that had much in common with *As You Like It*. No wonder Marie referred to these woods as their Forest of Arden. The very air of Wilton, its fragrances, birdsong, and caressing breeze, aroused images from the summer when I fell in love with John Donne. A bird trilled a plaintive melody in the branches, echoing the song in my heart. "Youth's a stuff will not endure." I shook myself. Forget nostalgia: you're a happily married man.

Birdsong followed me up the path to the house, melodic with a hint of melancholy. In the stable yard stood a recently arrived coach. I saw no passengers, just two men releasing the horses. The broader of the two looked familiar: could it be?

Moll Frith!

I ran toward her. "What are you doing here?"

"I was invited, what else?"

"But you don't know the Countess or her sons."

"As good as. I'm here with Henry, the Earl of Southampton, their great friend."

At the mention of Southampton I thought not of his part in the Essex rebellion but how he had been, years ago, beautiful Henry Wriothesley, "Risley," adored by both women and men. William Shakespeare dedicated his two long poems to him and glorified a young man resembling Wriothesley in his sonnets. Shakespeare imagined this youth to be a lover of his dark lady—presumably Amelia Bassano—a love triangle that prompted anguished poetry. Amelia had done no more than flirt with Wriothesley, but the imagination of a poet carries emotions far beyond their compass.

Some time later, Wriothesley married Elizabeth Vernon, chiefly to give her child a name, as he quickly abandoned her. Though a nobleman, he behaved only slightly better than Johnny had with Frances. Southampton had barely avoided execution for supporting Essex's rebellion. Apparently our new king thought more of Wriothesley's youthful promise than his collection of sins.

"King James freed him from the Tower and he wants to celebrate with the Herbert brothers, attend on the king, and see your play."

"When did Wriothesley make you his confidant?"

She laughed. "We met a couple of days ago in Bankside. Dreary place, what with the plague. Only a handful of taverns and brothels were open. Nothing jolly about them."

"You shouldn't have risked staying in London."

"As you see, I didn't. Wriothesley and I shared ale and jokes and he invited me to come along to Wilton. 'The Countess of Pembroke lacks a roaring girl,' he says. So here I am, ready to meet the king."

I grinned. What would King James make of Moll Frith?

"I shall have a chamber in the servant's hall all to myself, usually saved for the fool. For the king, I can play the fool in earnest."

"They say he has terrible manners and no one knows what he'll do at any moment. The Scottish sense of decorum differs from ours."

"Then I'm in luck, my friend. So too does my sense of decorum." Moll pronounced the last words with an exaggerated courtly accent. She slapped me on the back. "I'll be a player like yourself, making up my own lines."

"You'll liven the party, as will Wriothesley, if he's anything like he used to be. Did his time in the Tower chasten him?"

"Not so far as I can tell."

"Frances is here," I said as we walked out of the stable yard.

"Oh good. I'll sit with her at supper." She opened the gate to the kitchen garden. "I'm going this way. Time to make friends with the cooks."

"Don't you dare play the fool during our play, Moll. Knowing you, you'll sit on the stage."

"I'd rather sit at the king's feet."

An unforgettable sight, Moll in her flamboyant dress at the feet of King James, and I didn't doubt she'd manage it.

Inside, all was in a flurry as servants bustled one way along corridors carrying travel chests and in the other direction, platters of food. I hurried into the chamber that was to be our tiring room where the players gathered, most with a drink or cake in hand. I was last to arrive, giving a quick smile to Frances, arranging costumes on their rail. With a handful of cherries and a glass of wine, I perched on a bench by the clean-swept hearth, its massive bunch of blue-flowered rosemary perfuming the room.

Shakespeare was speaking to Robert Armin. "Don't worry, man. Touchstone's jokes will bring a laugh."

"Not if King James finds himself on the wrong side of the debate between Touchstone and Corin the shepherd." Armin spoke as Touchstone: "Why, if thou never wast at court, thou never sawest good manners; if thou never sawest good manners, then thy manners must be wicked, and wickedness is sin, and sin is damnation. Thou art in a parlous state, shepherd."

"Don't be silly, man." Burbage spattered cake crumbs as he spoke. "However folk here regard the king's manners, they were perfectly courtly in Scotland. He wouldn't consider them wicked."

"Exactly. Their debate is clever, not personal." John Heminges spoke in Corin's voice: "Not a whit, Touchstone. Those that are good manners at the court are as ridiculous in the country as the behavior of the country is most mockable at the court. You told me you salute not at the court, but you kiss your hands. That courtesy would be uncleanly, if courtiers were shepherds."

"You prove my point. Tell me the king's hands aren't uncleanly."

"Say your lines and make him laugh." Burbage brushed away the last of the crumbs. "I hope Queen Anne arrives soon."

"The king and queen appear to lead separate lives," Phillips said. "After the coronation, she and her ladies left London, but she wouldn't miss Wilton House."

Heminges set down his wine glass. "She exists, that's the point. As do their children."

"That's something new: a royal family with two sons." Trying to read Shakespeare's face as he spoke, I saw a fleeting look that suggested regret. I too missed Queen Elizabeth, but now we were the King's Men.

"An embarrassment of riches." Burbage laughed. "Whatever else King James must contend with, it won't be the succession."

"He'll be challenged to live up to Queen Elizabeth in every other regard." Heminges had the final word.

Shakespeare walked over to the rail and Frances, who'd been sitting quietly in the corner, handed him his costume for Adam, the trusty old retainer who escapes to the forest with Orlando. She helped us find our costumes and took our outer layers as we shed them down to our shirts. My back to the others, I fastened Rosalind's gown for my first scene, Ganymede's breeches beneath.

In the garden, we bowed low before King James sitting under a canopy. He wore oyster-colored silk with a wide collar, a black linen cloak edged in embroidery, and a banded hat rather than a crown. The blue-upholstered high back chair beside him stood conspicuously empty. I'd been as convinced as Augustine Phillips that Her Majesty, reputed to enjoy performances, wouldn't miss *As You Like It* on this idyllic stage as the sun slanted down in the western sky.

The play moved more slowly than usual, all of us speaking clearly to be sure His Majesty missed not a word. Robert Armin need not have worried. All through Touchstone and Corin's debate about court manners and country manners, the king's high-pitched laugh rang out. During Ganymede's courtship game with Orlando in the forest, he actually giggled, particularly when Celia pretended to marry us and we came within a breath of kissing.

Not until I spoke the epilogue in Rosalind's wedding gown did I speak directly to him.

> *I am not furnished like a beggar, therefore to beg will not*
> *become me: my way is to conjure you; and I'll begin with*
> *the women. I charge you, O women, for the love you bear*
> *to men, to like as much of this play as please you:*

The King, surrounded by a handful of courtiers and Moll Frith sitting on a stone just below, returned a rapt gaze as I continued,

> *and I charge you, O men, for the love you bear to*
> *women—as I perceive by your simpering, none of you*
> *hates them—that between you and the women the play*
> *may please. If I were a woman I would kiss as many of*
> *you as had beards that pleased me, complexions that liked*
> *me and breaths that I defied not: and, I am sure, as many*
> *as have good beards or good faces or sweet breaths will,*
> *for my kind offer, when I make curtsy, bid me farewell.*

When the audience rose to applaud, serving men whisked away their chairs.

The King's white-gloved hands clapped enthusiastically. From my place at the front of the women's line of dancers, I saw that Thomas Lupo's royal consort was larger than usual. Every skilled musician in London appeared to have escaped to the fresh air of Wiltshire. I wasn't surprised to see young Harry Lanyer in their number, as he was now officially apprenticed to his Uncle Innocent. But no Amelia, apparently still at Cookeham.

The musicians struck up the first bars, and Burbage took my hand, followed by the other three bridal couples. As we stepped onto the terrace where the audience had been seated, King James descended from the royal platform as men and women formed into lines. He took the hand of Philip Herbert, who'd started toward the men's line. All those who'd had a dancing master—actors and courtiers both—joined in.

Only four of us in *As You Like It* were dressed as women, Rosalind, Celia, Audrey, and Phoebe, and there were fewer ladies than gentlemen in the audience. Wriothesly and a couple of the youngest men followed Philip Herbert's lead, dancing in the women's line. The Scotsmen looked askance.

Suddenly the music stopped, and Burbage and I bumped into each other. Marie Herbert was kneeling before a woman wearing a feathery coronet who'd stepped from the glass door followed by four ladies. The musicians played a fanfare, and the dancers bowed or knelt. King James rose to his feet.

Queen Anne's entourage showed little evidence of travel, and I couldn't help being annoyed that she preferred perfecting her toilette to watching our play. The audience made space as she moved toward her husband, Philip Herbert vanishing from his side. Her gown was more simple than she'd have worn inside a palace, pale blue satin embellished with forest green and gold-threaded embroidery. A teardrop emerald hung from each ear.

All eyes were upon the couple, who greeted each other formally in voices too soft to hear. Then King James took Queen Anne's hand and moved to the head of the line of dancers. Her ladies joined the women's line, everyone rearranged themselves, and the pavanne resumed.

No changing of partners through the patterns with king and queen in the lead. King James did not appear built for dancing. His padded doublet gave his upper body an imposing shape, but he favored one of his spindly legs. Before the next dance began, he and the queen retreated to their canopied platform.

Beyond the gardens, summer's lingering sunset cast a roseate glow over the assembly. I shared a pattern with William Herbert who appeared sun-washed, hair gleaming and cheeks pink. His sharp look reflected a mind alert and discerning. I was relieved when he moved on to his next partner.

William Herbert's probing eyes made me uncomfortably aware of the layering of my identity, a girl playing a boy playing a girl. In Ganymede's shepherd costume, I'd feel less noticeable than in Rosalind's wedding gown of pale pink linen and the string of pearl-like beads against my bare throat. I would change out of this costume at my soonest opportunity!

When the musicians struck up a galliard, I breathed in music and joy, my worries vanquished by the jingling of Harry Lanyer's tambourine. Leaping footwork drove older folk to the side of the terrace and brought in the younger ones who'd stood apart with gusto. Who should jump the highest of all but Moll Frith, in ungainly splendor.

Earlier I'd seen Frances standing among Marie's household and Moll dancing at the end of the men's line, her scarlet plume waving. Now she grabbed Frances as her partner. They danced a few rapid steps before Moll lifted her high. Breathless, Frances turned away and Moll reached me just as the musicians built up to another volte. She lifted me high in the air, Rosalind's skirts awhirl, setting me down none too gently. I gasped with laughter. "I never dreamt I'd dance with Moll Frith!"

The king and queen remained in their royal chairs, the consort bowed, and guests began to move toward the pavilion for food and drink. Phillip Herbert called to the musicians, "Keep playing dance music!"

"Soon," Thomas Lupo replied, instead choosing a madrigal. As courtiers and ladies bowed and curtsied to king and queen on their way to the pavilion for refreshment, I saw Frances standing as near as she could to the royal couple, her eyes on Queen Anne in her chair of state.

I tried to escape to the tiring room but couldn't get past everyone in between, now compounded with servants bringing wine and confits to the king and queen and young men encircling the king. I gave up, and holding my skirts above the ground strode down the slope toward the river. Above torch-lit festivities, the purple sky was spangled with vermillion and silver clouds.

Shakespeare, who had shed Adam's costume after his part ended, fell into step beside me. "I have no appetite either."

"What a pleasure, to perform my favorite part here."

"As well it should be." Shakespeare laughed. "It's your longest part."

We were startled into silence by the penetrating voice of a nightingale, answered by another from the woods beyond. "I was reminded as I watched the end of the play from the tiring room," Shakespeare said as the song faded, "I don't have it in me to write another comedy like tonight's. I'm no longer the man who wrote this joyous frolic."

"So I gathered from *Measure for Measure* and *All's Well That Ends Well*."

"Most everyone suffered at the end of Queen Elizabeth's reign. Brightness had dimmed. But then we became King James' Men! He wants to see all our plays and be patron for new ones. Looks like our future is made." He shook his head with a mischievous smile. "Even though he believes in witches and all sorts of dire Scots superstitions."

"What sort of plays have you in mind?"

"My muse inclines toward tragedy. *Hamlet* has been a great success. Fewer plague outbreaks of plague in London every day. I'm sure we'll return to the Globe this autumn, and no doubt take the lead in the king's first Twelfth Night revels."

"I'm happy to hear that, Will. About time."

We turned toward the rising noise of revelers.

"We can expect much courtly display. King James must go some distance to match Queen Elizabeth for royal presentation, but he loves the idea of being monarch and Anne of Denmark delights in becoming the queen of England. In that, at least, they see eye to eye." He dropped his voice. "Who knows where the king's extravagance and wild Scots character will lead England, but all we must do is please him."

As we reached the lawn, now lit with intermittent torches, Frances hurried over to me and he took his leave. A new tune was starting up.

"You must dance with me, Sander. I have something to celebrate."

"Do you see what I'm wearing?"

"Of course I see. Rosalind's wedding gown with smudges of dirt on the hem. I can easily clean it."

"A woman's gown. Tell me your news so I can change back into my breeches and doublet."

"You're not the only actor still in costume. Armin is still Touchstone and Beeston is Celia. Besides, we'll be moving through the patterns. You won't stand out."

"I'll be less noticeable as a man."

"What if King James fancies you in your breeches?"

"Frances!"

"That's what they say." She flashed a mischievous smile and put a warm hand on my arm. "But look, there are more women than men here. Even the serving maids are dancing now that they've cleared the tables. We'll be telling our grandchildren we twirled with King James and Queen Anne."

"Dance together as women?" I laughed. But I'd danced with Moll Frith for a mad moment. Anyone who wasn't dancing would rather watch the clumsy Scotsmen, the Herbert brothers and Southampton in their rainbow of silken clothes and rosette-bedecked shoes, and the royal couple. I took her hand and we joined the pairs moving through patterns, our skirts swirling together.

The patterns fell apart in a few minutes, as most of those present, the Scots included, had never known a dancing master. So I could linger deliciously with Frances to the bright tunes of the Lupo consort. I'd lost thought of anything else, but she stopped after several rounds of the garden.

"Now you need to hear my news." We stood to one side where we could glimpse King James looking bored and Queen Anne dancing with William Herbert.

"I stood there," Frances pointed at royal chairs, "until Her Majesty motioned to me. When I stood up from my deepest curtsey, she complimented me on my embroidered bodice. 'I have heard of your skill, Mistress Cooke, and now that I see your work I have decided. You must be my Silkwoman.'"

"What wonderful news!"

"She told me I'm just the one to remake the late Queen's gowns for her." Frances looked around to be sure no one could overhear. "Of course I'll do as she asks, but I'm puzzled. I understood that Queen Elizabeth's wardrobe was to be a state treasure."

"Not locked away in cupboards, evidently." I took her hand. "If someone must cut up those gowns, well that you're the one."

Frances shrugged. "There's more, Sander. Queen Anne praised me for having my own business, rare in Scotland or Denmark. She intends to sponsor masques to outdo Queen Elizabeth's, and I shall design the costumes!"

"Masques?" It took a moment to sink in. I'd heard of masques, occasional revels for Queen Elizabeth's court. Shakespeare made scornful remarks, how they were more for ladies showing off, as court ladies could appear in elaborate costumes and sing a song or two in private performances. The few lines of these productions were spoken by actors—but none of us.

But elaborate costumes! She was waiting for my reaction. "What an opportunity, Frances. What did she tell you?"

"As the queen described her grand ideas, I understood that she wants gorgeous spectacles beyond any seen before. Masques are usually performed just once, yet no expense will be spared for costumes, music, and stage sets. And I'm to be in charge of designing costumes and delegating work to skilled seamstresses."

"Who better than you to create it?" I didn't say that to me, masques were the opposite of stage plays. All sorts come to hear our plays on a bare stage whatever we wear. Masques dazzle the eye of the noble few. "What about your shop?"

"I'll never give it up. Masques come and go, but my business is constant, and I have Joan and Rebecca."

"Congratulations, my love. All is going better than we imagined for us both. Now I really must get out of this gown."

When I returned properly dressed, Frances stood waiting. She took my hand as we joined the next dance, whispering, "Now we are Master and Mistress Alexander Cooke."

As Master Cooke, I proudly took my wife's hand. Frances' smile shone brighter than the torchlight and her fingers felt reassuring twined with mine. William Shakespeare may have tired of happy-ever-after endings, but ours felt hard earned. What joy to be united in our own Arcadia, moving together under the waxing moon.

A NOTE ON THE TITLE

"Bedtrick: sex with a partner who pretends to be someone else."
Introduction, Wendy Doniger, *The Bedtrick: Tales of Sex and Masquerade*,
University of Chicago, 2000.

Two of Shakespeare's plays, *All's Well That Ends Well* and *Measure for
Measure*, make use of the plot device called a bedtrick, an ancient motif
in stories—and occasionally in life, according to Wendy Doniger's study,
which shares a title with my novel. Like me, Doniger is intrigued by masquerade and pretense in sexual encounters—for her, from a mythic point
of view. Thus her definition of the term "bedtrick" is broader than that in
Shakespeare's plays, whereby a man sleeps with the woman he rejected,
believing she's the one he lusts after. The overall definition of a bedtrick is
a lie about sex, whatever form that lie takes.

In these two so-called problem comedies of Shakespeare, the man sleeps
with a woman who gives him her virginity while he believes she's someone
else, thus consummating a marriage with a reluctant groom. According to
Doniger, this sort of bedtrick was legal, and she documents cases to prove
it. She adds that in fact, such a deception could be regarded as a valid way
to secure a husband. Some men may agree with Stanley Wells' assertion in
Shakespeare, Sex, and Love, that a bedtrick is tantamount to rape: the man
does not desire union with this particular woman.

I encountered Doniger's book after I devised the plot—and title—of
this novel, and was relieved that her analysis is inclusive enough that my
fictional bedtrick warrants the name. Those perpetrating the bedtrick in
my book are fully aware of who slept with whom: the lie is to the world.

The historical actor Alexander Cooke fathered children. In my version,
Sander Cooke was born female. Pregnancy would destroy her male persona
and her acting career. Another means is needed for her to become a parent:
a bedtrick.

HISTORICAL NOTE

Alexander Cooke is an historical actor listed in Shakespeare's First Folio of 1623. The early critic of Shakespeare's work, Edmond Malone, credited Cooke with originating Shakespeare's principal female roles. The fact that the historical Alexander Cooke fathered children inspired this book as an explanation of how that could be, given that here, Cooke was born female.

Only men were allowed to perform on the London stage, and there is no historical evidence that a woman managed to do so by presenting herself convincingly as a male player. It's not impossible, however. History is full of women who got away with such a disguise, discovered only upon their death. In the last two centuries in the U.S., these include soldiers in the Civil War and the jazz musician Billy Tipton.

The central plot of *Bedtrick* is fictional within an historically accurate context. For the Essex rebellion, the death of Queen Elizabeth, and the accession of King James VI of Scotland to the English throne as King James, I rely on books such as *Elizabeth and Essex* by Lytton Strachey; *After Elizabeth* by Leanda de Lisle; and various biographies of Queen Elizabeth and King James. I found *1599: A Year in the Life of William Shakespeare* by James Shapiro particularly useful for the spirit and details of that time. *Shakespeare, the King's Playwright* by Alvin Kernan documents the plays performed by Shakespeare's company for King James I and his court, including floor plans of the royal performance spaces.

Amelia Bassano Lanyer, author of the first book of poetry published by a woman in England, *Salve Deus Rex Judaeorum*, 1611, was proposed as the Dark Lady of Shakespeare's sonnets by the scholar A.L. Rowse. Although not all critics agree, that identification of her serves novelists well, and so she is presented here.

Novelist's leeway shows in the private presentations of Shakespeare's plays for Queen Elizabeth and some of the dates of specific court performances. We can be sure the Queen would have dearly loved to see plays in an intimate setting, particularly late in her life when court appearances became onerous: this could well have happened. *As You Like It* was performed at Wilton House for King James a couple of months later than here depicted.

ACKNOWLEDGEMENTS

Huge thanks go to Hosking Houses Trust for my residency in Clifford Chambers during the summer of 2014. Sarah Hosking, Paul Edmondson, and the board of the Trust were kind, generous, and ever helpful. The residency gave me uninterrupted days to work on *Bedtrick* and the opportunity to attend plays and events at the Royal Shakespeare theatres in nearby Stratford-upon-Avon, conduct research in the historic houses and library of the Shakespeare Birthplace Trust and the Shakespeare Institute library of the University of Birmingham, and to visit sites throughout Warwickshire and beyond. Exhibitions such as *Shakespeare: Staging the World* at the British Museum gave me further insights.

The earliest reader of *Bedtrick*, Kate Wheale, offered valuable suggestions about plot, marriage in Elizabethan England, language, and many significant details. Nigel Wheale caught anachronisms and historical points that needed clarifying. I owe thanks to Jan Rudestam, Lenore Hughes, and to Mesa Writers, including Sharon Dirlam, Elizabeth Campbell, Susan Matsumoto, Betsy Johnson, Cynthia Martin, Fred Hunter, R.W. "Hap" Ziegler, and Lois Phillips. Early support of my work came from Jane Spitzer and the late George Spitzer of Nebbadoon Press. Special thanks to Ibrahim ben Salma for finding and translating the poem by Füzuli. Most deserving of praise and appreciation is Martha Hoffman of Cuidono Press, who gave me excellent editorial feedback and has been a delight to work with.

My heartfelt appreciation extends to the directors and actors of the many plays of Shakespeare I've been fortunate to see, from the Oregon Shakespeare Festival in Ashland and Theatricum Botanicum in Topanga Canyon, California, to the Globe performances in London, and a multitude of theatres in between. "The Roaring Girl Season" in Stratford-upon-Avon was a rare treat: Moll Frith's spirit is alive and well!